JOEY PISS POT

"No argument here," cunning cut throats. Iı your ... him killed for snooping around the way we did, it can mean any number of things, none of them any good."

"Meaning?"

"First off, the murder. Double murder. I don't imagine Rapino wants anyone knowing any of his business, never mind the issue of me following them, placing them near that house on Staten Island ... Then there's the reality that the mob often uses PIs, private investigators, to watch their own people, make sure they aren't plants or CI's, criminal informants working with the feds.... I can give chase and follow, but I'll have to be extra careful in case they have someone watching his back besides the FBI, not that I trust them not to tip him off."

"Tip him off?" Joseph said.

"You don't think they pull that shit?" Adler said. "The feds think they need somebody to make a bigger case, they'll warn the guy they need. If they can ignore nineteen murders, you better believe they'll tip off someone they need."

"Or I could just walk up to him and kill him myself," Joseph said.

"Catches the cadence and daily grind of organized crime grunts."

—*Publishers Weekly*

"There's terrifying verisimilitude to his criminals and their dwelling places."

—Barry N. Malzberg

"There are few writers (except possibly Elmore Leonard and George V. Higgins), who can write mob dialogue as well as Charlie Stella."

—Patricia Abbott

"The dialog flows so smooth you'd swear you were over hearing someone's conversation."

—Brian Lindenmuth, *Spinetingler Magazine*

"Charlie Stella is one of the best writers the crime genre currently has to offer."

—Craig Clarke, *Somebody Dies*

"Stella cares about his characters and he made me care about them too."

—Mike Parker, *Crime Fiction Lover*

"... every time you think you've got a handle on where it's going, Stella throws you a curve ball."

—Michael Scott Cain, *Rambles*

"Fresh, fast, and darkly funny."

—*Kirkus* *Starred* *Reviews*

Charlie Stella Bibliography

Novels:
Eddie's World (December 2001, Carroll & Graf)
Jimmy Bench-Press (December 2002, Carroll & Graf)
Charlie Opera (December 2003, Carroll & Graf)
Cheapskates (March 2005, Carroll & Graf)
Shakedown (June 2006, Pegasus)
Mafiya (January 2008, Pegasus)
Johnny Porno (April 2010, Stark House)
Rough Riders (July 2012, Stark House)
Tommy Red (September 2016, Stark House)
Joey Piss Pot (July 2024, Stark House)

Non-Fiction:
Dogfella: How an Abandoned Dog Named Bruno Turned This
Mobster's Life Around—A Memoir (May 2015, Da Capo Lifelong
Books)
The Voices in My Head: A Fictional Memoir (2021, Stark
House)

Plays:
Coffee Wagon (1983; Bruno Walter Auditorium)
Mr. Ronnie's Confession, Double or Nothing (1984; 45th Street
Theatre)

JOEY PISS POT

Charlie Stella

STARK HOUSE

Stark House Press • Eureka California

JOEY PISS POT

Published by Stark House Press
1315 H Street
Eureka, CA 95501
griffinskye3@sbcglobal.net
www.starkhousepress.com

JOEY PISS POT

ISBN: 979-8-88601-096-1

Cover and text design by Mark Shepard, shepgraphics.com
Proofreading by Bill Kelly

First Stark House Press Edition: July 2024

For Dave Gresham.

And all the teachers and coaches along my 68-year trip.

Anyone tells you teachers aren't important,
they're talking out their ass.

Acknowledgments

Thanks to all those who did first and final reads. I call them the *Hawkeyes*: Merle Drown (who is a great novelist and helped with the editing), Nicole Caliendo (the Bolshevik daughter), and Ann Cucci-Stella (the love of my life). The eyes have it.

1

"New?" Artie Adler said. He saw what Joseph was doing and added, "Oy vey."

He'd just let himself in the back door of Joseph Gallo's house. Adler was carrying a large shopping bag in one hand and a six-pack of Diet Coke in the other. Joseph, at 70, weighed 300 pounds, down 40 pounds from two months ago. He was standing at the kitchen sink with the front of his sweatpants pulled down enough to allow room for the small pot he was urinating into. The faucet was running hot. Steam rose from the sink.

"Meshuggeneh," Adler said. "Wish I had a camera right now. With a zoom lens."

Joseph flipped Adler the bird. He finished urinating and poured the urine into the drain with the hot water still running. He filled the pot with hot water to sterilize it, then emptied the pot into the drain. He refilled the pot with hot water, shut off the water and left the pot in the sink.

"I'll try again," Adler said. "New?"

Joseph turned to Adler and said, "Again with the Yiddish?"

"Fine," Adler said. "Nothing's new. How's your stomach? Still getting pain?"

Joseph pulled up his sweatpants and frowned at Adler. "You're the pain. What's in the bag?"

"Shabbot Shalom to you too."

Joseph frowned again as he took a seat at the kitchen table. "One more time," he said. "What's in the bag?"

"Deli," Adler said. "I was downtown Brooklyn this morning asking about your grandson and decided to cross the Manhattan Bridge for some Katz. We're gonna play cards, I'm gonna whip your fat ass again, you'll be less cranky if you eat something first."

"Not hungry," Joseph said. He pointed to the refrigerator. "There's ice in the freezer if you need it. Glasses in the drain board. What do I owe you?"

"A twenty-one Buick LaCrosse, one of your neighbors decides to swipe it from your driveway."

"Moron."

"You're the moron with the stomach pain doesn't go to a doctor."

"Putz."

"That's more like it."

Adler was Joseph's oldest and best living friend. The two met when Adler was 10 years old. He was 6 months younger than Joseph and a lot healthier. Adler, at 69, walked 2 miles a day. He was tall with broad shoulders and a flat stomach. What hair he still had was white.

He and Joseph had attended Public School 115 in Canarsie where they became instant friends.

They had played together in the Canarsie and PAL baseball little leagues. Both played varsity sports in high school, Joseph football at Canarsie high school and for Adler basketball at Sheepshead Bay.

Adler ripped open the six-pack of soda he'd brought, pulled out two cans, and grabbed glasses from the drain board. He set them on the table as Joseph took plates from a cabinet, then two forks and knives from a drawer. He sat at the table nearest the sink and slid one of the plates to Adler.

"You wash your hands?" Adler said.

"No," Joseph said. "Which sandwich is mine?"

Adler unwrapped a thick pastrami sandwich on rye bread. He said, "The other is corned beef. There are franks in the other bag, four of them. Fries in the other one."

"I'll be shitting all night after this," Joseph said.

"Lovely image," Adler said.

Joseph used his fork to spread mustard on one side of a piece of rye bread. "What do I owe?"

"Sixty-three bucks."

"Remind me before you leave."

They took bites from their sandwiches. Joseph swallowed his after a few chews. Adler, a naturally slow eater, took his time.

Then Joseph set his sandwich down and began to wrap it.

"What's wrong?" Adler said.

"Stomachache. You talk to your friend?"

Adler reached for his Diet Coke. He nodded as he pulled the tab.

Joseph winced from stomach pain, then held his stomach with both hands.

"Moron, if you're sick, you should go to a doctor."

"What did your cop friend say?"

"Okay, ignore me."

"What he say?"

"Looks like your grandson got himself involved. If my friend is right, Chris is definitely hanging around the wrong people."

"Shit," Joseph said. "He sure?"

"It's what he said. It's inevitable, you ask me. Between what happened to his father, the disappearing acts you say Chris has pulled, that decision to go to Iraq. Comes back and finds the country is a comedy with a moron con artist as president, the one girl he was crazy about finds somebody else ... hooking up with the mob is just another mistake he might as well make."

"He went to college," Joseph said. "He's gotta be smarter than that."

"I know half a dozen morons my own family got degrees can't change a flat. They can dial a number, get somebody to change the thing for them, but that's about it. My brother-in-law I don't speak to no more, that dumbass was a professor before he cheated on my sister with one of his students. Dumb fuck threw it all away. Teaches in some high school in Ohio now. Must've been hard-up for teachers there. Went from a fat salary and tenure to the sticks teaching mouth breathers."

Joseph was still holding his stomach. He held up a hand. "Hang on," he managed to say.

"Are you sick or what?" Adler said. "If you are, let me take you to a doctor."

"Chris ain't like that," Joseph said after the pain passed. "Kid has brains. Always did. Top of his class. Cost me some coin paying his way up in Albany. I was hoping he'd go straight to law school. Any law school. I don't know why he didn't."

"Fuck law school," Adler said. "Who needs another lawyer? I got three in my family, one dumber than the next. They spend a dozen hours a day at the office, they cheat on their wives, and their wives cheat right back. They all three look down on me, but push comes to shove, who do they call? Social retards is what they are."

"Can't use that word anymore?" Joseph said before taking a sip of his Diet Coke.

"Which word is that?" Adler said.

Joseph set the Diet Coke down as he winced in pain.

"You're a fuckin' spectacle, you know that?" Adler said. "How the fuck long you gonna ignore the pain? You're losing some of your tonnage. Even I can see that. What's the deal? You see a doctor or not?"

"You know what you need?" Joseph said. "A dog, something. A pet. Then you can play mother to it and leave me alone. Who'd your friend say Chris has been around?"

They two friends stared at one another a long moment.

"Hello?" Joseph said.

Adler said, "Montalvo's crew. Old crew, I guess. Montalvo is still away on a RICO charge and supposedly has cancer. He was on the short list to the hierarchy in the family until one of his own burned him. Jerry Galante is acting skipper for Montalvo's crew now."

"I don't know them," Joseph said. "Except what I read in the papers, the articles about the mob, and what you tell me. If Chris is hanging around shit like that, it won't end well."

Adler shrugged. "What're you gonna do? He's not a kid anymore. Look what happened to my kid. First time he got his noodle wet, he runs off with some Columbian broad gets him killed the first time he visits her family."

"And I lost mine to so-called collateral damage."

"I'll tell you this much," Adler said. "If I knew that twat's brother was connected to a cartel, I would've killed her and him myself. I was suspicious and kept my mouth shut because David was in love. They were gonna get married and whatnot. Meanwhile, he goes down there to meet her family, they hear he's a cop, they assume he's on the job, and he gets whacked for it. And she never steps foot back here again. Sends my wife over the edge and speeds her cancer. I think if I saw that broad again, I'd choke her. Not even a phone call. David's body was shipped back. How I found out he was killed. All the phone calls I made afterward to the police down there? I got nothin'. Fuck those people."

Joseph nodded at Adler. "What you say before? What're you gonna do?"

"Why I'm telling you to ignore what Chris is doing now. We both know he's making a mistake hanging around anybody connected to the mob today, but what good's worryin' about it? He's gonna do what he wants to do. It's a shame he blows his education for it, but it's out of your hands now. You did the right thing by the kid."

"I can talk to him," Joseph said. "I get the chance, I can talk to him."

"You can try, sure."

"I don't understand it. Why would he go that route? How'd you handle it, patrolling the neighborhood where your old man had the store? That neighborhood changed the same as Canarsie changed. You didn't change."

"The neighborhood changed all right, only a lot sooner than Canarsie," Adler said. "Good old Brownsville. I handled it. Wasn't bad the first few years, everybody knew me from when I worked in the store there. Jews owned Pitkin Avenue for a long time. Everybody got along. Then, over some more time, most of the stores were gone, the Jewish ones anyway. Either the people changed, or they moved out. The new ones didn't know I was a kid worked in the same neighborhood. Then I was a cop. The relationships changed. They shut down and I did the same. So, yeah, I did change. Put the hours in and punched out. The indifference was thick. That's when I started to hate being a cop, couldn't wait to retire. I think it's even worse now. I can't imagine being a cop today. Everybody hates cops now. It's what makes cops bond and hate right back."

"Not to mention they tend to shoot unarmed black kids."

"No excuse for that. They reap what they sow."

"Chris was an outgoing kid before his father was killed," Joseph said. "I think that changed him more than we realized. The disappearing acts after high school. Joining the Army. He was already in Iraq before he let his mother know. She was frantic back when he disappeared. We all were."

Joseph cringed as his hands covered his stomach again. Adler stared at him.

"What?" Joseph said.

"You're pissing me off is what. I can take you to the hospital right now."

Joseph rolled his eyes.

"You're a moron," Adler said.

Both men remained silent a while. Joseph continued to hold his stomach. Adler shook his head.

Finally, Adler said, "She still pissed at you, his mother?"

"Still pissed?" Joseph said. "The other day was the first time I heard from her since before my operation. How long is it now, two years? She's the one told me she's worried about him. He still disappears, he still don't call her. He even sounds funny, she said. 'Like one of those morons you know,' she said."

Adler chuckled. "Well, you were surrounded by a lot of them," he said. "Morons, I mean. Clearly rubbed off too."

"I didn't hang around mob guys."

"Please. You owned a bar in a mob haven and your brother-in-law was a wiseguy himself."

Joseph flipped him the bird again.

Adler smiled. "Feeling better, I guess."

• • • • •

Jerry Galante left his social club before the Celtics-Bucks game ended. He'd taken Milwaukee in a teaser with the Rockets and lost both ends, dropping more than $5,000. He was angry as he drove onto the Belt Parkway heading east. He called his wife on a burner phone and told her he'd be home late, then hung up on her when she started to complain. Galante checked his mirrors for a tail several times before missing his exit near the JFK expressway. He drove to the next exit and circled back using North Conduit Avenue to the Courtyard by Marriott Hotel. He drove around the parking lot two times before parking and making another call, this one to his boss's wife, Doris Montalvo.

She was waiting in a room on the eighth floor for Galante. When she let him into the room, she was wearing a one-piece black corset with matching panties, black garters attached to black thigh-high stockings, and black pumps. At 56, she was still a looker but was conscious of what time had wrinkled. Her grayish-red hair was recently dyed blonde. She wore a long string of pearls and black square glossy eyeglasses.

"Jesus Christ," Galante said as soon as he took her look in.

"Not quite," Doris said, "but neither am I the Virgin Mary."

They exchanged a kiss that quickly turned passionate. When they finished having sex, they used the bathroom, Galante first, then Doris. Afterward, Galante checked messages on his cellphone while Doris sat up in the bed craving a cigarette.

Galante stood in front of the dresser mirror and could see he'd gained a little weight. At 5'8", 195 pounds, he'd developed a pouch since being handed the reins as acting captain of his former boss's crew. He also noticed that his widow's peak was more defined. When he saw Doris looking him over from the bed, he turned and flexed.

"I've seen better," she said.

"Not Carmine," Galante said. "That old fuck had to be wrinkled top to bottom."

"Did I mention Carmine?"

Galante pointed at her and lost his playfulness. "Speaking of which, that guy you've been with is in the hospital now. Carmine found out. You're gonna do that shit, you better be more careful."

Doris looked at Galante as if he had six heads. "What guy?" she said. "What the hell are you talking about hospital? What hospital?"

"This young guy you were fucking," Galante said. "Eddie Russo? Carmine knew about him and sent word to take care of him. We did, but not what your husband wanted. That was too much."

"Carmine sent you a name? Jerry, what the fuck? What are
you talking about?"
"Relax, okay. I don't care who you're fucking as long as you
stay clean."
"You don't care ... Jesus Christ. Guess what, genius, there is
no other guy. I fuck you, Jerry. That's it. Just you."
Galante stroked the air with a fist.
"You have to be kidding," Doris said. "You don't believe me?
You believe Carmine? And you had someone beat up? Trust me,
I don't know Eddie Russo, whoever he is. I haven't fucked
anybody except you since before Carmine went away, and he
had the guy killed because he's a jealous lunatic."
"He had a guy killed because he can't have it on the street he
did nothing. Those are the rules."
"Rules? Please. That was ego. He made sure I knew he had
that poor bastard killed. This is the safest life I can have right
now, with you, and that's why I wouldn't screw around with
someone Carmine might kill because of his jealousy."
"Listen to me," Galante said. "He ever finds out about us,
we're both dead. You didn't screw this kid, then why would he
get word to me about him? How'd he get a name?"
"I don't know. Maybe he does suspect you."
"He did that, suspected me, I'd be dead already."
"Well, I haven't screwed anybody else since before Carmine
went away, and that's over six years already. For all I know,
you're the one killed that poor guy. Carmine made it clear my
life would be miserable while he was away. If some guy is laid
up in a hospital now, that's a mistake. You had somebody beat
up for nothing. Why didn't you tell me what Carmine said? I
could've saved the poor bastard. What the hell did you do to him
anyway?"
"Now you're sounding concerned for the guy."
"Oh, God, you're thick."
"Hey, I'm serious here. This is serious. Carmine isn't gonna
let it go when he hears the guy only caught a beating. He'll
break my balls all over again."
"Jerry, I wasn't fucking anybody else. Whoever this Eddie
Russo is, he's innocent. I don't know him, and I can assure you
he doesn't know me."
"Hey, Doris, this is a mess I don't need right now."
"Carmine must have a bug up his ass about something.
Either somebody fed him a bullshit story or he's going nuts
again. He hates me as it is, but now he's going nuts."

"Don't jerk my chain, Doris. Your husband made sure I got the name, so whoever this kid was you were banging, he was owed that beating, but Carmine wants him dead. My problem is now I can't touch this Russo guy, and Carmine won't let it go."

Doris stared at Galante a long moment.

"What?" Galante said. "Your husband wanted the guy killed. We weren't gonna do that, but now the kid caught the beating, we can't do anything. You gotta make a call or something. Back him off."

"You hit your head or something?" Doris said. "First of all, I don't call Carmine anymore. He calls me, and not very often. Probably when he's having a bad day with the cancer, and he feels like torturing someone. All he cares about is whether or not I'm miserable. He prefers I remain miserable until one or the other of us drops dead."

"Look, if you were banging this guy, you know I don't give a fuck. Like I told you, long as you're clean when we're together, fuck whoever you want. I already got a wife. But now we did it, put Russo in the hospital. Carmine is gonna want him dead anyway. You gotta back him off. I wasn't going that far, kill a guy, but I had to do something. Now you gotta back him off. I don't care who you screw on your own time."

"Yeah, you got a wife. You said."

"Don't break them Doris."

"I'm not fucking anybody else. If you beat somebody up, you did it for nothing. If Carmine claims someone tipped him off, he should think about why."

Galante sighed. "That's not good enough, even if you're telling me the truth."

"Why?"

"Because your husband is relentless. He won't believe it."

"Fuck what he believes."

"I need you to make that call. You have to back him off."

"You want me to talk about this shit over a prison line? Have you lost your—"

"Not the specifics, for Christ sakes. Just tell him you're pissed off about the guy was beat up and is in the hospital now. Tell him the guy is in the ICU or some shit. He's critical. Tell him he's a distant cousin or some shit. Maybe he lets it go."

"I don't like the idea of calling him. I hate the son-of-a-bitch. And he hates me."

"And he still pulls enough weight to make everybody miserable. You make the call and whoever it was you were fucking gets a pass. Understand? We can't do anything to him because the cops are already involved. Carmine won't let it go unless you can back him off."

Doris leaned her head back and closed her eyes.

"Hey!" Galante said.

She swallowed hard and looked at him.

"What?" he said.

"Twice," she confessed. "I was with him twice."

"Eddie Russo?"

"Duh."

Galante reached over and slapped her off the shoulder. She rolled to her left and cowered. "I'm sorry," she said.

"Why the fuckin' lying? I told you I don't give a—"

"He's a civilian," she said. "How the hell was he supposed to know who I'm married to? I hope you don't think I was gonna tell him."

"Where'd you pick this jerkoff up?"

"Nebula in Manhattan," she said. "And he picked me up. I wasn't on the prowl, if that's what you mean."

"Hey, it was none of my business until Carmine heard about it and ordered me to take care of it. Like I said, it's not like he don't hold a position while he's in the joint. It's not the same as he's on the street, but he could make my life a bigger pain in the ass than he already has."

Galante went to a window and looked down at the parking lot. Then he turned and positioned a chair facing the bed and sat.

"What?" she said.

"I need you to do this," Galante said.

Doris said, "Carmine is sixty-seven years old. He can barely get it up anymore, and he still has four years before he can even think about getting out. Plus he probably has stage four cancer and probably won't get out. But when and if he does, it'll be on compassionate release and you know it, or you wouldn't be screwing me while he's away."

"Yeah, but he sent word down to me to take care of this Eddie Russo you fucked. That means somebody spotted you two. Probably in that club in Manhattan. You're gonna fuck around like that, you need to be a lot more careful. Me, I know better, so I'm a dead man he finds out about this. Same for civilians. Your boyfriend was lucky to catch a beating."

"The rules? Please."

"Don't be a smartass, Doris. Yeah, the rules."

"Well, you didn't seem too concerned when you had your dick in my mouth."

"I wasn't then. I am now. I mean it, you gotta watch what the fuck you're doing. And you gotta make that call."

"Or else?"

"If your husband don't sleep nights until he knows this kid is dead, that's on me."

"This is such bullshit, what you're asking."

"No, Doris. Bullshit is what you were trying to do telling me you didn't fuck this guy. Somehow your husband found out and now it's a big fucking mess. You caused it, you fix it."

"Fuck you, Jerry."

"You call Carmine and you say whatever the fuck you have to, but you back him off having this guy killed."

"I said fuck you."

"Maybe again before I leave. In the meantime, I need you to get your shit together. I mean it. I don't know who it was gave you up. Maybe they go back to Carmine and Carmine thinks maybe he's still banging you."

"Then why would he believe me if I called?"

"Maybe he won't, but that's not the point. He's got that lawyer of his running back and forth to Pennsylvania telling me what to do and it's starting to get on my nerves."

"So, maybe you're the one needs to take a break," she said. "All the tail you get from those strips joints."

"Trust me, I don't let strippers do anything more than blow me."

"You're an icon of virtue, Jerry."

"I'm talking about how Carmine sees things here. He hears the guy is in some hospital and you give him shit for it, without admitting to anything yourself, maybe he backs the fuck off. Tell him this Russo guy is a relative or some shit, you went dancing with your cousin. Make him believe its mistaken identity. I don't care what you say. Bottom line, it's me getting all the *agita* otherwise."

"That's a bit dramatic. You're getting the stress? What about this, what you're asking me to do? Calling that psycho about somebody he thinks I was fucking? You have any idea what my life will be like after that phone call?"

"He not only thinks you were fucking somebody, Doris. You just said you did."

"Shit. I hate that bastard."

"Jesus Christ, you like to live dangerous."

"I like having a life. I'm not ready for some nunnery, Jerry. You seem to like that fact yourself. That bullshit rule about wiseguy wives having to wait home like nuns until their husbands are out of prison is ridiculous. And it's bullshit. I know at least two other wives married to wiseguys doing the same thing. I'm sure there are more. Some don't even wait for their husbands to go away."

"Yeah, well, let me know if one is my wife. Otherwise, I don't wanna know."

"I think you're safe until she's closer to my age, your wife. It's not like you'll be paying attention then anyway."

"You mean like when Carmine had some computer programmer catch you?"

Doris rolled her eyes. "Yeah, and Carmine is batting his shoe size with that. He caught me once. Wow. He smacked me around a little and it hurt, but I got over it. The full court press he gave me afterward only made me more determined. The more he kept an eye on me, the more I figured out ways to get what I want. How long was it before I had you once he went away, two weeks? You were supposed to be his spy, right? How'd that work out?"

Galante was rubbing his face with both hands.

"And you should think more about her needs," Doris said. "Your wife, I mean. At least once in a while. Save some of what you have down there for her."

"Now comes a lecture on my marriage? All I want to know is you're gonna make that fucking call and see what your husband has to say. Feel him out. The main thing is throwing him off. Get him to back off."

"This isn't fair."

"Fuck fair. I don't wanna hear it from Carmine again. Make the call."

Doris couldn't look at Galante then. Her shoulders went up and then down as she sighed.

"Make that fuckin' call," Galante said, then slapped a flower vase off the desk.

Doris let him throw his fit. Eventually he stormed into the bathroom. She heard the toilet flush and the sink water run. A few minutes later he came out from the bathroom and dressed without looking at her.

"I'm sorry," she said.

"Don't think I won't know if you called Carmine or not. You wanna save your fuck buddy, you'll make the call. You don't make the call, I'll cut this Eddie Russo's dick off before I shove it down your throat."

• • • • •

Carmine Montalvo was 67 and had recently been diagnosed with stage four lung cancer. A once big man with broad shoulders, he'd lost more than 70 pounds since his diagnosis 8 months earlier. Although federal prisons banned smoking, Montalvo managed to get some through the system's pipeline of corrupt correction officers making an extra buck selling contraband. He had reduced his daily smokes from 2 to 3 packs a day before prison down to 5 cigarettes or fewer the last two years of his incarceration. The reduction wasn't doing his lungs any good.

Three months after divorcing his first wife 15 years ago, Montalvo met Doris O'Shea in the aisle of a Boeing 737 redeye from New York to Las Vegas. Doris was sitting in an aisle coach seat alongside a girlfriend. Montalvo was seated in first class but needed to stretch and decided to walk to the bathrooms in the back of the plane. He saw her from a few feet away and noticed she was looking at him. She winked and he was hooked. On his way back to his seat, he invited her up front.

She introduced herself and her friend, then said, "I can't now, but maybe later we can get a drink. I'm staying at the Tropicana."

"Honey," Montalvo said, "we used to call it the Trop, but now it's a low rent joint. I'll put yous both in Caesars with me. Comped, of course."

Two days later they were married at the Chapel of Love. The rest of their stay, three more days, was their honeymoon.

For a few brief months after their wedding, Montalvo ignored business for the only time in his life and was coming up light on the tribute he sent to the head of their crime family, Aniello Fontana. Until then Montalvo had been a top earner for the crime family. He was sent for by Fontana and a sit-down on Staten Island ensued. Fontana demanded a penalty tax and issued a stern warning. Montalvo handled the tax without a complaint, but the warning he couldn't dismiss.

The next day he pressed his crew of 10 made men and 50 or so associates to earn and earn fast. Within weeks, one of his crew and two associates were disappeared, and the money began to flow once again. Within another few weeks, Montalvo was back in Fontana's good graces as a top earner.

Montalvo thought Doris was beautiful and sexy and more creative in bed than any other woman he'd ever been with, including the ones he'd paid for throughout his adult life. She was 46 years old, Montalvo, 57 when they married. Doris had been married before and divorced a few years later. She'd had one abortion and was never pregnant again. She didn't have siblings. Her parents lived in their three-floor brownstone walkup in Sunset Park, Brooklyn. Her mother remained in the house after her father had died six years ago, around the same time Carmine was incarcerated under a federal RICO statute.

Montalvo had started off crazy in love with Doris knowing full well that she probably didn't love him anywhere near the same. He was 11 years older and a lot less active than he should have been, but Doris played the role well enough to keep him both protective and adoring of her. She knew her husband had other women from time to time, but that was the life she'd married into, and she didn't really care. She made sure that none of his girlfriends, no matter their age or looks, could match how she made him feel. Doris Montalvo had Carmine eating out of her hands until the day computer spyware caught her in an affair with a trainer at a Bay Ridge gym where she worked out.

When the trainer disappeared a few weeks after the discovery, Doris threatened to leave her husband until he told her she'd be joining her dead boyfriend in the waters off the Jersey coast if or when she did leave him.

After her affair, Montalvo fell out of love with his wife and could no longer hold a conversation with her, but he still expected her usual performance in bed when he was in the mood. The only difference in the sex they had was the dirty names he'd call her while she performed.

He continued to have other women while she was precluded from having other men until he was caught in a federal roundup of key organized crime figures in the New York metropolitan area. Montalvo went away for 10 years. Relieved of his personal scrutiny, Doris resumed her extracurricular activities.

Today his attorney was visiting Montalvo on an alleged application for compassionate release based on his cancer prognosis. Montalvo had been in a bad mood the last few days and hadn't slept well the night before. He knew he was dying and that he'd probably never get out of prison without a compassionate release, but Montalvo also knew his chances of a release were slim.

He was cursing a blue streak when he spotted his lawyer sitting at the small table inside the private meeting room where inmates met with their attorneys.

Morris Greenblatt was 61 and a little overweight. He was bald but wore a light, curly-haired wig. He'd been a mob lawyer for 20 years and had taken over the firm after his father's death ten years ago. Greenblatt represented several clients aligned with the Cirelli crime family. Montalvo was his most newsworthy and valuable client.

Although prison protocol precluded the taping of legal meetings between inmates and their lawyers, both Greenblatt and Montalvo spoke to one another with a piece of paper covering their mouths.

"What he say?" Montalvo said.

"Jerry?"

"Yeah, Jerry."

"He doesn't know yet. He's still working on it."

"He tell you that or you protecting him? It's a fuckin' month already. At least that."

"Nobody is gonna speak up, Carmine."

"I'm grinding my teeth over here. I know what happened, fuck face. Eddie Russo caught a half-assed beating. He's still alive. Jerry don't know to follow orders?"

"They're nervous. The guy is a civilian."

"Now they're nervous? Now he can't be touched, that's what they think? That's what he's saying? Fuck that shit."

"There were cops involved when the kid was found. There's a police report now. I think they're nervous about that. It's too much attention if something else were to happen now."

"Balls."

"Jerry's doing his best, Carmine. It's not easy for him to watch her and run the crew."

"Listen to me. I know that cunt. She's not fuckin' her brains out while I'm in here? Bullshit. Some kid up here tips me got no reason to lie. If he heard it, it's onna' street. I'm no fuckin' *cornuto*, okay? I don't let my wife fuck other men. Not while I'm still breathing. I gotta', I'll have her and whoever she's fuckin' buried. Understand? And I have Aniello's okay on this. He understands the rules. He's old school just like me."

Greenblatt held up both hands. "Listen to me a second," he said. "Jerry isn't going to okay what you want on this. It's too much to ask while you're in here and sick. The attention it'll bring scares everybody."

"I'm a fucking captain here, counselor."

"I know, I know. But you gotta—"

"Hey, fuck face, don't tell me what I gotta, don't gotta. I want the motherfucker gone, okay? You just tell Jerry what I say and that's all you do. No lectures."

"It's advice, Carmine. It's sound advice."

"It's bullshit. If Jerry lost his stones, he can be replaced. I'm in here, but I'm not dead. I still have pull, okay? I'm not somebody gets jerked off by his own crew."

Greenblatt swallowed hard and then sighed. The frustration of dealing with assholes like his client seemed never ending. Some days he didn't know if it was worth it. The money was good, but it's not like he couldn't survive without it. He still didn't understand the how and why his father had put up with it for so long.

Montalvo was his client and Greenblatt was stuck with him and anyone else from that crime family seeking his help.

Greenblatt's frustration must've showed because then Montalvo said, "What?"

"I'm just saying. Jerry is being cautious. I can't blame him."

"You can't blame him? Who the fuck are you?"

This time Greenblatt sat back and nodded. "Fine," he said. "Okay."

It was what he hated most about dealing with the old timers, especially the ones in prison. They'd yet to come to terms with the changing nature of the times. The mob wasn't what it used to be. Not by a long shot. Leaving bodies in the street was no longer the way to go, which was one reason it didn't happen the way it once had. Guys like Montalvo were headstrong and arrogant and had to believe, or make believe, they were still powerful enough to call the shots on the streets back where they came from. The reality was that the only thing everybody on the streets wanted was to stay the hell away from where Montalvo had ended up.

Killing some kid because he'd fucked Montalvo's wife might've been how it was done back in the day, but times had changed. Today deals were cut before the handcuffs were on. The kid Montalvo wanted killed was a civilian. For all Montalvo knew, whomever had tipped him off about his wife might've had a personal beef with this Eddie Russo. Maybe the guy who'd brought Montalvo the tip, Paul D'Angelo, an associate of his crew, had a beef with Russo. Maybe D'Angelo was the guy who'd fucked Montalvo's wife.

Greenblatt had tried again and again to understand how the mind of a psychopath like Carmine Montalvo worked, but there was no understanding guys like his client. All he'd get was more frustration than he needed in his life. Montalvo was an angry, miserable, old bastard on his way out. Ordering murders was his way of believing he was still relevant. Reality was staring him in the face and with all his tough guy bluster, he couldn't face the fact he'd be dead and forgotten, probably within a month or two.

None of it mattered because there was no talking to a dinosaur like Montalvo. He'd made up his mind and was probably torturing himself in his cell with thoughts of his wife spreading her legs back in Brooklyn.

Greenblatt remembered back to when Montalvo first caught his wife cheating because somebody in IT at the law office installed spyware on her laptop for her husband. Greenblatt had advised his client to divorce her, but guys like Montalvo could never live with knowing their wife was out there having their own life. To guys like Montalvo, it was a betrayal they couldn't ignore.

Montalvo and his ilk preferred making a woman pay the old fashioned way, by keeping her like a slave to fuck or beat whenever the mood presented itself.

Did he stay with an unfaithful woman for the sake of making them both miserable? The cycle seemed unending, or why didn't he divorce or have her killed?

He'd become a snake eating its own tail, and now that Montalvo was dying in prison, his spite had become a poisonous obsession. He needed the satisfaction of ruining his wife's life. He needed her too afraid to live her own life.

Greenblatt had met Doris Montalvo a few times and was never fooled by the woman. She was a player getting up there in age who was married to a mobster for no other reason than what she could get out of it. Montalvo might've kept her in line after catching her that first time, because she knew what he was capable of, but now that he was inside, Doris Montalvo didn't seem concerned with his threats. If Greenblatt had to guess, what was going on with Doris Montalvo had to do with getting her last licks in before her beauty lost its luster.

And she obviously wasn't waiting for her husband's death to start.

Greenblatt decided to try one more time and said, "I think you should give Jerry the benefit of the doubt here, Carmine."

"I think you should stick to gettin' me out of here for the cancer."

"I told you that's not going to be easy. They might've if you were closer to the end of your sentence. They demand you serve seventy-five percent of your sentence or that you already served ten years. You still have four years on the sentence. We can try again in another year. Probably two years."

"Yeah, and I'm dyin' now. Cancer, counselor. The fuck else they want from me? I'll never see the end of my sentence with this shit I got now."

Greenblatt gave it a moment.

"What?" Montalvo said.

"What do you want me to tell Jerry?"

"I already told you what I want you to tell Jerry. What've I been saying for how many fuckin' weeks now? I want the kid fucking my wife to disappear. Nothing short of that. And if I don't hear this was taken care of in another week or two, I'll be speaking to someone else comes up for a visit."

"Who?"

Montalvo smirked. "Yeah, you better worry," he said. "You'll know when you know. Pro'bly after the fact. Meantime, you can tell Jerry the clock is ticking and I'm not dead yet. He better move his ass on this."

2

On a warm spring night, Joseph Gallo met his grandson at the Canarsie Pier. Several cars were scattered around the edges of the parking lot. Chris Gallo was waiting in a gray 2013 Honda at the far end of the pier. Bird droppings littered the car front to back. Joseph pulled his 1979 Oldsmobile Ninety-Eight Regency alongside his grandson's Honda. The men met between their cars.

"Gramps," Chris said, then pointed to Joseph's car. "You still drive that thing?"

Joseph ignored the question. "Your mother tells me you're MIA, maybe hanging around the wrong people. She says you disappear for months at a time and don't return her calls. You don't stay in touch. You aren't communicating with me, that's for sure. I just assume it's because your mom hates my guts, you don't wanna get in the middle. Why aren't you returning your mother's calls?"

"Oh, boy," Chris said, then yawned, stretching his arms over his head, then back behind him. At 5'11", 180 pounds, Chris was in prime shape. His body was rock hard from the exercising he'd never stopped since before he joined the Army. He'd inherited his father's thick, black hair and wore it straight back, something neither Joseph nor Chris's mother were crazy about.

"Look," Joseph said, "she still blames me for what happened to your father. She forgets he was my son, but this time she reached out to me to find out what's going on with you. That scared me. So, what is it? What's going on?"

"I've been busy," Chris said. "And I have a girlfriend now I think I might marry."

"A girlfriend. Months at a time she don't hear from you, your mother. She meet this girlfriend? She didn't mention one to me."

"Not yet, no."

Joseph moved to the fender of his car and leaned against it. "Try not getting married before they meet," he said.

Chris saw Joseph was looking at the Honda and said, "I'm gonna get it washed."

"Christ, I hope so. You know that bird shit'll eat right through the finish, right?"

"My girl's place is on the Island. Trees on both sides of the driveway."

"Maybe you should cut them down. Or park in the street."

Chris smiled.

"What's her name?"

"Haydee."

"Haydee? That's Spanish, no?"

"She's Greek."

"From there?"

"Second generation."

"Where on the Island?"

"Mom send you here to interrogate me?"

"When she calls and asks me to find out something, it means it's serious. So, now tell me what's really going on with you and your girlfriend and your bird-shit Honda."

Chris wet his lips, huffed, and then said, "I'm a grown man, Gramps. I have my own life now. I'm not answering to anyone about what I'm doing. A few years back, I did a little traveling without getting everyone involved and I've been interrogated ever since. I'm doing fine."

Joseph pointed to the Honda. "Yeah, I can see that. You're driving around in a car covered in bird shit."

"We have another car."

"We do, huh? So, you're living with this Greek girl? I'll ask again, your mother know about her?"

"You'll tell her. Come on, you know how she can be, my mother. She's still shitting her pants because of what happened to my father."

"He was caught in a mob dispute is what happened. All the shit that went down after Gotti was convicted. Your father was in the wrong place at the wrong time. An unintended target. Collateral damage they called it. I lost my son because he couldn't ignore the extra money he was making running football tickets like every other square guy looking to make a few extra coins. My son, your father, never wanted anything to do with mobsters. Mob associate they called him in the paper. Assholes. Mob associate my ass. He was hustling for a few extra bucks was all your father was doing. That orange fuckin' Bozo was in the White House, him and his greedy fuckin' kids, what's that called? That's a fuckin' crime family."

"I remember what happened, Gramps. I was eleven. I remember it all too well."

"If you remember it then you'll quit hanging around with dumbskis think they're in a fuckin' movie."

"Huh? Hanging around with who?"

"Your mother thinks you're playing with bad guys. Bad people."

"What people? Jesus Christ, this is what I mean. She's paranoid, my mother. You know that."

"I know she's a mother and mothers are always paranoid about their sons, especially when their husband, their son's father, was killed by the mob, mistake or no mistake."

"I'm not hanging out with mobsters, Gramps. And I'm not going to listen to her accuse me of it either. I'll call her when I get home, but if she starts again, I'm not gonna listen to it."

"Then take it from me, kid. If you are playing with those clowns, know that nothing good will ever come from it. Nothing. They're all full of shit. Every one of them thinks they're in a movie. They hate each other as much as they hate themselves. You let them, they'll change you. And if you stick with them and their bullshit because it all looks so enticing, in the end you'll wind up in one of two places, neither of them good. In jail or in the ground, take your pick."

"I'm not hanging out with mobsters, Gramps. How's Artie, by the way?"

Joseph gave it a moment, then said, "I wish I could believe you, Chris. Right now, I don't."

"Artie?"

"Artie's fine. Don't change the subject."

"Right," he said. "You don't believe me. Sorry you feel that way."

He started to walk away when Joseph said, "Hey, it doesn't mean I don't love you."

Chris frowned.

Joseph said, "I've been around the block too many times to not know when I'm getting jerked off."

"Goodbye, Gramps," Chris said.

Joseph watched his grandson get into the bird shit covered Honda. He waved as the Honda's engine started. He waited to see if his grandson would wave back. He didn't.

Joseph watched as his grandson's bird shit covered Honda entered the traffic circle at the entrance/exit of the pier and then veered right onto the entrance ramp of the Belt Parkway heading east. Thirty seconds later, Artie Adler's 2020 Ford Fusion followed the same path.

• • • • •

"Cute," Jerry Galante said. He pointed to the mug Morris Greenblatt had just poured a cup of black coffee into. The mug read: "Kill all the lawyers ... except me!"

As the acting captain of a crew, Galante was required to handle all communications between Carmine Montalvo and his lawyer. At 46, Galante had been an inducted member of the Corelli crime family just over 13 years. A protégé of the current underboss of the same family, Dominick Nucci, Galante had been involved in two murders, one before and one after he became a made member. Galante had spent time in prison only once, four years of a seven years sentence for a murder knocked down to a manslaughter charge.

Today he came to Greenblatt's office expecting another series of threats from his boss, Carmine Montalvo, by way of Greenblatt.

Galante was wearing blue jeans, a white polo shirt, and white Reebok sneakers. He'd brought his own coffee from a street vendor and sipped at it with part of the plastic cover peeled back.

"You know he's pissed off, right?" Greenblatt said.

"When isn't he pissed off?" Galante said.

"Now he's extra pissed off."

"More threats."

"Implied, but yes."

"He'll put somebody else in charge of the crew and what else?"

Greenblatt shrugged.

"You can't say it," Galante said before sipping his coffee.

"The point is, Carmine is unpredictable."

"Hey, fuck that," Galante said. "We have enough problems without whacking some civilian over this bullshit."

"What I tried to explain to him. Carmine wouldn't hear it, but killing someone over this? Way too far."

"You got that right. Who needs the extra attention? Especially now. Everybody cutting deals to stay out of prison. Nobody is getting whacked over his wife spreading her legs."

"Just so you know, he's especially pissed off with you, Jerry. How she got away with this in the first place. What he says."

"I can only sit on her for so long. I got other shit to take care of. I've since put one of my best guys watching Montalvo's wife, and I can't spare him either right now."

"I can't tell him that. He doesn't want anyone else knowing about her."

"Please. Everybody knows about her, and I can't have my guy be a babysitter twenty-four seven."

"He's gonna be transferred to Butner. His cancer is worse."

"Meaning no compassionate release. No wonder he's going ape shit now. He knows he's gonna die inside."

"Yep."

"Fuck me."

"Look, you know him better than me."

"I know he don't like excuses," Galante said. "None of the guys in top spots do. I've learned to distrust excuses too, but this is different. He wants to whack a civilian and keep his wife in chains. He should've whacked her before he went away."

"We both know he's headstrong. He'll still give me a headache when I go back down there to see him. He's worse than my wife when it comes to breaking balls."

"You don't have to tell me about wives breaking balls."

"Not like mine," Greenblatt said. "Mine don't even care the kids are out of the house. I can leave whenever I want. She don't care. She'll get half of everything and move to Florida full time. I almost wish she'd fuck around and gimme a reason."

Galante smiled as he pointed a finger at Greenblatt. "You were the guy fixed Carmine's computer that time, right? His wife's computer."

"One of our IT guys, yeah, but nobody is supposed to know that. How'd you find out?"

"Please, Carmine liked his Vodka. Then you can't shut him up. He brags."

"He should've divorced Doris. I never understood why he didn't."

"You know what he did instead, right?"

"No, and I don't want to know."

Galante smiled.

"Yeah, I know," Greenblatt said, "but ..."

"Yeah," Galante said, "you can't say that either. Isn't that convenient?"

Greenblatt shrugged. "What can I tell him about this kid fucking his wife?"

"My guy is on it. All I know right now is the kid is busted up pretty good."

"Specifically?"

"I don't know. Broken this, broken that. Missing a few teeth. I doubt he'll be looking to pork Carmine's wife again."

"The guys did it, they know what it was about?"

"I outsourced the beating so none of my guys got dragged in. I didn't tell the guy I gave to, so my assumption is the guys did it, they didn't know what it was about."

"Somebody is going to have to let Doris know. If the kid they beat up doesn't know what it's about, she should know so she doesn't go near him again."

"That's been handled already."

"Okay," he said. "That's good."

"Carmine's wife is a looker, even at her age," Galante said. "She's also a cum-dumpster. I doubt this kid was the only one she'd been spreading her legs for. Again, Carmine should've handled her before he went away. Now it's everybody else's problem."

"Cum dumpster, Jerry? That's a bit harsh."

"Please."

"Okay, but I don't need to hear that. It's smart your guys aren't involved. I agree."

"Apparently not. Carmine still wants him dead."

"He does. There a chance she'd divorce him? He's never getting out of there, not Butner."

"Why would she do that, divorce him while he's stage four with four years left to go? I'd think she'd be paranoid about what he can still do. If he wants some guy whacked, he can want the same for her."

"I guess."

Galante stretched his neck, then said, "Still, she's what, fifty-six, fifty-seven now? What she stands to gain in a divorce? She's waiting for him to die. A lot of people are waiting for that."

"Hey, I'm his lawyer, remember? He's got a Prenup with her. It isn't that much she gets either way. The house and her car. The other assets, all of them, go to his kids from his first wife."

"He left her anything, he's out of his mind, but that house is worth more than a million alone."

"What I tried to tell him."

"And?"

Greenblatt shrugged.

Galante finished his coffee and set the empty container on Greenblatt's desk. "It's none of my business anyway, so ..."

"Nor mine," Greenblatt said. "It's not like he listens to me anyway. The guy still talks like he's on the street. Doesn't want to accept where he is or how there's no one cares much anymore."

"What they call it in that Patton movie?"

Greenblatt squinted. "What movie?"

"The one about Patton. You know, World War Two. The one with George C. Scott."

Greenblatt shrugged.

"You know, where some German guy is burning papers or whatever, he's holding a picture of Patton before he tosses it in a fire. What he call him?"

"I saw the movie but that was a long time ago. I don't remember."

"Something old fashioned. I remember I had to look it up when I heard it. Anacharoid or some shit."

"Anachronism?"

"That sounds right. What's it mean?"

"Old fashioned, I think. Let's look it up."

Greenblatt grabbed a dictionary from a shelf of legal books behind his desk and looked up the word, then read it aloud: "A thing belonging or appropriate to a period other than that in which it exists, especially a thing that is conspicuously old-fashioned."

Galante smiled. "See that," he said. "What I said."

"Close enough for jazz," Greenblatt said.

• • • • •

A member of the Cirelli crime family, Giovanni Rapino was born in the small town of Pizzoferrato, Italy, 31 years ago. At age 11, his mother brought him to the United States to live with her brother in his home in the Williamsburg section of Brooklyn. It was shortly after 2001. His American born cousins, all 3 boys, were street kids. Their father, his uncle, was an American *mafioso*. His sons and Rapino would learn the ropes of the criminal life they would eventually pursue on the streets of Brooklyn. Although he would learn to speak English, Rapino's accent was still audible 20 years later.

Just under 6-feet, weighing 190 pounds, Rapino was a dedicated gym rat who used almost all of the equipment when doing superset cycles around the universal circuit 3 to 4 times a week. His dark complexion and thick curly blonde hair was an enigma to most of his fellow mobsters. Still considered a zip by some in the Cirelli crew, Rapino's reputation as a stone killer kept them from speaking such insults in his presence.

He'd only met Aniello Fontana once, on the night he was inducted into the Cirelli crime family, but the old man always kept track of his people. Now the 70-year-old boss was anxious to move Rapino up in the ranks of his Borgata.

Today Fontana sent his attorney, Frank Cusmano, to speak with Rapino at the Spumoni Gardens in Gravesend, Brooklyn. Rapino was standing alongside the entrance to the parking lot when Cusmano double-parked, blocking the entrance. Cusmano had just turned 60 and was having problems with his lower back. The attorney waived at Rapino to join him.

Rapino went to the front passenger window as Cusmano lowered it.

"Get in," Cusmano said.

"Park and we get coffee. I buy."

"I don't want coffee. Get in."

"Sure," Rapino said, then surprised the attorney by sitting in the back.

"What the fuck?" Cusmano said.

"What?" Rapino said.

"You think the car is wired?"

"What wired?" Rapino said. "I want to feel like the boss."

Cusmano frowned. He wasn't used to back talk or joking when representing Aniello Fontana. He shifted to his right in the seat, an uncomfortable position for him. He looked at Rapino as if to warn him to quit the smartass routine and was surprised when the gangster from Italy winked at him.

Their meeting had to do with Carmine Montalvo's wife and was being kept secret from other members of their crime family, including the captain Rapino reported to, Jerry Galante.

"What you want?" Rapino said. "I'm busy, eh."

"Fine. The situation with Montalvo's wife and her boyfriend. You know about it?"

"No. What about it?"

"His wife had an affair with some guy. Young guy. Montalvo got word to Aniello, and the boss says it's against the rules."

"The boss Aniello?"

"Yes, your boss. I already told you that over the phone."

Rapino was looking out the window and spotted an attractive older woman in tight white stretch pants.

"Hello?" Cusmano said.

"I hear you, Frank. What the boss wants?"

"He wants the rules enforced."

"He has a captain for that, no? Jerry is acting captain."

"He doesn't trust Jerry. Nobody should know about this. Nobody."

Rapino watched the woman in the tight stretch pants head inside the Spumoni Gardens restaurant. "And?" he said.

"He wants you to take care of it."

"Enforce the rules?"

"Yes."

"He wants I kill the wife's boyfriend."

Cusmano sighed.

Rapino smiled. "You don't say it, I don't do it."

Cusmano sighed again.

Rapino leaned forward, both hands on the back of the front passenger seat and said, "Come on, Frank. I says I'm busy."

"He wants you to take care of the guy."

"Take care like how? Buy him lunch. Get him a woman?"

"Jesus Christ, I'm not supposed to say it."

"And I'm supposed to do it, but I still don't know what the boss wants."

"Eddie Russo. He gets out of the hospital tomorrow."

"I bring him flowers?"

"Kill him. Okay? Your boss wants Eddie Russo dead."

Rapino patted Cusmano on the right shoulder. "There you go, Frank. Bada-boom, bada-bing. Is done now. Tell the boss I take care of it."

"Jesus Christ, you don't make it easy to –"

Rapino opened the back door and was out of the car heading toward the building where he saw the woman in the tight stretch pants go.

• • • • •

Soon after his meeting with Giovanni Rapino, Frank Cusmano was sitting in the living room of his client's home in Eltingville, Staten Island. Aniello Fontana, as head of the Cirelli crime family, rarely left the confines of his house and yard. He was in good shape for a 70-year-old. Just under 6-foot, he weighed 175 pounds. His hair was still thick but had turned completely white. He wore it combed straight back.

Aniello's daughter, Angela, was 47 and essentially a widow since her husband was serving 25 years to life on a murder conviction more than 23 years ago. She'd lived with her father ever since. A petite woman with short dark hair and dark eyes, she often helped her father doing surveillance on soldiers, associates, and new recruits for the crime family.

Now she set a tray of Italian cookies on the coffee table and poured 3 cups of espresso from a tall stovetop pot. She handed

Cusmano one of the cups, then sat at the far end of the couch from where her father sat. Cusmano was sitting in an armchair closer to his client. He thanked Angela and proceeded to complain about Rapino's attitude when he met the killer.

Aniello explained to his attorney the tragic details of Rapino's mother being raped and murdered back in Italy, and why he still had a chip on his shoulder. He also mentioned how valuable Rapino was to their organization.

"Okay," Cusmano said, "but I didn't know any of that. He was being a smartass with me. I think he enjoyed pissing me off."

"Because he don't respect you," Fontana said. "He's a wiseguy, Frank. A made guy. He's like me. He doesn't have to respect you. Unless I tell him to, and when have I spoken to him directly?"

Cusmano was still flustered. "Okay, I get it. I still didn't like it."

Aniello looked to his daughter and shrugged. Angela smiled.

"You gave him my message?" Aniello said.

"I did. He made me say it. I mention he sat in the back, as if the front was wired?"

"He made you say it, what I think you're talking about, just in case the car was wired, Frank. But it wasn't, right?"

"What? Of course not. Come on, Neal. How long have I been your attorney now? How could you ask me something like that?"

Aniello was looking to his daughter again. Both were smiling.

"Calm down, Frank," Aniello said. "I'm breaking your shoes. I'm doing the same as Rapino with you now. You gave him the message and that's all that counts. Eat something."

"I'm not really hungry."

"Eat something anyway. Have a cookie."

3

Rapino still wasn't sure of her name, but she'd been a decent fuck and wasn't clingy until the morning when it appeared as though she expected some kind of royal treatment.

"Hey, wake up," he said as he nudged the woman's bare shoulder.

He needed to wake her up and send her home. It would be a busy day that started with phone calls to arrange a sanctioned hit.

Rapino saw the woman's tight white stretch pants on the floor alongside her blouse and panties. Her jacket was draped across a chair and her flats were near the door.

She was wearing a gold necklace with a ruby at the tip of the letter J. Rapino went through her bag when he first woke because he couldn't remember her name. Her driver's license showed her name was Janice Bernstein and that she was born in 1978. He left the $63 dollars she had in her purse and examined her body as she lightly snored. Janice had a decent chest that must've been enhanced, he assumed, because it didn't sag. He was too drunk and horny to notice or care about her facial wrinkles or the cellulite behind her legs and on her ass last night, but now they were clearly visible and it turned Rapino off.

She'd been attracted to him when she spotted him waiting on line in the store. Rapino saw her smiling his way and winked. A few minutes later they were flirting openly while waiting to be served, and when he told her he wanted to marry and buy her a house, she agreed to have drinks with him and they left the place without buying a thing.

They went to a bar near his apartment. He drank a few Vodka rocks. She drank a few apple martinis. When she was clearly drunk, he told her he couldn't wait until their wedding night, and she giggled as he led her out of the bar to his car. Half an hour later, she was smoking weed while he went down on her. She made a lot of noise when she came, and it bothered Rapino because he never believed it when a woman was loud during sex. He remembered turning her around and doing it that way. Then again when she got on top of him and worked him back up to speed with her mouth. The last he remembered was her lightly snoring when he lit a joint for himself.

"Come, Janice, wake up, *bella.*"

"What time is it?" she said after stirring from her side onto her back. She draped an arm over her eyes to block the sunlight shining through a window.

"Seven o'clock, but I have busy day."

She smiled with her eyes closed. "You have an accent."

"Yes, we talk about last night. I'm from Italy."

"What time is it?"

"Janice, no bullshit now. Come, get up."

"I want breakfast," she said. "Can we call it in?"

Rapino gave up and pulled her up by an arm. She tried to pull back and struggled until he smacked her face hard.

"Hey, I don't have time, okay? Get up, get dressed and go home. I give you money for cab."

Janice had cowered after the slap and was still holding her cheek when he pulled his arm back to smack her again. She ducked around him and ran to the bathroom.

"Ah," he said. "*Finalmente.*"

• • • • •

Special Agent, Chris Gallo, working undercover as Charlie Mazza, didn't know what they were doing or why. Giovanni Rapino had called him in the afternoon and told him to park near 92nd Street in Brooklyn and to wait for him there.

Half an hour later, they were driving over the Verrazzano-Narrows Bridge onto Staten Island in a stolen 2018 Toyota Camry. Rapino parked on the corner of Jewett Avenue and Bache Street. He glanced at his watch and told Mazza to get behind the wheel and to wait in the car. Rapino went to the back of the stolen car and opened the trunk. Mazza looked at the rear and side view mirrors but couldn't see Rapino. He waited until the trunk closed and he could hear footsteps crossing the avenue before glancing at Rapino again.

Rapino was carrying a black bookbag in his right hand. Mazza watched him until Rapino disappeared around the corner.

Mazza was recently spoken for by Rapino and assigned to his crew within the Cirelli crime family. What he knew of Rapino came from other associates with the same crew, his FBI briefings, and Rapino himself.

Mazza knew that Rapino's mother, after taking him to the United States at the age of eleven, had returned to Italy to care for her husband during his final stages of pancreatic cancer. One month after her husband's death and two weeks before she returned to her son in New York, Maria Theresa Rapino was raped and murdered in the home where she had lived with her husband and son.

Once he learned about Rapino's mother, Mazza understood the gangster's desire and intention to return to Italy and avenge his mother. It was the only thing Rapino had ever personally shared with Mazza about his past.

Now Mazza was doing what associates did when on the road with a made member of a crime family. It was either everything or nothing. Today, at least so far, it was nothing.

• • • • •

Giovanni Rapino had spoken for Charlie Mazza three months ago after taking him on a few collection errands for the acting skipper of their crew, Jerry Galante. Thus far the 27-year-old from Brooklyn was handling himself. Mazza didn't ask questions and seemed fearless. Today he'd become an accomplice to murder without knowing it.

Rapino had made his boss's attorney say the words. Once said, the young man fucking Carmine Montalvo's wife had to be killed. This old rule of *Cosa Nostra* couldn't be ignored. If there was to be any honor maintained within *Cosa Nostra*, the young man, Eddie Russo, had to die for fucking a made man's wife.

The hit was arranged by calling one associate to steal a car and another to drive. Charlie Mazza would be the driver. Eddie Russo had been released from the Staten Island University Hospital earlier in the day and was convalescing back at home.

It all came together within two hours. Rapino gave Mazza an address and followed him to the location on Station Island where they both parked. From there Mazza drove them in the stolen car near Eddie Russo's home address.

Rapino didn't mention what it was about. Mazza didn't ask.

A Baretta 9mm and a sound suppressor were hidden in the trunk; the handgun under a blanket and the suppressor taped under the donut spare.

Rapino put both inside a bookbag. He slammed the trunk shut, then carried the backpack in his right hand as he crossed the street. He looked back at Mazza one last time before turning the corner and heading to Eddie Russo's address.

The house was near the middle of the block. Rapino went halfway down the driveway and dropped to a knee to remove the Beretta and sound suppressor from the bookbag. He put on a pair of blue surgical gloves and then went to the back of the house. He climbed a short stairway to the back porch and then opened the screen door. He tried the back door, but it was locked. He knocked on the door four times and waited. An older woman with short white hair and a gray housedress came to the back door. Her brow was furrowing a moment before Rapino shot her two times in the chest through the window. He used the bookbag to push the rest of the broken glass out of the frame, then reached in and unlocked the door. He was careful going through the rooms on the ground floor, wielding the Beretta in front of him in a shooting stance.

The television was on in the living room. A snack tray with a cup and cookies was positioned near the couch. Rapino looked up the stairs, then took them two at a time. There were two doors near the top of the stairs and one further down the hall toward the front of the house. He checked the room closest first, quietly opening the door. He took two steps in and could see the man he was there to kill. He had bandages around his head, a badly bruised face, swollen lips, and a cast on one arm. A hospital tray was positioned to his left. The man was watching a television to his right.

"Eddie?" Rapino said.

Eddie Russo turned to Rapino. His eyes opened wide a moment before he was shot three times, twice in the chest and once in the forehead.

Rapino headed back down the stairs and left through the front door.

• • • • •

Charlie Mazza was a little nervous when he saw Rapino had taken a bookbag from the trunk, but there was no way he could question him about it. He could only hope Rapino would tell him afterward. The few times he'd been with the gangster, Rapino hadn't said much beyond what had happened to his mother back in Italy.

Mazza clocked the time Rapino left at 8:02. When he caught movement on his left again, 14 minutes later, he saw Rapino returning. The gangster made a fist of his right hand and turned twice to the right. Mazza assumed he meant start the car and did so.

"Go," Rapino said once he was inside the car.

Mazza put the transmission in drive and pulled away from the curb. As he navigated his way back to Route 440, he wondered if Rapino would say something.

Rapino had placed the bookbag on the floor and covered it with his feet. He remained silent until Mazza asked, "Brooklyn?"

"Not yet," Rapino said. "One more stop."

Neither spoke again until they approached the exit for Bradley Avenue. Then Rapino said, "Here, take this exit. Bradley."

Mazza turned his blinker on and exited the Staten Island Expressway at Exit 11. When they approached Bradley Avenue, Rapino said, "Right here."

Mazza turned right onto Bradley Avenue, then Rapino said. "Left there."

Mazza turned left onto Ramsey Lane.

"Park," Rapino said.

Mazza pulled up to the curb and parked.

"Come," Rapino said as he opened his door. "Leave keys."

Mazza left the key in the ignition, then followed Rapino across the street. Rapino opened the door of a Navy Blue, Chevy Equinox. He sat behind the wheel. Mazza walked around the front and used the passenger door. Rapino started the engine, then pulled away from the curb. He turned right onto Gannon Avenue South and then veered left into the entrance for the Staten Island Expressway. Twenty minutes later they were back in Brooklyn. Rapino turned right onto 92nd Street, then parked on the corner off Battery Avenue. He fist bumped Mazza before telling him he'd call later. Mazza walked back to his car, a 2019 Buick Encore, on Battery Avenue. He sat in the car a few minutes before driving up to 92nd Street and turning left. He took 92nd to 4th Avenue, then turned left and stayed on 4th Avenue until he hit Shore Road. He turned right onto Shore Road and headed for his apartment in Bay Ridge.

•   •   •   •   •

Rapino drove back to his street. He brought the bookbag up to his 4th floor apartment. He closed the blinds in his living room and kitchen, then removed the sound suppressor from the Beretta. He then disassembled the Beretta and placed the 16 major parts in separate small black plastic bags. He wrapped the bags with black duct tape, then showered. He called a Chinese prostitute he'd used since he moved into the building. She lived on the second floor with another Chinese woman. He'd been with both a few times. He was glad Li-Jie was home.

Twenty minutes after they were finished having sex, he told her he had an appointment and that he'd call her again when he was back.

Rapino put the 17 black plastic bags back into the bookbag. He brought them down to his car and set them on the floor under the front passenger seat.

He drove to New Utrecht Avenue and turned left under the El. He stopped at a few commercial garbage containers along the Avenue and tossed one black plastic bag at a time into a container. He continued doing so until he turned onto Fort Hamilton Parkway and stopped at the garbage containers behind a few different fast-food restaurants.

He tossed the last of the plastic bags into a Burger King container near the Greenwood Cemetery, then stepped inside and ordered a Whopper, fries and a vanilla milkshake before returning to his car. He ate the fries and drank the milkshake while heading home. He developed a slight stomachache as he parked the car.

Rapino was thinking he might need to use the bathroom and maybe take a nap before calling Li-Jie again.

4

"This where he lives?" Joseph Gallo asked Artie Adler.

They were sitting in his Ford Fusion across the street from the apartment building where Adler saw Chris Gallo enter the day before.

"He was clever when he left the pier where you met him," Adler said. "He drove one exit to Starrett City, parked on Pennsylvania Avenue and walked to the Ford Fusion parked here on Shore Road."

"He switched cars? Why?"

Adler shrugged. "I followed him back onto the Belt. Kept my distance until I seen him get off at Exit one. Then he does a roundabout back to Fourth Avenue and back to the bridge, turns right on Shore Road and takes that a few blocks before he finds a spot and parks. I laid back in a hydrant spot and waited. He walked into the building across the street. That's his car. Next day he drives a little ways back toward the bridge. I thought he might take the bridge into Staten Island, but he winds up on some shit side street near Ninety-Second Street. Battery Avenue. Parks there and walks up to Ninety-Second where some guy in a 2019 Toyota Camry picks him up. I follow them over the bridge into Staten Island and they wind up parked around the corner from where those two people were killed. The guy picked him up took a bookbag from the trunk and came back with the same thing. This time they get on the Expressway and off again at Bradley Avenue, park nearby and switch cars. They take off in a Chevy Equinox. I took down the license number and have a guy can get me a name and address. I assume the Camry was stolen. Then they return to Brooklyn and the guy drops your grandson off on Ninety-Second Street and takes off. Chris waits a few minutes and heads back to here."

"Fuck me," Joseph said.

"It was a hit, Joe. And your grandson was the driver."

"Stupid fuckin' kid."

"I'll find out who the shooter was."

"Alleged shooter."

Adler sighed. "Come on, Joe."

"Whatever," Joseph said. "The shooter, fine. What now?"

"I'll find out who the shooter was while you try and flip your grandson. It's the only way to get him out of it now."

"If Chris was in the car, he can't testify. What's he gonna say. I drove the guy to this place, waited for him, and then went home."

"With a couple of car switches between start to finish," Adler said. "Not to mention that Camry was likely stolen."

"Hey, we have to figure this out, Art. I have to."

"We're talking a double murder, Joe. What's to figure out?"

"Jesus Christ."

"You know better. The hell is he gonna do?"

"Can I at least question the kid first?"

"Of course. In the meantime, I'm gonna see who his friend is."

"You're not staying?"

"No. You can grab a cab back. I don't advise getting in your grandson's car though. Just grab an Uber or something."

"Right," Joseph said.

Adler patted Joseph on the left arm. "I'll call you."

• • • • •

Internal Affairs Investigator, Tommy Stone, pulled three twenty-dollar bills from his wallet and set them on the kitchen table on his way out of the house. It was a few minutes after 8 o'clock in the morning and he wanted out before his wife came downstairs and broke his balls about money again. Last night had been a push, except for the interest on the three $500 losses in baskets.

Win three, lose three, you still pay 10% on losses, which amounted to $50.00 per loss, a total of $150.00.

He'd had worse days. A lot worse.

He was at least five years from retirement, a retirement he wouldn't be able to afford unless he nailed a Pick 6 at Belmont with at least two longshots in the mix. His wife had become impossible to be around of late. If it wasn't money he was shelling out for their daughter's private high school, twenty-one grand a year, it was a bathroom renovation, or a new car, or the vacation they hadn't taken in the three years he'd been gambling.

The list was long and annoying, and his wife knew just how to ruin any sense of positive energy he might have before picking a team or a horse to try and dig himself out of a hole.

Four weeks earlier the hole was $3,500. Three days ago, he'd built it up to $7,000. He was desperate and had considered trying to remortgage the house one more time but doubted the bank would go for it, especially while he was late on mortgage payments. Then he'd been gifted a $4,000 get-partially-out-of-the-hole-free card in the form of sending a couple of goons to bust up some guy on Staten Island. Why the hard guys didn't want to handle it themselves, Stone didn't know or care. Four grand was four grand, leaving him just $3,000 in the hole and maybe some room to bet again.

He'd been playing with fire the last three years, betting with a connected bookmaker he did the occasional favor in exchange for credit or cash. It was risky and dangerous, but so far he'd been fine. At least he didn't know if he wasn't.

Gambling had changed the way he thought, and it started the night he met a woman, the wife of a cop he'd been investigating. He'd gone to her house to interview her claim about being hassled by her husband, a dirty cop she'd claimed. They were estranged, her husband living with his brother, another cop.

A few drinks into the interview she climbed on Stone's lap, and they wound up in her bed. Afterward, she wanted to date. She said she hadn't been on one since before she was married. She was going to file for a divorce the next week and thought an afternoon trip to Belmont was a good way to see if her decision to divorce was a lucky one.

They got there after the 5th race and Stone backed her picks in the 6th and 7th races. He hit a late daily double for more than $2,200. She'd won $200 and rewarded him with a blowjob while he drove her home.

Their affair lasted just a few more dates over the next few weeks, but by then he'd been back to Belmont several times and was almost even, losing back $1,800. He'd been careful at home with his wife and started using condoms just in case he'd picked something up. Then he went to a doctor and was cleared and he could fuck his wife again, but the gambling needle was firmly in his arm, which led to him betting sports.

At first he started small with 10 and 20 time bets, $50 and $100, and eventually graduated to nickels and dimes, $500 and $1,000. He'd been up and down a few thousand over time until he hit a bad streak and lost almost $9,000. He'd backed the bookmaker off until a meeting was requested by the guy behind the bookmaker. Jerry Galante, a wiseguy with the Cirelli crime family, had cut Stone off from betting until they met. That's when the favors began and working for a wiseguy became his second job. He did favors until he worked his debt off and was allowed to bet again.

He mostly provided information he could get through his internal affairs investigations, claiming a confidential informant's tip on one of the detectives within the organized crime unit justified his investigation. It was a front to gather information on who the task force was looking at and who might be making deals. He provided license plate numbers, phone numbers and street addresses until he was watching mob associates for a potential rat.

As soon as he was given a green light to bet again, Stone lost big. He continued to lose and win and lose again. Then, a few weeks ago, he hit a harsh cold streak. Coupled with household and tuition bills, it was the biggest financial mess he'd ever backed himself into.

He didn't pay his daughter's tuition. He was late on his mortgage and cable bills. There was little to nothing in their bank account, and the money his wife managed to squirrel away disappeared when he found it wrapped with a rubber band in a cereal box.

Now he was reading about a double murder on Staten Island that appeared to be a mob hit. A guy named Eddie Russo and his mother had been shot to death in a house where Russo had just returned after being released from Staten Island University Hospital hours earlier.

"Fuck me," Stone said.

He wasn't about to call Jerry Galante and find out what it was about, but Stone knew it couldn't be good. If they were going to kill Russo, why have Stone arrange a beating for the guy beforehand? Why arrange a beating for him at all?

Galante called from a burner phone an hour after Stone left for work. Stone answered the call without saying anything.

"The office," Galante said. "After six."

"Shit," Stone mouthed, then killed the call.

• • • • •

"I brought a present," Special Agent in Charge, Connor Kelly said.

He removed two small bottles of Manhattan Special coffee sodas and set them on a milk crate. He used a bottle opener connected to a keyring to pop the tops. He handed one of the bottles to Doris Montalvo and said, "*Sláinte*."

Doris frowned. "You're in a good mood," she said.

"Once I heard the nervousness in your voice, I had a feeling the worm was finally turning."

"Don't be smug, Kelly. I haven't made up my mind yet. I'll need guarantees."

They were in the basement apartment where her mother lived on 55th Street in Sunset Park, where she usually met lovers she was shielding from her husband's spies. Doris had dealt with the FBI twice before, but only to protect herself from her husband after getting caught having an affair. She'd told them what she knew, none of it helpful to their investigations, but she was more concerned with law enforcement having a record of her complaints and fears in the event she disappeared someday.

In the event she was killed, Doris wanted law enforcement to know as much as possible about whomever ordered her death, which more than likely would be her husband. Although they listened and recorded her story, there was nothing they could offer her in the way of direct protection. Not unless she could provide something substantial they could use against Carmine Montalvo or his associates in organized crime.

The second time she dealt with the FBI was six months ago when she realized she was being followed by someone other than Jerry Galante. Frightened that her husband had finally ordered her death, she called Kelly again and the two met in the back of a hair salon. After hearing her story, Kelly assured her yet again there was nothing they could do without something they could use to bring down her husband's crew or anybody else associated with mob related criminal activity.

Frustrated and fed up with the FBI, Doris seduced the man Jerry Galante had following her.

Today was different. Since she'd received word from her husband's lawyer that Carmine would be moved to a medical prison in North Carolina, she became more nervous than usual. Her husband was about to die and she feared he might be anxious to make sure she did so as well.

Kelly said, "This latest anxiety attack of yours. Anything to do with this guy all the fuss was about getting murdered along with his mother in the home on Staten Island?"

Doris huffed. "He was a kid for Christ's sake, twenty-eight years old or something."

"You know who did it?" Kelly said.

"How would I know that?"

"Because you called your husband."

"That was because of Jerry. He wanted me to call Carmine."

"And?"

"And what? Carmine wouldn't take the call."

"And his lawyer?"

"Greenblatt only calls me to pass on messages. This one was about Carmine going someplace in North Carolina."

"FMC Butner," Kelly said. He took another sip of his soda, set the bottle down and said, "Well, somebody carried out Carmine's wishes and killed Eddie Russo. They also killed his mother. Let me ask you this, did you grieve yet?"

"Go fuck yourself, Kelly."

"Well?"

"Why would I want some guy I fucked twice in six months killed? If someone hadn't ratted on us, I'd've fucked him again. Probably a few more times."

"I hope I didn't buy those Manhattan Specials for nothing, Doris."

"Yeah, you're a big spender."

"Look, Carmine going to FMC Butner—"

"To die, I hope," Doris said.

"Doris, one minute you're nervous he might die and want you dead first, the next you're wishing he would die. Which is it? I mean, you lose a lot of leverage once he goes. I'd be cheering for him to survive as long as possible, I was you."

"Meaning?"

"Jerry Galante still has an envelope brought to your house, right? That's tribute their rules say has to be done."

"It's a small tribute, Kelly. Just enough to pay the bills."

"And still better than nothing, which it will be once your husband does croak. So, maybe it was an act of desperation, this guy he wanted dead for a month or so now finally gets killed along with his mother. If you know something, like maybe who did the hit?"

"What?"

"Eddie Russo?"

"Holy shit, you think I wanted that?"

"I know your husband wanted it. Maybe you have an ulterior motive. I don't know."

"Ulterior motive such as?"

"Jerry Galante know about it or not?"

"Jesus Christ."

"Well?" Kelly said.

"I fuck Jerry Galante, Kelly. For my own purposes. I don't order murders. Besides, all Jerry does is complain about what Carmine wants him to do."

"Now, if you could get some of that on tape … I'm just sayin' here."

Doris frowned. "Yeah, right. Get Jerry on tape whining about Carmine, and if he finds the recorder, he kills me and loses the tape. No thanks, buster."

Kelly sipped from his bottle of Manhattan Special again. "I love this stuff," he said afterward. "I can drink six bottles of this, but then I want to die from gas later in the day. Not to mention I wouldn't sleep for a day or two."

Doris ignored him. "You want the details of what Jerry tells me in the heat of getting laid or what he says when he lets his guard down?"

Kelly took a deeper drink from his coffee soda, finishing more than half the contents.

Doris said, "You know, when he caught me cheating with the computer thing, the thing Carmine wanted most from me were the details. In bed that's what he wanted to hear. How far down my throat I could take it and so on."

Kelly yawned.

"Am I boring you?" Doris said. "You can always make believe you give a shit, Kelly. At least turn off whatever recording device you're wearing under your shirt or jacket or wherever the fuck you cops put them."

"I'm not recording, Doris. You should know that."

"Why would I know that?"

"Because we're here in your mother's house, in the basement apartment where you fuck Johnny Rapino. I hope Jerry Galante never learns about that, by the way."

"You agents think you're all so smart, don't you? How many agents do you waste a day following me around?"

"None," Kelly said. "We don't even bother with warrants. Not against you or this house. Nor would I record if we were at the JFK Marriott, where you fuck Jerry Galante. Recordings are only made with warrants. You're not a target, Doris. Remember, you're the one who contacted us, and more than once. Actually, we picked that up about you and Rapino six or so months ago. I guess from when Galante told Rapino to follow you around."

Doris snickered. "And follow me he did."

"So we weren't following you, Doris. We were following him."

"Bullshit."

"Whatever. It's not relevant. Do you have something for me or not? I already finished my soda."

Doris huffed. "Carmine accused me of fucking Eddie Russo. I have no idea how he learned about that. Maybe it's one of your people told him. That wouldn't surprise me, not an iota, using me as bait. I wouldn't know. Jerry now knows I was fucking the guy. I had to admit it. It's Carmine I'm worried about maybe wanting to have me killed too now. I tried to back Jerry off and said I only fucked him, nobody else. That after they put Eddie Russo in the hospital. Jerry claims Carmine wanted Eddie dead. Now he is. I don't know who told Carmine and I don't know how Jerry was so sure I was fucking Eddie Russo, but eventually, like I said, I had to admit it. Jerry didn't sound like he wanted anybody killed, especially a civilian, he said. That seemed to be a big deal, killing a civilian."

"It is."

"They have their rules. All I'm worried about is them killing me, which is why I called you."

"And you don't know who told Carmine about Eddie Russo?"

"I don't. I just said so two seconds ago. Neither does Jerry know. He was worried about that too."

"Because he's fucking you and the same set of rules can get him whacked as well."

"Whatever. All I know is that Carmine is nuts. Maybe it's the cancer and maybe he's decided he should have me killed now in case he dies before he can give the order. I have no idea, but he told Jerry about Eddie and then I tried to sell it as bullshit. Jerry knew it wasn't. He's an arrogant fuck just like most of them, but he's not stupid. Besides, all those guys are paranoid now. Jerry for sure. Carmine's just crazy. Between his cancer treatments and who knows what's going through that sick fuck's head."

"I still don't have enough to hide you. You have to know that."

"I know you won't move a muscle until I'm dead. That's what I know. Jerry said if I didn't call Carmine, which I did, he threatened to kill Eddie, cut off his dick and stick it down my throat."

"Yeah, well, whatever it is he does for you, you should know he doesn't have much respect for you. Talks some nasty shit about you."

"Jerry Galante served my purpose."

"And Rapino?"

"He serves another purpose."

"And now this poor bastard, Eddie Russo, and his mother are dead. What purpose did they serve?"

"Fuck you. I have recordings. I made some."

Kelly smiled. "Really?" he said. "And when can I hear those?"

"When I know I'm going to be protected."

"Doesn't work that way, Doris."

"Well, it'll have to for me."

"You don't get it," Kelly said, frustrated then. "You still don't get it."

"Get what, Kelly? What don't I get?"

"You have competition you can't compete with. These guys today, the mob, a lot of the old timers and almost all the young ones, they have no intention of doing serious time once they're arrested for anything that'll put them away for more than five years. Some of them can't even do that. How many decades is it now they've been turning state's evidence? Soldiers and captains and the bosses themselves now. They no longer have the juice they had in the past. They started cooperating en masse after the RICO statues. Whatever power that was left by the 80s was obliterated by those RICO statutes. Now everybody wants to make a deal the day they're arrested. You don't have what those guys have. You don't have the shakedowns, the union corruption, the construction, sanitation, or the murders. You have talk. Talk without corroboration. You knew what you were involved in how many weeks after you married Carmine? If it even took that long. Did it?"

"Back to smug again."

"I'm not being smug, Doris. I'm being honest. If you're still afraid of them, get on a plane and find somewhere else to live. The mob has no reason to do anything to you anyway. What you give them is free, whether they serve a purpose for you or not. Maybe it's mutual. If so, God bless. If you want to stay, you should stay. It's up to you, but a federal prosecutor won't justify witness protection or anything else just because you fuck an acting captain and one of his soldiers. If you can't give me the person or people who killed Eddie Russo and his mother, if you can't corroborate it when you do have it, then we both have nothing. These days, mob guys making deals are a dime a dozen. Almost all of them flip. The guys that don't, they do long stretches and everything changes by the time they're out again. Nobody cares they were stand up and did time. The new guys will still turn on them first time they're facing time themselves. We have more than a few wiseguys who were twice burned. Shit, we had one made it a hat trick."

Doris was squinting then, her face flush with anger. "So I'm better off going to the press is what you're saying? Because I will if I have to."

"There's nothing I can do," Kelly said. "That's what I'm telling you, but if you go to the press, then your life will be in danger. That's a given, and the order won't have to come from your husband. We both know of at least two out there that'll raise their hand to volunteer for the work."

Doris swallowed hard, gave it a moment, then stood up and pointed at the basement door. "Then you're right, Kelly," she said. "What the hell do I need you for?"

• • • • •

When Jerry Galante learned about the murder of Eddie Russo and his mother on Staten Island, he went ballistic. He threw a 10 minute fit, during which he'd broken two lamps, a coffee table, and then put a hole in a basement wall with a crystal ashtray.

His wife came down to the basement after hearing the noise. It had happened before when Galante lost it and broke a few things, but never like this, at least not to her recollection.

"Jerry, what the hell?" Regina Galante said.

Galante glared at his wife a moment, then turned away.

"Jerry?"

"Nothing. Go back upstairs."

"No. What's going on?"

He glared at her again. Regina set her hands on her hips and shifted her weight onto one leg.

"What?" Galante said. "What do you think happened, something good? You see me smiling? Opening a bottle of champagne, something?"

"No, but tell me instead of breaking up the house."

She pointed at the hole in the wall and looked down at the crystal ashtray still in one piece.

"Jesus Christ," she said. "That thing must weigh ten pounds."

"I'll have the wall fixed, don't worry."

"And the lamps and coffee table?"

"What about them? You can't replace them? What are they fuckin' relics or something? Buy new ones."

"Are you going to tell me?"

"What do you think? No."

Regina frowned, then turned and headed back upstairs. Galante waited until he could hear her footsteps, then punched a second hole in the wall. Her footsteps returned to the basement door upstairs.

"Asshole!" she yelled.

Galante punched one more hole in the wall, cutting two of his knuckles on his right hand. He wiped the blood on his pants, looked at his bruised knuckles, and yelled, "Cocksucker!"

Somebody had gone ahead and killed Eddie Russo, a civilian, and his civilian mother. The law enforcement heat such a stupid move would generate would be enormous. Galante grabbed a burner phone from a desk drawer and dialed Morris Greenblatt.

"Jerry?" Greenblatt answered.

"Yeah, it's Jerry. You see what happened?"

"I did."

"And?"

"Not on this line."

"Did you know about it?"

"No, but not on this line."

"Asshole," Galante said, then killed the call.

He started to call Doris Montalvo next, then stopped himself. Her phone had to be bugged. He called his mob mentor and the underboss of the family instead. First he had to call a coffee shop in Dominick Nucci's neighborhood. It was a screening method Nucci insisted on for the sake of security. The callback could take anywhere from 20 minutes to an hour. If it exceeded an hour, Galante would call one of two social clubs to try and locate Nucci. At least he could leave another message for a callback.

Galante spent the next half hour trying to figure out who in or outside his crew would have killed Eddie Russo and his mother. If Nucci wasn't aware of the hit, and Galante couldn't imagine he was aware of it, then someone had gone rogue on Carmine Montalvo's behalf, and that could mean he'd be replaced as the acting captain of their crew.

Nucci called after 40 minutes.

"Dom," Galante answered.

"Tell me you didn't order that," Nucci said.

"What? Of course not. I'm racking my brains here trying to figure out—"

"Come to the house."

"Now?"

"Right now."

"I'm on my way."

5

"You make a lot of noise," Giovanni Rapino said.

"And you grunt like you're pushing a car," Doris Montalvo said.

They were sitting across from one another in the basement apartment in Sunset Park. Doris continued to use visits to her mother for the extra-marital affair she'd been having with Rapino and where she had met with the FBI Special Agent in Charge, Connor Kelly. The times she and Rapino could spend together always depended on when he was supposed to be spying on her. Either then or when he knew that his boss, Jerry Galante, another of her lovers, was too busy to keep an eye on her.

Today he'd entered the basement from around the block, hopping a backyard fence, then taking the stairs down to the apartment. Doris was waiting for him in a royal blue lingerie outfit. He picked her up and brought her to her the bed, then ripped her royal blue panties off and turned her around. It was aggressive sex, the kind they both preferred. When it was over, Rapino sat on a folding chair facing Doris. She remained on the edge of the bed, a cigarette already in her hand.

"I grunt because you like, no?" he said.

Doris set her cigarette in an ashtray. "I like what you're doing, yeah. So?"

Rapino waited for her attention. "I don't believe noise."

"I do that for you," she said.

"Bulla'shit."

"Okay, I like it too. It turns me on."

"You like because it's me."

"Yeah, don't ever mistake that for more than what it is."

"You do for Galante, make noise?"

"Jesus Christ, you too?"

"Me too what?"

"Gotta know the details," she said. "What is it with men? Every one of you has to know how big another guy's dick is, who is a better fuck, although none of you ever really wanna know the truth about that, right? Not really."

"You do for Jerry or no, bitch?" Rapino said, a touch of anger in his tone.

Doris winked at Rapino. "I do it for every man I'm with, hon," she said. "Gets things over with quicker that way."

"I'm'a no quick," Rapino said.

She ignored him and pointed to her torn panties on the floor. "Those cost seventy-five dollars."

"You can afford."

She took a long drag on her cigarette. The fact that both Galante and Rapino had been with her was dangerous. Rapino didn't seem to care, but Jerry Galante would have both her and him killed if he ever learned about them.

"Where he goes today?" Rapino said.

"Where who goes? Jerry?"

"He tells me to watch where you go."

"And here you are."

"Don't make stupid, eh? He tells me today, somebody else tomorrow. What he says?"

"Jerry or Carmine?"

"Motherfucker."

"Don't get angry," Doris said. "Carmine doesn't talk to me. Ever. Jerry is cautious like you. He doesn't say much either."

"Why he's watching you? You fucking around?"

"He obviously thinks so."

Rapino leaned forward to grab one of her cigarettes from a pack on a night table. He used her lighter to put fire to it, then set the lighter back on the night table.

"So, who killed Eddie Russo?" Doris said.

Rapino let the smoke escape his lungs. "What?"

"Eddie Russo was killed. And his mother. Who would do something like that?"

"You write book?"

"No, but the kid was only twenty-eight. I don't know how old his mother was."

"This the boy your husband want to kill?"

"You know it is."

"I know nothing."

"Yeah, right."

"Don't fuck with me, eh? I don't know who kills this man and his mother."

Doris put out one cigarette and started on another. When it was lit, she said, "Carmine sent word from prison for Jerry to kill him."

"And his mother?"

"You're making fun of me now."

"How you know this about Jerry?" Rapino said.

"How you think?" Doris said. "It's all he could talk about the other day. He pissed and moaned about it. He made me call Carmine."

"You still fuck him?"

"Carmine?"

Rapino leaned forward and aimed the cigarette at her. "I put out in your fucking eye next time," he said.

Doris moved back on the bed. "Relax," she said. "Jerry only fucks me when he can, which isn't often. And yes, you're a better lover. You have a bigger dick."

Rapino smiled. "I know this. I see his little thing in restaurant *pishadoo*. You like a'still fuck baby cock he has?"

"I a'still fucking him because I need to know what my husband is up to. That psycho wants me to live like a nun now that he's out of the picture. That or he'll kill me too."

"Husband is sick, no? The cancer?"

"Stage four."

"He gets out or no?"

"I doubt it. If he does, he'll be in no condition to run his crew. He'll be on chemo or something that keeps him in a bed."

"He comes home, then what you do?"

"What Jerry and everybody else is waiting for him to do. Die. I do nothing but wait."

Rapino smile. "You are cold cunt, eh?"

"Cunt?"

"I like this word."

"So do I, but not when it's aimed at me."

"You full a'shit. I like knowing this. Never to trust."

"I could give you up as easy as Jerry, you know."

"Then you're dead too. No, you choose already. Is safe that way. Your husband dies and I fuck you when I want."

"And Jerry?"

"I fuck Jerry."

"Aren't you the cocky one? Or maybe I missing something here."

"Cocky? Like big cock?"

"Close enough," she said, then opened her legs.

Rapino stood up off the folding chair. "Okay," he said. "Once more time."

•   •   •   •   •

Joseph came back to Chris's apartment building and found a spot out front. He was leaning against the passenger door when his grandson finally exited the building.

"What the fuck?" Chris Gallo said.

"That was gonna be my question to you," Joseph said. "I waited out here more than two hours yesterday before I gave up and went home to get my car. Then I decided I'd come back today and wait again. Now, finally, here you are. I don't see the bird shit Honda anywhere, though. Where you park that, on the Island where you live with your Greek girlfriend? This supposed to be a fuck pad or something? That what you're gonna tell me now?"

Chris said, "How'd you find me? Artie do that for you?"

Joseph nodded. "What's going on?"

"You're gonna get me killed is what's going on."

"Like those two on Staten Island yesterday? Killed like that?"

Chris squinted at Joseph. "Excuse me?"

"You heard me. That what this is about, your life now?"

"Artie followed me again? Great. Are you fucking crazy? Is he crazy?"

"Yeah, and your boyfriend there is a made member with the Cirelli family. Still wanna sell that bullshit about who you're hanging out with? They aren't bad guys?"

Chris kicked Joseph's front fender hard.

"Hey!" Joseph said.

"Hey, your ass," Chris said. "You have no idea the kind of mess you're creating pulling this shit."

"Then why don't you explain it to me?"

"No. Fuck you, Gramps. No fucking way. I don't answer to you. I don't answer to my mother either. And you better warn Artie that he's in over his head on this. Following me might get both of us killed, so tell him to back the fuck off. You back the fuck off too."

Joseph stared at Chris.

"What?" Chris said. "You don't know, okay? You don't have a fucking clue, except you're putting me in danger."

"Like your father?"

"Close enough."

Joseph sighed.

"Go!" Chris said. "Please, if you give an iota of shit about me, just go. And mind your own business going forward. Stay the fuck out of my life."

"He's a murderer, Chris," Joseph said. "Your friend from yesterday. A stone killer."

"Goodbye." Chris started to walk away. "Don't be here when I get back."

"I'm you, I leave the country now. Do it while you can."

It was frustrating having to keep his family in the dark, but if Chris was exposed as a federal agent, neither he nor his family would be safe. The mob had become weakened over the last three decades from government deals. Chris feared that sooner or later those seeking to restore order would break the rule about not going after family members of those who testified for the government. The only thing worse than having to deal with rats was allowing a federal agent to infiltrate their operations.

He hated having to be cruel about it, but Chris raised his right arm and flipped Joseph the bird. Maybe if his grandfather was insulted enough he'd back off. It would be even better if, temporarily at least, Joseph disowned his grandson, but Chris didn't believe that could happen, not even for a second.

Joseph was more hurt than angry. He felt a pang in his heart as he watched his grandson step inside a Buick Encore. He waited until the car pulled away from the curb and made a quick U-turn to drive the other way.

• • • • •

In the dentist office a couple of days ago, Thomas Stone had taken more abuse from Jerry Galante than he was comfortable with. He knew Galante's mood wasn't from the money Stone owed. He'd owed as much in the past.

Stone wasn't sure what Galante was so angry about, but Stone had his own problems. He needed money and he needed it soon. Before they left, Stone asked Galante if he could have the cash instead of knocking off some of his gambling debt.

"It's been a week almost," he told Galante. "I'm counting on that cash. I need the money."

"Fuck you. It was going toward your bill, buddy boy. You weren't getting that in cash no matter what."

"Yeah, but you also said it would let me back in. I had two winners this week would've got me out of shit with the old lady. I'm serious. I'm about to lose my house. I can't pay my kid's tuition."

"Because you're a degenerate fuck."

"I know I am, but I can't make it back without that money."

"Hey, asshole, you want a street loan, I'll send you to somebody, but then you'll pay points on money you'll never pay off. You keep betting after that, you'll wind up in a landfill somewhere."

Stone had swallowed hard. He wished he didn't leave his weapon in his car. He would've shot Galante in the mouth.

Instead he said, "How much can I get?"

Galante smirked. "You sick fuck."

"How much?"

"What's your nut?"

"Total?"

"Total, yeah. How much you need?"

"I don't know, about twenty-five."

"How much of that is to make your next bet?"

"None of it. It's what I owe."

"Bullshit, but if that's what you want, I'll okay twenty and then you'll pay two points a week until you fuck up. The standard rate is three points. You'll get two points. Then it jumps to three when you miss enough times. You miss on three and I'm Pontius Pilate. I wash my hands."

"How soon can I get it?"

Galante glared at Stone and said, "Think about it a couple, three days. You still want it, I'll send you to a guy. Think hard, my friend, because maybe all you really need is fifteen or ten and that's a lot easier at two points than three."

"Can I call you in the morning?"

"No. What I just say, you degenerate fuck? Two or three days. And don't let me find out you're betting again until you wipe the slate. I do find out, like I said, I'm Pontius fuckin' Pilate. My hands are clean. Cop or not cop, you're left to the wolves."

He'd had to put up with Galante's bullshit in the past, but this was over the top. As for the thing with Eddie Russo, Stone had done his job and hired two former confidential informants to throw the guy a beating. They'd done a good enough job. Galante had been fine with it.

Learning the guy and his mother had been murdered was another story, but Stone had nothing to do with that. He never would've taken a job that required someone get killed, never mind some old lady. He figured it was why Galante had been in such a bad mood in the dentist office.

Now Stone was eating dinner while he watched ESPN on a 14" television he'd bought for the kitchen a few months ago. It was on the counter across from where he sat, something his wife didn't appreciate for the extra lack of attention she received the few nights when he was home.

Tonight, when it was apparent her husband was focused on a basketball game on the television, she stood in front of it with the latest notice from their daughter's school in her right hand.

"Hey, what the fuck?" Stone said.

"You need to see this," she said, holding out the notice.

"I'll see it later. Move."

"I'm not moving. You need to see this now."

"Jesus Christ, Lee."

"If I thought Jesus could pay the tuition, I'd bring it to him."

Stone took the notice from her, glanced at it no more than 10 seconds before tossing it on the table.

"And?" his wife said.

"And what? I don't have it."

"Because you lost again."

"Because I lost again. Very perceptive. Maybe you should've been the cop."

"Maybe I should've."

"Please move."

She sat at the table and frowned at her husband while his eyes remained glued to the television.

"They're not going to let this go on," she said. "That was a final notice. Jenny will have to leave Fontbonne."

"For what they charge, they'll be doing us a favor. Twenty-one grand for one year of high school. Fuck Fontbonne Hall Academy, the fucking thieves."

"She loves it there. She loves it and it's where her friends are. And she's doing great. How can you keep betting knowing she'll have to wind up in some shithole public school?"

"Yeah, I know. And I'm on the street risking my life. I think I'm entitled to make a few bets."

"I can't believe you. What's next, Tom? We remortgage the house again or sell it because you don't win your bets and we're close to strapped."

"Don't worry about it, okay? I'll handle it."

"We owe Fontbonne four thousand dollars. Can you handle that?"

"I'll get it."

"They want it now."

"I'll get it this week."

"You'll get it, but you can't bet it. I have to pay them."

"Jesus fucking Christ, will you give it a break?"

Lisa swallowed hard, then left him alone in the kitchen. She didn't make it up the stairs before she began to sob.

• • • • •

"What the hell can I do?" Joseph said. "He told me to fuck off."

"He's likely guilty of murder," Adler said. "Whether he knew what was going on or not, he's guilty as an accessory. That's how it works, Joe. You know that."

They were in Joseph's kitchen again. Adler had brought a pizza. Joseph took one bite but couldn't finish the slice. Adler had taken a few bites of his slice and noticed his friend wasn't eating.

"You get any sleep?" he said.

Joseph frowned. "What do you think?"

"It's a shit situation. You tell his mother yet?"

"Are you crazy?"

"Might be better coming from you than she hears it on the six o'clock news."

"Why would she hear it on the news? You tell one of your cop friends something?"

"Don't be an asshole. Of course I didn't tell anyone. I won't either, but if I could latch onto where Chris was, you better hope some Organized Crime task force wasn't paying attention. Think about the number of ways Chris can go down. There are plenty, the least of which is Rapino flipping someday."

"What hurts as much as knowing this about him is how he spoke to me," Joseph said, his eyes getting wet. "It was nasty. Hurtful. I tried to fend it off, but by the time I got back here, I was full on bawling like some four year old."

"You think this is about his father?"

"That doesn't make sense, Artie. Was a pair of moron wannabees killed his father."

"And nothing happened to them, right?"

"Because nobody would talk, but one of them is dead now and the other is upstate someplace on a drug conviction. Clinton, I think."

"Dannemora," Adler said.

"Right. Where those two escaped from, what is it now, five years ago?"

"More like eight, ten years ago. The two killed your son, that was back when most people didn't talk. Witnesses, I mean. You gotta go back sixty-seventy years ago when wiseguys held their water. It's different now. Most wiseguys can't wait to make deals, and people today, what they consider civilians, aren't as afraid to talk anymore."

Joseph winced from stomach pain. "I don't know," he said, then took a deep breath. "Until that confrontation, I was concerned about him getting involved with those assholes. Now I'm feeling like everything I ever did was wrong. I can't take him hating me."

"I'm sure he doesn't hate you, Joe."

Joseph sipped from a glass of water. Then he felt another stomach pain and struggled to get over it.

"You okay?"

Joseph nodded.

"You're gonna have to pee again you keep drowning yourself," Adler said.

"And that bullshit about a girlfriend, living on Long Island with her. I'll bet that piece of shit car he was driving when he met me on the Canarsie pier, I'll bet that was stolen or something."

"If he's involved with the Cirelli family, he's lost, Joe. There's no coming back from it now, not after what happened on Staten Island."

"He disappeared for months at one point, Artie. Something like five, six months. Nobody could contact him. We were afraid he rejoined the Army or something. He never bothered to tell anyone about it. The why of it."

"You're obsessing, Joe."

"Yeah, I'm obsessing. He's my grandson. My son's son. Why the fuck would he hook up with those assholes. He knows better. He has to know better."

"I still think you better talk to his mother."

"And get accused of this too? No thanks."

He took another few sips of water from his glass.

"This Rapino came over from Italy," Adler said. "He's a zip. OC thinks he's linked to two murders."

"That they can't prove."

"Yes, until the right wiseguy gives him up."

"So, what? Yesterday makes four."

"And Chris gets linked to those two. The mother and son."

"Meaning?"

"He has a card to play."

"Jesus Christ."

"That's not the card, Joe. You know what the card is. He does it now, he may get immunity."

"And how am I supposed to convince him of that? He told me to fuck off and he meant it."

"So, we both go and talk to him this time. He knows I retired from the force. Maybe that'll help."

"He's already blaming you for following him. I doubt he'll want to talk to either of us."

"Why don't we take a shot and see?"

Joseph sighed, then pushed himself up from the table and went to the sink. He reached for his pot and said, "First I gotta pee."

Adler rolled his eyes. "I'll wait in the car."

• • • • •

Chris Gallo had been involved in two long term relationships, both ending when he decided to leave the area and pursue his career. The first was a college girlfriend he'd been with just over a year before joining the Army and going to Iraq. Holly Cohen thought she was in love. So did Chris. They had an intimate relationship until his deployment to Iraq. The two exchanged letters for a few months before the one that ended their relationship arrived at camp Bravo at the Basra International Airport.

"Dear Chris, I'm so sorry," she'd written. "I met someone and I think I love him. Please forgive me."

"Yeah, right," he'd said after reading it half a dozen times. "Forgive yourself."

He was brokenhearted over her letter and dealt with it by volunteering for deadly night patrols. Somehow he'd survived them.

Whether it was the possibility of Chris being killed or maimed or she really had fallen in love while he was in Iraq didn't assuage his anger. If she fell in love, it meant she'd been intimate with someone else. He hadn't been intimate with anyone except Holly. To his mind, she'd cheated and that was the end of it.

His second relationship lasted long enough to leave him wanting more. Her name was Katherine Grady. She was a southern woman from Georgia, his age and a lawyer. They met after a car accident in Quantico on J. Edgar Hoover Road as she entered an FBI Academy parking lot.

Katherine worked in Stafford, Virginia. The first thing Chris noticed about her was her red hair and green eyes. She was there regarding a civil case for one of the Quantico staff. Chris was leaving the same lot and turned into her Subaru Forester left front panel. Their exchange afterward left Katherine more interested than angry.

"Hey, my fault," Chris had said. "At least partly."

"Partly?" she said.

"Well, I was looking at your face and didn't see your car. You have beautiful eyes and I've always been partial to redheads."

"That's some corny shit, mister."

"And that sounds like a southern accent," he said.

"And you're clearly a Yank," she said.

"Chris Gallo," he said. "Soon to be Special Agent Chris Gallo. And you are?"

"Katherine Grady."

"Soon to be dating Special Agent Chris Gallo."

"Really? You think so? Just like that? You hit my car and we have a date?"

That's how it started. Chris paid for her repairs, a smashed front panel and a headlight. They exchanged phone numbers and once her car was repaired and paid for, they agreed to a date the next day he was free from training. Katherine told him she'd drive until he practiced enough so he didn't get them killed.

They became intimate soon after, but when it was time for Chris to make a commitment to their relationship, his decision to train for undercover work ended everything. Katherine didn't like the idea of being involved with someone who would disappear for days or weeks or months at a time. She had not only seen the *Donnie Brasco* movie and didn't like it, she'd also read some of the book by the federal agent doubling as a mob wannabe.

Katherine and Chris spent a last night together before he headed for undercover training.

He hadn't been with a woman since and hadn't stopped thinking about Katherine Grady. He managed to remain focused on his job and eventually, between the training and the undercover work, he was able to forget that he'd fallen in love.

Privacy had been the trajectory of his entire adult life, especially after his father was killed. He hadn't taken to the sympathy shown him at school after his father's murder, nor did he appreciate the bullies who joked about it. He spent a lot of time working out with weights and running and researching the mob. By the time he graduated high school and was ready for college, he preferred anonymity to a social life. Infiltrating the mob wouldn't catch the men who'd killed his father. One of them had already died. The other would die in jail sooner or later. Infiltrating the mob was both a challenge and something Chris felt would serve as an homage to his father and to justice in general.

Now that he'd infiltrated the mob, he was upset about how he'd inadvertently been part of a double murder. He wasn't as interested in the undercover aspect of his job as he was in seeing Giovanni Rapino arrested for the crimes. It's what he was thinking about as his boss, Special Agent in Charge, Connor Kelly, reminded him of who and what the bureau was trying to accomplish.

On the blackboard were pictures in a pyramid formation with names on index cards below each picture. At the top of the pyramid was the boss, Aniello Fontana. On a sub-level to the top of the pyramid were the underboss and consiglieri of the Cirelli crime family. At a second sub-level were the captains, including Carmine Montalvo, a onetime powerful captain in the crime family.

Kelly pointed to it and said, "We want to focus on this clan because after this kid and his mother were killed, we expect all hell to break loose."

"It was Rapino and I was his driver," Chris Gallo said.

"You were Charlie Mazza," Kelly said.

"Doesn't change the fact I was there."

"Yeah, it does."

"How so? There's a police report about this guy, Eddie Russo. He's out of the hospital in the morning and gets killed the same day. He and his mother get killed in her house. Won't somebody wanna know why?"

"NYPD homicide will, sure. What does that have to do with you working undercover?"

"Jesus Christ."

"I doubt he cares either."

"Was this guy bait, this Eddie Russo? Did we know anything about this guy?"

"Why would that concern you?"

"Because I was there, damn it."

"Again, did you know he was going to kill those people?"

"No. So, we're gonna ignore this? I drove a killer to a double murder and we're going to ignore it? Won't this create a bigger problem down the road?"

"Only if your grandfather pokes his nose in the wrong place and gets you killed."

"He doesn't know anything. It's his friend, Artie Adler, an ex-cop who did the snooping."

Kelly shrugged. "Why we moved you."

"I'm still not comfortable with it."

"We pull you now, it'll look even worse. If you remain undercover, it covers you and everybody else. You, Charlie Mazza, didn't know what Rapino was up to when he called you, correct?"

"Correct. So?"

"So, he never told you what he was about to do, correct?"

"Correct."

"And he never told you afterward what he'd done, correct?"

"Yeah, but—"

"Correct or not? He never told—"

"Correct."

"Then there's no problem, Charlie Mazza. This is how it works. You didn't know there would be violence, much less a double murder, which, by the way, has yet to have been established. And if you didn't know, you were under no obligation to try and stop it."

"Except now I do know what happened."

"Do I really have to go through it again, Charlie Mazza?"

It was part of the job he'd come to hate. Seeing and knowing how the bureau used Orwellian doublethink to justify its immoral and outwardly illegal actions to protect itself and/or to bolster its cases. Chris had joined the bureau for the sole purpose of putting away the kinds of men who had killed his father. Now, because he was undercover, he couldn't let his family know, least of all his mother. When his grandfather suddenly showed up outside the apartment building it was because Chris had been followed by an ex-cop.

If an ex-cop could find him that easy, so could someone else. The people who loved him didn't realize the situation. They were in danger of blowing his cover and getting Chris killed.

Not to mention the doublethink lesson he was getting from his immediate supervisor, the Special Agent in Charge. It was difficult for Chris, whether playing the role of Charlie Mazza or not, to ignore a brutal double murder he'd inadvertently taken part in with a hit man in the crew he had infiltrated. Giovanni Rapino had kept the work and subsequent double murder to himself for obvious reasons. Charlie Mazza could never say he knew what was going on, except to lie and say he did.

The problem for Chris was his working an undercover assignment as Charlie Mazza, an associate of the Corelli crime family who had been spoken for by Giovanni Rapino. He still didn't understand why they couldn't arrest Rapino. He knew they wanted a bigger fish, which meant at least for the time being, the double murder would go unsolved, even though they damn well knew who did it.

He wondered if the bureau knew about Eddie Russo all along. He wondered if the poor bastard had been bait. He wondered if they gave a damn about Eddie Russo's mother.

Connor Kelly, along with FBI officials, knew about the murder of Jack Gallo, Chris's father, by mobsters back in 2011. They also knew Jack's father was doing nothing more than hustling football tickets out of his father's bar. He'd been killed by accident when a mob hit when awry and unintended victims like Jack Gallo were killed. The papers referred to Gallo and two other men, one killed along with Gallo, the other severely wounded, as "the kind of collateral damage the mob wasn't usually guilty of."

Once Chris had gone through training in Quantico and received his FBI badge, he volunteered for undercover work against the New York mob, and was immediately put into an intensive program for undercover field work. Almost a year later, after a total immersion into his new life as Charlie Mazza, a rogue criminal and former marine who'd served in Afghanistan and Iraq, Chris Gallo was no more.

A phony police record of assaults was created for Charlie Mazza and his introduction to the Cirelli crime family came from a Cirelli wiseguy who had become a criminal informant for the bureau two years earlier. Charlie Mazza's first test came the day he was told to rough up a dirty carpenter union shop steward for skimming from payouts by his rank and file. Mazza pummeled the shop steward without regard for FBI restrictions, mostly because the shop steward had robbed from workers. It was the first time he used doublethink to doublespeak with the bureau itself, not that he believed for a second they cared.

The next time was more serious and Mazza had to make a decision regarding whether to pull the trigger or walk away. They were in the backroom of a Brooklyn bar when he was handed a Ruger 9mm and told to shoot the bartender. Banking on the bureau's CI in the crime family, Mazza didn't hesitate. He aimed the handgun just over the head of the bartender in case the informant was wrong about it being a mock execution. He swallowed hard when he pulled the trigger. He pulled the trigger a second time when the Ruger didn't fire. When he turned to the others in the bar he'd been with, he saw they were all laughing.

It had been a test. A sick test, but he'd passed.

Giovanni Rapino immediately spoke up for Mazza and claimed him. There wasn't a discussion since the Underboss of the family, Dominick Nucci, was there to affirm Rapino's claim.

At the end of their meeting, Kelly assured Chris Gallo/Charlie Mazza, that he was covered as far as the double murder went. What Kelly needed to know next was whether or not Rapino was planning a personal coup against the acting captain of the Montalvo crew, Jerry Galante. It would require asking questions and asking questions could be dangerous when undercover.

• • • • •

Joseph couldn't tell his daughter-in-law about her son's involvement with organized crime. It was too much too soon. He did his best to convince himself that there wasn't enough evidence anyway, no matter what Artie Adler had learned from his surveillance or his connections.

What he planned to do was immediately after meeting with his daughter-in-law, Joseph would return to the apartment building where he'd had a confrontation with his grandson and beg him to turn himself in or leave the country.

Mary Gallo had married Joseph's son in 2000. She was 25, her husband, 24. She had always been a cautious woman and feared for her husband working at his father's bar for extra money. When she learned about the illegal football tickets her husband was hawking, she was extra upset because she knew the entire operation was being run by gangsters.

When her husband Jack was killed delivering the take from football tickets, her fears turned to hatred and it was all aimed at Jack's father, Joseph. The two had barely spoken since her husband, his son, was buried. Mary and Jack's son, Chris, was 11 going on 12 at the time of his father's death. She had since become overly cautious with worry for him.

When she met up with Joseph outside his home, she brought a container of coffee and refused to go inside. She spoke to him from inside the front gate while Joseph moved to the stairs and sat there.

"What's going on?" she said. "Did you find out?"

Joseph frowned, "Hello to you too, Mary."

"I didn't come here to be friendly, Joseph. What's going on with my son?"

"I don't know," Joseph said. "He won't talk to me either."

"You saw him?" she said. "You met with him?"

Joseph was sticking to his first meeting with Chris. "The Canarsie pier," he said. "He didn't stay long."

"What did he say? What did he look like?"

"He looks fine, Mary. His car looked like shit, but he looked fine."

"What about his car? What do you mean it looked like shit?"

Joseph ignored the interrogation about his grandson's car. "He said he's got a girlfriend he's living with now. Out on the Island."

"Jesus Christ. Why won't he tell me these things?"

"He says you pester him."

"He's my son."

"He knows that, but you gotta admit, you're a little over the top with Chris."

"Yes, I am. I should let him hang around with the kind of people that killed his father. Of course, I'm over the top. I'm his mother."

"I told him that."

"He doesn't need you to tell him that."

"I'm doing my best here, Mary. I'm trying to fill you in."

"This is like when he joined the Army. No notice to me. Nothing. I learn about it the day he lands in Iraq. He's playing war in the Middle East and I can't sleep for almost two years. It's not fair."

"He probably didn't want you to worry more than you already do."

"I don't care what he thought. I'm his goddamn mother, Joseph. I have to know where my son is and what he's doing. Jesus Christ, he went off to play war against people who could kill him!"

Joseph sighed.

"Am I bothering you, Joseph? Is my concern for my son too much to handle? Maybe if you had the same concerns about your son he wouldn't have been dealing with mobsters and gotten himself killed."

"He wasn't dealing with mobsters, you stupid ..." Joseph stopped himself from saying more. He felt a sharp pain in his side and held it with one hand. Then he said, "Jack was trying to earn an extra buck. He walked into the wrong situation at the wrong time. That's all that happened. It was no different than if he was hit by a car crossing the street. It wasn't my fault any more than it was your fault. Why can't you come to terms with that? Maybe if you lightened up a little, your son would contact you."

"Stupid what, Joseph?"

Joseph looked up at the sky, then at Mary again. "Nothing," he said. "Forget it."

"Fuck you, forget it. You're a fat piece of shit."

"I apologize. My temper got the best of me."

"They still call you piss pot? You're a disgusting man."

"Yeah, yeah, I know. Jesus Christ, you'd make me wanna join the army."

"They wouldn't have you."

"Probably not."

"I hate you."

"Yeah, I can see that."

She threw her empty coffee container at the stoop just below where Joseph was sitting. "Tell my son to call his mother."

Joseph struggled to stand, then gave her a salute. "Yes, Ma'am."

"Asshole," she said as she walked away.

6

"They got me on this shit now," Carmine Montalvo said. "Aceta-whatever the fuck. Means I'm for sure dying and soon."

Greenblatt looked at his client's medical sheet and said, "Acetaminophen."

They were in the hospice ward at FMC Butner. Montalvo was barely sitting up in bed. He'd lost more weight and looked very frail. The color had been drained from his face. He looked about to die.

Morris Greenblatt was doing his best to look sympathetic. The fact was he couldn't wait to get out of there and hoped Montalvo was dead by the time his flight landed back in New York. Before he had left New York for the trip to North Carolina, the Underboss of the Cirelli's, Dominick Nucci, had told Greenblatt to learn what he could about the double murder, and that before he left, he should tell Montalvo that he'd been shelved.

"And make him feel it," Nucci had said. "Say it with balls, counselor. Let him know his last act as a member of *Cosa Nostra* cost him his honor. Make it sting."

"What's it called?" Montalvo said.

"Acetaminophen."

"Yeah, that shit," Montalvo said.

"Making you nauseous?" Greenblatt said. "I know it's one of the side effects."

"Only when I eat."

"I'm sorry, Carmine. I really am."

"At least it was taken care of, that prick fucking my wife."

"That was a surprise," Greenblatt said. "Jerry didn't know anything about it. He was very upset. So was Dominick."

"Fuck them, Galante and Nucci."

"It's causing a lot of unwanted attention, especially since the guy's mother was killed."

"Fuck her."

"Jesus, Carmine. She had nothing to do with your wife."

"I look like I give a fuck? I'll be dead myself in a couple, three weeks, if not sooner."

"Everyone is trying to figure out who did the work back home."

"You asking me, counselor? Because if you are, I can tell you this much, go fuck yourself."

"Your underboss wants to know who you gave the order to."

Montalvo spit on the floor. Greenblatt knew it was meant for him. He'd been told to let Montalvo have it, to let him know he's been shelved and to insult and piss him off. Greenblatt wasn't comfortable playing the role he'd been assigned, but if anybody could get him to hurl insults, it was Carmine Montalvo. Then his client removed phlegm from his mouth with a finger and tried to toss it at Greenblatt and that did the trick.

"Great," he said. "Well, since you are going to die and nobody can stand to hear your name anymore, I'm going to pass along a message from your former underboss."

"Fuck you and him," Montalvo said.

"You're shelved, you miserable prick."

Montalvo looked up with a dead stare at Greenblatt. A threatening stare his attorney knew meant nothing now.

"That's right," Greenblatt said, deciding to use his best litigation skills. He'd been a master of cross-examinations in court and was about to do so again now. He said, "That make you feel better when you stare like that? You think that actually works in here? You can do that staring shit all you want, Carmine. Nobody cares anymore. I don't even care. I'm talking to you with total and absolute disrespect, the way I was told to talk to you. 'Make it sting,' Nucci told me. I hope it does because all you are now is a dying *cornuto*. Everybody knows your wife fucked around on you. Everybody. Nucci says he knows the guy you put in charge has been banging your wife. Your acting captain has been fucking your wife from within a week or so when you went away. How's that taste, you miserable prick?"

"I'll have you fucking killed," Montalvo struggled to say.

"You aren't having anybody killed, you miserable bastard. You're done, old man. You can make all the threats you want, but by the time I get back to New York, if you're not dead already, you'll know that your wife is spreading her legs for half a dozen different guys and everybody else knows about it. Maybe that'll kill you. If not, it'll haunt you, that's for sure. Imagine, a macho man like yourself staying married to a woman who fucks a guy in his crew and anybody else who winks at her? Seriously, Carmine, you really are a cuck."

Montalvo became as animated as he could and raised his right arm a few inches before it dropped. "Get out of here," he said. "Get the fuck out of here."

"Enjoy your last few days, you prick. Enjoy knowing she's still getting fucked while you die."

"My head," Montalvo said. He leaned forward to rest his head on his left arm.

"By the way, Carmine, that acetaminophen? It's fucking Tylenol, you stupid guinea. That's all they're giving you now, Tylenol, and it's the cheap version. If your head hurts, that's why."

At that Montalvo tried to spit again but his mouth was too dry.

● ● ● ● ●

Jerry Galante was waiting on Doris Montalvo at the JFK Marriott. He'd gone there after a captain's meeting at which the underboss, Dominick Nucci, issued an order from on high.

"Carmine Montalvo has been shelved," Nucci said. "This thing that happened on Staten Island is not to be discussed, per usual, but Montalvo has no authority for anything going forward. The old man was always loyal to our thing, but now he's gone off the reservation. Maybe it's the cancer. Maybe it's the medications he's taken, but he can no longer be trusted with anything. It's possible he gave people up. We don't know. Not for sure, so nobody is to contact him or take any messages from him or anyone representing him. His lawyer went to see him and let him know he's shelved and that he's already dropped him as a client. Hopefully the old man dies soon. Very soon."

That was a couple of hours ago at a restaurant on Cross Bay Boulevard in Howard Beach, not far from the JFK Marriott. Galante had hung around to talk to Nucci alone afterward. A few days ago, Nucci had told him something was going on with possible indictments and that everyone should stay on their toes and play it safe.

Then there's a double murder and nobody knows who was involved, except civilians had always been off-limits. Not only was someone who'd already been assaulted and put in a hospital with a full police report on the assault killed, so was his civilian mother. The orders had to have come from Carmine Montalvo, but nobody knew who the killer or killers were.

When Galante finally spoke with Nucci after the meeting, it was outside the restaurant in the parking lot. Nucci was sucking on a short Cohiba Robusto cigar. He led Galante toward the waterside of the lot and leaned against the fence pole. Boats were docked up and down Shellback Basin.

"So?" Nucci said. "Anything?"

"Nobody unaccounted for that I know," Galante said. "Is it possible he reached out to another family?"

"Shit, anything is possible. Especially with that old fuck. Montalvo had his hands in a lot of different pies. He had Fontana's ear, that's for sure, but that was before. Fontana didn't seem to mind we shelved Carmine. That was my idea and the old man didn't flinch. I'd bet big money on Fontana shitting his pants every time his doorbell rings."

Galante said, "That hit couldn't come from Aniello. I can't believe that. If it was Fontana, why would he put Carmine on the shelf now?"

"Because Montalvo is gonna die is one reason. Who knows? Probably wasn't Aniello. Could be one of our associates, or one from another crew. Bottom line is we're fucked right now. Two civilians? Feds are all over us again. Them and their task forces. NYPD, everybody. Our inside guys are afraid to talk to us now. Half a dozen associates rounded up for bullshit yesterday, another half dozen today. One of them is guaranteed to talk after six hours in a lockup. This was bad. Very bad."

"I only have two shooters could even pull it off, and only one of them has the stones to cowboy it the way it was done."

"Rapino?"

"Yeah, but it wasn't him. Couldn't have been. He's had eyes on Montalvo's wife."

"Eyes on her or his dick in her?"

"No, not Giovanni. That guys gets more tail than a toilet seat. Mostly at the gym. He likes them young. A lot younger than Doris Montalvo."

"Okay, but somebody did the old fuck's bidding, and we need to find out who before something else turns to shit."

Galante left a few minutes later but was stuck in traffic from an accident on the Belt Parkway. It had been raining hard most of the day. Traffic on the Conduit was just as bad from the overflow. It took him more than an hour to circle back to the Marriott side of the Belt. He booked a room and sent the room number in a text to Doris Montalvo. Half an hour later she knocked on his hotel room door.

Galante had been watching the news from the end of the bed. He stood up, opened the door and saw she was wearing a white raincoat and hat and that both were wet. She was also carrying a white leather shoulder bag. He stepped back and let her in. Some of the eyeliner she'd put on had run.

"Let me get you a towel," he said.

"It's okay," she said. "I'll get it."

He used the remote to switch to ESPN. A few minutes later, Doris stepped out of the bathroom with her raincoat still on. Galante used the remote to turn off the television.

"What's up with the raincoat?" he said.

Doris Montalvo let the raincoat drop to the floor and Galante's eyes opened wide. She was wearing a black corset, garter belt, black stockings, and a large string of pearls around her neck.

"Jesus Christ," Galante said.

"Never mind him," Doris said. "Let's get busy, Jerry. We have something to talk about after."

• • • • •

Giovanni Rapino said, "Tell the truth, man, you never have Chinese before, right?"

"Never," Charlie Mazza said.

Mazza was still high from the blunt they'd shared half an hour ago, twenty minutes after a 23-year-old Chinese woman had attempted to jump his bones in one room while a 25-year-old Chinese woman made it happen with Rapino in the living room. Afterward, Rapino paid both women $100 each before they left.

"They work fast, Chinks women," Rapino said. He was pouring Vodka from a bottle fresh out of the freezer into a juice glass. He held the bottle up for Mazza.

"No thanks," Mazza said.

Rapino downed half the glass of Vodka, coughed twice, and then poured another glass full. He put the bottle back into the freezer, then sat back in his recliner. He pressed the buttons alongside the right arm of his recliner and adjusted his back as the chair slowly reclined.

"Jerry catch hell," Rapino said.

Mazza was careful not to ask why. "Huh," he said instead.

"Wants we take orders, he doesn't."

Mazza remained silent.

Rapino said, "What she do, Li's friend?"

"The girl?"

"Blow job or fuck?"

Mazza feigned a smile. "Both."

"Use bag, I hope."

He couldn't take the chance of not going through with it in case the girl mentioned it afterward. He limited the sex to exposure and the start of a hand job, then told the woman he couldn't make it happen because he was too high. He couldn't admit that to Rapino. He nodded and then lied. "Of course," he said.

"They live in here," Rapino said. "This building."

"The one you call Li?"

"Second floor. Sometime she cook. Good. Real Chinese, eh?"

"Convenient."

"She is married. Husband in jail."

"Seriously?"

"Crazy Chink. She like Italian *Salsiccia*, eh? She do both, swallow and the ass."

Mazza was thinking he could shoot the son-of-a-bitch now and do what his grandfather had suggested, leave the country.

"You okay with Jerry?" Rapino said.

Mazza shrugged. "I guess."

"He is fuck the boss's wife."

"Huh?"

"Montalvo, his wife Jerry fuck."

Mazza put both hands up. "I don't wanna know."

"Smart, eh? But is okay now. You with me. We alone."

Mazza wasn't biting.

Rapino said, "She's old but good fuck."

"None of my business."

"Not your business but is true. Old but good."

Mazza was tempted to ask how Rapino knew but managed to suppress the question.

"Anyway," Rapino said, "Jerry has trouble without he fucks the boss's wife. He doesn't do what is told. He fucked up."

Chris changed the subject. "You want me to collect this week?"

"Huh?" Rapino said. "Oh, okay. Yes, in Queens. Strip club there owes."

"Owes?"

"Three, four weeks. He has money, give him slap to reminder, eh?"

"And if he doesn't have it?"

Rapino shrugged. "Break his face, but don't kill. Not yet."

Mazza was thinking he'd like to break Rapino's face. Instead, he said, "I'll leave now. I'll grab some coffee at Dunkin' and head to Queens tonight."

"Watch him first," Rapino said. He looked about to fall asleep. "He goes to club before it closes."

"You okay?" Mazza said, a smile on his face.

"Chink knock me out, eh?"

Mazza forced a smile. "I'll see you later."

• • • • •

Mei-Ling was recently brought into Brooklyn by way of Shanghai, San Francisco, Fort Worth, Georgia, West Virginia and Chinatown in Manhattan. Her journey took more than two years. She'd recently turned 23 years old and already had two abortions, the last of which ended any chance of her becoming pregnant again. Li-Jie had taken a similar route to America, except hers started in Hunan and began when she was 11 years old. She'd been in the states 14 years since first arriving in San Diego and was now a few months from turning 26.

Both were married to Chinese gang members still awaiting trial on Rikers Island. Both had been forced into their marriages.

Now they spoke in broken English to one another while sharing a joint.

"I don't like you boyfriend," Mei-ling said. "Too much like Lǐ Nà. Bossy all the time."

"You will learn," Li-Jie said. "I use Italian same as Ming. Gangs all fading now. All falling apart. We do our own now. For us. You and me."

"Lǐ Nà will kill me."

"Lǐ Nà will be in prison another year or more. Fuck Lǐ Nà."

"And his friend Ming and your husband?"

"Fuck Ming. Fuck husband. Chén is no husband. We our own now. No need for them."

Li-Jie had been planning an escape from the man she was married to, a 22-year-old punk she'd never met before being told he would be her husband. Chén Wáng was arrogant and stupid. Li-Jie had no respect for him or for all the angst she'd been through as an illegal immigrant shuffled through the system by criminal gangs. Forced into prostitution at age 10 back in China, hooking had become her trade in America from the day she'd illegally arrived on a container ship.

Her plan was to secure enough funds to make the move to Europe and start life anew. She had recruited Mei-Ling just over a year ago, Mei-Ling's husband was arrested on a manslaughter charge. Neither of their husbands had the money for bail and insisted their wives make it on the street. Thus far they had lied to their husbands about the money they'd been saving, always claiming it wasn't enough yet to retain good criminal lawyers.

When Li-Jie's husband sent another gang member to threaten her and Mei-Ling, she'd turned to Giovanni Rapino for help. Rapino met with the gang member under the guise of giving him money and broke both of the gang member's arms with a baseball bat instead. That was three months ago. Neither Li-Jie nor Mei-Ling had heard from either of their husbands again.

"Europe soon?" Mei-Ling said.

"Upstairs get us passport," Li-Jie said.

"Free?"

Li-Jie chuckled. "Nothing free. One thousand dollar. Each. Two thousand dollar."

"When?"

"Maybe this week."

"And we go?"

"And we go."

Mei-Ling smiled.

"Come, now we shower," Li-Jie said.

Both women wrapped their arms around each other's waist and headed to the bathroom.

• • • • •

Thomas Stone was surprised at how easy it was to take the money. The night before he'd been up thinking about the consequences if he couldn't pay the street loan back. He'd asked for $15,000. At 2 points a week, it would cost him $300 in vigorish alone. He could pay $300 in juice a week for a full year and still owe $15,000.

He didn't discuss it with his wife because she was too smart and pragmatic to even try and kid her. Sooner or later, especially if he didn't quit gambling, he'd fall behind in payments and would lose everything anyway. His wife would know better than to take the money, but Stone couldn't resist. Stone was looking ahead to his next bet.

Even if it cost him his job.

Or jail time.

He could also be killed, but he doubted it. Even the mob knew better than to kill a cop.

Not that going to prison would keep him from getting killed.

His mind had spun in circles the night before, precluding sleep. It left him in a fog in the morning. Then he showed up where Jerry Galante had said and there it was, fifteen dimes he counted twice before a few thousand was pulled back.

He'd gone where Jerry Galante sent him for the money, a bodega on 4th Avenue in Brooklyn, less than six blocks from the 72nd Precinct. He asked a heavy Hispanic man behind the counter for a cup of coffee with extra icing.

"Icing?" the Hispanic man said.

Stone said, "Jerry sent me."

"One minute," the Hispanic man said.

He came out from behind the counter and locked the door. He flipped the open sign to closed and returned behind the counter. He grabbed an envelope from a shelf under the counter and set it on the counter. Then he looked at Stone and said, "Count it."

Stone looked over his shoulder, then up at a camera aimed at the counter.

"Don't worry, it's off," the Hispanic man said.

Stone opened the envelope and saw two bundles of hundred-dollar bills wrapped with rubber bands. There were also loose hundred-dollar bills. He counted both banded bundles twice, then put the money back in the envelope and nodded. The pricks had taken what he owed on his bets. What was left was $11,300.

When he was back in his car, Stone recounted the cash. He'd have to give more than half of it to his wife for their daughter's school tuition and the back payments on his mortgage. He'd have what he assumed would be left for gambling, except some of it would have to be put aside for the 2 percent interest on the $15,000 he'd have to pay the following week.

First, Stone had to stop in Queens and do his job. The officer he'd been investigating the last month was a woman working patrol in the 114th Precinct, Officer Sharon Kwan. A 32-year-old Korean-American, Kwan had been accused of shaking down store owners along Roosevelt Avenue in Jackson Heights. Stone had followed up on Kwan using confidential informants running their own scams in the same neighborhood.

Today he found her eating a slice of pizza while leaning against a patrol car parked car on Roosevelt Avenue under the El at 79th Street. Her hat was inside her patrol car. She was a tall, thin woman, with sharp facial features, dark brown eyes and short dark hair she'd recently had clipped.

"Pay for that?" Stone said, pointing at her slice of pizza.

"Ah, the rat squad," Kwan said. "I'd offer you a bite but then I'd have to throw it away after you touched it."

"That nice?" Stone said.

Kwan flipped him the bird.

"I hope you know you still have time to fess up, Officer Kwan. I mean, words out on the Avenue about you."

"What word is that?"

"What you've been accused of. Shaking down shop owners again."

"Again? I wasn't aware there was a first time."

"You lucked out the first time. Now we have owners fed up and ready to testify."

"Testify to what? I protect some of these assholes to use their bathrooms. I don't even take a soda when they offer. I use their bathrooms to pee. If that's shaking them down, I'm guilty."

"Your partner doing the collecting today?"

"Fuck you, rat. My partner is clean. On the job less than a year now."

"You know, I wouldn't be such a hard-on if you worked with me a little. A confession won't get you tossed. You tell them you didn't know any better about the sandwiches or slices of pizza. You don't have to admit to taking coin. Worse that happens, you'll get a reprimand and a warning."

"I don't take sandwiches or pizza without paying."

"You do realize they have videos in those stores, right?"

"I also realize I might pay for my food outside the restaurant, or in passing inside."

Stone frowned. "Like I said, you'd do well to work with me."

"Work with you how, snitch?"

Stone shrugged.

Kwan shifted her weight onto one leg. "You really think I'd snitch?"

"We all know there's higher priced corruption above your pay grade. Whatever you're jamming down your bra is peanuts compared to it, Kwan."

"You're a real asshole, Stone. You know that, right?"

"Yeah, but I got the power."

"Power my ass. You gonna bring me up on charges? Good luck with that. If you think some CI is gonna come out of the woodwork to testify, you're out of your mind. They may tell you one thing, but they won't appear in court, and without an appearance, what have you got?"

"And if they do appear what happens to them," Stone said. "You just inferred a threat. Not to mention if you're muscling in on street gangs. There are still remnants of the Green Dragons around. I don't think you want to butt up against them."

Kwan finished her slice, except for a piece of crust. She held it out to Stone. "Want?" she said.

"No thanks."

Kwan popped the piece of crust into her mouth and chewed.

"Okay, you've been warned," Stone said. "I don't go this far for most, but I like your style, Kwan. You've got balls."

Another uniformed officer approached from around the corner. He was Hispanic, short and stocky. He looked to Kwan, then motioned at Stone with his head.

"Rat squad," Kwan said.

The stocky officer chuckled.

Stone winked at Kwan. Kwan grabbed her crotch and said, "You wish."

Twenty minutes later, the money he'd borrowed on the floor of the passenger seat, Stone was heading home hopeful that his wife wouldn't grill him about the sudden influx of cash into the Stone household.

7

"He wasn't there," Artie Adler said. "I greased the super and knocked on every apartment door in the building. Super said someone moved out the other day, a guy by the name of Charlie Mazza, but he'd only been there a few months. A single guy. Described your grandson. If he's with a Cirelli crew, makes sense he used a phony name. Bottom line now is, he's gone, Joseph. On the lam."

Joseph was urinating into his pot in front of the sink in his kitchen. Adler had just arrived through the back door. He waited for Joseph to finish cleaning the pot and his hands before taking a chair at the table.

"Coffee?" Joseph said.

"If it's made, sure."

Joseph poured two cups of coffee. He set one in the middle of the table for Adler and one in front of himself. Both men sipped their coffees, then Joseph said, "What do you think?"

"What I said. Looks to me like he's on the lam."

"Shit."

"I can look around about this Rapino character, see if he's still around, but if Chris is gone, my money'd be on Rapino being gone too."

"Because he killed a pair of civilians."

Adler sipped his coffee, then set the cup down. "That's a big no-no for the NYPD and the feds," he said. "Nobody is gonna look the other way over that one."

"I told him he should leave the country."

"Maybe he did."

"I'll tell you, Art, I can't bring myself to believe this shit. I can't. You try searching for that name the super gave you?"

"Nothing so far. I'm gonna talk with a guy working the task force tonight, I hope. If he's with Rapino, this Charlie Mazza, my guy will know."

"You're not gonna tell him—"

"No, of course not. I'm just gonna fish around, see if he knows the name. He asks why, I'll say it's got something to do with a friend owes some bookie."

Joseph took a big sip of coffee, then said, "This kid had everything going for him. Why would he get involved with those assholes? It's not like I didn't have talks with him about those clowns. He always wanted to know who it was, which family, which wiseguy, did it, killed his father. I'd tell him it didn't make a difference. They were all the same. They were all cut throats and they've been proving it the last forty-fifty years now. They'd crawl over their mothers to fuck their sisters if they thought it'd keep them out of jail."

"No argument here," Adler said, "but they're also very cunning cut throats. If your grandson said we could get him killed for snooping around the way we did, it can mean any number of things, none of them any good."

"Meaning?"

"First off, the murder. Double murder. I don't imagine Rapino wants anyone knowing any of his business, never mind the issue of me following them, placing them near that house on Staten Island. Then there's the reality that the mob often uses PIs, private investigators, to watch their own people, make sure they aren't plants or CI's, criminal informants working with the feds. They learned to watch their own, wiseguys and the new kids on the block, the ones they're recruiting. Once I know about Rapino, whether he stuck around or not, I can give chase and follow, but I'll have to be extra careful in case they have someone watching his back besides the FBI, not that I trust them not to tip him off."

"Tip him off?" Joseph said.

"You don't think they pull that shit?" Adler said. "The feds think they need somebody to make a bigger case, they'll warn the guy they need. If they can ignore nineteen murders, you better believe they'll tip off someone they need."

"Or I could just walk up to him and kill him myself," Joseph said.

"That's not remotely funny, Joseph."

"It isn't meant to be funny. What the hell do I have to worry about? I'm almost dead as it is. I'd be doing the world a favor along with my grandson."

"Yeah, well let's keep that fantasy on hold for now, okay?"

Joseph finished his coffee and pushed himself up from the table. He felt another sharp pain and winced.

Adler said, "Asshole, you need to see a doctor. Whatever the hell is going on with you, you need to get it checked."

"I need to piss again," Joseph said. He turned and faced the sink.

When he reached for the pot, Adler frowned and said, "I'll talk to you tomorrow."

• • • • •

"This is confirmed?" Dominick Nucci said. "He's dead?"

"Murdered," Morris Greenblatt said. "His throat was cut at two a.m., according to the prison official who called me this morning. Ear to ear, one side of the throat to the other. I asked for more details, but they weren't anxious to share any."

"They don't know who did it? It's a fuckin' hospital, no?"

"I don't think they care. But no, not yet."

"I know I don't care," Galante said.

Nucci said, "I know we didn't have anything to do with it. He was on his way out anyway with the cancer."

Greenblatt nodded. "He was."

They were on the Canarsie pier, their cars parked alongside one another behind a patch of pavement that used to house a connected Italian restaurant, *Abbracciamento*. The pier was fairly crowded at noon with mostly Hispanics and West Indians cooking food off the backs of vans and setting up at the picnic tables.

"Now what?" Jerry Galante said. "He was shelved, right? Can't have a funeral."

"Fuck a funeral," Nucci said. "He'll get burned whether he wanted to or not, the prick."

"His wife won't have a problem with that," Galante said.

Nucci's said, "Speaking of that twat, we sure she's clean?"

"Meaning?"

"She talking with the feds? Somebody with the task force? She didn't have a problem spreading her legs, maybe she did it for a fed or two to protect herself."

Galante shrugged. "I can check. Have somebody go through her place with electronics. She has bugs in there, we'll know."

"Do that. Doris Montalvo isn't some cupcake didn't know her way around the block."

"I have to take care of his estate now," Greenblatt said. "Speaking of Doris."

"His estate," Nucci said. "Fuck his estate. We should siphon off that asshole's estate and split it."

"I already protected some assets from his kids. I didn't expect him to pay his fee in full."

Galante smiled. "I knew you were a fuckin' snake, Greenblatt."

"Comes with the territory," Greenblatt said. "Power of attorney."

"Pull that shit on my kids and I'll come back and strangle you," Nucci said.

The three men laughed.

Greenblatt pointed to the barren spot where a restaurant used to be. "Weird how this place turned out, huh?"

Nucci said, "When I was a kid, a young kid, my grandfather used to take me crabbing off this pier. He told me there was a bait house on a dock and a boat that took you on rides for, like, a quarter, fifty cents."

"I remember that, hearing those stories," Greenblatt said. "I had an uncle used to come here. A great uncle, I guess. Nate was in his eighties when he died two years ago."

Nucci pointed at Galante and said, "In case you haven't figured it out yet, tag you're it. You're running Montalvo's crew now."

Galante gave Nucci a thumbs up. "About time," he said.

"Calm your jets, Jerry. It's not the rosy promotion you think it is. We still have a rogue out there did Montalvo's bidding on that kid on Staten Island. We have to know who that was. Cops already busted three of our offices. Feds'll go straight to our online operations next."

"Nobody is gonna volunteer and take credit," Galante said. "Why I think it was some other family."

"Or Montalvo made a deal," Greenblatt said. "He gives up X amount and word is leaked to someone through the feds."

"Or they do it themselves," Nucci said.

"Motherfuckers," Galante said.

"Here's the thing," Greenblatt said. "You look at what happened to the Vignieri crew. First a captain or two flips. Then the underboss, and then the boss. What are the rest of their people gonna do if their boss flips? After that it was like dominoes, one after another. They'll be crippled for years, and with technology the way it is, the deals the feds offer, it'll never be the same again. It's just a fact of life now."

"I hope you're not giving that speech to any of your clients," Nucci said.

"Most times I don't have to. With some of them, one minute they're my clients, then I don't hear from them because they've got new counsel and a deal. Feds know to keep the ones they can flip away from me."

"That what they call conflict of interest?" Galante said.

"No, but it keeps me from tipping you guys off when someone does flip."

Nucci looked to Galante. "You believe this guy?"

"Not really," Galante said.

"Haven't I always been accurate?" Greenblatt said. "It's not without risk and why I'm not allowed at trial sometimes. They waive attorney-client because of prior incidents. Crime-fraud exception, like I'm some gangster."

"Stop the shit, counselor," Nucci said. "Most of your clients today never see the inside of a court room."

"And if they wanted to, the courts would block me from representing them," Greenblatt said. "Mostly because I'm good at what I do. Especially in a court room."

"He does have a couple big wins," Galante said to Nucci.

Nucci stroked the air with a fist.

Greenblatt turned to Galante. "He doesn't like to admit it."

Nucci waved Greenblatt off. "Just make sure that broad isn't talking to anyone, Jerry."

"Will do."

"Carmine really turned on her after my IT guy loaded that spyware on her computer and caught her fucking around," Greenblatt said.

"You sure that was your guy?" Nucci said, then laughed. "Look, Carmine was away for six years before last night. What the hell can she have isn't about him?"

"Nothing on me," Galante said.

Nucci frowned. "Make sure," he said, then glanced at his watch. "Meantime, I gotta be somewhere in half an hour and it's an hour away."

"I'll call you tomorrow," Galante said.

Greenblatt said, "My wife is making latkes for her family on Long Island. They're in town haunting today. I'm going home to eat a few before they're all gone."

Nucci turned to Galante and said, "Latkes. This fuckin' guy."

• • • • •

Between layovers and connecting flights, Giovanni Rapino's trip took nearly 30 hours. It started when he left for Newark Airport at 8:40 in the evening. A Lufthansa flight to Frankfort, then to Milan, and finally to Abruzzo International Airport in Pescara.

He arrived in Pescara, Italy, in the early morning. Twin cousins he hadn't seen in more than 20 years met him at the airport. Alfredo and Rafael were 31 years old and the same height. Alfredo was thicker with more muscle than his brother, but both had the same blondish curly hair as Rapino. They had stayed in touch over the last few years, with Rapino sending

money to maintain the relationship and to pay for the help he'd
need to avenge his mother.

The twins had offered to kill the two men responsible for his
mother's rape and murder several times over burner phone
conversations with their American cousin, but Rapino insisted
the revenge was his to take. He explained to them that he
needed to do it himself and that he'd be there as soon as he
could leave. With all he'd left in his wake in America, it was a
good time for Rapino to leave the country and avenge his
mother. Although he'd been able to block out her rape and
murder from his mind for months at a time, whenever he did
think about her being held down, raped, and then strangled,
the muscles of his body would tense with adrenaline.

Now that he was back in Italy, he'd get his revenge. He'd use
a stiletto because a bullet was too merciful.

Alfredo did the driving while his brother sat shotgun up
front. Rafael told Rapino one of the two men involved with what
had happened to his mother was being held in an apartment on
Via Calore, a 6-minute drive from the airport. Rapino was
anxious to kill him, but his cousins wanted to get him settled
first.

Their home was on the outskirts of Pescara. Rapino didn't
recognize his cousin's place. Terramontara was a 15-minute
drive from Pescara and the Adriatic coast. The cousins had
moved twice since they were young boys. Rapino's mother was
originally from the town of Pizzoferrato, a commune and town
in the Province of Chieti, in the same Abruzzo region of Italy.
Pizzoferrato was in the mountains, an hour and change drive
from Pescara. Rapino hoped to visit the mausoleum where his
parents were entombed in *Cimitero di Gamberale* before
returning to New York in three days.

He remembered how his mother was especially proud of her
hometown when she learned from relatives in America that one
of its famous wrestlers in New York, Bruno Sammartino, was
from the same town. Rapino remembered his mother telling
him the stories of Sammartino and when he brought it up with
his cousins, they told him there was a statue of the wrestler in
Pizzoferrato.

"Wrestling in America is no real," Rapino told his cousins.
"Is bulla'shit. Acting. Entertainment. Big business, but
bulla'shit."

"Your mother wouldn't hear of it," Alfredo said. "She swore it
was real."

Rafael said, "And let's face it, what else do we have here to be proud of?"

"Is crazy," Rapino said.

Talking about his mother brought him back to the task at hand. Rapino didn't want to waste time while he was in Italy. He was anxious to get what needed to be done and head back to New York. After showering at Rafael's apartment, he took a brief nap. An hour after he awoke, Rapino was brought to the apartment building where one of his mother's murderers was tied to a chair. A third cousin, Augusto, was at the apartment when Rapino arrived.

He didn't know or recognize Pietro Alvino, the man tied to a chair with a thick gag in his mouth. He looked to be about 50 years old. He was thin and had a full head of black hair. He also had a small scar over his left eye. Rapino was relying on his cousins for a valid identification, but the thought of what his mother had gone through upon her return to Italy after leaving her son in New York enraged him. He removed the gag from Alvino's mouth and spoke Italian to the man.

"*Ricordi cosa hai fatto a Maria Teresa ventuno anni fa?*"

"He speaks English," Alfredo said.

"*Chi?*" Alvino said, his eyes squinting as he tried his best to appear confused.

Alfredo walked up behind Alvino and smacked him hard off the back of his head. "English, motherfucker," he said.

"I'm don't know this woman," Alvino said. "Maria Theresa? Please, I don't know."

"Who was with you?" Rapino said.

"We know who he is," Augusto said in broken English. "Don't a'fuckin' lie."

"Wait," Rapino told his cousin. "I want to hear it from him. He tells me, I break his legs and let him go."

"I don't know this person, you say," Alvino said.

Rapino removed a stiletto his cousin had given him earlier. He let the blade out and held the tip to the bound man's chin.

"Who was with you, *pezzo di merda?*"

"Please, I don't—aye!"

Rapino shoved the tip of the blade into Alvino's chin. "Next time I cut your eyes out," he said. "Who were you with and who did what to Maria Theresa? She was raped and murdered."

Alvino began to sob. "Carlo Gentile," he said. "I didn't touch this woman. I was outside. Carlo Gentile."

Rapino turned to his cousins. Alfredo stuffed the gag back into Alvino's mouth. He stepped back and nodded at his cousin.

Rapino, in a fit of pure rage, jabbed the stiletto's blade into Alvino's left eye. Alvino's head shifted left to right over and over. The muffled scream was barely audible. Rapino then grabbed Alvino's hair and then ran the blade left to right across Alvino's throat before he stepped back from the arterial spray. One of Rapino's cousins covered the spray with a towel.

Alvino shook in the chair as he continued to gurgle almost a full minute before his body stopped moving.

They left the body in the empty apartment and returned to Rafael's home. Rapino showered again, ate a hearty meal of veal and pasta, and had a few glasses of homemade wine with his cousins before heading to bed.

He would deal with Carlo Gentile the next day.

• • • • •

Dominick Nucci crossed the parking lot to the white van with commercial plates and fish logos on both back doors. He knocked on one of the back doors a few times before it swung open. Special Agent, Connor Kelly, extended a hand to Nucci to help him up into the van.

Both men sat on plastic milk crates across from one another. A coffee carrier with three capped Dunkin Donuts coffee containers was on the floor between them. Kelly picked one from the carrier, peeled the lid off and took a sip.

He held it up to Nucci. "Take one," he said.

Nucci waved it off. "I'll be up all night," he said. "You get it?"

"We got it."

"That fuckin' lawyer had a big mouth."

"Doing his job."

"Doing your job, you mean."

Kelly smiled.

Nucci said, "Although he did make a good point about you guys and Montalvo. You farm it out for the old prick or what?"

"Come on, Dominick. If we did, which we didn't, could I tell you?"

Nucci smirked. "Sure," he said. "So's you did."

Kelly shrugged. "Look, it's not like you're the only guy working with Uncle Sam. All five families have members on the street who already cut deals. Another good percent have deals in their pockets. Nobody with half a brain would want in on the top spots anymore. Full functioning brains keep them on the sidelines. Dozens have turned down the opportunity to get straightened out. It's a bit less dangerous as far as prison time goes if they remain associates."

"The dirt you guys do doesn't absolve you either," Nucci said. "That shit yous pulled on Montalvo's wife. Computer program. Greenblatt even know his IT guy was an agent?"

"Now why would we want him to know that?"

Nucci sarcastically smacked himself in the forehead. "Right, what am I thinking? What you get on that dirt bag anyway?"

"Remember the Bruce Cutler fiasco with Gotti?" Kelly said. "Pretty much the same thing here. The prosecutors in the Vignieri case, one of the sons, I forget which, contended Greenblatt may have known about criminal activity. No attorney-client bullshit since he might be called as a witness."

"Didn't the kid plead out?"

"Yeah, but not with Greenblatt's help. He knows he's on thin ice in federal court. I have a question though."

"What's that? Or should I say what else?"

"Funny. Rapino took off for Italy the other day. He coming back?"

"I don't know anything about it."

"He ask permission? Leave notice?"

"Not that I know. I can ask Galante."

"Do that."

"You think it was him on Staten Island?"

"Maybe, but we know the story about his mother. We're wondering … you know?"

"And you won't go through Interpol or notify the law over there in Italy because you think you can flip him here."

Kelly yawned long and loud.

"It's understandable," Nucci said. "You say you know about his mother, so the idea that he's going back to where he was born for the first time in his life has nothing to do with him going after the people who murdered his mother. Sure, makes sense. He just wants to visit his relatives of a sudden. Makes perfect sense."

"I'm the one who informed you," Kelly said. "About him going to Italy? You didn't know, or so you say. The other thing they did to his mother was rape her. That'd make most men want revenge."

"It would me," Nucci said.

"And you don't know anything about it."

"You enjoy fishing like this? Why would I keep knowing about that from you?"

Kelly shrugged.

Nucci smiled. "Right, sure," he said. "You don't know nothing about anything. Right."

8

For the first time in a very long time, Lisa Stone didn't care where her husband found the money to pay their daughter's tuition not only for the months owed, but for the rest of the school year. He also had money for the mortgage owed and all their other bills. She was so grateful for the economic relief, she couldn't stop kissing him in their kitchen.

Thomas Stone was grateful for the affection and responded in kind until he remembered there were two games he wanted to look over before dinner. He managed to stop the lovefest by asking for the newspaper. Lisa excused herself to use the bathroom. When she returned, Stone was focused on the sports pages of the Daily News.

"Can you take a long enough break to go upstairs?" she said.

"Five minutes, sure," he said.

"I'll make it worth your while," she said.

He looked up at her and smiled. "Gimme two minutes."

She was determined not to fight tonight. Not after the way he came through like he'd never come through before. Tuition, mortgage, bills, all paid for with the money he'd brought home to her. She quietly watched him going through his routine with the newspaper, but after a few minutes she couldn't help herself.

"I'm afraid to ask where the money came from," she said.

Stone tapped at the NBA lines in the newspaper. "Right here, kiddo," he said. "I nailed two parlays and four reverses. The worm has turned, baby."

"That's great, Tommy, but now that we're okay again, flush, I mean, do you have to keep betting?"

"We're okay because I was betting."

"Couldn't you take a little break? Let us enjoy this for a while."

"Don't start, Lee, okay? I know what I'm doing."

She wanted to try and convince him to forget the betting for a few days at least but knew there was no point. He was going to do what he wanted no matter what she said. She gave up and headed downstairs to do the laundry.

Stone used a pen to do the math on a page he ripped out of one of his daughter's notebooks. He had $3,100 left. He could pay down two grand on the principle of his street loan plus the interest he owed on $15,000 grand, which came to $2,300, leaving him with $260 in weekly interest on the $13,000 balance.

Or he could set aside the $300 vigorish, and bet the balance, spreading it around between the ponies, the NBA, or maybe the NHL. He'd have to wait on the NFL. The season was still months away.

Tonight, Stone liked the Knicks getting six against the Nets. Stone believed in taking underdogs, especially in hometown rivalries. The game was being played in Brooklyn, but the Knicks had been playing aggressive defense of late. Stone phoned Galante's bookmaking office and asked for the betting lines on the Knicks-Nets game, plus the over/under. Because the office knew he usually bet an underdog in point spreads and the over in point totals, he was told the over/under was set at 230 points. Stone knew it was bullshit and decided to use their practice of moving a line based on who was calling against them and took the under. It would help keep them more honest in the future when he won.

Stone also knew that the average point total thus far in the season for the entire league was 228.8 points. He called the office back and bet a one dime reverse on the Knicks and the under. Assuming those bets were a lock, Stone then searched the horse charts for Aqueduct in search for an exacta box that would at least double his return. When he was finished doping out the horses, he put a late daily double bet in on the 7th race at Aqueduct, boxing an 8:1 horse with a 9:2 horse. The payoff could be substantial on a $50.00 box costing him $100 to bet.

Once he was finished betting, he remembered what he'd told his wife about heading upstairs. He almost made it to the basement door before he stopped himself to make one more bet with money he didn't have.

● ● ● ● ●

Jerry Galante was growling as he ejaculated inside Doris Montalvo. He finished his business, then rolled off to his left. He could tell she had faked her orgasm but didn't care. He went into the bathroom to shower the smell of her strong perfume off.

He was there to try to find out if she'd been talking to the feds. Nucci had planted the thought in his head and Galante was determined to learn what he could. They were in her house and had fucked in her bed, in her dead husband's bed. Instead of their usual place to meet, at the Marriott JFK, Galante had come to her home bearing what would be the last of any money she was entitled to as the wife of a captain while he was in jail. Normally, the money was dropped off by one of his crew's associates. Now that he was dead, the money she was entitled to would end, but Galante wasn't there to tell her that. He was using the money to keep her off guard. If she was talking to the feds, Galante needed to know for sure.

Carmine Montalvo had been a big shot. Even after he'd been shelved and then murdered, appearances had to be kept up.

At least for the sake of drugging Doris Montalvo.

Galante had already slipped Doris a mickey, a grounded-up Roofie he'd dropped into her highball when he was making them drinks. Galante needed to check her home for electronic bugs and/or recording devices and couldn't do that while she was awake.

When he returned from his shower, Doris was sitting up in the bed smoking a cigarette. "Carmine let you smoke in bed?" he said.

Doris turned to him. He was naked, a towel slung over his shoulder.

"Carmine is dead," she said with a sleepy smile.

"And I'm still bringing you money," Galante said. "Not everyone gets that bonus once a guy dies."

"And here I thought you came for me," Doris said.

"That'd make you a prostitute since he's dead."

Her words began to run together and slur. "I don't mindthelabel, as long as sexisgood."

Galante smirked. "I'm honored."

He saw her highball glass was empty. It was the perfect opportunity to make her another drink. He did so, then watched her drink half of it before yawning. Then she handed him the glass and tapped the bed alongside her. He sat sideways to face her.

"Who killed him?" she said.

"Not us. You know?"

"How'd I know that?"

Galante shrugged. He was staring into her eyes looking for a sign that she was lying. "The good news is he was shelved before he died," he said.

She yawned. "He's be-what?"

"Mob speak. He was out. I'm running the crew now. He lost all his privileges, even before somebody cut his throat."

"Meaning?"

"Meaning I can bring you your money without having to send it. Meaning we can fuck without worrying going forward."

"Yeah?" she said through another yawn.

He could see her eyes were getting heavy. "What's wrong?" he said.

"Sleepy."

Then she yawned again.

"Maybe you need to take a nap," Galante said.

"Before wefuckagain?"

"Yeah, you look a bit pale."

"Make menother drink."

"You sure?"

"Please. And water. Bring aglassawater."

Galante went to her kitchen for the water first. He poured a glass from the faucet, then went to the liquor cabinet in the dining room. He made her another highball, then added what was left of the Roofie he'd ground into a powder. He stirred the drink with his finger, grabbed the glass of water and headed back to her bedroom.

Doris had kicked off the bedsheet and was lying with her head on a pillow. Her eyes were closed. Galante took a chair, glanced at his watch, and then he watched her until she was lightly snoring.

● ● ● ● ●

The beaches along the Pescara coast were clean and packed with both tourists and locals. Rapino was there with two of his cousins to meet a second cousin. She worked at one of the seafood restaurants on the beach. They parked on *Lungomare Columbo* and spent the early afternoon on the beach at *Spiaggia Libera - Porto Turistico.*

Rapino had been to the beach twice as a child when visiting these same cousins. It had been a favorite vacation for him and his parents before his father became ill.

The second cousin he finally met was 25 and beautiful. She had been the manager at the seafood restaurant the last two years and was intrigued when introduced to her American second cousin. Like his mother, she was also named Maria Theresa. Her surname was Costantini.

Maria Theresa was short like Rapino's mother, but was also curvaceous. Rapino couldn't believe how beautiful she was and couldn't stop telling her.

"Sei così bello," he kept saying. *"Non ci posso credere."*

To which she replied, "*Smettila, mi stai facendo arrossire.*" Then she turned to her other cousins and said, "Seriously, make him stop. He's making me blush."

When he learned she spoke English he said, "I'm sorry, *cugina*, but you are beautiful. I'll stop now, but I won't sleep tonight from thinking about you."

The two continued to flirt, glancing at one another the rest of the time they were together. After she left to do her job, Rafael said, "You two should get married, eh? You can take her back to New York and make a lot of *bambini*."

It was exactly what Rapino had been thinking, but he'd only be there another couple of days and still had business to take care of.

"Does she know what I am?" he asked his cousins.

"She's not stupid, eh," Alfredo said. "She knows."

"She asked about you," Rafael said. "Then she learned the story about your mother. I think she knows why you're here."

"Which is why she wouldn't marry you," Alfredo said. "She's a lefty, eh? *Comunista.* She has no use for *cosa nostra.* If you want to spend time with her, don't bring it up."

Rapino frowned.

Then Rafael said, "Hey, it's not like there aren't any beautiful woman in New York, right?"

"Not like her," Rapino said. "Not Italian. Not from Italy. Not from Pescara."

It had been a sore spot since he first had sex when he was fourteen. He had been dating a young girl, and they had experimented, and eventually had intercourse. She was a blonde girl from the Williamsburg neighborhood where'd he'd been living with his mother's brother and his sons. His strong accent had been the cause of many fights he'd had as a kid. When the people he dated didn't have an accent, he thought less of them. They were for sex. An Italian woman, a real Italian woman, had become his standard for love and marriage. Women like his mother.

Now he finally met one. Maria Theresa, his second cousin.

He and his cousins left the restaurant at five o'clock. His cousins had clocked Carlo Gentile's routine a few days before Rapino arrived. They expected Gentile to leave the bar where he hung out around six o'clock. Gentile had parked a red Nissan Versa in front of an Italian café on *Via Titburtina Valeria.* Rapino and his cousins were in place across the street from Gentile's car a few minutes before six o'clock.

When Gentile turned the corner and started for his car, Rapino, wearing a dark wig, approached him as if to ask for directions. Gentile was in his early-sixties. He was short and fat and moved awkwardly with a slight limp.

Rapino held the stiletto hidden behind his right leg and said, "*Mi scusi. Ricorda Maria Teresa?*"

Gentile looked confused as he forced a smile. "*Chi Sei?*"

Rapino switched to English and said, "You raped and murdered her. She was my mother, you piece of shit."

Gentile took a step back as Rapino brought the Stiletto out from behind his leg. The blade went into the right side of Gentile's stomach. Rapino pulled it across to the left. Gentile grunted from the sudden pain but couldn't speak as blood spilled from his mouth. Rapino pulled the blade out, grabbed Gentile's hair, and then slashed his throat.

A few seconds later, he was back in the car, his shirt and pants stained with Carlo Gentile's blood.

• • • • •

"He could've killed you, Doris," Special Agent, Connor Kelly said. "You're lucky he didn't."

The three small magnetic audio recording devices were on a paper napkin on the night table. All three were smeared with Vaseline and stained with spots of blood.

Doris Montalvo, sitting on her bed in a blue robe, pointed to the recording devices. "And now he knows I'm a snitch," she said. "What's my life worth after this?"

"Doris, you're home free after this," Kelly said. "He went for humiliation rather than death. Probably because he knew we'd be watching. If you were dangerous to them, Galante would've killed you. He was likely acting on a tip. What I need to know is who tipped him off."

"What you need to know?" Doris said. "Fuck you, Kelly. Fuck you!" She pointed to the recording devices again. "He put those up my ass. You find out which drug he used yet? Isn't that rape? Isn't that assault?"

Kelly frowned. "You really want Jerry Galante arrested on those charges after you've been fucking the guy since your husband first went away? You make that kind of trouble for Galante, you do that, have him arrested, and then they will look to kill you."

Doris couldn't stop looking at the recording devices. "What the fuck good are you or the FBI?" she said as she turned to Kelly. "You won't help me until I'm dead, I can see that."

"You don't need protection anymore," Kelly said. "I don't know how many times I have to say this, but you don't have enough to do anything to anybody. A good lawyer, which they all have, will piss on what you have, and federal prosecutors won't touch it anyway. Look, it's over now. Carmine is dead. He can't have you killed anymore, and the worse that could happen has already happened. Galante drugged you, he found the bugs wherever you had them, and he put them where you'd know he found them. Be grateful he used Vaseline, for Christ's sakes."

"You can't even say it, can you?"

"Say what?"

"Where he put them. Up my ass, Kelly. Mr. Special Agent in Charge piece of shit. He raped me. He had to put his fingers inside me to do what he did. That's rape and all you can do is make believe he did me some kind of favor."

Kelly sighed.

"What?" Doris said. "You're bored now? I was raped as far as I'm concerned."

"Then you need to contact the NYPD and make a charge."

"You motherfucker."

"We don't have jurisdiction, Doris. You know that. If you feel you were raped, then you should call the NYPD. I can make the call if you want. I'll make the call and then you can ask them for help because once you have Jerry Galante arrested, aside from his lawyer laughing you out of court, with the trouble you'll have caused him with the head of his family, not to mention his wife, you'll be in real danger."

"Get the fuck out of here," Doris said.

Kelly frowned.

"Just go. I'm done with you FBI assholes. No more. Take your fucking bugs and stick them up your ass. The next place I go is to the press with this. I'm sure this will make a good story."

Kelly went to take the magnetic recording devices, but Doris stopped him. "Oh, no, buster. I paid for those in pain. I'll bring those to the press."

Kelly grabbed a tissue from the box on her night table, grabbed the bugs and then stuffed them in his pocket. "Sorry, those are ours. I have to account for them, Doris."

"You prick. You're taking those things, those bugs, after what he did to me?"

"I think you'd better think it over," Kelly said. "I'm not kidding about what your chances are if this winds up in some newspaper."

"Get the fuck out of here," Doris said.

"Fine."

He stood up and headed for the back door. He stopped before leaving. "You have a nice day," he said, then left.

Doris gave it a few minutes before reaching under a couch pillow and stopping the recorder.

• • • • •

Mary Gallo still refused to step inside Joseph's house, so her conference with her father-in-law and his friend, Artie Adler, took place on the front steps again. Rain was forecast, and it had already started to drizzle. Joseph sat on the top step and held a newspaper over his head. Adler sat one step below to Joseph's left and pulled the hood on his sweatshirt over his head. Mary stood in front of the stoop with one foot on the first step.

"You're the ex-cop, right?" she said to Adler.

"You know he is, Mary," Joseph said.

"I wasn't talking to you."

"I'm the ex-cop, yes," Adler said.

"Where's my son?"

"We don't know."

"Why not? Why can't anyone tell me anything? I'm going to report him missing."

"I don't know that's a good idea," Adler said.

"It's not a good idea," Joseph said.

"Why the hell not?" Mary said. "One minute you're talking to him and then what? What's going on? I know you know, Joseph. If he's hanging around mobsters, I know you know about it."

"Jesus Christ," Joseph said. "You need to get over hating me already. At least for your son's sake."

"The hell is that supposed to mean, for my son's sake?"

Adler said, "Why don't the two of you give it a break already? Fighting each other isn't going to help Chris."

Mary said, "I asked you to do one thing, Joseph. One fucking thing."

"He took off again," Adler said. "I went back to the apartment building where Joseph found him and he's gone."

"What apartment building? Fatso told me he met him on the Canarsie pier."

Joseph said, "Forget that. I told him to call you, but he didn't seem enthused about the idea. It was like this when he went off to war and then again a couple years ago, right?"

"You knew where he was living and lied to me, you fat fuck."

"I told him not to say anything," Adler said.

"What business of it was yours?" Mary said.

"We're looking out for him, the both of us. You need to trust us."

"Yesterday was his birthday," Mary said, her voice choking up. "Why does he hate me?"

"Would you stop with that bullshit already?" Joseph said. "He doesn't hate you. He may hate me for looking for him, but I'm sure he doesn't hate you."

"Okay, enough of this bullshit," Adler said. "He may be in trouble, Mary."

Joseph kicked at Adler's legs. "Damn it, Artie."

"What do you mean, trouble? What kind of trouble?"

"We don't know," Adler said. "It's just his taking off and not staying in contact makes no sense. We don't know what he's doing, but the way he took off can't be something good. That's why I said maybe he's in trouble. Maybe."

"It's the mob again, isn't it?" Mary said. "That I do blame on you, Joseph."

"We don't know it's the mob," Adler said.

Mary pointed at Joseph. "Why doesn't he say so?"

"We don't know it's the mob," Joseph said.

"Asshole."

"Right."

"Well, I'm going to the police anyway," she said. "You two are full of shit and I don't trust him."

"We're telling you that's not a good idea," Adler said.

"You're telling me nothing."

Adler turned to Joseph.

"No," Joseph said. "Fuck it already. If something happens, let it be on her head this time."

"What's that?" Mary said.

"You can cause more problems for Chris going to police than if you wait for him to call you," Adler said.

"Bullshit."

"Oh, what's the point, Artie?" Joseph said. "Fine," he said to Mary. "It's bullshit. Go call the police and fuck everything else up for your son. Knock yourself out making it a bigger mess than it already is."

"I will."

"No wonder he ran away."

"Oh, fuck yourself, Joseph! Fuck yourself!"

She stormed off as the rain began to come down hard. Both men watched her cross the street to her car. They remained on the steps in the rain as she pulled away from the curb. Both waved when she flashed them the finger.

Joseph said, "What can I do. We tell her what we know, and she'll definitely go the police. Maybe this way she thinks about it and backs off."

"I hope you're right about that," Adler said.

"Yeah," Joseph said. "Me too."

9

Sheila Greenblatt was a petite woman with a big bust and crystal blue eyes. She'd been a legal secretary at her husband's firm for several years before retiring six years ago. Sheila knew her husband's business inside and out, and never cared for the mob clientele he'd inherited from his father. The day Carmine Montalvo and his bodyguard showed up to their office for a consultation was the day Sheila decided to retire. She did so the following week.

Lately she'd been looking forward to retiring to Coral Gables, Florida, the wealthy Miami suburb, where both her daughters and six grandchildren lived. Only her son remained in New York. Although her husband was upset with their son's decision to avoid the legal profession and become a professor instead, Sheila knew that Morris was more upset with their son being gay than anything that had to do with not becoming a lawyer. Their son was busy and had an active social life in Manhattan. The estrangement between her son and her husband made it worse.

Sheila could only see her son from time to time, and although she missed him, her daughters and grandchildren were living in Florida, and she could be with them as much as she liked.

When she learned about one of her husband's mob clients being murdered in prison, Sheila had had enough. Morris had been down to the federal prison center in North Carolina and back several times over the last few months, always complaining about his trips and the crap he had to put up with from an evil man he and everybody else wished would die already.

Now that Carmine Montalvo was dead, apparently murdered, according to Morris, Sheila wanted to sell their house and move.

She told her husband so when he returned from work.

"That animal was murdered and that's enough," she said when Morris entered the house through the back deck door. "I want to sell this place and move to Florida."

He stood in the kitchen holding his briefcase. He looked exhausted.

"You hear me?" Sheila said. "I said that's enough. Either you retire and come with me, or you can stay here, but I'm going to live with the girls and our grandchildren."

"And what brought this on?" Morris said.

"Your work with those animals," Sheila said before pouring him a glass of water for his Metformin pills.

Morris set his briefcase down and sat on a kitchen chair.

"Here," Sheila said. "Take them before you forget again."

Morris took the two Metformin pills for his diabetes and chased them with a sip of water. He set the glass back down on the table and said, "What's for dinner?"

"Meatloaf. Did you hear what I said, Morris? I'm not kidding."

"What do you want me to do?" he said. "Montalvo is dead. I don't have another case with any of them right now. Just a backlog of appeals we'll never win anyway."

"And you're not worried? The way those people kill one another?"

"As long as they kill one another, I'm not worried, no."

Sheila sat at the table with him. "I found a place," she said. "Two places. A condo or a house. Either way."

"The condo is less work," Morris said.

"But not as private. There are handymen for a house."

"If you want to pay through the nose."

"We aren't destitute, Morris. We can pay a handyman."

"It's still a stranger in the house."

"Stranger shmanger. Who cares? I won't know the men doing the lawn and fixing things in the condo either. I can live with it."

"And if I don't want to leave?"

"This time I'll go alone. You can join me later or not, but I'm not going to worry myself over these animals you defend. They should all be lined up and shot."

"Defending them is my job, Sheila."

"It'll get you killed someday."

"That's a little dramatic."

"It's not dramatic. Look at how they kill one another. How long is that going on? Forever. And if they don't kill you, they'll get you in trouble."

"Not the documentaries again, please."

"Never mind. Bobby Simone in Philadelphia, Bruce Cutler in New York. I don't want to hear my husband's name on the six o'clock news someday. Morris Greenblatt, indicted for this or that. We don't need that, Morris. We can retire and enjoy our grandchildren. I will if you won't."

"Can we talk about this tomorrow?"

"Talk shmawk, Morris. I'm moving to Florida."

• • • • •

Maria Theresa agreed to visit Rapino's hometown in the mountains. She took the next day off from the restaurant and met up with her cousins at their home in Torremontanara. Alfredo and Rafael drove a rental Chevy Sport. Maria Theresa wore tight, light blue stretch pants and a tight, white pullover. Her sneakers were pink and blue Nikes. She also had a light, white sweater with her for the mountains.

Rapino and Maria Theresa sat in the back for the hour and ten minutes' drive to Pizzoferrato. Rapino couldn't stop looking at her. She smiled each time she caught him.

As the temperature cooled, Rapino offered her his windbreaker, but she draped her sweater over her shoulders instead. Alfredo parked in a small lot off *Via Ettore Casati*. The statue was in an enclosed area that appeared to be part of a school for young children. Rapino allowed his twin cousins to walk ahead to create some distance from them so he could talk to Maria Theresa.

"You have my mother's name," he told her.

"*Si*," she said. "There are three more of us in the family. An aunt and two first cousins of mine."

"I asked them to take me to see Bruno Sammartino's statue because my mother loved him."

"Everybody in this town loved him, but I think most people knew he was more an actor than a wrestler."

"He was a strong guy. You have to give him that."

"I've seen pictures. Yes, very strong."

"Have you been to America?"

"Never, no."

"Would you want to go there?"

"*Si*, but not yet. I have college to finish here."

"College? You're a manager. What do you study?"

"Italian literature."

"Really? How does it pay?"

"You are a true American, Giovanni."

Rapino laughed. "No, I'm still Italian. I'm American when I have to be."

"For the mafia?"

Rapino shrugged.

"I heard talk around here, but then I looked up a few things on my computer and saw your name. Why?"

"America is very different than here."

"But the mafia is the same everywhere."

"Here they are stronger. In America they are weak and getting weaker."

"So, why? Why become part of that?"

They reached the fenced-in schoolyard where the statue of Bruno Sammartino stood. Rapino took his cousin's hand and went to the plaques in front of the statue.

Alfredo and Rafael sat on a bench near a plastic jungle gym smoking cigarettes.

"If I could take it back," Rapino said. "If I had a woman like yourself, I never get involved. Never."

"And now it's too late?"

Rapino shrugged again.

"*Obelisco di Alfredo Sammartino*," Maria Theresa said. "The town made this an historical landmark."

"I think he died a few years back."

"In twenty-eighteen. He lived in Pittsburg, was married and had three sons."

"Wow," Rapino said. "I'm impressed."

"Anyone from this town, the ones a generation older than us, know everything about him. How many discussions at dinners. You hear it enough, you remember. It's crazy."

"I could give it up," Rapino said.

Maria Theresa looked confused.

"For you," Rapino said. "I could give it all up for you."

"*Cugino*, that can't happen."

"Why not?"

"First, we don't know each other. Second, you didn't even ask if I'm with someone."

"Are you?"

"No, but I know what you have to do for the mafia. I can't live with that. I'm sure our *cugini* told you. I'm not someone who accepts the mafia. I'm very far to the left of anyone who thinks the mafia are good. They're not good."

"But I could change. I could leave them."

"I'm not a naïve woman, *cugino*. If we knew each other well and were in love, I couldn't accept what you have to do for them."

"What if I told you I'm already in love with you?"

"I wouldn't believe it."

"But I am. You were the thunderbolt for me."

"No, I'm a fantasy for you. I'm attracted to you too, *cugino*, but I'm not foolish enough to think it's more than that. We're very different people with very different lives. You're not in love with me. You're in love with the idea of being in love. I know this. I've done it myself. Love doesn't come so easy, I don't think."

Rapino frowned.

"Aside from all of that, I think I know why you're here," she said. "What you came here for."

"I had business."

"To avenge your mother. All these years you haven't come, except for now."

Rapino looked away.

"I understand, *cugino*, but I can't accept it. Whatever you did or you are going to do, I could never accept it."

"This is a shame," he said. "The biggest mistake of my life, eh? I lived with a *zio* is mafia there, in New York. His sons are mafia. He brings me up to be mafia. I don't know anything else."

She took his hands then. "You can still do what you said you'd do for me," she said. "Maybe for the next woman in your life?"

Rapino removed his hands from hers. "No," he said. "I'm afraid it's too late. I have nothing without them. All my life, I'm them. I'm lost now."

Maria Theresa said, "It's a shame if you believe this, *cugino*."

They looked at each other a long moment before both of them frowned.

"Now, let's catch up with Alfredo and Rafael," Rapino said. "I want to pass by the house I was born in if it's still around. I fly home tomorrow."

"*Via Pineta*," Maria Theresa said. "Just a few blocks from where Bruno Sammartino was born and the same street as the statue."

Rapino wasn't listening. He no longer cared about where he was born. He led the way back toward the street. When Maria Theresa went to take Rapino's hand, he pulled away.

"That will make it worse," he said.

"I'm sorry," Maria Theresa said.

He couldn't lie to her. He was telling himself as much as he was telling her.

"Don't be sorry," he said. "Is my fault."

• • • • •

Charlie Mazza, wearing a long blonde wig and black shirt and pants, hid in the men's room of the Sticky Fingers strip club on

Queens Boulevard until it closed at 6 o'clock in the morning. He'd been there for two hours waiting on an opportunity to catch the owner, Barry Rosenfeld. He'd been looking for him since leaving Giovanni Rapino's apartment a few days earlier. Rosenfeld was going on his fourth week of missing payments, more than $2,800.

Mazza had met with the club owner twice before, the last time was two months ago when Rapino wanted Rosenfeld to know who to pass the weekly $700 payments off to going forward.

Rosenfeld had made good for four weeks before turning bad. The disappearing acts he'd been pulling on Mazza aggravated Rapino to the point of making a threat over the phone. When Rosenfeld no longer answered phone calls, Rapino instructed Mazza to handle the situation. A slap if Rosenfeld had the money he owed and a lot worse if he didn't have it.

It was Rosenfeld's habit to stay late on the mornings they closed at 6 o'clock. He left earlier on weekends, but since it was a Wednesday morning, he'd likely be hanging around after hours.

Mazza couldn't stand strip joints. Not the men who managed them nor the bouncers who kept things in line. He knew how the operation worked. Everything inside the clubs was transactional. Managers picked favorite dancers and offered them favored shifts. Sometimes they picked based on looks, but most times it was based on the sexual favors they could get in return; sexual favors or cash kickbacks.

Although he often felt bad for the woman, most conducted their business in the same transactional way, the same as the men they worked for. Some dancers gave it away willingly to managers and bouncers for the favors they received in return, whether it was a good shift or a few hours in the VIP room. They all stripped for the money and the chance for an occasional sugar daddy who might pay their rent and other luxuries for services rendered.

Mazza found that bouncers were the ultimate opportunists, however, charging the dancers kickbacks for the rooms they worked or by taking it out in trade. Nothing was gained without paying a price.

So it wouldn't be difficult for Mazza to throw Rosenfeld a beating, no matter the FBI rules he was supposed to follow regarding not engaging in violence. He reminded himself of the doublethink: *I'm undercover working to take down the bad guys.*

He heard someone step inside the bathroom. He assumed it was Rosenfeld and crouched on a toilet seat. He heard a urinal flush and then the sink water run.

Then he heard a ring tone before Rosenfeld said, "Fuck me." Mazza listened to the one-sided conversation.

"I don't know, Jenn, in a little while. I have shit to do here."

There was a brief pause before Rosenfeld said, "Receipts, Jenn. I need to check receipts the same as every night. Go back to bed and I'll see you when I get home. Okay? Good. Love you too."

Mazza was thinking he should grab Rosenfeld now and not worry if there was anyone else in the club. He gave it another moment and Rosenfeld said, "Jesus Christ, I can't take much more of this shit."

It was then Mazza hopped off the toilet seat and pulled the stall door open. Rosenfeld was surprised. He looked from side to side a moment before he said, "What the fuck? You fall asleep in there?"

"Don't recognize me?" Mazza said as he stepped closer.

"Who—Oh, shit."

Mazza nailed him in the solar plexus with a right uppercut. Rosenfeld gasped once as his body folded at the waist. A second later, he spewed and began choking as he tried to catch his breath. Mazza stepped back to avoid the vomit. He let Rosenfeld catch his breath before punching down at the manager's right temple with a hard right. Rosenfeld dropped to the floor, his face in his spew. He was breathing but unconscious.

Mazza ripped open Rosenfeld's pants pocket and took a wallet and a small money clip. The money in the clip came to $705.00. Another $62.00 was in the wallet. He stuffed the cash into his front pants pocket, rolled Rosenfeld over onto his back, and then used a plastic Zip Tie on his hands. He used another Zip Tie for Rosenfeld's ankles and left the bathroom. Mazza then took Rosenfeld's cellphone and dropped it in the nearest toilet.

He double-checked the scene before covering his head with both hands and exiting the Men's room. He navigated his way through the club's kitchen and then out to a parking lot through a back door.

When he was back to his car, he put in a call from a burner phone to the local NYPD precinct for them to check on an apparent robbery at the Sticky Fingers strip club on Queens Boulevard.

• • • • •

"Rapino was in Italy," Artie Adler said. "He's just back and the task force will be all over him."

They were sitting in Joseph's kitchen. Adler had just come from a meeting with a friend on the NYPD Organized Crime Task Force. Joseph seemed to be in pain as he twisted every so often on his chair. Adler didn't notice at first.

"All over him how?" Joseph said. "They arrest him?"

Adler took a can of Diet Coke from the refrigerator, pulled the tab and then sat across the table from Joseph. "No, but they're focused on him because of Staten Island," he said. "He's going nowhere without a tail."

"What about Chris?" Joseph said.

"My guy said Rapino was alone. Flight manifests. Nothing with the name Mazza or Gallo."

Joseph cringed from back pain as he leaned to his left. "And where is he now, Rapino?"

"Out and about or home is my guess," Adler said before taking a deep drink of soda from the can. He excused himself after belching into a fist and said, "He's definitely back in Brooklyn."

"Do we know where he lives? You got an address?"

"We can't go near it while it's under surveillance. Not if we want to protect your grandson."

"I can."

"No, you can't. You get caught up in this, they get you on film, which they're definitely using, and then something goes down with your grandson ... no, you can't go."

Joseph twisted in his chair again. "Meaning you won't tell me where he lives."

"I wouldn't if I knew. No. Besides, we still don't know if your daughter-in-law went to the police. If she did that, you definitely want to stay the hell away."

"Meanwhile I'm sweating out my grandson being involved in murder."

"Double murder, in case you forgot."

"I hope you're not trying to be cute, Artie."

"I'm emphasizing how serious this is, you big dope. If Chris is on the lam, he might be better off right now."

Joseph held up a hand as he felt another back pain. He paused a few seconds, then said, "You think they'll bust this Rapino?"

"For sure, soon as they have proof he's the killer. Then they'll flip him. The fuck is wrong with you? You hurting?"

"No. Go on."

"The task force assumes Rapino will flip once they have him for the murders. Why I wanted you to get Chris to flip."

"If they don't have Rapino on the murder, proof that it was him, that he did it, then Chris flipping wouldn't do them any good either. I doubt Rapino told Chris he was driving them to kill a couple of people."

"My guy did say there are moles in the crew he's with. He didn't say who. Could be anybody, other wiseguys, associates, who knows? Bottom line is if anybody working with the feds knew about it, the Staten Island thing, Rapino would've been pinched when he got off his Alitalia flight."

"I have to do something, Artie," Joseph said as he gasped for breath. He needed another few seconds before he could continue, then said, "I can't just sit back and watch."

"There's nothing you can do, Joe. This has to play itself out. Jesus Christ, what is it with you and not seeing a doctor?"

Joseph frowned, then said, "I don't need a doctor. I already know."

"Know what?"

"Cancer. I have cancer."

Adler was incredulous. "What?"

"You heard me."

"Fuck me. How bad?"

"Bad."

"You don't smoke much beside that stupid pipe and I haven't seen you with that in months. Where is it, the cancer?"

"Pancreatic."

"Jesus Christ," Adler said. "Why the fuck didn't you say something sooner?"

"The pain's gone from my stomach to my back. I'm losing weight, believe it or not. I can't control the diabetes. I'm pissing maple syrup."

"You dumb fuck. What are we talking about here, Joe? Stage three or four?"

"Four, I guess. I haven't been back to the doctor for a few months. I was three the last diagnosis."

"And you kept this to yourself why? You want to die? Are you fucking crazy?"

"There's nothing anyone can do now anyway."

"You idiot. Of course, there is. I'll take you to the doctor's right now."

"No."

"You're going to let that shit eat you alive?"

"I'm going to go down swinging, I'll tell you that much."

"Jesus Christ, you're nuts sometimes. Get me your doctor's office number."

"No."

"No? Seriously?"

"No."

The two friends stared at each other, Adler frowning and Joseph emotionless.

"You're an idiot," Adler said.

"Go home," Joseph said. "I gotta pee."

• • • • •

Rapino was angry during his flights home. He couldn't stop thinking about how Maria Theresa was right to reject him and how it was his own fault. Why would an intelligent young woman with a full life ahead of her tie herself to a mobster and the disastrous life it would be for her? What could she get from such a life?

Rapino remained depressed about the situation. She was right. It was best she didn't even consider spending a night with him, never mind running off with him. He belonged to a criminal organization that had no sense of honor. Mob movies from back in the day showed a nostalgic reality that had never existed. Nor was the life ever good enough to justify if one believed in a judgment day.

Rapino understood that now. He understood how anyone with an iota of education and decency could never accept the world of organized crime. What made it worse was that it had been his choice to pursue the life he resented now. *Cosa Nostra* was why he could never have someone like Maria Theresa.

Rapino also knew that had she gone with him, had they married and had children together, he'd wind up treating her the same as men in his world treated all women, as appendages with little value outside of housework, pregnancy, and raising children. Her natural beauty would fade with age and pregnancies and he'd wind up with the younger prostitutes he currently paid for, or the middle-aged women he picked up for a night or two of sex.

The genuine love he had felt for Maria Theresa would wilt over time and eventually turn to contempt.

There was no turning back, not even if he walked away from the life. He'd always be someone who'd beaten and extorted and killed for an organization of criminals. At 31, Rapino couldn't change. He knew he wasn't strong enough to live a legitimate life. He knew he couldn't resist the perks of his criminal life. He'd live and die a criminal. At least he had taken revenge for his mother's rape and murder, but that was the only good thing that had come from his choices.

Maria Theresa was a fantasy he'd have to get over. She was smart and beautiful and completely out of his league. He would continue to have the kind of women who didn't care what he was or what he did, the kind he could never respect or love.

Nor was his life in the mob proving worthwhile. Having to take orders from a punk like Jerry Galante was demeaning. Although he had an inside track because the boss of the family liked him, Rapino knew such things were fleeting and too tenuous to count on. He finally understood how nothing in this life was sacred. Nobody in the crime family could be trusted. Any of them would flip under the right circumstances. What good was money and power when both could disappear overnight? What could possibly come from his dedication to *omerta*, when most so-called men of honor betrayed it without a second thought? What good was the mob anymore when everything about it was a fantasy?

By the time his last flight was nearing JFK, Rapino realized he'd given up everything for a mirage, an illusion as fictional as *The Godfather* movies. It was all a lie. What it had become was pathetic, and he was embarrassed to be associated with it, ashamed of being a sworn member of it.

He learned over time how the mob had always been a part of his family's life. His father had been harassed by a local *mafioso* shortly after Rapino was born. His mother had explained how they extorted his father's construction business and forced him to pay for the ability to take on new projects. He learned how two of the men associated with the local *mafioso* pressed his mother to make the payments she could no longer afford and how they eventually took his father's business.

Shortly after he was brought to America because his mother knew that staying in Pizzoferrato was too dangerous for them both, it was already too late. When he learned what had happened to his mother after she returned to Italy to care for his father, he no longer believed in a legitimate life.

His mother's brother was a gangster in America. His uncle's sons, Rapino's first cousins, would become gangsters too. From age 12 on, all that young Giovanni Rapino knew and heard came from the mobsters he would live with until he could live on his own. By then, he knew nothing else. By then, he wanted nothing else.

Now all he could do was regret his choices if they ever were choices. He'd made them while growing up in his *zio's* house in the Williamsburg section of Brooklyn. Life on the streets of Brooklyn would teach him to survive. The boys and men he eventually befriended were both apprentices and professionals of a criminal society. As much as he knew he'd soiled his mother's hopes for him, Rapino refused to become the victim his father had been before he died.

Nobody was going to fuck with him and not regret it.

By the time he was inducted into the Cirelli crime family, Rapino had proven himself a stone killer.

As his flight made its final approach, Rapino wasn't sure what he would do once he was face to face with Jerry Galante again. When he closed his eyes, all he could see was himself shooting Galante in the face.

10

"Where the fuck you been?" Jerry Galante said.

Giovanni Rapino had just stepped out of the Harbor Fitness gym. Galante had been waiting for him.

"Italy," Rapino said. "Just a few days."

"And I gotta come here to find you? You can't call?"

"Was business."

"Business my ass. A few things went down we need to talk about, you and me."

Rapino sighed. "Yes, boss," he said, then pointed to Galante's SUV parked across the street. "The truck?"

He started across the street without waiting for Galante. He walked around the front of the SUV before reaching for the passenger door handle. It was locked when he did so. He looked up and frowned at Galante a moment before the doors were unlocked.

"*Stroonzo*," Rapino whispered.

He set his gym bag between his legs as Galante sat behind the wheel.

"So?" Galante said. "You get it out of your system, whatever you did over there?"

"I do nothing over there," Rapino said. "I visit family. See Bruno Sammartino's statue where I was born. I see *cugini*. One is beautiful, a second *cugini*, Maria Theresa. I fall in love, but she doesn't bother with us, *cosa nostra*. She has her own life. She goes to university, eh? Maybe she's a *Professoressa* someday. She has no use for mafia."

Galante pulled into traffic and drove along Fourth Avenue heading north. "Fuck her then," he said, trying to calm himself. "I hope you did that much if she's so beautiful."

"No, not this woman. Don't talk like that, eh? Maria Theresa is a beautiful woman, and virtuous. I respect her. I don't fuck her."

Galante rolled his eyes. "Whatever," he said. "Long as you got what you wanted over there."

"I visit my family," Rapino said. "It was nice, but these fucking flights. So long the flights. Hours and hours. I have headache now. Bad headache. Even in gym, I don't workout. I sit and watch the televisions. The news. This fuckin' guy, Donald Trump. He's fucking clown, eh?"

Galante was surprised. "You don't like Trump?"

"He's fucking idiot, please. Why he pays porn star to fuck? He has beautiful wife at home, he fucks porn star. Is ugly too, no? Orange face, that fucking wig. Is an asshole, that guy."

"His wife is hot, but the guy's the President. I think he should be allowed to fuck whomever he wants," Galante said. "The Playboy model was even hotter than the porn star and his wife."

"He pays her too. How he respect himself? He is president and he pays for women? Stupid fucking man."

"I guess. Okay. But now I gotta ask you a question and I hate to ask it."

Rapino shrugged.

"The civilians murdered on Staten Island," Galante said. "No names, but the one was somebody Montalvo wanted killed. Then there was another person."

Rapino shrugged again.

"Do you know about it?"

"What I'm gonna know? No."

"You know Montalvo died?"

"No. Is dead?"

"Is dead. Somebody cut his throat in prison. The hospital prison in North Carolina."

Rapino shook his head. "I don't know this."

"Anyway, it's a big mess here now. Cops are laying it into us because of this Staten Island thing. Nobody seems to know who did it."

Rapino shook his head no.

"Nucci is hot about it," Galante said. "Disobeyed orders and whatnot."

"But Montalvo dead is good, no?" Rapino said.

"For me, yeah. It's good. I'm official now. I'm a skipper."

Rapino nodded.

Galante was instantly annoyed. "Usually what you say is congratulations or something," he said. "I'm happy for you, boss. Good for you, boss. Great news, boss."

"I'm happy for you, boss," Rapino said with no emotion.

"Oh!" Galante yelled. He pulled the SUV to the curb and slammed on the brakes. He turned to Rapino and said, "Hey, I'm trying not to be angry over this shit you just pulled taking off to Italy without telling anyone. People wondered where the hell you went and did you talk to the feds. I'm trying my best to hold my temper with you, and you've got an attitude all of a sudden. If you have a problem with me, you need to get over it or do something about it."

Rapino sighed, thinking if he had a gun with him right then, he would have shot the asshole.

"Well?" Galante said. "Which is it?"

"I'm tired, boss. Exhausted. The flights, the time change. Sorry. I'm happy for you."

"Jesus Christ," Galante said. "Sometimes I don't know about you."

"I'm good, boss."

Galante forced a smile. "I hope so," he said. "You're my best guy. You're the guy I'd want to take over from me if some other crew doesn't steal you away."

Rapino was still depressed from his exchange with Maria Theresa back in Italy and his thoughts on the flights home. He was fed up with assholes like Jerry Galante and the other members of the Cirelli crime family. He knew he'd have to snap out of his depression and soon. Having to listen to Galante shoot his mouth off wasn't easy. Rapino didn't respect Galante and didn't think he was much of a leader. He took orders like all the captains took orders from those above them. Then there was the fact Galante had been screwing his captain's wife while Montalvo was alive in prison, and long before Rapino had screwed the same woman. Galante broke the rules the same as everybody else. He was no one to bring them up now.

Rapino was tempted to tell him, "*Yeah, I killed those two on Staten Island. I killed them because the boss told me to kill them. He doesn't tell you because you don't have the balls, eh? You're afraid of your own shadow, which is why I'll be killing you too, stroonzo. You only think you're a skipper now. My orders came from the top, you punk.*"

He didn't say anything. It would be a lot easier to take him out when Galante's guard was down.

"We were supposed to see Nucci when you got back," Galante said. "I'll tell him you're exhausted and whatnot. I'll drop you off, but make sure you're over this shit when we meet with Nucci, okay?"

"Okay, boss. I'm sorry."

Galante shoved Rapino's left shoulder and smiled. "Forgetaboutit," he said. "I'll drop you home. Get some sleep. Maybe a blow job to help you sleep. I'll call you soon as I set up a meet with Nucci and we'll get this over with. He's gonna wanna know about Staten Island and why you went back to Italy. We both, me and Nucci, think we know about Italy, but he won't press you on it same as I didn't. We understand."

"Thanks, boss."

"Forgetaboutit. Just get some sleep after I drop you off."

"I will, boss. Thanks."

• • • • •

The women had double-teamed a recently released prison gang member sent to threaten them. Ming Tao showed up while they were sitting outside on the stoop of the apartment building smoking cigarettes. He parked in front of a fire hydrant and waved at both women. He was a friend of Mei-Ling's husband, Lǐ Nà. Mei-Ling didn't wave back.

Ming Tao demanded the money her husband had requested. Lǐ Nà had called her several times over the past few days demanding she visit him and deposit money in his inmate account for commissary. As of last night, Mei-Ling refused to answer her husband's calls.

Mei-Ling knew Ming Tao from when she was living in Chinatown in Manhattan with her husband. Ming Tao was tall and thin and 26. He'd been in Rikers as a co-defendant with her husband, released when a friend was able to post bail for him. When Ming Tao approached the two women, Mei-Ling spoke in the broken English she'd been learning.

"What you want, Ming?" she said. "I don't have money for Lǐ Nà."

"Then we go upstairs to fuck," he said with a mocking smile on his face.

Mei-Ling was about to tell him to fuck off when Li-Jie stopped her.

"We fuck, no money?"

Ming Tao gave it a moment, then nodded. "For today."

"For week," Li-Jie said.

Ming Tao shrugged. "One week."

"Okay," Li-Jie said. "Come."

She took Mei-Ling's hand and headed inside the apartment building. Ming Tao followed them inside and up the short flight of stairs.

Once they were inside the apartment, Li-Jie and Mei-Ling told Ming Tao to get himself a beer from the refrigerator. They went to the bathroom together to whisper to one another while the water ran. They removed their clothes and stepped back out of the bathroom. Li-Jie waved at Ming Tao to use the bathroom.

"Wash yourself," she said. "Make dick clean."

Ming Tao frowned at her as he headed for the bathroom with his beer.

When he was back, Li-Jie waved at him to join her on the mattress that lay on the floor.

Ming Tao said, "No, her first. Mei-Ling."

Li-Jei shrugged.

Mei-Ling sat on the mattress. Ming Tong pointed to his crotch. "First this," he said.

"Lay down," she said.

"Why?" he said.

"Lay down."

He guzzled the rest of his beer, then set the empty can on the floor as he lay on the mattress. He slowly turned over to lay on his back. Mei-Ling dropped to her knees on the mattress and fondled his testicles. Ming Tao closed his eyes a moment before Li-Jie went to hand Mei-Ling an industrial razor. Mei-Ling shook her head no. Li-Jie made the cut herself, deep into the left side of his penis. Ming Tao hesitated a moment before he sat up, saw and felt what had happened, and then screamed. He grabbed at his penis as Li-Jie handed him a towel.

"Go hospital," she said.

"I fuckin' kill you!" he yelled.

"Go now. They stitch your cock."

Mei-Ling had a large square band aid. She handed it to him. Ming Tao took the band aid and applied it to the wound, covering the left side of his penis. Li-Jie handed Ming Tao's underwear and pants to him. He was threatening them as he quickly dressed himself. Li-Jie took a Smith & Wesson, M&P® BODYGUARD® 380 from a kitchen drawer and turned it on Ming Tao.

"Go hospital," she said.

He told her in their native language that he would come back and kill them both. Li-Jie waved him off.

She had already put their escape plan to work. The counterfeit passports had cost her $2,000. The tickets to Madrid in Spain another $3,200. They would take flights from within Spain to either Portugal or somewhere in France. They hadn't made up their minds yet.

They had already packed and kept their suitcases in the single closet in the apartment. Their flight would leave from JFK in two days. Li-Jie had one more move to make before heading to a motel near the airport.

She watched from a window as Ming Tao, clutching his crotch, sat inside his car. She waited until the car pulled away from the curb and sped down the block. When he was gone from view, Li-Jie said, "Now Italian. Now we get money."

• • • • •

"Where you go?" Li-Jie said.

"Italy," Rapino said. "I don't want anything today, ladies. I'm taking a few days alone. To get my schedule back."

"What schedule?"

"Nothing. I'm tired. Busy couple of days. What do you want?"

"Money."

"Huh?"

"We want borrow."

Rapino's brow furrowed. "Why?" he said. "You make money now."

"We starting our own."

"Own what? *Putana* house?"

"For girls. We manage."

"Where?"

"Apartment across the street."

"Won't your husbands want a piece?"

"They locked up. One of Mei-Ling's husband's friend comes today to steal money."

Rapino was smiling. He liked their balls but wasn't sure if he could take them seriously. "And what happened?"

"I cut dick with razor."

Rapino laughed. "Are you fucking with me?"

"I cut dick with razor."

"Christ. And when they come back?"

"You protect."

"I protect?"

"Like last time. Yes?"

"And what do I get for that?"

"What you always get."

"I think you a little crazy, eh?"

"Ten thousand dollar, yes?"

"You know what it'll cost you?"

"Two point."

Rapino laughed.

"What?" Mei-Ling said.

"What funny?" Li-Jie said.

"How do you know about points?"

"Husband."

"Husband, huh? Why not borrow it from him?"

"He in jail. No money. Piece of shit."

Rapino smiled. "It's three points on the street, but I give it to you crazy bitches for two. You know what that means?"

"Two hundred a week."

"You're a smart cookie, eh?"

"I know business."

"I can see that."

"When?"

"When what?"

"Money."

"*Gesù*, you're in hurry."

"Deposit. We need for deposit."

Rapino shrugged.

"Ming come back."

"Who?"

"Mei-Ling's husband friend. I cut dick."

Rapino put his arms up. "You're making me dizzy."

"Need money now."

"You sure?"

"Now."

"Fine, fine," Rapino said.

He went to the cabinet under the sink and opened it. There was a small safe inside behind rolls of paper towels. He opened the safe and removed one of three stacks of bundles of cash secured with a rubber band.

Mei-Ling looked to Li-Jie, eyes wide open. Li-Jie shook her head no.

"Here," Rapino said, holding out the bundle of cash. "Count it."

"No count," Li-Jie said.

"Count it or I don't want to hear about it being short."

"Short?"

"Count the money."

Li-Jie removed the rubber band and counted the hundred-dollar bills.

"Okay," she said. "You want now? Sex?"

"No," Rapino said. "I want to sleep. Go do deposit."

"Thank you."

"Don't thank me. You owe two-hundred next week. Plus the ten thousand you have now."

Li-Jie nodded. "Okay."

Mei-Ling nodded also.

Rapino stretched his arms as he yawned. "Good luck," he said.

Both women left his apartment. He followed them to the door and locked it. He went to the window and saw a gypsy cab was double parked in front of the building. A minute later he saw both women carrying suitcases leave the front of the building. They sat in the back of the gypsy cab, their suitcases on their laps.

"Never lend to women, eh?" Rapino said with a smirk.

•   •   •   •   •

Chris Gallo broke into his mother's house through a basement window shortly before dawn. He remained in the basement until he was too hungry to ignore what he knew would be upstairs in her refrigerator. He removed his shoes and took the stairs carefully and quietly.

His mother was a light sleeper and was usually up before 8 o'clock in the morning. He prepared a fresh pot of coffee but didn't plug in the electrical cord because the smell might wake her.

He wasn't going to avoid his mother, but he wanted to eat something before she became hysterical when he told her why he hadn't called for so long. Her reaction would be over the top dramatic, probably more so than the day he broke an arm playing two-hand touch football as a kid.

Chris thought about telling his grandfather instead, but it was dangerous because Joseph wasn't the type to freeze from fear. If anything, he'd want to know details about the undercover work in the event something went wrong. Joseph might do something on his own that could jeopardize his job, not to mention his life. It was from love, Chris had no doubts about it, but Joseph still had friends like Artie Adler who could cause trouble for everyone.

Telling his mother instead was a calculated risk Chris was willing to take because he knew that his mother would become paralyzed with fear. Chris doubted she'd ever even tell Joseph.

The bureau had moved him to Forest Hills in Queens after he explained about his grandfather showing up at the apartment building in Brooklyn. The apartment was a studio on the sixth floor of a building called the Howard Apartments, a group of apartment buildings off Queens Boulevard. He joined a nearby gymnasium under the name of Frank Minelli, the identifications provided by the bureau.

None of that information could be passed on to his mother, but he would have to fill her in on a few things. The only thing that had saved him from her going to the police and filing a missing person report was the fact he'd disappeared so often in the past and for a lot longer than he'd been on this assignment.

He was in Iraq for 10 of the 15 months before he called to let her know. She hadn't even known that he'd joined the Army. Then he was home for a short time before disappearing for more than 30 weeks of training at Quantico, Virginia, with the FBI for his badge and then undercover work. He never returned home during or after his training but would sporadically call his mother and lie about the traveling he was doing.

Special Agent in Charge, Kelly, knew Chris would be visiting his mother and had arranged a hotline for her to protect Chris. In the event he had to go silent with her again, she could call an answering service that would contact Kelly directly.

After making his way upstairs from the basement, Chris was eating a ham and Swiss cheese sandwich with a dab of mayonnaise when he heard his mother's footsteps upstairs. He'd already drunk half a quart of milk and was anxious to drink some coffee. He plugged in the coffee pot and it began to brew. He heard the toilet flush upstairs. A minute later, his mother was halfway down the stairs when she suddenly stopped.

Chris figured she was frightened and called out to her. "Ma," he said.

"Chris?"

"Yeah, Ma, it's me. Come down, I put up the coffee."

He could hear her quicken the rest of her steps down to the living room. Her eyes were opened wide when she saw him.

"Oh, my God!" she yelled. "Chris!"

He hustled to her, and they exchanged a long hug. Mary kissed his cheeks, his forehead, and then one side of his mouth before her eyes watered with tears and she needed his help to make it to the kitchen to sit.

"My God. I was so scared for you," she said. "How are you? What have you been doing? Does Joseph know you're back? Why didn't you call?"

"Take it easy, Ma," Chris said. "Everything is okay."

"I need to wash my face," she said as she stood. "I'm so happy you're home!"

She grabbed his head with both hands and kissed him half a dozen times before releasing him and heading for the bathroom.

"I'll be right back," she said.

Chris poured two cups of coffee while his mother used the bathroom. He set them on the kitchen table across from one another. He took spoons from a drawer and napkins from a holder on the counter. A sugar bowl and a matching packet holder stuffed with Sweet-N-Lows was centered on the table.

When Mary returned, she was still wiping tears from her eyes.

"Milk?" he said.

"No," she said, then pointed to a swivel tray on the kitchen counter. "I use the creamer."

Chris grabbed the creamer and handed it to her. Then he sat and waited for her to use the creamer and stir her coffee. She added sugar, stirred, and then smiled at her son.

"I'm going to tell you where I've been and everything else, Mom, but you have to remain calm and swear it doesn't leave this house. You cannot tell Gramps or anyone else. Okay?"

"Tell me, please," Mary said.

Chris told her a series of lies to cover himself. He admitted to being an FBI agent working undercover, but told her it had to do with drugs, not the mob. Her eyes were wet with tears throughout his explanation. It became worse when he told her she couldn't know where he was living and that he'd have to go silent for months at a time until his undercover work was finished.

"Drug Cartels?" Mary said. "Those people, Chris? They're killers."

"Not the ones in Mexico, Ma," he said. "The smaller outfits here in New York. They aren't like the ones you hear about it Mexico."

"It sounds so dangerous. How much longer do you have to do this?"

"I don't know, Ma," he said. "It takes time. Sometimes years. Sometimes we get a break and it's over sooner than later. But you can't freak out if you don't hear from me. I'm going to give you a phone number to call when you haven't heard from me in a while. My supervisor will tell you whatever he can without jeopardizing the investigation or my cover. It's not a number you should call every two weeks. You have to give me time to get back to you. And the key is you have to keep this to yourself. Everything I'm telling you now has to remain between us only."

"Who am I going to tell, Chris? Please."

"Joseph. I know you're still angry with him, but I also know you spoke to him. He told me."

"Angry? I hate him."

"Okay, but you two might talk again and you can't tell him any of this."

"I'll never speak to that man again. You have my word."

"Ma, I'm not a fool. I know you went to him looking for me."

"One time."

"One time too many. I'm not kidding, Ma. If I'm exposed in this investigation, it could be dangerous. Please, say nothing to my grandfather. Nothing."

"I call him by his name. I'll never call him your grandfather."

"Fine. Whatever. He can't know I was here today or anything I told you."

Mary ran two fingers across her mouth.

"I mean it, Ma," Chris said.

"Zipped," she said. "Can you spend the day with your mother at least?"

"No, but I can hang around for lunch."

"What should I make?"

"You got gravy?"

"I can make it fresh. Which kind of pasta?"

"Anything. Spaghetti is fine."

"Spaghetti it is. Pay attention and you can make your own sauce."

"Gravy."

"Sauce."

"Ma, don't start."

"You don't start. The world calls it sauce. We're second-generation Italians. You're third generation. It's sauce."

"Okay, I'll watch you cook, but it's still gravy."

Mary stared at her son until they both laughed.

11

Aniello Fontana was watching a small portable television in his backyard while doing 10 pound dumbbell curls with his right hand off his right knee. He switched from right to left hand after a set of six repetitions. He was sitting on the edge of a bench under a table umbrella to shield his skin from the sun. He wore a white wife beater T-shirt and black sweatpants.

Jerry Galante stood on the edge of the grass and waited for Fontana to finish. Earlier in the day, he'd been summoned by one of Fontana's sons. The drive from Brooklyn to Eltingville, Staten Island was a quick one. Galante had been told to park in the driveway of the house on Lyndale Avenue. There were two cars already parked in the driveway. Galante parked on the street instead.

Fontana's daughter, Angela, led him through the house out to the back porch where her brother, Vito, and their father's bodyguard were sipping iced-teas on the deck. Fontana paused the show he'd been watching before turning to Galante. The two hugged and cheek-kissed each other. Fontana then sat at the table where he had been doing preacher curls.

The temperature was in the mid 70's, but without a breeze it felt closer to 80. Galante removed the black windbreaker he was wearing and folded it over his left arm.

"JG," Fontana said as he rubbed his right elbow. He pointed to the bench opposite where he sat. "Hungry? What'll you have?"

"Nothing, thanks," Galante said. "What are you doing still lifting weights at your age?"

"I atrophied when I was in the hospital last year," Fontana said. "Two months of laying on my back, taking an occasional walk up and down the hallways there, what was that gonna do? I atrophied and now I'm trying to get back some of what I lost."

"Mr. Olympia next year?"

"Fuck that. I don't like it when my arms shake because the muscle died. The only muscle that used to count, that one I can't do nothin' about anymore, that one is dead for two years now."

"Well, you got me by two decades almost and I'm not doin' so good there either."

Fontana shrugged. "Except for that pin cushion, Montalvo's wife, no?"

Galante swallowed hard.

"It's okay," Fontana said. "He's dead now so nobody cares."

"It was only a couple times—"

"Stop," Fontana said. "What's done is done. Whatever it was can't be undone, but I have something I need you to take care of for the family."

"Anything, sure."

Fontana waived to his son Bruno up on the deck. "Bruno, tell your sister to bring us something cold," he said.

"Ice tea okay?" Bruno Fontana said.

"Ice tea okay?" Fontana asked Galante.

Galante nodded. "Sure," he said.

Fontana nodded at this son. He removed a small pack of Muratti Italian cigarettes from his sweatpants pocket and held the pack up to Galante.

"No thanks," Galante said.

Fontana pulled a cigarette from the pack and lit it with a lighter. He inhaled twice before his daughter appeared on the deck holding a tray with a small pitcher of ice tea and two glasses. She brought them down to the table and set the tray down.

"Thanks, hon," Fontana said.

Fontana waited for her to disappear inside the house. "Angela," he said. "Poor kid. You know her husband?"

"Never met him, no," Galante said.

"Richie. He's doing life. Now he's in Leavenworth, but they move him every few years. Maybe he can get out in a few more years. Twenty-three years he's been inside."

"Jesus."

"My oldest has been in and out twice and my son-in-law is still inside."

"That's a long time, twenty-three years."

"Last of the Mohicans that kid."

"Will he get out?"

"We hope. Couple more years. Too late for my daughter to have kids, unfortunately. That's the real curse in all this."

"Sorry," Galante said.

"But she's a trooper, Angela is. Does work for me, believe it or not. Not this kind," Fontana made a gun from his hand. "But other stuff. She's good at it too. Has a good eye."

Galante nodded again.

Fontana shrugged before taking a sip of iced tea. "What are you gonna do?" he said. "Life throws a lot of shit our way, right? We have to deal with it. Angela too."

"Sure."

"I'm watching this series on the HBO, *Succession* it's called. It's about a rich family like the Brits own Fox. Or maybe Trump's family. You know, spoiled brat kids don't know their asses from their elbows. The old man built everything and now they gotta pull the shit Trump did to take control or something. Who knows? I like it though. Get to see how the respectable pricks get away with the shit we go to jail for."

"I think my wife has been watching that series."

"It's a good one."

"I'll have to check it out."

"Speaking of the shit life throws, today I have to ask you to do something you're not going to like."

Galante straightened up before he shrugged. "Anything," he said. "What is it?"

"It's for the family, but it's also for you."

Fontana stared at Galante then. Galante knew not to look away.

"Nucci has to go," Fontana said.

Galante's eyes opened wide.

Fontana nodded. "He's gone to the other side."

"Jesus, Aniello. Nucci is a rat?"

"At least six months," Fontana said. "At least. So, if there's anything he can have you on, remember it if you have second thoughts about clipping him."

"I do whatever you say, Aniello."

"No second thoughts?"

"None. If he's gone that route, I agree, he has to go."

"You're closest to him, Jerry. Why it has to be you."

"I understand."

"Nobody else."

"Got it."

"Don't go to him. Don't set up a meeting. Wait for him to call you."

"He already did," Galante said. "He wants to meet with one of my guys. Johnny Rapino went to Italy without telling anyone. I met him the other day, but Nucci wanted to ask him about that thing with the mother and son here. I think we know why Rapino went to Italy, but Nucci wants to hear it firsthand about Staten Island."

"Nucci thinks it was Rapino?"

"I don't know, but I don't think so. Johnny Rap didn't even know about Montalvo being killed."

"Okay. Good. Just make sure you're out of view when it goes down. And make sure to strip him of any recording devices he has on him. Remember, no body, no crime."

Galante nodded.

"*Capische?*"

"I got it."

"Good. Now, that thing on Staten Island. I know Dominick told you it wasn't sanctioned. It was, so there's no need for you to know who was involved. It wasn't Rapino."

Galante raised both his hands. "No problem."

"Good. Now, drink your iced tea. That how we say it? Iced or ice?"

Galante shook his head. "No idea," he said. "Ice tea, no?"

"Exactly," Fontana said, "Ice before, iced after."

Then he winked at Galante.

• • • • •

Stone had the Boston Bruins to win the game and the series versus the Florida Panthers in game seven. In total, between each of the six games, his wins and losses, Stone was effectively laying $11,250 to win $5,000. All of it rested on the final game of the series. The Bruins had set the NHL record for most points in a single season. It was the safest bet he could find and although he didn't have the $11-plus thousand to pay if he lost, he went with it anyway.

The series had started off great with the Bruins winning three of the first four games. Then the Panthers won the next two games, including a wild one in game 6 when Stone threw his remote at the television screen in his kitchen, breaking both the remote and cracking the small 14" screen. Game 7 would decide the series. Of course it went to overtime and of course the Panthers won the game and the series. It was the worst luck he'd ever had and it left him out $11,250 on the Bruins alone. He was also out another $2,300 on NBA playoff games he'd lost.

Down $13,550 in action alone, and without a dime to pay any of it off, he went to meet Jerry Galante at the Broadway Junction, East New York stop on the 14th Street-Canarsie L line. The two stood on the southern end of the Canarsie bound platform, one of the highest elevated platforms in the city. Stone wondered if he was about to be tossed off the platform.

He'd told Galante their meeting was an emergency. Galante already knew about the gambling debt and was in no mood for an explanation. Stone couldn't help but offer one.

"The fucking Bruins, Jerry," Stone said. "Who the fuck thought they'd blow it? The way they did it, at home? They set the record during the regular season for points and they choke in game seven at home? Who the fuck had the Panthers to win that series? Motherfucking choking dog cocksuckers is what the Bruins are."

"Admit it, Stone, we could've jacked those odds to minus three hundred and you still would've bit. And then you took the Knicks and lost there too. The fuckin' Knicks. What, you think they were going to upset the Heat in Miami? On their home court? You're a fucking loser, Stone, and now you owe more than thirteen dimes, plus the juice on your street loan. You got it? Any of it? No, of course not."

"I can sell my house."

"Yeah, right. I'll make a bet with you right now that thing is mortgaged for every nickel its worth. Fuck you, you degenerate piece of shit."

Stone's jaw was clenched tight.

Galante noticed and said, "What? You gonna do something?"

"I'm still a cop, Jerry. You can't kill a cop?"

"Yeah, no shit. And I can't get blood from a stone either. You know what I can do, asshole? I can bury you with your own people. We don't get paid, neither do you, except you'll have to deal with lawyers and we won't. They'll make it even worse for a cocksucker like yourself." He listed off his fingers. "You'll lose your job, you'll go to jail, and then you'll lose your house and wife and kid. Who wants to kill you? Not me. Nobody. Either we bleed you dry first or we let your people do it."

"This is wrong, man. You knew I had a problem."

Galante laughed. "Here we go with that line of shit," he said. "Every gambling loser piece of shit I ever dealt with has the same story come the end of their miserable betting lives. Motherfucker, I'm the one told you to get help with this shit. How many times did I tell you?"

"What can I do?" Stone said. "Is there anything I can do?"

Galante stared at him a long moment. He was thinking: *Yeah, there is something you can do, but I'm not supposed to have help with it. Then again, what's the difference if they never know I had help with it?*

• • • • •

Bruno Fontana was at Rapino's apartment early in the morning. He brought a small box of pastries and two containers of double espresso. Rapino was up from a restless night of sleep. The two exchanged a hug and cheek kiss before Rapino led him to his kitchen table.

"You know my father named me after Sammartino, right?" Fontana said with a smile.

Rapino returned the smile. "Then you should make the trip I just made," he said. "They got a statute there with a landmark for that and where he was born. Pizzoferrato. It's up in the mountains but beautiful."

Fontana nodded. "Abruzzo, right?"

Rapino nodded. "It's beautiful. I could retire there."

"You have family there still. That's great."

"Not many left, but, yeah."

"Any troubles over there?"

"None."

Fontana opened the pastry box and grabbed one of two *sfogliatella*. "I can't resist these things. I swear if I ever retire, I'm gonna buy a pastry joint and live in the back."

Rapino took a cannoli and bit into one end. "Mmmm," he said before swallowing.

"So," Fontana said, "there's gonna be open spots soon. My father wants you to know, you're entitled. He's gonna bump you up."

"That's appreciated."

"He knows. He also knows you're old school. Like my brother and I, and our brother-in-law, that poor bastard. Richie is inside now more than twenty years, but he held his water. Pop knows you'll do the same anything happens, God forbid. Not many do clam up these days."

"Like Nucci."

"Like Nucci."

Rapino took another bite from the cannoli. "And Galante?"

"He did something as bad in my father's eyes," Fontana said. "I'm sure you figured out the old man is old school. No straying outside the lines. He goes way back with this thing of ours. What Jerry was doing with Montalvo's wife can't be ignored, not to my father."

At that point Rapino knew he was safe or Bruno Fontana would've already killed him. "It'd be my pleasure," he said.

"You'll have help," Fontana said. "Me and my brother."

"I can do it myself."

"We're fixed to be the new leadership, the three of us. It's best we're all involved."

Rapino shrugged. "Sure," he said. "Okay by me."

Fontana nodded. "Good," he said.

A few minutes later, the two hugged and exchanged another cheek kiss. Rapino walked Fontana down to the street and watched him get in his Mercedes and pull away from the curb, the message delivered. It was still cool enough outside to enjoy the fresh air. He decided to have a cigarette before heading back upstairs. He was close to finished with the cigarette when a white Toyota with dents along the right rear fender pulled up to the curb in front of the apartment building.

Two Asian men stepped out of the car. Both had black steel telescope batons. Rapino exchanged a stare with one of them as the Asian men passed him and headed inside the building. Rapino waited a few seconds before heading inside himself. He saw the two Asian men had stepped onto the 2nd floor landing and disappeared in the direction of the apartment where the Chinese women who had ripped Rapino off for $10,000 lived.

He headed upstairs to his apartment and didn't look down the hall when he heard loud banging he assumed with the telescope batons against a door. He went to his apartment, then to a closet where he had two separate drop boxes in the floor. He removed a GLOCK® 45 Gen5 9mm, Suppressor Ready, Semi-Auto Pistol from one drop box and the sound suppressor from the other drop box. He screwed the suppressor onto the Glock and headed back out of his apartment. He took the stairs down slowly until he was on the second floor. He could see the door at the end of the hall was partially open. He headed down the hall holding the Glock along his right leg. When he got to the apartment door where the two Chinese women had lived, he pushed the door open and saw the two Asian men rummaging through the apartment.

They saw Rapino at the same time. One, Ming Tao, grabbed his telescope baton off a table and held it up over his shoulder. Rapino stepped fully inside the apartment and closed the door behind him. The baton bounced off the door and his Rapino in the back. Rapino shot Ming Tao in the chest. The other Asian, Feng Zhao, grabbed a pot off the stove and threw it. Rapino sidestepped the pot.

"Fuck you," Zhao yelled.

Rapino shot him in the forehead, then walked over to Ming Tao and shot him in the forehead as well.

When he was back in his apartment, Rapino wiped down the Glock and the suppressor and put them in his gym bag. He'd get rid of them come nightfall.

He figured the dead Asian men would start to stink in another day or two. By the time the smell was reported, and the bodies were found, enough time would have passed for the police to have a chaotic situation on their hands. The women had fled with Rapino's money and the men who'd been abusing and exploiting them were dead. The men's likely arrest records would explain at least some of what had happened to them.

The way Rapino looked at it, the women had scored on both ends. Losing the money to them sucked, but taking out two punks made it a push.

• • • • •

There were 3 Rapino's in the Brooklyn white pages when Joseph searched for the Italian surname. Two were men. Eliminating the women and a man too old to be the Rapino he was looking for, Joseph chose Giovanni Rapino as the prime suspect in the murders of a mother and her son on Staten Island, the same murders his grandson might be legally guilty of being an accessory to because he'd driven the killer to and from the murders.

The address was on the border of Sunset Park and Borough Park in Brooklyn. The building faced 58th Street, off Fort Hamilton Parkway. Joseph wasn't as familiar with those sections of Brooklyn as was Artie Adler, but there was no way he could ask his friend to join him

He drove there in the afternoon and found a street crowded with NYPD cruisers as well as several onlookers. Joseph was forced to park on Fort Hamilton Parkway and walk back to where the police vehicles were parked. He watched from the corner as two black bags on gurneys were removed from the apartment building and brought to a white van with a blue stripe. He saw it was a Medical Examiner's van. He didn't want to ask anyone in the crowd of onlookers watching the scene what had happened but began to wonder if his grandson's body was inside one of the black bags.

The Medical Examiner van left a few minutes after the bodies were loaded. Then an NYPD tow truck removed a late model white Toyota with damage on the right rear fender from in front of the apartment building. An hour passed before two of the four police cruisers left. A few minutes later, one of the two cruisers left. Joseph decided to leave when he saw a police cruiser relieve the cruiser that had been there for hours.

Joseph called his friend Artie Adler and asked about the Medical Examiners and where they brought bodies picked up in Brooklyn.

Adler wanted to know why he was asking.

Joseph told him where he was and what he'd just witnessed.

"Are you trying to get him killed?" Adler said. "Are you trying to get yourself killed?"

"Artie, relax," Joseph said. "Chris is my grandson."

"And you're my friend, dumb fuck that you are sometimes. You can't go near this situation, Joe. It's dangerous. I kid you not. It's fucking dangerous."

"Where's the ME van going?"

"Up your ass."

Joseph hung up. He was on his own.

• • • • •

Jerry Galante prearranged the job hours earlier. He picked the 2019 Chevy Caprice from the used car lot on Merrick Road first. A Walther PPK with an attached sound suppressor was under the driver's seat. A Smith & Wesson .38 was inside the glove compartment. Galante moved the .38 from the glove compartment, checked to make sure it wasn't loaded, then slid it under the passenger seat. He drove Northwest on Merrick Road until Arlington Park where he slowed to a stop alongside a bus stop shelter. He beeped once and Thomas Stone, disguised with a blonde wig and wearing a military jacket and high-top sneakers, stepped out of the bus stop shelter. He sat up front alongside Galante.

"What are we doing this time of the night?" Stone said.

"We're heading out to Bay Shore," Galante said. "Then you're gonna arrest a guy."

"Arrest a guy?"

"I speak Chinese?"

"Why? What for?"

"For starters, to knock off half of what you owe on bets."

"Who's the guy?"

"You don't know him."

"What's he owe?"

"His ass. A lot more'n you."

"You're not gonna kill him, I hope."

"With a cop in the car?"

Stone let out a deep breathe. "I'm just sayin'," he said. "I got enough stress in my life right now."

"Wife?"

"Like you wouldn't believe."

Galante laughed. "Yeah, wives can give a guy an ulcer. So can betting more than you can afford."

He headed back to the Belt Parkway and took it to the Southern State Parkway heading east. Both men lit cigarettes.

"Seriously, you know you gotta quit betting, right?" Galante said.

Stone nodded. "I do, but then there are those streaks like last time and I think I can stay ahead of it."

"You'll never stay ahead with the volume you play. Never. Gambling operations aren't gambling, trust me. The more volume the more profit. Why we look out for sharp bettors. I'm not talking about occasional streaks. I'm talkin' like this guy used to run a clothing operation in the city. Guy was gold on baseball. Who can bet and win on baseball, all the teams, sixty, seventy percent of the games. The volume of action guarantees we stay ahead. Offshore can't get enough baseball action. You, my friend, need an intervention with that shit. You need to give it up and never look back."

"Soon as I'm done with this debt, I'll give it a real shot."

"No, you won't. You're destined to hit bottom first. I had to bet, that's what'd be on, you bottoming out. Lose your house, your wife, all self-respect, maybe lose the job while you're at it. Sooner or later, unless you go cold turkey and stop jerking yourself off, you'll hit bottom. Then you won't have a way to bet, unless you count those poor bastards you see outside bodegas blowing their social security on scratch-offs."

It was a phony conversation Galante felt he had to make to keep Stone somewhat calm. The Internal Affairs cop had become a total detriment with his gambling. Sooner or later he'd get pinched by his own squad of police rats and he'd spew his connections to Galante for a deal.

They drove in silence the next 20 minutes. Galante took the exit for the Robert Moses Causeway and then the exit for Sunrise Highway. When they were near the Fire Island Ferries, Galante took the exit for Clinton Avenue, then Gibson Street east to Maple Avenue south toward the Fire Island Ferries. He pulled into a clam house parking lot and parked three spaces from a 2020 black Mercedes C Class coupe. The rest of the lot was empty.

Stone said, "Its three o'clock in the morning."

"Then we're early," Galante said.

"Early for what?"

"You forgot already? The arrest."

"Am I pulling a badge on this guy, whoever he is?"

"It'd probably help. You bring a piece?"

"What? No, I didn't bring a piece."

"Under your seat. Don't worry, it's not loaded. Just for show."

"Jesus Christ, you're making me nervous."

Galante turned to Stone and rolled his eyes.

Stone was still nervous. "Okay, so I arrest him and then what? Where will you be?"

"Hiding."

"Hiding? For what?"

"So the guy don't see me, you dumb shit. He knows me and he owes more than you."

"Jesus Christ. Don't tell me you're gonna whack a guy. You said you weren't."

"Once you arrest him, I'm gonna bring him to the people he owes and they'll do whatever they're gonna do. All you gotta do is arrest him, make him think he's being pinched, and he'll get in the car. I'll take him a few blocks from here while you keep an eye on him in the back. Then we drop him off and go home. Okay with you? You can even help him get in the back. You know, careful so he don't hit his head."

Stone could see Galante was smiling.

"You're jerking my chain," Stone said.

"Don't worry about it, okay? He'll go right there to get his car, the Mercedes, and you pop out showing your badge."

"What if he runs?"

"He won't run."

"What if he does?"

"Jesus Christ, you always piss your pants like this? No wonder you're not a cop on a beat."

Stone finally let it go. Ten minutes later, Dominick Nucci appeared around a corner of the clam house. He was looking at his cellphone as he walked. He brought the phone up to his ear as he approached his car. Stone stepped out of the Chevy and held up his badge.

"Hands up," he said loudly and clearly.

"What the fuck?" Nucci said. He looked left and right, as if his head was on a swivel. "Who're you?"

"Put your phone on the hood of your car and raise your hands high," Stone said as he walked toward Nucci.

"What is this?" Nucci said. He continued holding his hands up, the phone in his right hand.

Stone said, "One more time. Put the phone on—"

The first shot hit Stone in the middle of his back. He fell forward, his right arm stretched out ahead of him. The next shot struck Nucci in the left shoulder as he turned to run back towards the clam house. Nucci lost his balance and nearly fell. He managed to stay on his feet and tried to run again. Galante had been hiding behind the Mercedes. Now he stepped out for a cleaner shot. He squeezed off two rounds, both hitting Nucci in the back, dropping his former mentor to the pavement. Galante then walked up to the body and fired one more round into Nucci's head, then ripped open the dead man's shirt and removed a wire taped to his chest. He grabbed Nucci's phone on his way back to the Chevy.

Then he fired one last round into the back of Thomas Stone's head. He checked for a wire, but didn't find one. He then walked back toward Maple Avenue where a navy blue 2019 Dodge Caravan had been left for him. Twenty minutes later he was on his way back to Brooklyn.

12

"I was in Italy for a few days," Rapino told the homicide Detectives investigating the double murder in his apartment building. They had returned the next day for interviews they'd missed the day before. "I was home to visit relatives in Pizzoferrato in Abruzzo. I'm born there in Pizzoferrato. I'm just come back today. Is all a surprise. Who does this killing?"

The interview was no longer than ten minutes. Rapino fed them a line of shit and they didn't seem interested one way or the other. He knew they would be back when his name was tied to the Corelli crime family, but he'd already gotten rid of both the Glock and the suppressor. Unless they had an eyewitness, and he was pretty sure they didn't, he was home free on the two Asian men he'd killed.

Charlie Mazza showed up an hour later. He brought cash from Rapino's loansharking business and word about the double murder the night before on Long Island.

"Galante?" Rapino said as he counted cash. "Somebody kills him?"

"No, no," Charlie Mazza said. "It's in the papers today. Dominick Nucci and some cop they think was dirty. Internal Affairs cop, I think. Both of them shot out on the island somewhere. Bay Shore, I think. I left my paper in the car. You want it?"

Rapino waived him off. "No, *aspettare*. Wait. They kill a cop?"

"That's what the paper says. One of the cops rats out other cops. An internal affairs cop."

"They think a cop did this?"

Charlie Mazza shrugged. "No idea. They didn't say in the papers, except they claim it was gangland style."

"MS thirteen maybe? Mexicans?"

Charlie Mazza forced a smile.

"Is big deal. Nucci is underboss. Not good."

"Scary is more like it."

"This fuckin' life is no good, eh?"

"I hope it is. I'm too invested now."

Rapino finished counting the cash. He looked up and said, "You're smart, Charlie, you go make pizza someplace. Buy a place. Work for yourself."

"I don't have the money or the skill. Maybe a few years from now if things aren't better."

"Better? Things get worse, you watch. Always worse. Nothing get better anymore."

Charlie Mazza nodded.

Rapino set the cash on a kitchen counter, then moved back into the living area. "Anyway," he said, "the women are here last time. You remember?"

"Sure."

"The two noodle women. They rob me. Ten grand."

"Seriously?"

"Like the heart attack. They give me bull'a shit story and I make mistake and give them money. They go right out to cab and poof, away goes the money. They don't come back."

"Ten grand? Ouch."

"I'm told many years ago never to give money to women. Never to lend. I don't listen and poof."

"Never have and never will."

"And then two other noodles, men, they come to do something to the women, break into the apartment. Somebody shoots them."

"That thing in the news?" Charlie Mazza said. "I didn't pay attention, but I heard about it. That was here, this building?"

Rapino nodded.

"Shit," Charlie Mazza said. "The women got away?"

Rapino shrugged. "I don't know where they goes, but they take suitcase. Who knows, eh?"

"Did you at least enjoy your vacation? How was Italy? Must've been beautiful."

"Is beautiful, yes. And my *cugina*, how you say, second *cugino di secondo*, *Madonna mia*, what a beautiful woman. Gorgeous woman. But is relation, eh? I think I fall in love when I see her, when I talk to her, but then she says no *mafioso* for her. She knows what I am. My people there know. They are associates, eh. Some *cugini*, they accept. Is what it is, eh? But no her. Maria Theresa, same name as my mother."

He slapped his hands twice and said, "And that's that. Nothing. I come home depressed. I can't believe what I do to myself with this bull'a shit we do. *Cosa Nostra*."

Rapino spat on the floor. Charlie Mazza remained silent.

"My mother was raped and killed over there," Rapino said. "The bastards do this ... fuck them, eh?"

Charlie Mazza acted as if he hadn't heard the same story half a dozen times before. "Jesus, sorry about your Mom," he said.

"Now, for you, Charlie," Rapino said, turning to Charlie Mazza then. "You want in, eh?"

Charlie Mazza squinted. "On what?"

"Us, to be straightened out. Become one of us, a wisea'guy."

"Of course. Yeah, sure I am."

"Okay. You get chance soon."

"Cool. Great."

"Maybe this week."

"I'm ready."

"Okay. Now I'm gonna sleep. You can stay you want."

"Nah, I got something I have to do."

"Good. Go make money."

"The name of the game," Charlie Mazza said, then exchanged a cheek kiss with Rapino and left.

• • • • •

His wife had been a good and caring wife, but Sheila Greenblatt could never ignore why defending mobsters had been so profitable. She believed they were evil people who would never let go once they had their talons in a person. A person like her husband, Morris.

Aside from the legal fees, the inside information regarding investments, both legal and illegal, there had been windfalls her husband couldn't ignore. The Greenblatts' net worth was in excess of $7 million dollars, some of which was directly related to his association with his clients, many of whom were members of organized crime.

Morris had only been unfaithful a few times during his marriage. Twice with a woman he'd met through Carmine Montalvo, once with a woman from his office, and once with a stripper from one of Montalvo's clubs. He wasn't a flashy lawyer, although he did enjoy the extra dose of respect and fear he received from his status as a high profile mob lawyer. Attorneys with heavyweight clients from the world of La Cosa Nostra possessed the kind of clout most other lawyers admired.

What Morris wasn't was a man who enjoyed confrontations, whether in his job or in his home. He'd already had a few nightmares from the way he'd spoken to his former client, Carmine Montalvo. The fact he was told to do so by the underboss of the Cirelli crime family hadn't sustained the momentary confidence he'd used to call Montalvo names the last time he'd seen him.

In his nightmares, Montalvo was 30 years younger and tracking Greenblatt down a long hallway with a meat cleaver. Sheila Greenblatt was the exact opposite when it came to confrontations. Over time, she'd worn Morris out.

He didn't mind moving to Florida to be with his daughters and grandchildren, but Coral Gables wasn't the Big Apple. Morris enjoyed being a New Yorker and couldn't imagine living amongst a bunch of conservative, wealthy hicks. He'd told Sheila more than once that if he had to live in Florida, it would have to be in a high-rise condominium on Miami Beach.

"Why, so you can look at all those floozies with their asses on full display in those bikinis they wear nowadays?" his wife had said to him. "They might as well go naked."

Yeah, Morris had been thinking at the time. *Why not?*

They'd been together more than 36 years. They'd been happy most of those years. Their issues began when their son, the baby of the family, ignored the legal profession Morris had wanted for him. Upon learning he was gay, an estrangement began that would last forever. It wasn't that Morris was homophobic, but many of the men he dealt with were, especially his clients. Whenever someone asked why his son wasn't married, Morris lied and said Jeffrey was having too much fun playing the field.

Now that it was apparent Sheila was going to move south to be with their daughters and grandchildren in Florida, with or without him, Morris felt the urge to let her go while he did something similar, except it wouldn't involve his daughters or his grandchildren, or moving to the same geographical location. Learning about Dominick Nucci's murder changed Morris's mind about remaining in the Big Apple. Now he was thinking there was a distinct possibility that the people he'd represented so well in the past might be looking to cut all ties to Montalvo and Nucci, including their lawyer.

The fact that a lawyer for the former President was required to testify against his client under the crime-fraud exception wasn't helping. Greenblatt realized the Department of Justice could use the same crime-fraud exception against him. If any of his organized crime clients felt he could hurt them, and some knew he could, they'd likely seek to eliminate the problem.

Morris wasn't sure that Aniello Fontana had sanctioned both murders. Taking out his underboss was one thing, especially if he'd been wearing a wire. Whacking a cop was much more serious, something the mob didn't do. If Fontana was looking to clean house, if the old man perceived Greenblatt as the same kind of threat as his underboss, the attorney was probably already on a kill list. Morris Greenblatt wasn't about to wait around to find out if that was the case. There was nothing keeping him from making his own move.

He would try the FBI first, even if it meant implicating himself. It would be better to serve time under witness protection of some kind than to be found in the trunk of some car.

And if the feds couldn't help him, he'd have to flee Aniello Fontana's reach. It wasn't as if the mob had the same clout as they once had. Their reach had become significantly curtailed since Sammy "the Bull" Gravano was doing podcasts. If he could get away fast and far enough, Greenblatt was thinking he could have a chance at a new life.

•   •   •   •   •

When he learned the two dead men taken from the apartment building he'd gone to were Chinese gang members, Joseph paid an orderly at the Brooklyn Office of Chief Medical Examiner $50.00 for the information and then drove home. He spent the next two days doing what his friend, Artie Adler, told him to do, which was stay away from the building where the Chinese men were killed.

Then he gave up on waiting for more information and returned to the building. He was about to get out of his car when he saw his grandson leaving the same building. Chris crossed the street and walked half the block to a blue Honda Accord. Joseph waited until the Honda pulled away from the curb, then followed his grandson from a distance to the corner where Chris turned right onto Fort Hamilton Parkway. Joseph maintained a good distance, leaving two cars between himself and his grandson. When he saw Chris turn right on Bay Ridge Parkway, he waited an extra few seconds before making the same turn.

Chris parked about halfway up the street alongside McKinley Park. Joseph remained double-parked on Bay Ridge Parkway until he saw his grandson disappear into the public restrooms in the park. Then Joseph drove up to the corner, turned right and parked on 7th Avenue. He could see the entrances to the restrooms and waited for his grandson to come out.

Fifteen minutes passed before Chris exited the bathroom. He was with another man a few years older wearing a light gray suit and sunglasses. Joseph had a decision to make. Follow his grandson or the man Chris was talking to before they split up and headed in different directions. When Joseph saw Chris get into a different car than the one he'd driven to the park, he decided to follow the other man.

A black SUV picked the man up on 7th Avenue, less than 10 yards from where Joseph was parked. Joseph followed the SUV from a distance and nearly lost him once they were on the Brooklyn-Queens Expressway. The SUV headed for the Battery Tunnel. Joseph didn't have EZ Pass and had to wait to pay a toll. He lost ground in the tunnel, but managed to find the SUV, or one that looked like the one he'd been following, on Trinity Place. Trinity became Church Street and Joseph sped up as they headed north until Worth Street, then right onto Worth. The SUV parked in front of 26 Federal Plaza.

"Fuck me," Joseph said. "He's snitching."

• • • • •

Special Agent in Charge, Connor Kelly, stopped to grab a bottled water from the refrigerator in the kitchen. He drank half of the bottle where he stood. It had been a busy day, from the early morning when Kelly tried to convince the NYPD members of the task force to attend the funeral of the slain Internal Affairs Investigator, Thomas Stone, to his meeting with two field agents on Staten Island. Kelly was disappointed when he learned that none of the NYPD task force were interested in attending what they considered a rat squad funeral.

Then Special Agent, Chris Gallo, operating undercover as Charlie Mazza, contacted him for an emergency meeting in Brooklyn's McKinley Park. The double murder out on Long Island was possibly bearing fruit. Chris Gallo/Charlie Mazza claimed that Giovanni Rapino suggested the possibility of Mazza being straightened out, the mob parlance for becoming inducted into *Cosa Nostra* as a made man.

"He told you that?" Kelly had said.

"He did," Gallo/Mazza said. "He hinted about Jerry Galante breaking the rules with Montalvo's wife last time I was with him. I don't think Galante has long for this world."

"Fontana is as old world as it gets. He wouldn't give a pass for screwing a made guy's wife."

"What about the woman?" Gallo/Mazza said. "She in any danger now?"

Kelly shrugged and said, "This is the most active the mob's been in years. And if it was one of them who killed that cop on the island, somebody'll sing soon enough."

"We know who did that?"

"Could've been anybody. We had Nucci in our pocket, but killing the cop doesn't make sense. We have to assume he was dirty."

"Working for them?"

"Yes, but it still doesn't make sense. It's a no-no, killing a cop. Worse than killing a civilian."

"And the woman?"

"Montalvo?"

Gallo/Mazza had nodded.

"I doubt it," Kelly said, ending their conversation except for expectations going forward.

When they were about to leave the men's room in the park, Gallo/Mazza said he had information about the double murder in Rapino's building.

Kelly waived him off. "Not now," he said. "None of our business. That's NYPD's headache."

Gallo/Mazza put both hands up. "No problem," he said and then left.

Kelly headed back to Federal Plaza where mob attorney, Morris Greenblatt was waiting in a conference room. After the murder of the Cirelli crime family underboss, Kelly assumed the attorney had had his come to Jesus moment.

"Need anything?" Kelly said. "Coffee, water?"

"I'm good, thanks," Greenblatt said.

Kelly wasn't surprised the mob attorney was dressed in casual clothes instead of a suit. "Take the day off?" he said.

"Once I learned about Nucci? You bet your ass I did. I haven't been in the office since. This works out today, I'll never go back. I hear Arizona is a little hot during the summer, but Flagstaff is up in the mountains and gets snow in the winter. Summers are livable. Eighty to ninety during the days. Gets cooler at night. Forty-fifty. I can live with that range."

"And you have a mountain of evidence you're ready to hand over for the sake of what? Nobody in this office is building a case against you, counselor."

"I'm not worried about a case, my friend. I'm worried about my life. Somebody took out the underboss of a family, they can take out a building full of lawyers."

Kelly rubbed his chin. "You have some kind of friendship with Nucci?"

"Let's not pull each other's chain," Greenblatt said. "This all started with Montalvo and his connection with Fontana. I was Montalvo's attorney, but I wasn't in that loop. He didn't discuss mob business with me."

"But you were in the Nucci-Galante loop," Kelly said. "We have that on video when you three met at the Canarsie pier not long ago."

"And now Nucci is dead. What does that tell you? I know what it tells Aniello Fontana, the boss of the family."

"And since Nucci might've spoken so boldly in front of you, you're worried now the guy wearing the crown wants to tie up loose ends?"

"It's obvious he was playing nice with you guys. How Fontana found out, I don't know, but maybe he thinks the same about me now."

"Which tells me you're keeping something more we should know about. I mean, fearing for your life and all, the prosecutor, he's gonna think the same thing. Did I mention he's an ambitious motherfucker, Mr. Nimitz? Wants to be a Senator someday, not to mention President."

"I defended several members of *La Cosa Nostra*. Fontana knows that."

Kelly nodded.

Greenblatt said, "Ever hear of Bobby Simone? You know, the attorney handled Scarfo and the Philly mob? Well, I know things too. Simone got four years for his entanglements. He was willing to go away rather than be killed. Same here, Kelly."

Kelly smiled. "Entanglements. Isn't that what that actor's wife called sucking their son's friend's dick?"

"Stop it. I know things. You know I know things."

"You're not Bobby Simone, Morris. You're more a remora than a shark. Like most lawyers get in bed with mobsters, you got off on the celebrity of it all."

"I know about union funds being siphoned off," Greenblatt said. "Some of it to my benefit, so there's something to prosecute me with, if that's what you need."

"Yeah, Montalvo left us a little tape about that."

"Then you know I'm in danger."

"Not from us, Morris. Over time, your clientele tends to give us what we need all on their own. We don't need you unless you've got something big enough to bag a bigger prize."

"I didn't deal with Aniello Fontana or his sons."

Kelly shrugged. "That's a shame, isn't it?"

"That union fund was worth more than a million dollars."

Kelly smiled. "We know, and I guess I can refer you to the IRS for that. I'm sure they'd make a deal. What about the mob, Morris? Sorry to disappoint you, but nobody here gives a shit about you."

"Come on, Kelly, you know I have more than that."

"Then make a proffer, but understand we don't have to take it seriously."

"And why would I do that before I have a deal."

Kelly stood up. "Look, I've had a shit day already. I'm gonna go to my office, have a cup of coffee to move my bowels. Then, hopefully, I can take a shit. The prosecutor you need is Nimitz. He'll be here when he gets here, and he'll tell you exactly what I just told you. Unless there's something you can give us on Fontana, you can lick his balls all you want. Like I said, the guy is ambitious. I'll leave word for him to buzz me, and I'll come back. In the meantime, I'm not playing hide the salami with you. Either your cock is loaded and ready to spew or it's not. Personally, I don't give a shit, so I'll see you again when I have to see you again."

Greenblatt frowned as Kelly left the room.

• • • • •

"You piss yet?" Artie Adler said.

He was standing in the foyer leading to the backyard with a bag of bagels. Joseph was examining a map at the kitchen table. "You ever knock first?" he said.

"I brought bagels."

"There's cream cheese in the fridge."

"I brought that too."

"You want a parade?"

Adler pointed at the map as he sat at the table. "What are you doing, planning an invasion?"

"Eat a bagel, Artie," Joseph said as he folded up the map.

"Hey, fatso, I'm here to talk sense into you."

"He met with the feds. He's flipping."

"You don't know that."

Joseph had the map folded. He put it in a kitchen counter drawer. "Yeah, I do," he said. "I followed the fed, the guy he met, right to Federal Plaza in Manhattan, the FBI building. They had their conversation in the bathroom at McKinley Park before. About ten-fifteen minutes they were in that bathroom. He's flipping."

Adler removed a plain bagel and a container of cream cheese from the bag. "You dumb shit," he said. "You ever think the kid is working for them?"

"Working for who?"

"Jesus, you're thick sometimes."

Joseph took steak and butter knives from a drawer and set them on the table. "What, the feds?" he said. "That's flipping, isn't it?"

"Were you dropped on your head at birth? I mean it. Were you?"

"Make your point, for fuck sake."

Adler cut the bagel neatly in half. "Ever think he's an agent, you big dope?" he said "Ever think he's working undercover as an agent?"

"The fuck are you talkin' about?" Joseph said as he sat across from Adler.

"Remember the Donnie Brasco thing? The movie about Pistone, the agent went undercover? Al Pacino played the gangster. Johnny Depp played Pistone. They filmed it in Little Italy."

"Chris? You think he's an agent?"

Adler smeared cream cheese on half his bagel. "I think he could be," he said. "We don't know, though, do we? Another reason to stay the fuck out of his way."

"And why wouldn't he tell us, his family? Why wouldn't he tell his mother?"

"Because it's dangerous shit, Joe. Going undercover with those people, the mob, it's dangerous. It's life and death for anybody undercover, and if he's sidled up with this Rapino, a stone killer, it's a lot more dangerous."

"Jesus Christ."

"Exactly, so maybe it's time you back the fuck off before you get the both of you killed."

"And Mary? What about her?"

"I'm sure she's the last person the kid would tell. If she worries as much as she's already shown, he's doing her a favor keeping it to himself."

Joseph grabbed an onion bagel from the bag. "How do I confirm this?" he said.

"You don't," Adler said before taking a bite from his bagel. "You wait for your grandson to tell you."

"I'm supposed to guess which is which, he flipped or he's undercover? No thanks."

Adler watched Joseph cut the onion bagel and smear a large glob of cream cheese on it, start to take a bite, then put it down. "Your stomach?" he said as Joseph winced.

Joseph nodded.

"See a doctor yet? Make an appointment? Again, want me to do it for you?"

"Come up for air with your questions."

Adler said, "You're not doing anyone a favor by dropping dead, Joseph. Not Chris or anybody else."

Joseph sipped his coffee. His free hand rested on his stomach. "I have to know which is which," he said. "Either he's gone bad or he's gone crazy. There's no percentage in going undercover with the mob. They rat themselves out every other day."

"If he's going by a fake name, it's more likely he's an agent."

"That Charlie Mazza bullshit?"

"Yes, that Charlie Mazza bullshit."

Joseph huffed.

"You have to stay away," Adler said. "I mean it, Joseph. Don't go looking for something can get your grandson in the shit. Keep your distance. He'll let you know what's going on when he thinks it's safe."

"You're the one wanted me to convince him to turn himself in," Joseph said. "What changed your mind?"

"What you told me today, moron. He's talking to a guy at Federal Plaza, that's FBI. Chris isn't a gangster, what you told me. What happened to his father and all, it makes sense now. I had to bet, it'd be on he's an agent working undercover. You blow that, you could get him killed."

Joseph held a hand up as he clutched his stomach again. "What if I call and ask about him?" he said through clenched teeth. "This fucking stomach. What if I called and asked?"

"If he's undercover they won't tell you shit."

"And if I go down there? To Federal Plaza, I mean."

"They still won't tell you shit. You're gonna have to wait it out. When Chris is ready to tell you he will. Meanwhile, let me take you to the fuckin' hospital already. I don't like seeing you in pain. Not like this."

"What if he's not an agent? What if he's with those assholes?"

"Then he's fucked. Sooner or later, he's fucked. Like I told you, I had to bet, it'd be he's an agent working undercover."

"Like that movie?"

"Yeah," Adler said. "Like Donnie Brasco."

13

The sun was setting outside the restroom in McKinley Park. Chris Gallo sat on a bench, his back to 73rd Street, as Special Agent in Charge, Connor Kelly, stood a few feet away with his cellphone to his right ear. Chris checked the time twice before Kelly finally ended his call.

"You're sure about Galante being in danger?" Kelly said.

"Yeah, same as I mentioned yesterday," Chris said. "It's the impression Rapino gave me. He's mentioned it more than once."

Kelly bit his lower lip. "Something's up," he said. "The Fontana boys have been on and off the reservation a lot the last few days. We don't have the resources anymore to follow everybody, but NYPD gave us that."

"That thing on the island had to be Fontana, no?"

"Probably, he's old world. Which means it was someone he trusted or someone he's going to disappear first chance he gets."

"Galante?"

"Could be."

"Then Rapino moves up to skipper."

"Probably, but someone has to fill Nucci's spot. Probably Bruno Fontana."

"He's the older son?"

Kelly nodded.

"Would the kids spill?"

"The law of averages say they would, but that's a tough family. None of their relatives have flipped to date. Even the son-in-law, that poor bastard, hasn't so much as squeaked since he went away a long time ago now. I don't know about Fontana's sons. Bruno's been away twice, but never for more than a few years. Vito hasn't busted his cherry yet. Maybe him. A guy is facing life, ten, twenty years or more, who knows?"

Chris said, "If they move Rapino up, that could be an opening."

"If he's tight with Fontana, maybe. If he's not, you're not safe either."

"I'm still just his gopher."

"Depends you get approached or not by one of the other skippers or one of the sons."

"That only happens if Rapino is moved up, no?"

"Or Galante. If they're not looking to get rid of him, who knows anymore. That shit on the island, Nucci and that cop, that's one hell of a curveball, and what do you do with a curveball?"

"Time it," Chris said. "Wait on it."

"Right," Kelly said, "and you can't miss when you take your swing."

• • • • •

Joseph was parked across the street from his grandson's car on Fort Hamilton Parkway. When he spotted him leaving the park, he stepped out from behind a tree and called to him. Chris looked up, then stopped in his tracks. He turned to head in the opposite direction before turning his head back around. He continued walking to the curb. Joseph had started to cross the street when Chris yelled, "Stay there!"

Joseph stopped walking. Chris waived at him to get back in his car. Joseph walked around to the driver's side of his car and waited. Chris headed across the street to Joseph's car.

"I told you to back off," he told Joseph.

"You a rat or an agent?" Joseph said.

Chris felt his jaw tighten. He paused a moment, then pointed to the car. "Get in," he said through clenched teeth.

Both sat inside Joseph's car.

"Well?" Joseph said.

"You talk to my mother?"

"Your mother doesn't talk to me."

"Adler?"

"Stop the bullshit. Are you an agent?"

"You can't wait to get me killed, can you?"

"Chris, answer me."

"Yes, I'm an agent," Chris said. "Happy now? I'm working undercover, and if anybody is watching me with the crew I'm with right now, I'm fucked."

"That guy you were talking to, he your boss?"

"He's the SAC."

"The fuck is that?"

"He's the Special Agent in Charge of a task force. Yes, he's my boss, my handler. I go by the name of—"

"Charlie Mazza," Joseph said. "Artie Adler learned about that. Why couldn't you tell us? We're your family. What did you think, we'd sell the information to the mob?"

"Don't tell me Artie Adler is still following me? He's not as stupid as you."

"I should smack you for that."

"You should mind your own fucking business is what you should do."

"At least now I know you're not one of them."

"Does that make you proud, gramps? How about if you compromise me and they kill me? Then I can be the family fucking martyr."

"Hey, all we are is worried about you, damn it. You're my grandson. You don't tell us anything and we find out your hanging around a killer for the mob. We find out you might've been involved in a double murder on Staten Island."

"Jesus Christ, don't even mention that. God damn you, Gramps!"

"What are we supposed to think? The bureau going to keep you out of the shit for that? I thought you guys couldn't allow people to get killed."

"Look, I have to get out of here and I can't have you following me."

"I didn't follow you today. I waited here because I saw you with that other guy yesterday. I assume this is where you do your business. I didn't see you pull up twenty minutes ago, I would've left. I got lucky."

"Yeah, well you getting lucky can get me killed."

"Where are you living?"

"Fuck you."

"You really want me to follow you again?"

Chris opened the passenger door and stepped out of Joseph's car. Joseph watched his grandson go to the car he'd parked earlier, then pull away from the curb burning rubber. Joseph didn't bother following.

• • • • •

Her father sent Angela Fontana-Sforza to Brooklyn to observe Giovanni Rapino. She could only do so if he left his apartment, so she waited in her car off the corner. An hour or so later she saw another man and Rapino exit the apartment building. They each smoked a cigarette before Rapino headed back inside the building. Angela decided to follow the other man when she saw him get in a car.

It was a hunch, nothing more than that, but she'd learned to follow her hunches. Although her husband might be released in a few years, Angela couldn't forgive the men who had testified against him. She remembered what he had told her once and never forgot it. "I had a hunch the motherfuckers would flip."

Because of the conviction, Angela had no children. She had no excitement in her life. She served her father and two brothers and dreamed of what might have been had her husband followed his hunch.

She followed associates of her father's crime family with pleasure because it gave her something to do while possibly exposing future turncoats against the family. Her father had hired private investigators to do it, but when one turned out to be feeding law enforcement, Aniello Fontana had the PI crushed by a car pancake compactor in a Bronx junkyard.

She'd never met the man who'd been smoking with Giovanni Rapino before, but her hunch was enough to feed her curiosity. She kept her distance following him, but when he parked alongside a park not far from where Rapino lived, Angela drove up ahead of him and parked off the corner of Bay Ridge Parkway. She used a Canon 4000D Camera with TWAIN Driver & Face Finder to snap half a dozen picture of the man who'd been with Rapino. Then she saw another man in sunglasses and a suit and she was sure he was an agent. She snapped several pictures of him as well, then put the camera down and waited after both men entered a public restroom.

When the man who'd been with Rapino appeared again, it was about 20 minutes later. Both men went their separate ways, except Angela saw the man she'd initially followed was talking with an older, heavyset man in the street before getting in the older man's car. She snapped a few pictures of them and the car before setting the camera down and trying to follow the man wearing the sunglasses. When she turned onto 7th Avenue, it was too late. The other man was gone, but there was traffic ahead on both sides of a fork splitting 7th and 8th avenues. She chose 8th Avenue and gave a short chase to see if she could spot him in one of the cars ahead of her. She gave up at Bay Ridge Avenue and headed back to Fort Hamilton Parkway. By the time she returned to McKinley Park, both the man she'd originally been following and the older heavyset man were gone.

Angela checked her camera for the digital pictures she'd taken, then headed back to her father's home in Eltingville, Staten Island.

• • • • •

Jerry Galante, wearing a blue suit with gray pinstripes, a white shirt and blue tie, dress slacks and glossy shoes, kissed his wife on the porch before descending the stairs to his driveway where Giovanni Rapino was waiting for him. Galante tossed Rapino the key fob.

"That was Vito Fontana," Galante said. "We're heading to Jersey. Keyport. He said take the Garden State."

Galante walked around the back of the SUV to the passenger side. Rapino opened the driver's side door and stepped up and into the driver's seat. He adjusted the height and mirrors before starting the engine. Rapino was well dressed in a dark gray sports jacket, a blue shirt and purple tie, gray slacks, and black shoes.

"Don't we look good?" Galante said as Rapino slowly backed out of the driveway.

"You look great, boss," Rapino said.

"Thanks. You seem back to normal."

"I am, boss. I had a shit couple of days with the traveling and that bull a'shit in my building. I'm better now."

"That was some crazy shit there where you live. Chinks, right?"

"Two of them, yeah."

"How's Mazza doing?"

"Good. So far he's solid."

"Good, because the books'll likely open once all the shit dies down. Between Staten Island and then Long Island, we're lucky we can still earn a few coins. Cops and feds are all over the place. Speaking of which, you have a tail coming here?"

"No, but I watch now the mirrors."

"Good. Stay sharp. This don't happen very often, meeting with the boss twice in ten days, whatever it's been. My guess is they're gonna open the books and move a few people around. They owe me, so I'm hoping for something more now than skipper. That happens, you'll probably fill my spot heading our crew."

"*Grande*," Rapino said. "That would be nice. Very nice."

"I'm just guessing here. I don't know for sure about anything. Could just be a party."

"At least we dressed for it, eh?"

The trip took less than an hour. Rapino drove across the Verrazzano Narrows Bridge onto the Staten Island Expressway to Route 440, and over the Outerbridge Crossing into New Jersey. He then took Route 440 to the Garden State Parkway and found exit 120, where he took local roads to the Keyport Marine Basin.

Rapino pulled behind a limousine parked near the building. Both men stepped out of the SUV. Vito Fontana, also dressed sharply, stepped out of the limousine. He exchanged hugs and cheek kisses with both Galante and Rapino. Fontana then led them through a canvas shielded walkway to a floating dock and a 32' 2023 Beneteau Gran Turismo 32 outboard. Bruno Fontana was waiting on the cabin cruiser, a scotch in his right hand. After untying the boat from the dock cleats, Vito was the last on board. He grabbed a drink his brother had made for him and headed straight to the captain's chair. He fired up the twin 300 Mercury engines.

"This is some beautiful boat," Galante said to Bruno.

"Up from Florida a few days ago," Bruno said. "Four hundred grand plus."

"You buy it?"

"Me? Hell no. Borrowed it. The old man is waiting for us on another one at Point Pleasant. A bigger one than this. Wait'll you see that thing, you think this is impressive."

Galante raised his glass. "Salute," he said.

Bruno touched glasses. "*Cento anni*," he said.

Rapino had taken a seat on the bench in the stern. He sipped his scotch on the rocks and looked toward the dock as the boat pulled away.

"This thing got a name?" Galante said as he sat on the stern bench a few feet from Rapino.

"*Bella figura*," Bruno said as he took a seat on the port bench. "A friend of the family owns it."

Twenty minutes later, as the boat passed between Keansburg and Ideal beaches, Galante had slumped over from the rohypnol-laced scotch and soda he'd been drinking. Bruno directed Rapino down inside the cabin where a trunk rested on a piece of loose carpet.

"The bag is inside the trunk," he said.

Rapino opened the trunk and removed a black body bag.

"Weights are in the bench in the back," Bruno said. "Careful you don't scratch anything. They're wrapped. Just don't drop them."

Vito let the engines idle as he joined his brother and Rapino in putting Galante inside the bag and then adding eight 25 lb. weightlifting plates onto the body. They tied the bag with rope so the weights wouldn't shift and remained on Galante's chest. Then Rapino grabbed one end of the bag, Vito the other end. They moved onto the bench seat with their knees, then lifted the bag onto the twin engines. Bruno went to the captain's chair and looked over his shoulder.

"Go," Vito said.

Bruno moved the throttle up and jerked the boat forward as his brother and Rapino pushed the body bag off the twin engines into the water.

• • • • •

When Morris Greenblatt showed up at Doris Montalvo's house dressed in a light blue NYU sweatshirt and grey sweatpants, he looked more like a jogger than a lawyer. She said, "You know there are cameras all over the place, right?"

Greenblatt said he was there to settle his client's estate. He removed a legal redwell from the gym bag he was carrying.

"This is business," he said. "I need your signature on some paperwork."

Doris let him inside, then led him to the kitchen. She wore a pink robe and white slippers.

"Sit," she told him. "Coffee?"

"Sure," Greenblatt said. He sat at the head of her oval table and removed paperwork from the redwell.

Doris poured two cups of coffee and set one down in front of Greenblatt. "Milk?"

"No, thanks."

"Sugar's in the bowl there," she said, and then sat mid-table to his left and sipped her coffee.

"The kids are going to contest unless you take what they're offering," Greenblatt said.

"Which is?"

"The house and the car."

"Which car?"

"The Lexus."

"Not the Mercedes."

"Not the Mercedes."

"Hmmm."

Greenblatt sipped his coffee.

"How much am I being scammed for?"

"Carmine's net worth? That I'm not sure of. What he's hidden, I mean. What I know of is about two million. He's probably worth another five, six."

"I can get one plus for this place, I think."

"You can get closer to two. I'd take it, I were you."

"I like the Mercedes, Morris."

"You get yourself a nice condo somewhere, you can trade in the Lexus and buy one."

"That mean you won't give them a counteroffer?"

"It means I'm retiring and really don't give a shit what you do."

"That why you're dressed like that?"

"Yeah. You going to sign or what?"

"Of course, I'm going to sign. I want all of this in my rearview mirror."

Greenblatt handed her a series of papers with yellow stickers for where she was to sign or initial. Doris read before signing, then shoved the papers back to him.

"You really retiring?" she said.

"You read the papers, see what's going on?"

"The mob murders?"

"Not to mention a cop and the mother of some guy your husband thinks you screwed."

"What does that have to do with you?"

"Please."

"It's a bit tame for a mob war, no?"

"Tame?"

"I'm not reading about bodies being found all over the place."

"One was enough for me. A little too close for my comfort."

"Let me guess ... Dominick Nucci?"

Greenblatt frowned.

Doris said. "Oh, come on, Morris. I'm sure you know about Galante and the shit he pulled on me."

"I don't. What shit?"

Doris ignored his question. "I'm the one who was sweating out an early departure. Carmine was a genuine piece of shit and took his pleasure from ruining my life."

"Eddie Russo?"

"That poor bastard, for one, although I thought the beating ended that situation, and I felt like shit for it. When I saw they killed him and his mother ... I wanted to run to the FBI."

"Why didn't you?"

"Who says I didn't?"

Greenblatt took a deep breath. "You want to be honest here?" he said. "Seriously."

Doris shrugged. "Can't hurt now."

"I tried that," he said. "The feds."

"And?"

"They weren't interested."

Doris stared at him.

"I tried," Greenblatt said. "Honest to God. No luck."

She continued staring at him.

"You waiting for more?"

She moved up in her chair.

He said, "They suspected you of the same, but Galante said he'd do the checking."

"So you do know."

"No, I don't. What?"

"Jerry and I were intimate. For a while actually."

"I assumed so when he said he'd check, but Nucci's the one who was suspicious. He felt you were too smart not to have an out. 'Sharp,' he said. You're too sharp."

"I'm still here, if that's what he meant."

"And he's not."

"And you're worried you might be next."

"I don't know about next, but it's enough to worry about."

"I don't see why you'd be in any real danger."

"Why not?" Greenblatt said, picking up his cup of coffee again. "You have any idea how many wiseguys I've defended since my old man passed? It's all I've done is defend wiseguys like your husband. Psychotics who think they're generals issuing orders to some private."

"Carmine spoke well of you."

Greenblatt chuckled.

"What?" Doris said.

"Carmine hated me the same as he hated everybody else, including you," Greenblatt said. "Not to mention he might've made a deal before someone cut his throat. At least somebody thought he made a deal. So, yeah, I don't feel comfortable lawyering any longer. Not with a mob war going on. Tame as you think it is. They've killed two civilians and a cop. Trust me on this. That's not tame."

Doris sat back in her chair. "Is this serious? You're really worried."

"It's why I met with the feds. I wasn't happy to hear they didn't care, but that settled it for me. Delivering these papers is my last official act. Once I drop them in the mailbox, that's it for me and the legal profession. I'm neither brave enough nor stupid enough to wait and see what happens next. The feds already know my culpability in a few things with Carmine. Carmine's people knew all along."

"You're going to run?"

"I'll probably drive."

"Taking your family?"

"My family, the kids, are grown and on their own."

"What about your wife?"

"I don't think she'd mind if I went out for the milk and never came back. At this point in our life, with the grandchildren she can't wait to spoil, she wouldn't miss my ass."

Doris sighed. "So, you want to know what Jerry did to *my* ass, the prick."

14

George Nimitz, age 50, was an Assistant U.S. attorney for the Southern District of New York. An ambitious man with a distinguished resume, Nimitz became anxious to leave his office for a political career the day President Biden appointed someone else to the position of United States Attorney for the Southern District. All he wanted now was a high-profile prosecution and conviction that would garner the same kind of fame his legal hero, Rudy Giuliani, had managed to obtain during his days in the same office.

Nailing one of the remaining mob bosses was a path to glory, and Nimitz had no problem with how it might be accomplished.

During his meeting with mob attorney, Morris Greenblatt, Nimitz didn't feel there was enough information proffered to do anything. He'd told Greenblatt, "If you're worried they might kill you or yours, I suggest you get on a plane and move to Israel. You'll have beautiful weather at least five months out of the year, universal healthcare, and if you get fed up and need to release some anxiety, you can always shoot a Palestinian. The IDF on the Israeli side of the wall in Gaza will give you a medal if you kill a Palestinian."

Greenblatt said, "The public know you're an anti-Semite? Your surname comes from the Russian word *Nemchin*, which means German."

Nimitz smiled at Greenblatt. "You do know the Russians are the ones who liberated most concentration camps, right?"

"Right," Greenblatt said. "Sure."

Nimitz held the conference room door open for Greenblatt to leave.

A few days later, Special Agent in Charge, Connor Kelly, was in Nimitz's office for a meeting. Kelly sat in one of two arm chairs facing the Assistant U.S. attorney.

"So?" Nimitz said.

"Galante hasn't been home for two days," Kelly said.

"There's that."

"And?"

"Resources. We don't have enough men to cover everyone. Galante wasn't on our radar. If Nucci was wearing a wire when he was killed, whoever killed him took it. Rapino took that trip to Italy, and now we have word two associates with the Abruzzo mafia were killed while Rapino was there. There's history behind it. The two were suspected of raping and killing

Rapino's mother when he was a kid. The Abruzzo mafia is allegedly tied to the *Ndrangheta* mafia."

"We can't let the Italians arrest him and expect a deal."

"No, we can't. We likely won't have to worry about it because if Rapino did those two, he covered his tracks well enough visiting family there."

"I'll bet."

"The bottom line is we need whoever disappeared Galante to flip and we don't know who that was. We had people on Aniello Fontana, but that was a waste of time because the old man doesn't leave his Staten Island compound. His sons have been in and out, but again we don't have the resources to follow them. A camera from a marina in Keyport, New Jersey, has a limo belongs to one of Bruno's businesses, but that's all we have, plus a boat that left the marina with people we can't make out on it. The thing never came back, so it likely went somewhere further south on the Jersey coast. Another marina or whatever. All we have on Galante is from his wife. He was dressed when he left the house. Well-dressed. Suit and so on."

"Could be they were making someone, no?"

"Could be, but that hasn't hit the street. Nobody newly made puffing their chests that we know of."

"Any chance one of the sons handled Galante?"

"Sure, but if I had to bet, it'd be Rapino."

"Do we have him?"

"Kind of. We're pretty sure he's the one killed the mother and son on Staten Island."

"The kid was screwing around with Montalvo's wife?"

Kelly nodded. "One of ours drove Rapino to the location, but Rapino never told him why they were there."

"Can't he lie and say Rapino did tell him?"

"I think you'd rather we have something better than an undercover agent's word. Defense attorneys might eat that up. On the other hand, there was a double murder where Rapino lives in Brooklyn. Somebody killed two Chinese gang members who were apparently inside the apartment of two Chinese women married to gang members inside Rikers. The women seemed to have fled."

"So the women are the suspects now."

"According to NYPD they are."

"Shit."

"If Galante is gone, and we're pretty sure he is, it could've been him who did Nucci and that cop. And if that's the case, Fontana might've used Rapino to do away with Galante. That might be an angle we can pursue. There's no way Rapino would make that move without Fontana's blessing."

"Then Rapino is the one to flip. Can our undercover guy get him on something?"

"Our undercover thinks Rapino might've proposed him for membership."

"I thought that only comes from a captain?"

"Rapino is now a captain."

"Acting or for real?"

"Word on the street is the vacuums have to be filled. If he isn't a captain now and is just acting as one, he'll be the real deal soon enough. When that happens and they open the books, we'll have a decision to make about our undercover. Do we pull him or let him go through with it?"

"I want Fontana, and I don't care how we do it," Nimitz said. "Bring me that old bastard on Staten Island and I'll put him away for the rest of his miserable life."

"That'd be a hell of a feather in your cap," Kelly said.

Nimitz winked at Kelly, then said, "Yeah, it'd be that too."

● ● ● ● ●

"Okay, so now you know why you can't go near him again," Adler said. "At least he's on the side of the good guys."

"The side that allows a killer to remain on the street?"

"Rapino?"

"You followed Chris to Staten Island, right? The good guys allow something like that? The murder of a mother and son by some hitman they're investigating?"

"The feds aren't angels, Joe. Cops weren't when I was on the force, and they're still not. When they want somebody, they'll ignore a lot of shit to get who they want."

"Isn't that something to be proud of?" Joseph said with sarcasm.

"Now you're pissed off he's an agent instead of a gangster?"

"I didn't say that. I'm afraid for him same as if he was a gangster. What if those mutants find out he's an agent? What then?"

"Why I've been telling you to lay the fuck off him," Adler said. "You keep sticking your nose in and they will find out he's an agent. Just back off."

"He spoke to his mother. I know that much because he asked me if I spoke to her."

"Then he told his mother the same thing he told you. Back off."

"I don't trust the FBI any more than I trust the mob."

"And you're right not to trust them, so don't think they wouldn't sacrifice an agent to make a case."

"I want some backup for him," Joseph said. "The press or something."

"Yeah, that's a great idea. Fill them in and it'll be a headline tomorrow morning, and you'll never see Chris again."

"I meant in case, you putz."

"Just make sure you don't do it while he's still on the job."

"I should wait until something happens to him?"

"You should wait, full stop. You can't make this public knowledge unless you wanna be some kind of asshole like Geraldo Rivera. You know what your grandson is doing now, so let it go. He's one of the good guys."

• • • • •

Bruno Fontana handed Giovanni Rapino a series of pictures his sister had taken outside McKinley Park in Brooklyn. "Your sidekick is an agent," he told Rapino.

Bruno gave Rapino a moment and then said, "The guy wearing the shades is a Special Agent in Charge. Your guy is undercover."

"Fucking Charlie," Rapino said.

"He's no Charlie," Bruno said. "Whatever his name is, it ain't Charlie."

Rapino flipped to a picture of an older man. "And this one?"

"We don't know yet. We're looking into it."

"He's a cop maybe?"

"The fat guy? Maybe. I doubt it. His age and shape. We'll know soon enough. Angela got his back plate and we'll get the address run. The thing about the agent is we can't kill him. Not while he's on the job."

"We can't kill? The son-of-a-bitch drives me to—."

"We cut him off, but we can't kill him."

"And he testifies?"

"You tell him what you were doing?"

"No. Of course not."

"Then what's he going to say? He drove you someplace. If they have it on film, they're not using it yet. If they had it on film, they would've arrested you already. Without film of you doing the work, you can just as easy say he did it. They're looking to nail you with him, so we can do one of two things, jerk him around or cut him off. The old man says to cut him off."

"Then he knows we know. Why I don't tell him bulla'shit he reports? I can feed him bulla'shit, no?"

"The old man isn't keen on that. He's worried somebody slips. We cut him off, it's just as good. They figure it out and he's out of action. They either make an arrest or they're back to start. At least on you they are. They'd probably have to pull him off the streets, this Charlie whatever the fuck his name is."

"This fucking guy," Rapino said. "I start to like him. I was to propose him when I'm captain."

"Better we know now than later."

"Fuck me."

"He would've, but now he can't."

"Why not he disappear?"

"Pop said no."

"Like Jerry. He's goes to ocean someplace."

"Look, Giovanni, we'd all like to lose this motherfucker but it'll cause a ruckus none of us can afford. They're still not over that cop they're trying to pin on us. We kill an agent, we might as well close up for a year. No, the old man is right on this one. Just cut him off. Let him know without telling him. He's not welcome anymore."

"Motherfucker," Rapino said. "Piece of shit, motherfucker."

• • • • •

When Giovanni Rapino didn't return his calls, Charlie/Chris began to wonder if the killer had also been clipped. It was already on the street that Jerry Galante had disappeared. On top of the underboss of the family getting killed along with an Internal Affairs cop suggested a mob war was already in progress, maybe an internal war. If Aniello Fontana was having people in upper management clipped, nobody below them was safe, including Rapino.

Then there was the fact Rapino had killed two civilians, a son and his mother. Two strikes against the Italian born killer. If they'd take out Rapino, Chris/Charlie wasn't safe either.

When he called the SAC on a burner phone, Kelly confirmed it was time for him to come in off the street.

Chris said, "What's going on?"

"You've been compromised."

"By who?"

"We don't know, but word is on the street to ignore you. You go down to the Galantes' old social club, they won't let you in. You've been burned, that's all we know. Come in and we'll go over what we can, and then you have the few months' time off you're owed. At least that."

"If I disappear, won't some of them assume I really disappeared?"

"They get a freebee for that, yeah. It'll make a few of them nervous for sure. Upper management cleaning house and all."

"Fuck."

"Come on in and we'll talk."

Chris decided to contact his family on the way in. He called his mother first, but she didn't pick up or wasn't home. Then he called his grandfather.

Joseph picked up after a few rings.

"Hello?"

"It's me," Chris said.

"Chris! You okay?"

"I'm fine. I'm heading into the city. I'm being pulled from the investigation."

"What? That's great."

"Maybe. I tried calling my mother but she didn't pick up."

"Probably out shopping. She'll be thrilled. I know I am."

"They may want to keep me off the street for a while. Give me another assignment out of state."

"Because?"

"Think about it."

"I don't understand."

"I was compromised, Gramps. They know I'm an agent."

"Then you need to get out of New York, no?"

"Probably what they'll do, send me someplace, but I'm going to see Mom first."

"Do they know who you are? Your real name, I mean."

"I don't know. Can you get her to your place?"

"Your mother? She hates me."

"If you tell her I'll be there, she'll go."

"I can try. You're coming here?"

"Soon as I'm finished debriefing."

"What time is that?"

"I don't know. Maybe tomorrow."

"Okay, just call and let me know. I'll get in touch with her in the meantime."

"Thanks."

"Are you sure you're safe?"

"I don't think the mob wants to off an agent. I'm probably fine."

"Probably doesn't instill confidence. Make the pricks you work for give you some security."

"I can't make them do anything, but I'm sure they'll do their best."

"Okay. Just call when you're ready and I'll have your Mom here."

"Thank you."

"I hope you don't blame me for getting exposed, but if it gets you from under the mob, I'm glad it happened."

"Talk to you later."

Chris killed the call.

• • • • •

Vito Fontana visited Rapino outside the Harbor Fitness on 4th Avenue in Bay Ridge. He'd spent the night at his girlfriend's apartment in the same neighborhood. He was carrying a few messages, one of which was that his brother had been elevated to the consiglieri position in the family. Vito himself, once he was made, would be taking an acting skipper role with another crew in the family based on Staten Island, and Rapino was being groomed to be underboss within a year of his new title, captain of what was the Montalvo crew. The name of the family was being officially changed from Cirelli to Fontana, and going forward the name Cirelli was not to be spoken and only referred to by touching or pulling one's nose.

Vito demonstrated by using his thumb and forefingers to tug on the end of his nose. "Pop loved that someone shot Mussolini and hit the tip of his nose," he said. "Yeah, some Mick broad shot him. Violet Gibson, her name was. I only know this because my old man repeats the story ten times a year. She wound up in a British nuthouse the rest of her life. She was something like a commie back in the day. Whatever she was, it took stones to take a shot at him in Rome."

Rapino was embarrassed about not knowing the details surrounding Benito Mussolini and blamed it on his move from Italy to America at age eleven.

"There's also a few people my father wants out of the way," Vito said. "I'm taking care of one of them. We have another covered, but we need help with that lawyer, the one Montalvo and some others used. Greenblatt. Has an office, downtown Brooklyn. The old man doesn't trust anybody can hurt us."

"I take care of the lawyer," Rapino said.

"Great. The old man knew you would."

Rapino pulled his nose.

Vito smiled. "Yep," he said. "It'll take some getting used to but that's how he wants it now."

"*Nessun problema.*"

"Huh?"

"No problem."

The two hugged.

Vito left Rapino a set of phony credit cards, a fake identification, an envelope of cash, and the address for Morris Greenblatt's home and office and a single telephone number. Rapino walked Vito downstairs where he could survey the street for suspicious cars. After exchanging another hug and a cheek kiss, Rapino leaned against the stoop railing and smoked a Marlboro. He watched as Fontana drove off in his 2023 Corvette. Rapino walked to the curb to see if any cars followed Fontana. He waited until the Corvette turned right at the far corner, then headed back upstairs to his apartment.

He filled his espresso pot with *Medaglia D'oro* grinds and heated a small pot of water. Rapino was still conflicted about what he'd been told regarding Charlie Mazza. After learning that Charlie Mazza wasn't Charlie Mazza, and was instead a federal agent, feelings of revenge resurfaced for Rapino. He hated the fact that he wasn't allowed to kill someone who'd been a rat, especially someone ratting on him.

His feelings of guilt about the life he'd chosen were gone again. He no longer thought about Maria Theresa, except to think she was a fool to think her way of life was any better than his. People like his second cousin, beautiful and educated, faced the same shit as everybody else. Their choice of men cheated on them the same as any gangster might. Their friends betrayed their trust the same as some mobsters betrayed their oaths. The educated struggled to make a living and had to put up with bosses the same as everybody else. Who cared if she was beautiful? There were millions of beautiful women in the world. Who cared that she was educated and had a university degree? There were millions of educated women in the world. Beautiful and educated guaranteed them *niente*.

Nothing.

If Aniello Fontana was dangling the underboss position for Rapino to stay loyal, that was fine. Rapino already believed he was as much his own boss as a servant to the head of the family. Whether he was moved up to underboss or not, there were only a few more rungs on the ladder before he was the boss. When that happened, he'd clean all the shit out of the family and start a *Borgata* of his own. If he did make it that far, there wouldn't be any silly pulling on the nose to identify him. He was Giovanni Rapino and proud of it.

He liked the idea and sounded it out. "Rapino *famiglia*."

It would be difficult climbing the last few steps to the top because of Aniello Fontana's sons. When the old man finally passed away, his eldest son, Bruno, would likely take over. The younger one, Vito, had yet to do time and wouldn't garner the same respect as his older brother.

It was silly to think so far ahead of where he was at the time, but Rapino still didn't like the idea of allowing a federal agent to walk away from whatever information he'd collected without so much as a beating.

Rapino wanted to kill Charlie Mazza, whoever the fuck he really was.

When he finally received word on who the older fat guy was in a few of the pictures Angela Fontana had taken, Rapino decided to perform some due diligence of his own. A cop he paid inside the NYPD ran the fat guy's license plate and Rapino learned where he lived in Canarsie. A deeper search using Google told Rapino that the old man was retired and had owned a bar back in the day, and that he lived alone and had a single grandchild, a grandson. When he learned that Joseph Gallo's son had been killed accidentally by members of the Vignieri crime family 12 years ago, Rapino felt as though he'd put it together.

Was it possible the agent using the name Charlie Mazza was the old man's grandson?

•   •   •   •   •

When she couldn't contact Morris Greenblatt, Doris Montalvo became frantic enough to carry the Smith & Wesson Model 642 .38 Special Pink Revolver whenever she left the house or answered the door for food deliveries. She assumed Greenblatt was dead and assumed she was also marked for death. They had discussed taking off together, but Doris felt Greenblatt was probably in more danger than herself and opted to remain in Brooklyn until a better opportunity presented itself.

If Greenblatt was dead, and Doris might never know if he was, it meant the head of the Cirelli crime family was likely cleaning house. Greenblatt had mentioned that Carmine

Montalvo, before his throat was cut, had made some kind of a deal with the FBI, and that maybe his making a deal was the reason he wasn't allowed to die from his cancer. Doris also had to assume that Jerry Galante had told somebody about the bugs he'd found in her apartment. When she told Greenblatt about them, he couldn't believe Galante hadn't killed her instead of embarrassing her.

"You searching for the right words, counselor," Doris had told him. "He stuck those things up my ass. He wanted me to know he found them."

"And now he's dead," Greenblatt had said.

He was right about that, and it somehow lessened her fears when he said it. Then she tried to contact the lawyer again, and again there was no answer. She tried his office and learned he hadn't been in for several days. She knew he'd been ducking his office, but she couldn't explain herself to some receptionist. What she did instead was panic and retrieve the handgun Carmine had given her after they were first married, except that one didn't have a pink handle. The pink handle was the one she bought herself, first as a backup, then as the main weapon she'd keep on her. The original was under her bed pillow, left side of the bed.

She was no longer wearing lingerie or expecting visitors outside of grocery deliveries or Chinese takeout. Sometimes she used Grubhub deliveries from Italian or Indian restaurants.

She tried Greenblatt's cellphone again and again the voicemail picked up.

"Fuck," she said aloud.

It was her birthday. According to her birth certificate, Doris had turned 57 at 11 o'clock in the morning. She decided to treat herself by researching places to move to online. She spent two hours visiting condo rentals and sales in six different states before finding one she felt was remote enough to consider. She could use a real estate agent to sell the house while she visited condos across the country. She had more than enough money to leave ahead of the sale. She could survive for several months, maybe a year if she was careful.

When she finally settled on a condo development, it was in Las Cruces, New Mexico. She looked at condo rentals in the college town and found several gated communities that were more than affordable. One-bedroom apartments went from $1,100 to $1,500. She was about to email for more information when her doorbell rang.

Doris hadn't ordered food and was immediately suspicious. She grabbed her pink handled .38 and peeked out from behind a living room blind.

A man she didn't know was standing there. He was short and stocky, and his blonde hair was slicked back. He also wore sunglasses, a black shirt and black slacks. Doris was suspicious and tried to find a bulge in his clothing but couldn't see any.

The doorbell rang again. She ignored it but kept the man in view through the blinds. It rang another few times before he glanced at the windows, then headed back down the stairs. There was security system in the kitchen pantry with a 19" flat screen television on a wall she had installed with an HDMI Network Extender shortly after her husband was convicted. She ran to it then and viewed each of the four separate screens.

The first was a camera view from the roof of the front porch. She'd already seen the stocky man had left. The second camera was a view from the top of the front porch roof to the street in front of the house. Again, the stocky man was no longer in view. The third camera was mounted above the garage door and viewed the driveway. She didn't need the fourth camera, which was mounted above the back deck, because the stocky man was using a tool to open the door alongside the garage door. She grabbed her cellphone and dialed 911 as she headed to the basement door and opened it. She removed her slippers and quickly and carefully took the stairs to the basement.

"This is 911, what is your emergency," a female call taker said.

"My house is being broken into," Doris whispered.

"Where is the location of your emergency?"

Doris gave her address and asked them to please hurry. Then she turned her phone off from fear the stocky man might hear her.

A door that led to the laundry room and garage was off to her left. She positioned herself a few feet from the door and took a firing position with her .38 as soon as she heard the outside door open.

Whoever was breaking into her house wasn't using stealth. He'd walked into something before she saw light appear under the door. A few seconds later, he tried the doorknob but the door was locked. It was a regular door lock she expected him to figure out quickly enough.

Doris swallowed hard when the lock seemed to give. The door started to open and she fired three shots at the center of the door. She heard a thud, but was careful as she stepped toward the open door. The stocky man was on the floor alongside her Lexus. Large blood stains appeared on his chest, but he was still alive and was dragging a handgun with a sound suppressor along his right leg. She shot him in the chest again, this time more centered. The handgun slipped from his hand to the floor. Doris stood there a long moment to make sure he was dead.

Then she heard the sirens.

15

Finding the attorney wasn't easy until the Fontana's put a private investigator on him. He'd left for North Dakota a few days before Rapino caught up with him in the city of Minot. Morris Greenblatt arranged to rent a small house in the most innocuous section of the small city, a flood area decreed Zone X. The city had experienced several floods dating back to 1881, including five floods within seven years starting in 1969, but the worst came in 2011, when the Mouse River flooded more than 4,100 homes, including the one Morris Greenblatt had rented.

Rapino's plans were simple and direct. First he had to take care of Greenblatt. There was no way the attorney was using his real name. The private investigator the Fontana's had hired said that his name under the rental lease was Dean Ólafsson, with a foreign accented O. Rapino had also used a fake name for his flight to Minot. His was Tom Jones, like the famous singer, except he pretended to be a local Alderman looking to greet the new people in town.

Rapino wore a long dirty blonde wig to go along with the Nordic name. He left from LaGuardia Airport in the late afternoon. There was a stopover in Minneapolis-St. Paul before he landed in Minot at 11:00 p.m. Instead of pre-booking a room, he rented a car under his fake name using a fake credit card. He drove to a hotel near the airport, the Grand Hotel, and was offered a room on the same level as the pool. Rapino preferred one facing the main drag, State Route 83, which would turn into North Broadway, then South Broadway, and then State Route 83 again. He spent the night in his room getting familiar with a local map and the address he'd been given for Mr. Dean Ólafsson/Morris Greenblatt.

Rapino had never met Greenblatt before. As far as he knew, Greenblatt didn't know who Rapino was either, except possibly by name. He'd learn for sure in the morning.

Rapino was anxious to get this work done and then return to New York. He intended to learn about his former sidekick, Charlie Mazza, or whatever his name was. Rapino was going to start with the fat old guy he'd seen in the pictures taken by Angela Fontana.

He slept well, woke up early and watched the local news in the morning. He was hungry after showering and grabbed breakfast in the hotel restaurant. He was back up in the room afterward and anxious to get going after using the bathroom. He hit the road again before 7 o'clock and took a quick tour of northern Minot from North Broadway, passing the University and several local fast food joints. He turned off North Broadway onto 4th Avenue Northwest, which turned into 3rd Avenue Northwest, the street where Dean Ólafsson/Morris Greenblatt now lived.

As it turned out, his disguise didn't matter. The recently retired attorney, wearing blue pajamas, opened the door to answer Rapino's knock and didn't suspect a thing until the stiletto was deep inside his stomach cavity. Greenblatt gasped a moment before blood appeared from his mouth as he folded at the waist and back-stepped deeper inside the house.

Rapino stepped inside and closed the door behind him. He'd left the knife in Greenblatt's stomach and bent down to remove it. He next took a pillow from a loveseat and used it to smother the former attorney. He leaned on the pillow a long two minutes, or what it felt like, before pushing the pillow to the side and checking Greenblatt's neck for a pulse.

When he was satisfied the attorney was dead, Rapino went through his pants and wallet, took the seven hundred-dollar-bills, a fifty and three twenties he found, and then wiped down the knife and set it under a couch pillow. He went to the kitchen and grabbed a bottle of water from the refrigerator, drank it, then wiped it down and tossed it in a mostly empty trash can.

When he was ready to leave, Rapino went to the front room and checked the street from behind the blinds. When he felt it was safe, he left the house. He began his drive to Fargo in the car he'd rented, using the GPS. It was a four-hour trip. It was another three and a half hours to Minneapolis-St. Paul, where he caught the 3:48 p.m. flight back to New York's LaGuardia Airport. He then took a taxi back to his apartment in Brooklyn.

Now he was anxious to eat a decent meal, catch up with what was going on in the street, and then looking into the old fat guy seen with his former sidekick, Charlie Mazza. It pissed Rapino off that until he found somebody he could trust enough to pick up his street money, he'd have to do it himself. It was exposure he didn't like.

There would also have to be a meeting for the sake of the different crew captains to clear the air about what was going on. If the Fontana's were really cleaning house, it wouldn't surprise Rapino if a few of the other captains didn't show up.

He took a quick shower and a nap. He grabbed a newspaper from the hallway when he awoke. He read it while a pot of espresso was brewing. He did a double take when he saw Doris Montalvo's picture on the front page and the headline that read: *Mob wife takes down apparent assassin.* "What the fuck?" Rapino said before reading further. "What the fucking fuck?"

• • • • •

"Why didn't you call me?" Special Agent in Charge, Connor Kelly said. "Or at least someone from the bureau?"

Doris Montalvo was wearing purple stretch pants and a white pullover. She hadn't put on makeup in two days. The signs of age were visible, including Crows feet, wrinkling eyes, and sagging skin around her jawline.

Today she didn't care.

Nor did she care that the man she'd tried to get protection from in the past was suddenly concerned about her reporting her act of self-defense to the press.

They were sitting in the kitchen of the house she had already listed for sale. This time Kelly had to ask for a cup of coffee. Doris set a cup and the pot on the table. She let him pour his own coffee.

"I called nine-one-one while the hitman they sent to kill me was breaking in. I didn't have time to call you or your useless fucking bureau. I had a gun and I wasn't going to let him kill me. I called the nine-one-one number, gave my location, and didn't bother staying on line because I could hear the prick on the other side of the laundry room door, which led to my garage. I waited for him to force the door open and then I killed him before he could kill me. I'm sure you talked to the detectives. They were doing their job when they questioned me. I told them everything I could about what I believed it was about. And then today I contacted someone from the New York Post to make sure the same exact story is published, which includes the fact that the NYPD put a car in front of my house since it happened and it's still there. So much for your cooperative task force, Kelly. I told the Post about the fact that I had been in contact with the FBI three fucking times about my fears and they weren't interested unless I could give them somebody worth more than my life. They were more interested in their case than protecting me."

"I never said that, Doris."

"Fuck you, you didn't say that. You did too. You didn't have the balls to put it that way, but that's exactly what you meant. I was expendable unless I could give up something that made my life worthwhile again. If anything, I was bait, so fuck you, Mr. G-man."

"You have to know that your life will be in more danger now than before," Kelly said.

Doris feigned a loud laugh. "You kill me," she said. "Now I'm in danger? Not according to the NYPD. They think I won't be touched now that I spilled the story. The mob took its shot and missed."

Kelly said, "Yeah, kid yourself all you want, but maybe not today or next week or next month, but as soon as enough time has passed, and if the same people are running the show as your husband's former friends, you're the first one they'll look to find."

"Like Sammy the Bull? Please. That guy put away how many mobsters and now he has a podcast. How many other former so-called made men have podcasts? Hell, they appear on cop podcasts now. The mob doesn't have the resources or the balls to follow-up on all their bullshit oaths and the consequences of breaking those oaths. The tough guys are more afraid than I am now."

"Yet you're going to move," Kelly said. "Why don't I believe you're no longer afraid?"

"Because you're desperate about the articles that will depict you and your fucking bureau as the useless pieces of shit that they are. Why I'm moving is none of your business, except to say I want nothing to do with this shit city and all its corruption anymore. I made a mistake and fell for the baubles Carmine Montalvo once provided. Now he's dead and I'm long over those baubles. I have enough to live out my life in relative comfort and that's what I intend to do, but never assume I won't have a few guns placed around wherever I live just in case. I killed one of their assholes and I'll kill a dozen more if I have to."

"And you think Las Cruces, New Mexico is the place to do that, live out your life?" Kelly said with a smirk. "That's pretty close to the border down there. El Paso, in fact. You don't think they can contract something out to one of those Beaners crossing the border? Those guys will kill for an ice cream cone."

"That a threat, Kelly. Are you seriously implying that I'll be killed now that I embarrassed you?"

"Not at all, Doris. All I'm saying is be careful down there in Las Cruces. There's plenty of crime crossing the border every day. I'm suggesting you be careful."

"Sure," Doris said. "Now you're looking out for me. Right. It is interesting how the FBI is taking an interest on where I'm going to live. I mean, I'm not so sure it's the mob that would put a contract out on me anymore. I'm thinking it'd be one of your people, the fuck-ups in the bureau. I trust the FBI as much as I trust the mob, which is not at all. You're two sides of the same dirty coin. Scumbags, the both of you."

"Sorry you feel that way," Kelly said.

"Sure you are. I think it's time you go now."

Kelly frowned as he stood up. "Goodbye, Doris," he said.

"Yeah, don't let the door hit you in the ass," Doris said.

• • • • •

"Well, I'm glad you're out of that shit," Joseph told his grandson.

"I'm not out of anything," Chris said. "I'm still an agent, gramps. I was undercover for a while and now I'm not, but I'm still with the bureau. The upside is I have some time off. A lot actually."

"They pulled you off the street," Artie Adler said. "That's good."

They were in Joseph's kitchen. Adler and Chris sat at opposite heads of the table. Joseph was seated in his usual spot mid-table nearest the sink. An Entenmann's coffee cake was on the middle of the table. Joseph was wearing his sweatpants and a green and white, Joe Namath, New York Jets football jersey. Adler was wearing worn blue dungarees and a gray New York Giants T-shirt. Chris wore faded blue dungarees, a white T-shirt and a loose blue and white checkered shirt. They were waiting for the coffee to finish brewing.

"I was compromised," Chris said as he turned to his grandfather.

"It could've been worse," Adler said.

"Yeah, it could've been."

"You two finished with your attempt at making me feel guilty?" Joseph said.

Chris shook his head. Adler chuckled.

Joseph said, "I only ask because the coffee is done and both of you can get to the pot faster than I can."

Adler held a hand up at Chris as he stood. "I got it," he said. "Wouldn't want fatso to pull a muscle standing up or something."

"You see what you left me with when you disappeared?" Joseph said to Chris. "Day after day I've had to put up with his bullshit."

"You two haven't changed," Chris said.

"You kidding me?" Adler said. "He can't change. He's coming down a little now. His weight, I mean, but for a while there it was a wonder he could even walk. Waddle was more like it."

"Yeah," Joseph said, "and wait'll I have to take a piss. Figure my second cup of coffee."

"I always thought that was a myth about you," Chris said.

"Myth my ass," Adler said as he poured the coffee.

Joseph pointed to the small pot alongside the faucet.

"Because you can't do the stairs?" Chris said.

"Never mind how I piss or why I use a pot. What's going on with those animals you were undercover with? You see they tried to kill some woman. She was lucky to kill the moron they sent first."

"They farmed it out, that fiasco," Chris said.

"Farmed it out to who?" Adler said.

"Some Russian, but that's just a rumor I picked up at the office. Now I took my time off, I don't care who shoots who. I'm not sure it's true about the Russian connection though."

"Well, whoever he was, he wasn't very good at his job, the piece of shit," Joseph said.

"The woman who killed him was some big shot's wife," Adler said. "What I read about her in the papers anyway."

"There are rumors about her too," Chris said. "Some pretty nasty ones, but I can't get into those now."

"You should write a book," Joseph said. "That Pistone guy did, right? Made a movie about it too."

"I'm not as enamored with the bureau as Pistone was. A lot of shit went down I'm not proud of."

"Staten Island," Adler said.

Chris nodded. "Except what you did could've gotten me killed, Artie."

"I did that because your grandpa over there, the nosey one, insisted I do it. He was pretty frantic about you, to be fair."

Joseph said, "What about what's going on now? It's been a while since the mob was dropping bodies all over the place. What's that about?"

"From what I know, Aniello Fontana is very old school and intends to clean house. Any of the old rules that were broken, he intends to rid their family of those who broke them. The kid on Staten Island allegedly screwed Montalvo's wife. The same woman who killed the guy in her house. The kids' mother on Staten Island was collateral damage."

"What they called your father," Joseph said. "They called my son collateral damage."

Chris said, "They want the old man more than anybody, but they don't have the resources they used to have, the bureau. Between the right wingers Trump stirred up and everything else going on down at the border, they can't pursue the mob up here the way they used to, but I suspect that's also why there hasn't been something like this, an internal mob war, in a while. They lost a lot of clout with all the defections into witness protection. They get to build back up now because they've been quiet and nobody much cares about them anymore."

"Well, that's a fucking mistake," Adler said.

"They don't have the power they used to have," Joseph said.

"They can still buy the occasional dirty cop," Chris said, "but they can't reach into the DA's office anymore. No more judges and so on. Not like they used to. They're on their own and figuring out it's over, their heyday. And then there's the technology. You wouldn't believe some of the shit we can do now with bugs and so on. They're definitely in decline, so I suspect gramps is right. They don't have the power they once did."

"Not to mention the new breed of gangster is a spoiled brat who can't imagine not having air conditioning running while they watch pornos on their computer screens," Adler said. "The new breed isn't as inclined to do time. They may get wood watching mob movies, but when push comes to shove and they're facing the jungles that are prisons today, reality sets in and it's help me Jesus."

"Neither is the old breed so anxious to stand up," Joseph said, "unless you didn't read about them giving each other up since Gravano. All those big shots in that one family who flipped? Those guys weren't kids."

"He's right about that," Chris said. "The so-called old school guys flip like fish fresh out of the water too now. That one crew, how many was it flipped? Associates to soldiers to captains to an underboss, and then their boss too. Not so tough, were they?"

Adler said, "And the few, the very few, who took it on the chin, stood up, what the hell will they get for their loyalty? Imaging spending twenty or more years in one of those hell holes and coming out knowing if you step back into the shit, there'll be wires and informants all over the place waiting to send you back. That any kind of a life?"

"I joined the bureau because of what they did to my father," Chris said.

"We figured," Adler said. "Although you did a good job of scaring the shit out of both of us. Your grandfather especially. I couldn't keep him from snooping. From wanting to know. Same as your mother. It's out of concern and love they wanted to know, Chris."

"I know that," Chris said. "And I can appreciate it, but sticking his nose into an undercover operation ... well, you know."

Adler nodded.

"You two make me sick," Joseph said. "And now I gotta pee again. Go for a walk, something."

• • • • •

The Assistant U.S. attorney for the Southern District of New York, George Nimitz, wasn't surprised that the FBI had removed Special Agent in Charge, Connor Kelly, from the organized crime task force and put him behind a desk pending an investigation into his actions during the last few months. The suspension was routine during an investigation. A possible termination was down the road.

All Nimitz was concerned about was how or when the head of the Cirelli crime family, Aniello Fontana, would be arrested and put away for life. It would be the conviction he needed to launch a career into politics, starting with the 11th congressional district, a seat representing all of Staten Island and parts of southern Brooklyn. Staten Island would carry the way because it was where the bulk of New York City Republican voters lived.

If Nimitz was going to break into politics, there was no better way than to bring down a major criminal organization or a potential terrorist cell. The truth of the matter was both types of criminal behavior were on the downswing, except the FBI had managed to stir the shit on the organized crime side of the aisle and maybe overshot their legal authority by passing off messages to the mob inside and outside of prison walls.

Now he had a new Special Agent in Charge to work with since Connor Kelly would never hold that position again. Ayaz Ozdemir, a Turkish American, had come up through the ranks working undercover during an investigation into a crew in the Chicago Outfit. He was average height and weight, but dark skinned enough to pass for Sicilian, which is what he had done while working undercover in Chicago.

He had recently been appointed Special Agent in Charge of the task force investigating the Cirelli crime family. Ozdemir had been fully briefed on the situation and was more than up to speed. He had ideas he wanted to put into place. Ideas that Nimitz was fully behind because the time to announce for a Congressional campaign was close at hand.

After hearing Ozdemir out on his plan to bring down Aniello Fontana, Nimitz said, "Okay. If you think that'll work. If you're confident it'll work, then go for it. I'm just not sure turning Vito Fontana is much different than what the previous game plan was. How would you implement it, since it couldn't be done before you?"

"It might not be all that legal," Ozdemir said. "I'm not sure you want to know."

"Well, you're not going to get caught, I assume. If you're talking about going out of bounds, as long as it's not way out of bounds, we have some wiggle room. Is there anything you can tell me?"

"The kid the bureau just pulled off the street. I want to bring him back for something."

Nimitz smiled. "Not murder, I hope. I don't have wiggle room for that."

Ozdemir's returned the smile, then said, "No, of course not. But I have an idea to use him as bait for something. Something they would have to respond to, something taboo in their world, although they already broke that rule out on Long Island."

Kelly smiled. "Yeah, the NYPD and their Internal Affairs division is still taking heat for that mess. It's difficult not to appreciate that. The shit the NYPD pulls on us sometimes would make your stomach turn. Jurisdictional bullshit. They can't stand playing second fiddle."

"This would be to draw one of the Fontana brothers out," Ozdemir said. "The young one, Vito Fontana."

Nimitz put both hands up. "I think this is the part I don't want to know."

"Probably not," Ozdemir said.

"Okay, then," Nimitz said. "You have my blessing." He made the sign of the cross and added, "Go now and do whatever you gotta do."

16

Joseph had just finished washing the dishes and frying pans from his breakfast. There were onion skins on the cutting board he was gathering with a wet paper towel. He started to pour himself the last of the coffee in the pot when his daughter-in-law stepped inside his kitchen from the back door.

"Where is he?" Mary Gallo said. "It's almost a week and he's gone again. Call him if you have his number."

"Mary," Joseph said.

"I know my name. Where's my son?"

"I'm not sure. Why?"

"I just said. I haven't heard from him in a week. He hasn't come home in a week."

"That so unusual? He's on vacation from the job. Leave or whatever they call it. Maybe he took off someplace. Maybe he's got a girl he's hiding."

"Don't break them, Joseph. He was living in my house in the basement. Then, all of a sudden, he's gone again. If you don't know I'm calling the FBI again, those bastards."

"Sit down, have a cup of coffee," Joseph said. "I'll make a fresh pot."

"I'm not here to socialize," Mary said as she sat at the head of the table nearest the door. "I don't know why that kid has to make my life so fucking difficult."

Joseph had started to clean the coffee pot, dropping the grinds in the plastic trash can before using a sponge to clean out the pot. "Let me give Artie a call," he said. "He might know somebody who can find something out."

"Somebody better know something or I'm going to the FBI office in Manhattan to raise hell," Mary said. "I take milk."

Joseph went to the refrigerator for the milk.

"I don't use Sweet-N-Low," she said.

Joseph grabbed the sugar bowl from the counter. "Here," he said, pushing it toward her.

Mary opened the lid and frowned. "When was the last time somebody used this?" she said. "It's all stuck together."

"Break it up with your spoon."

She did so, frowning the entire time.

"Has he talked about a girlfriend?" Joseph said. "Maybe he's with her now, visiting or something."

"He didn't mention one to me," Mary said before sipping her coffee and then making a face. "This is a little strong. How the hell many spoons of grinds you put in?"

"Four."

"Four? What you use, a ladle?"

Joseph chuckled. "Do you have his phone numbers?" he said.

"Of course, I do," Mary said.

"The two-one-two or three-four-seven?"

"Both, I just said. Did you call?"

"No. I didn't think to. You?"

Mary's brow furrowed. "Me what? Call? Of course I called. Both numbers."

"And?"

"Moron, why am I here? What have I been asking since I got here?"

"I haven't called," Joseph said.

"Do you enjoy making me this angry?"

"Honestly?"

Mary was glaring at him then.

"Yeah," he said. "Because you're so unreasonable."

"Really?" she said, loaded with sarcasm.

"You still blame me for my son's death."

"He was murdered."

"You still blame me for my son's murder."

"I do."

"That's unreasonable."

"That's a fact. You gave him that stupid fucking job he didn't need working with mobsters."

"He was doing that for you and his son, making extra money, and he wasn't working with mobsters. He was hawking football tickets, getting twenty-five percent on tickets he sold to customers at my bar. He earned from fifty to a'hundred and change extra a week with those tickets. All he did was deliver them when two assholes shot up a place. He was killed by idiots."

"Which never would've happened had he not been delivering those football tickets, yes or no."

Joseph sighed. "Jesus Christ," he said.

Mary stood up from the table, grabbed her coffee cup, and threw it at Joseph.

• • • • •

Giovanni Rapino was positioned for big jumps within the organization. If all went well, he'd be going from soldier to captain to underboss in a very short time. Still, he couldn't get beyond the fact he'd been fooled by some federal agent posing as an associate looking to be made. There was also the issue of Mazza driving him to a successful hit. Killing a civilian, never mind his mother, was a death penalty at worst, or a life sentence at best. To Rapino, eliminating someone who could testify against him was the only way to handle the situation. He didn't appreciate the Cirelli position regarding federal agents being untouchable.

He'd gone to North Dakota to take out a mob lawyer the boss of the family felt was still dangerous because of the amount of information he held on several fronts. Rapino was fine doing the work, but once he learned an attempt to kill a woman was farmed out and then botched, he resented the work he'd been given.

The aborted attempt at killing Doris Montalvo had to be an embarrassment to the Cirelli crime family. First off, it wasn't supposed to happen, the killing of family members, especially women or children. Secondly, farming it out made it worse and more of a disgraceful act. The Cirellis were lucky the woman had killed the idiot sent to kill her. At least he couldn't talk and give anyone up.

Rapino was disappointed to learn how the woman he'd been fucking was talking to the FBI. He liked Doris Montalvo. She was a good fuck and a tough woman, but knowing she was giving up information was something he'd kill her for without hesitation.

Nor would he have botched the job.

It was weak for a crime family to farm out work that was already considered taboo and against the rules, especially when the person sent was killed instead.

Not to mention the fact that he'd been sent to North Dakota. Why hadn't Aniello Fontana sent someone else to North Dakota to take out the lawyer? While Rapino couldn't admit he'd been with the wife of a fellow made man and captain doing time, he might've talked them into letting him do the work. Doris Montalvo may have been street smart, but Rapino never would've let her get the jump on him. Not in a million years.

Jerry Galante had originally sent him to look after Doris Montalvo, which is how and why he wound up in an affair with her. Now that an attempt on her life was foiled, she couldn't be touched again. The fact she'd foiled the hit herself was something Rapino admired.

It was also a bad sign of things to come, whether he was upped to underboss or not. If the boss of the family and his eldest son, the consiglieri, couldn't pull off a hit on a woman with one of their own, there was nothing to be confident about going forward. If they were truly cleaning house, how did he know he wasn't on their kill list?

He wondered if there would be an issue with the Russians now that one of their people was killed by a 57-year-old woman on her birthday. The Russians had to be as embarrassed as Aniello Fontana.

Today he was making a pass at the address of the old fat guy in a picture Bruno and Vito's sister had taken while following the undercover agent. The street was a busy one, but the driveway was deep. The mental notes Rapino made had to do with logistics. Whether he'd approach through the front door by knocking on it, or head to the back. He would need another sound suppressor either way. That would cost him, whether he made one himself or paid through the nose for one with someone outside family connections. He preferred to pay the price rather than get one from somebody within the family. Rapino always did his best to avoid providing someone with snitch ammunition that could be used against himself in the future.

Now he made a few more passes by the home of Joseph Gallo before heading into Manhattan to see a friend with expensive gun connections. He'd already decided there was no way he was allowing a federal agent to testify against him.

Charlie Mazza, whomever he really was, was a dead man.

•   •   •   •   •

The new Special Agent in Charge, Ayaz Ozdemir, had told Chris to do his best to lure Vito Fontana into a fist fight, and to make sure the gangster took the first swing. He was to make it as innocent a provocation as possible, preferably in front of the gangster's girlfriend or wife.

"Start with a curse or something," Ozdemir had said. "Do a DeNiro on him. 'You lookin' at me?' Call him a pussy. Insult his wife if you have to. Just make sure he gets out of his car to come after you. Get him to take that first punch. Ask him if his wife swallows or something. Be prepared for a cheap shot. Then feel free to beat the shit out of him."

"And if he has a weapon?" Chris said.

"There will be half a dozen eyes on you. All of them close enough to stop him. Besides, Vito is the bodybuilder brother. He'll puff his chest out and probably flex, maybe even pose, before he throws a punch."

"The half dozen eyes going to stop a bullet?"

"If he pulls a gun, we'll stop him. We'll have somebody on a roof. A sniper."

"I can get that in writing? For my mother's sake?"

Ozdemir frowned. "You don't have to take the assignment," he said. "It's an ask on my part."

Chris was originally glad they asked him back into the investigation, but he wasn't sure about being bait. He didn't mind taking down Vito Fontana. He'd been trained enough to handle some musclebound punk, but he also knew that guys like Vito Fontana couldn't accept being beaten in a fight, and that that was when they were most dangerous, after they caught a beating.

The goal was to arrest Fontana on a cocaine distribution charge the bureau was going to make by planting evidence in the gangster's car. The subsequent goal was to get him to flip and testify for what journalists had nicknamed Team America. Even if the case went south, they might get an idea of Vito Fontana's tolerance for prison. If he was as spoiled a brat as they assumed, it wouldn't take long for him to seek a deal and testify against his brother and father. It wasn't as if that hadn't happened in the past.

It was dirty business and illegal for law enforcement on any level to pursue, but nobody involved in the operation was going to mind. Not if it was in an effort to take down a prize as big as the Cirelli family leadership. Entrapments and/or the planting of evidence wasn't unheard of by law enforcement.

To be sure he could maintain his stamina in a fistfight, Chris spent three days of training with a private jujitsu specialist he'd met while training in Quantico. He'd been well trained in hand-to-hand combat there and had kept up his physical conditioning since.

Agents had been watching Vito Fontana's home for two days without seeing him. On the third day, they observed him kissing his wife before driving his 2023 Corvette out of the garage. Fontana was followed to his father's home on Staten Island, and then later to Brooklyn where he parked outside a mobbed-up restaurant in Bay Ridge for half an hour. When he left, Fontana had a young woman with him.

Agents then followed Fontana to the Liberty View Brooklyn Hotel on 4th Avenue in Brooklyn, at which point Chris was notified to wait near the parking exit on 29th Street. He wore a fake mustache and sunglasses and was wearing a Burger King shirt.

The couple remained inside for little more than two hours.

One agent had put a GPS tracker on Fontana's Corvette after he pulled into the subterranean parking lot. When Fontana left the hotel parking lot, he was forced to wait because of the car blocking his way on the street.

The shouting began after Fontana had leaned on his horn several times. Gallo acknowledged him with the middle finger of his right hand. Fontana moved up to within inches of the bureau issued Dodge SUV. When he looked up at the SUV's driver, he saw a smile and a hand waving at him to get closer.

"Motherfucker!" Fontana yelled before putting the Corvette in park and getting out of his car.

Chris was already out of the SUV and had moved to the front of it with both hands on his hips. He laughed at the sight of Fontana's outfit: red khaki shorts, a red and black striped polo shirt and brown moccasins.

"The fuck is your problem?" Fontana yelled. "I'm trying to get out of here."

"Yeah, I know," Chris said. "Get back in your car and wait."

"Excuse me?"

"You heard me."

"Listen, Burger boy, move your fucking car."

Chris folded his arms across his chest and smiled.

"Asshole, I'm not gonna ask you again," Fontana said.

"I'll move when I'm ready, jerkoff."

"Jerkoff? You're calling me a jerkoff?"

Chris smiled again as Fontana moved further into the street. When they were chest to chest, Chris said, "Yeah, so?"

Fontana smacked Chris hard with his right hand, knocking the special agent's fake mustache and sunglasses off.

"Now move before I break your face," Fontana said.

Chris stepped up to Fontana again, except this time he smacked him first. Fontana went into a rage and started throwing wild punches at Chris, landing one or two before being head-butted on the nose.

Fontana growled as he grabbed at his nose. Blood flowed through his fingers as Chris laughed. Then he grabbed Fontana by the throat and slammed him into the driver's side door of the SUV.

The young woman who'd been with Fontana in his Corvette was out of the car and yelling for Chris to stop. She had her cellphone in hand and was out in the middle of the street, her back to the car, while another special agent dropped a brick of cocaine wrapped in a towel onto the passenger floorboard of the Corvette. The same agent then joined the young woman and asked if she saw what happened. By then Fontana, his face and chest a mess of blood from his broken nose, was pinned to the street by both of Chris's knees.

"Leave him alone!" the young woman shouted.

"What are you doing with this piece of shit anyway?" Chris said. "You know he's married, right?"

"Fuck you," Fontana said.

Chris slapped Fontana hard across the face.

"Call NYPD," the other agent told the young woman.

"No!" Fontana yelled to her. "Don't call the cops."

"He's embarrassed," Chris said. "I'll bet you thought he was a tough guy, huh, honey?"

"Fuck you," she said.

"Get off a me!" Fontana yelled.

"Uh-uh, tough guy," Chris said. "Not until the cops get here."

There were two cars behind the SUV leaning on their horns to pass. One was driven by Angela Fontana. None of the agents noticed her. An agent who'd been on the corner approached the cars and held up traffic on 4th Avenue so the cars could back out onto the Avenue.

"You're fucking dead," Fontana said.

"Am I?" Chris said.

"Yeah, definitely."

"How you gonna do that from your back?"

Fontana tried to turn to one side and Chris slapped him again.

• • • • •

Six hours after the arrest of Vito Fontana on drug charges outside a hotel garage in Brooklyn, an attorney for the Fontana family, Frank Cusmano, sat at a conference table in the U.S. Attorney's Office, Southern District of New York, in Manhattan. A smiling Cusmano engaged in a minute long staring contest with Assistant U.S. attorney, George Nimitz.

When he finished staring, Nimitz turned to Fontana and said, "Well, your attorney is here now. Do you have anything to say?"

Vito Fontana, his face bruised, his broken nose bandaged after being brought to the New York-Presbyterian Brooklyn Methodist Hospital emergency room, shrugged as he turned to his attorney.

"You're joking, right?" Cusmano said to Nimitz.

"Not at all," Nimitz said. "A key of cocaine isn't remotely funny. Technically more than a key."

"Right," Cusmano said, still smiling. "How about the fact it was planted? Or that my client was provoked into an incident outside a parking garage where I'd bet dollars to donuts, not a single camera was working, but had been working right up until maybe half an hour before my client pulled into that garage. And where is the agent who started this fiasco in the first place? My client and the young woman he was with claim your agent's mustache was a fake my client slapped off his face. He in hiding now, your agent? I'm sure the other agents involved are."

Cusmano then turned to Special Agent in Charge, Ayez Ozdemir. "Your people couldn't be more obvious if they tried."

"The young woman who was with your client, Doris Hoffman, was it?" Nimitz said to Vito. "That your girlfriend or just someone you met this morning?"

"That's none of your business," Cusmano said.

"You know, he had a much bigger mouth out on the street earlier," Ozdemir said. "From what I was told, he was full of piss and vinegar until he made the mistake of picking on the wrong guy. From what I understand, he got his ass kicked."

"Fuck you," Vito Fontana said. "I was japped."

"Sure you were."

"Isn't it a shame you don't have that on video," Cusmano said. "Shame that garage camera broke down when it did, but maybe there were other cameras in the area. I've already sent investigators from our firm to check and see."

Nimitz said, "Be that as it may, a key of pure Columbian cocaine was found under the front passenger seat of your client's corvette. Nice car, by the way."

"And you haven't even booked him yet," Cusmano said. "I guess you're looking for my client to do something for you. Is that what this fiasco is about?"

"I'm sure you're aware of the recent killings and disappearing acts of certain associates of your client and his father. If he had something to tell us about them, who knows what might happen to these potential drug charges."

"He's not even under arrest."

"I'm sorry, does he want to spend the night in jail? Does he want his father to post his bail? I'm sure it'll be substantial. A key of cocaine is nothing to sneeze at."

"Are you going to arrest my client on this bullshit setup arrest or what?"

Nimitz shrugged. "Sure, why not?"

• • • • •

Angela Fontana brought a pitcher of lemonade and two glasses on a tray into Aniello Fontana's living room. She set the tray on the coffee table alongside an envelope, then poured a glass of the lemonade for Frank Cusmano. He'd arrived a few minutes earlier from Assistant District Attorney's office. He thanked her and she left them alone.

Aniello Fontana was sitting in his favorite armchair and Cusmano on the couch.

"Vito will be released in a few hours," he said. "They know it's a total bullshit case, and they'll drop it before embarrassing themselves in court. They don't and I'll have a press conference set up in the morning."

Fontana pointed to the envelope on the coffee table. "Those are for you," he said. "Pictures of what happened to my son."

Cusmano grabbed the envelope and removed a set of a dozen pictures. He smiled as he went through them.

"The guy Vito was fighting with and without a mustache," Fontana said. "Then a guy, an agent no doubt, walking alongside the car and putting something inside after the broad got out of the car. Nice and tidy, huh?"

"I won't even ask where you got these." Cusmano said.

"Good, because I wouldn't tell you unless we went to trial. I already sent a check for the bail. We work with this bondsman all the time. He takes a bank check."

"I'm sorry you have to lay out a dime," Cusmano said. "It really is a bullshit charge. These pictures will clear it up."

"And then we can sue the FBI."

"Or sell the pictures to some newspaper and let them do it for us."

"Maybe," Fontana said. "It's the cost of doing business for both sides. That said, it won't help with the other families. The Vignieri people want a sit down. They get ahold of this, a drug charge, bullshit or not, it makes us look bad. The law is harassing all five families now. They can point to this as another example. Strengthens their hand in negotiations."

"Everybody knows you're old school, Neal. Nobody is gonna believe this shit the feds pulled."

"My boys think I'm too old school," Fontana said. "They watch the Godfather movie, that scene with the Turk, and they think its unavoidable changing the rules. A made guy fucks another made guy's wife? I can't look the other way. A guy gets nailed in a drug bust, he flips before they cuff him. The old way is the only way. I can't get past that."

"They planted the cocaine, Neal," Cusmano said, holding up one of the pictures. "The feds did. We have it right here. It's a scam they pulled."

"They didn't pull it without a reason, Frank. They know what they're doing."

"Stirring the shit?"

"More than you know. The feds, the cops, they're no different and no better than us, except they have better technology and more resources. One thing I learned since before Gravano flipped on Gotti was that it was just a matter of time before somebody that high up did. Somebody high enough up for anyone below them to justify flipping. How can we expect a guy doing the grunt work, the collections, the intimidation, all the hustling, the work, to kick up and stay silent when the boss of an operation gives up everybody else? Once that happens, a captain, an underboss, and then a boss flips, it's open season on everybody else. They've collected a boss now. How long before they collect another one? I don't like having to deal with the other families. In some ways it's suicide what you're giving up just meeting them."

Cusmano pointed a finger at Aniello and said, "They're still cheating, Neal. The feds, I mean. You should've heard that bastard bring up your son's girlfriend. He was bluffing, except he wasn't. They don't care what they do as long as they can score some points. Rumors are Nimitz is gonna make a run for Mayor or maybe Congress. I hope he gets hit by a car."

Aniello chuckled. "Mayor. Congress. Talk about organized crime."

"Yes, exactly right," Cusmano said. "Talk about organized crime is right. Think about the shit that goes on in government. Criminals, every one of them. From insider trading to the bribes they take as campaign contributions, to the scams they run for their legal defense funds when they're caught with their pants around their ankles. Trump, Giuliani, Biden, and his kid. All of them."

"They're not so different than you, counselor. Licenses to steal, eh?"

Cusmano frowned.

"Don't be upset," Aniello said. "I wish one of my sons were disciplined enough to go to law school. I wish one of them could get through college. They're both spoiled and don't know any better. It's too late for them. We're all part of the same stupid shit. I wanted to straighten things out. Go back to the old ways, when there was structure and discipline, but how can I? I don't blame you for what you do, how you bill. You're worth every dime. It's the world we live in. No need for a mafia, a *cosa nostra*. Everything is dirty now. Everything and everybody is corrupt. Some get to call themselves legitimate. I swore by capitalism my whole life and now that I'm seventy, I know why. Because the corruption is built into the system. So, some get to call themselves legitimate, but they're full of shit too. That's the only difference."

Cusmano was still frowning.

Aniello laughed. "What, you don't like it when I lecture?"

"I watched an episode of that series you told me about?"

"Really? The HBO thing, *Succession*? What'cha think?"

"It started okay."

"Only one episode?"

"I deal with people like that almost every day. Present company excepted. They don't impress me."

"The old guy is good though, no? The one plays the father. And the kid, the young one, I read somewhere he was in one of them kid movies from back in the day. *Home Alone?*"

Cusmano shrugged. "My wife or daughters'll probably know. Or the grandkids, I guess."

"That was a funny fuckin' movie, that *Home Alone* thing they did. Even the second one was good, the sequel."

"I think they made a few more. Probably not with the same kids."

"Milk the thing for what you can, right?"

"Sure," Cusmano said, then glanced at his watch. "I should get going, Neal."

"You want something to take home. Angela made some Italian cheese cake. It's out of this world. She's an excellent baker."

"Thanks, no," Cusmano said as he stood up. "Vito should be home soon. I'll give him a call tomorrow."

"Safe home."

"Thanks, Neal. Good night. Say goodnight to your daughter for me."

"Night, counselor," Angela said. She was standing in the kitchen doorway.

17

Giovanni Rapino met Bruno and Vito Fontana at the St. George Terminal of the Staten Island Ferry. After entering the ferry, they went to the concession kitchen for coffees. Vito still had black eyes from his beating. He wore sunglasses and a Yankees baseball cap.

Bruno was dressed business casual with gray slacks, black shoes, and a light blue untucked shirt. He was holding his cellphone up for Rapino to see the pictures of the young woman who'd been with his brother during Vito's arrest. She was naked in the pictures.

"She let you take these?" Rapino said.

"I think she gets off doing that," Vito said.

"Nice," Rapino said.

Bruno said, "He says she can take a load down her throat and keep going."

"Yeah?"

Vito was rubbing his forehead with the middle fingers of both hands. "My fuckin' head hurts," he said.

Rapino was still looking at the picture. Suddenly he stopped and pointed to Charlie Mazza. "Wait, that's that motherfucker," he said. "That's Charlie Mazza."

"That's Charlie Mazza?" Vito said.

"That's a fed," Rapino said. "Remember, your sister took his picture before."

"This is the same guy?" Bruno said.

"Look," Rapino said. "Mustache, then no mustache."

"I knocked his mustache and glasses off," Vito said. "I thought he looked familiar. The motherfucker."

"Your sister was there when this happens?"

Bruno nodded. "Her idea, yeah. She does it for us once in a while. Usually she follows new guys or people we're suspicious of. Pro'bly my father told her to keep an eye on my brother because of all the shit going down. He's still afraid there'll be another mob war because of that cop on the island."

"You give pictures to lawyer?"

"He has them," Vito said. "That fugazy mustache will put that bullshit drug charge to bed. It was a setup. Start to finish. Including that brick of—"

"Cocaine, yeah," Bruno said. "You know what this is about, right?"

"You out on the bail, no?" Rapino said.

"Couple hundred grand, yeah."

"They're looking to flip you," Bruno said.

"No doubt," Rapino said.

"That case will get flushed down the toilet," Vito said.

"Maybe," Bruno said. "The feds are devious motherfuckers, little brother."

Vito waved his brother off. "That coke was planted," he said. "That entire thing was a setup. Look at the pictures. The guy gets in my face. He japs me and the fight starts, and then Jennifer gets out the car and they plant the shit when I wasn't looking. They obviously didn't know about Angela. If that guy is an agent, it's obvious what they were pulling, no? Cusmano's people, the PI's, they found two other cameras on the street there the feds didn't know about."

"Cusmano?" Rapino said.

"Our lawyer," Bruno said. "Pray you never have to use him. He's good, but he's also a thief."

"Lawyers? They are all thief, eh?"

Vito said, "Cusmano said it'll go away without a trial. He said they had to break every rule in the book to pull that shit off, especially because of the cameras they didn't account for. And the one they missed. Ours. Angela's camera."

Bruno said, "The feds killed those other cameras. They'll have a cover story for that and their agent."

"That prick pushed it until I was ready to take a swing, and then he japped me and broke my nose."

"There were probably agents all over the place," Bruno said. "We already know that guy, Mazza, he was undercover. They fucked up big time with this move. Shame Dad had to pay any bail."

Vito shrugged. "The price of doing business, Pop says."

"Yep," Bruno said. "Says it all the time when shit goes down."

"All I know is I'm not going away for some bullshit like this."

Rapino said, "Still want me to leave him alone?"

"Not me," Vito said. "Blow his fucking head off far as I'm concerned."

"Except for Dad," Bruno said.

"Give me okay and I kill this agent," Rapino said.

"You have it from me, the okay," Vito said.

"Jesus, hold up," Bruno said. "It's not that simple."

"Sure is simple," Rapino said. "I find him. I kill him." He clapped his hands, left over right, then right over left. "Boom, is done."

Vito looked to his brother and said, "Boom."

"We're talking about a federal agent here," Bruno said. "We're still feeling the heat from that fucking internal affairs cop. Didn't take them long to figure he was dirty, but that didn't stop them from breaking our balls. The other families weren't thrilled about it either."

"Maybe we get rid of all the heat at once. What the hell else can they do?"

"The cops or the other families? Think, little brother."

"I think for you," Rapino said. "He goes like Galante. Nobody find."

"That makes sense," Vito said. "The old man will know but he won't know. Not really. Just us three."

Bruno frowned, then gave it a moment and said, "Nothing gets back to him, the old man. Nothing."

"Is us, right?" Rapino said. "Who is to talk?"

"So, boom it is," Vito said.

Bruno frowned.

"He's gone," Rapino said. "No body, no crime, eh?"

"Boom already," Vito said.

"Okay," Bruno said. "Boom."

• • • • •

Chris Gallo bypassed the receptionist and walked into the office of Katherine Grady while the attorney was on the phone. She held up a hand without looking at him.

"I'm sure we can work something out, Tom," Katherine said as Chris sat in one of two armchairs facing her desk. She squinted at him as she smiled.

"Sure, Tom," she said into the handle handset. "Thanks again. Bye."

"You're still beautiful," Chris said when she hung the receiver in the desk cradle.

"If it isn't the Special Agent who can't drive," Katherine said as she stood up.

"Tell me you're still single," Chris said.

"Hello? How about a hug first."

Chris stood and met her halfway around her desk. The two hugged for a long moment before separating. Katherine sat in the other armchair in front of her desk. Chris sat back in his.

"Jesus, you look good," he said.

"So do you. Are you still playing Donnie Brasco?"

"I was," he said. "Then I wasn't, and then I was again. Now I'm not again."

"Way to confuse a girl," Katherine said.

Chris looked her up and down. "Your eyes and your hair and that dress. Perfect. Now answer my question. Still single or am I torturing myself?"

Katherine smiled. "I see someone now and then," she said. "It's nothing more than that."

"Skip the part where you tell me it's just for sex."

"Okay, I'll skip that part."

"Ouch, woman."

"Ouch, man. How have you been? Where have you been?"

"Me? You know how hard it was for me to track you down, a Georgia girl practicing law in New York?"

"You're FBI, Chris. It probably took you less than an hour."

"Ten minutes, but why up here? What made you leave Virginia?"

"A job offer. I make the big bucks now."

"Too big to be seen with a copper?"

She smiled as she shrugged.

"That's more than enough of an opening," Chris said. "Can I buy you lunch in the hotel I'm staying at. It's convenient as all hell. We can eat before or after."

"Hmm, that might be tempting. Do you have a clean bill of health for STDs on you?"

"Always."

"I can see you haven't changed. The shy boy at first appearance and then you learn he's a wolf."

"I already know about you, but it's been forever for me."

Katherine closed one eye. "Sure it has."

Chris made the sign of the cross on his chest. "And hope to die," he said.

Fifty minutes later they were in her apartment. It was two blocks from her office, in the Dumbo section of Downtown Brooklyn. They shared a cold leftover pasta and shrimp dish in Katherine's refrigerator and barely made it to the bedroom before they were naked. Katherine made him use protection and was surprised when it was over so quickly.

"You weren't kidding," she said from underneath him in the bed.

"I wasn't," Chris said. "Not since the last time. Not with somebody else."

"You poor man. Can you go again?"

"I might need some help. That or a nap first."

"Right," she said. "Sure. Roll over, Donnie."

She helped him get there and they did it again. Afterwards, they sat up in bed and shared a cigarette.

"Since when you smoke, by the way?" Chris said.

"I don't normally," Katherine said. "That pack has been in my night table for about a month."

"That the last time?"

"Shush."

Chris grabbed one of her hands. "Look, I have a lot of time owed me," he said. "Especially since they asked me to come back for a single operation. I'm free again now."

"You're done with undercover?"

"I'm not even sure I'll stay with the bureau, but undercover, absolutely. I'm finished."

"That bad, huh?"

"You wouldn't believe it. Most of it."

"Don't kid yourself. I co-chaired a few criminal cases now. I know what defendants are up against."

"We don't have to have kids right away, but I do want a couple. Eventually, I mean."

Katherine rolled her eyes. "Tell me that wasn't a proposal."

"It's practice. I've been told practice makes perfect."

"You were told to practice your driving skills so you didn't kill us on a date."

"Something like that, yeah."

"I'm not going to marry you this fast, Chris."

"Tomorrow is fine."

"Stop joking. I mean it. We'll have to spend some time together first. I also want children someday, but not until I can afford them enough to work part time. And I need to know you won't disappear, whether it's because of your job or some young blonde who turns your head."

"I'm not a blonde type of guy. Always been partial to reds."

"And I'll have to meet your family. And you'll have to meet mine."

"Yours are from Georgia. They won't like a Yank."

"And yours?"

"Just two left. My over protective mom and my streetwise, always too nosey grandfather."

"How did you get into the FBI with an overprotective mom? You never explained that."

"And Iraq before that? It wasn't easy."

"Ready for round three?"

"Jesus, you're a nymph."

Katherine punched him in the shoulder before she climbed on top of him.

• • • • •

Aniello Fontana was re-watching the last episode of the *Succession* HBO series from his armchair in the den when his sons arrived. He paused the show while Bruno and Vito sat at opposite ends of a brown leather couch. Angela brought a tray with three cups of espresso and three bottles of water. She set it on the coffee table in front of the couch, then brought one of the espressos to her father.

"Pastries?" she said.

"*Sfogliatella*," Bruno said. "Thanks."

Angela left them.

"They want a sit-down," Aniello said. "They're sending Carneglia."

"Where?" Bruno said.

Aniello shook his head. "Don't know yet, but somewhere public. They'll know that."

"We know what it's about?" Vito said.

"Everything," Aniello said. "Pro'bly the woman. That was some sloppy shit."

"You talk to Shevchenko yet?"

"He's out of town."

Vito chuckled. "I'll bet he is."

"It isn't funny," Aniello said.

Angela returned with a tray of pastries. Two *sfogliatella,* two cannoli and two cream puffs. She set the tray with some napkins on the coffee table.

"Thanks, Ange," Bruno said as his sister left. He took one of the *sfogliatella* and bit into the crusty shell.

"That's why you're getting fat," Aniello said.

"That and he doesn't work out anymore," Vito said.

"I can still kick your ass," Bruno said.

"Bullshit," Vito said.

"Enough," Aniello said. "Stop clowning. This is serious. I don't know if they're serious or they're looking to do something. Maybe I send back-up for you two. I don't like you're alone together like that. Not the two of you."

"If it's a public place, I don't think they'd do anything," Bruno said. "We make it middle of the day or something. Lots of civilians around and whatnot."

"Of course, but that doesn't mean they can't do something."

"What, a rifle?"

"Yes, a rifle. Why not?"

"Still too dangerous. They miss and hit someone else? I don't think we have to worry."

"You won't be able to carry. You know that, right?"

"How about something small?" Vito said.

Bruno looked to his brother. "Your Tomcat?"

"That or a Ruger LCP."

Aniello said, "Whatever you choose to do, do it smart. If Carneglia asks, you show him if you're carrying. Tap your pocket or whatever. Don't try to conceal if he asks. Tell him I told you to carry."

"He'll be alone?" Bruno said.

"For the meeting, yes," Aniello said. "When you talk. He won't go there alone. He'll have backup too, and we don't know where yet."

"You think they'll ask for something?"

"To keep the peace, of course."

"Money or turf?"

"Turf is money. Probably something here on the island."

"Can we give them a piece of Port Richmond?" Vito said.

"There's still drug money in Port Richmond," Aniello said. "No."

"Let's worry about it when we get there," Bruno said. "Maybe it won't amount to much. Maybe they just want to be heard."

Aniello said, "You've got much to learn, my sons. Meantime, either of you watch this show about the billionaire guy and his kids? Supposed to be about the guy owns Fox News, I think. Reminds me more of Trump."

"I think you need to get out more," Vito said.

"I'm serious, you little shit. It's a good show. Good actors too. The old guy there and the kids. Good actors. There's a redhead in it I would mind spearing I was younger. A lot of intrigue. They got ass kissers and ball washers too in that world, the corporate world. You two might learn something about taking over some day. That's what the show is about. Which of the three kids is gonna take over the old man's business. They make it real cutthroat."

Bruno looked to Vito.

"What?" Aniello said.

They both laughed.

"Okay, get the hell out of here," Aniello said as his sons stood up off the couch. "Two morons. Try to teach you something."

"Okay, you taught us," Bruno said. "We'll bring an axe when we meet Carneglia."

"Think you're funny?" Aniello said. "You should be a comedian."

At that Vito broke out laughing hysterically.

"Another moron," his father said.

• • • • •

"He showed you a picture?" Adler said. "Hey, don't do that. Not now."

Joseph flipped him the bird as he faced the sink and grabbed his piss pot.

"God damn it," Adler said. He stood up and headed out the back door. He stood on the small porch and lit a cigarette.

Joseph could hear him grumbling as he did his business with the pot. When he was finished, Joseph rinsed his pot out with hot water and set it on the back ledge of the sink next to the faucet.

"You finished in there?" Adler said.

"Fuck yourself, Artie."

Adler returned to the kitchen and frowned at Joseph.

"She's gorgeous," Joseph said. "Redhead. Great shape. A lawyer, no less."

"You meet her?"

Joseph sat at the table. "Not yet, no."

"You have the picture?"

"Put your tongue back in your mouth. No, it was in his wallet."

"His mother meet her yet?"

"I doubt it. Maybe."

Adler sat across from Joseph. "Well, good for him," he said. "It's about time."

"If this is for real, and he thinks it is, he's talking about leaving the bureau and working for her law firm as a PI."

"That's great, Joseph. I hope it happens for him. Think the old lady'll like her?"

"No, but she won't like any woman Chris brings home," Joseph said. "Let's have a toast, eh?"

"Beer in the fridge?"

"Always, but not that shit. Let's have a real toast. Grab my Chivas bottle from the liquor cabinet inside."

"You sure that's a good idea with your stomach and all."

"Go get the bottle, putz."

Adler headed into the dining room. There were six bottles of scotch standing on the shelf behind the glass. Three of them were Chivas, two of them unopened. Adler opened the cabinet doors and grabbed the opened bottle of Chivas. It was less than half filled. He brought it to the kitchen and saw Joseph cracking ice.

"You wash your hands?" Adler said.

"Before I picked my nose," Joseph said.

"You're disgusting."

Joseph dropped a few ice cubes into both rocks glasses. He set them on the table. Adler poured about a shot in each glass, then set the bottle on the table.

"Let it chill," Joseph said.

"You mean water down the Chivas," Adler said.

"You're a Neanderthal."

"You're a fat Neanderthal. I'm not sure this is a good idea, you with the scotch."

Joseph picked up his glass. Adler followed. They touched glasses and drank.

Joseph set his glass down and felt a sharp pain in his right side. "Fuck me," he said.

"You don't fuckin' listen," Adler said.

Joseph sat. He was still holding his side.

Adler walked around the table and stood alongside Joseph. "You okay, moron?"

Joseph shook his head. "This one hurts more than usual," he said. "Really hurts."

Then he spat up blood and nearly fell off the chair.

18

Bruno and Vito Fontana came to Manhattan on the Staten Island Ferry and then walked along the water smoking cigarettes while looking out for federal agents. They had come for a meeting with the underboss of the Vignieri crime family, 67-year-old Eugene Carneglia. The Vignieri crime family was representing the other three crime families regarding the series of arrests the police were still making since an NYPD Internal Affairs investigator was found murdered on Long Island. All five families were losing money due to the harassment the NYPD was using to pressure the mob to either give up the killer of one of their own, or at least produce the shooter's body.

The Fontana brothers were dressed business casual. The bruises on Vito's face had turned yellow. His nose was covered with an aluminum nasal splint.

They stopped near the East Coast Memorial in Battery Park. They had come early, hoping to spot whoever might be following Carneglia. They went to the railing and watched one of the Statue Cruise boats leaving the dock. Passengers from the prior trip had already dispersed in both directions.

"I never went," Bruno said.

"Me neither," Vito said.

"I don't get the appeal. Gotta be hot inside the statue."

"Very hot during the summer. Then there's the walk up the steps. Fuck that."

They'd remained mostly silent during the ferry ride from Staten Island. Now, as they both leaned their backs against the railing, they scanned their surroundings. The memorial was straight ahead of them.

Bruno said, "We're going to have to protect ourselves with Rapino."

"I was wondering about that," Vito said. "This is not from Dad, though, right? You didn't—"

"No way. Nothing to do with Dad. This is between us. He takes out that agent, we're both fucked they ever get something on him."

"You think he was wired?"

"You remember what Dad told us? Sometimes you gotta do what you gotta do."

Vito nodded

"If you gotta wonder about it, you best take care of it," Bruno said. "Look at what happened to Richie. He knew, had a hunch, but he didn't act. Twenty-five to life. Besides, with the other guy, Rapino'll make two. That'll get you straightened out. Bottom line is he's gotta go. We can't leave him the option to flip on us.

"I'll do whatever I have to."

"I'll be there for backup and verification, so don't sweat that."

"You mean in case I fuck up?"

"You can't fuck it up with Rapino. He's too dangerous. I'll be there. Dad'd be pissed at me if I wasn't. Probably kill me if I let you get whacked."

"Dad'll be pissed we do this without his permission no matter what happens. He likes Rapino."

"Why we never mention it."

"He's taking this old rulebook too serious, don't you think? One should be enough. Galante, I mean."

"It's his prerogative, Vee. Don't forget how far back he goes with this. Nearly fifty years. Plus you're his son and you don't have a prison record. That's what bumped me up as much as a couple of hits. He can't show favoritism. It's how he was brought up. Old school and old school rules. It could be a help long term. If we can find enough people don't shit their pants over prison time."

Vito nodded. "Okay, so where do we do it?"

"Can't be his apartment until we know he's not on camera."

"Then where?"

"We send for him. Tell him he's stepping up."

"Won't that tip him off? Especially once he whacks that agent. I mean, I'd be suspicious, I was him. He might think its Dad gave the order."

"We'll have to be careful, that's for sure. Rapino is a stone killer. He gets the jump on us, we're fucked."

A loud series of whistles sounded. It came from somewhere to their right as they stood at the railing. Suddenly armed men and women appeared from a park walkway. They surrounded an elderly man the brothers realized was Eugene Carneglia. There were loud shouts for him to put his hands up before he was guided to his knees. Both his arms were tugged down behind him before he was handcuffed.

Vito and Bruno turned around and headed back toward the ferry. They were surprised when no one stopped them.

• • • • •

Assistant U.S. attorney for the Southern District of New York, George Nimitz, and Special Agent in Charge, Ayez Ozdemir, had listened to the tape several times. Nimitz stopped the recording and sat back in his chair.

"Can we use it?" he said. "Can we let those two go through with it?"

"Legally?" Ozdemir said. "That's a hit those two are talking about."

"It would be a score if they did it."

"Except for the tape in our possession and the possession of whomever delivered it."

"Vignieri squad," Nimitz said. "Shit, we have to inform him."

"Be risky if we didn't."

"Shit."

"Letting Rapino hear it might flip him."

"You believe they had parabolic mics set in trees every ten feet. Two were dug in the ground. One aimed at where the Fontana brothers were talking near the water. Whomever they have in that Borgata is linked in big time."

"Carneglia is a good pinch, and he's already talking, but the big goombah for me in this is the guy nobody has touched in forever, old man Fontana."

Ozdemir said, "What made them make the arrest before they met up, the brothers and Carneglia?"

"Huh? Oh, the old man was carrying," Nimitz said as he moved forward on his chair. "Believe it? It was a hit. Probably because of all the shit the Cirelli people stirred the last few weeks. Carneglia was there to take them out, both brothers. He was coming from his apartment on Mulberry. They picked him up on Hester Street. They weren't even following Carneglia. They were following the driver. The car was bugged and Carneglia gave his driver instructions, including where they'd lose the gun."

"They have all of that?"

"Soon as he learned about it, Carneglia joined team America."

"And the driver?"

"He's on hold. They don't really need him unless he's got a tale or two to tell."

"They had the driver all the way. How lucky was that?"

"Extremely. Then they grabbed his driver on State Street after they arrested Carneglia. That old bastard was gonna whack the two brothers and start a mob war."

"Or end one before it started," Ozdemir said. "The Vignieri people take out Fontana's two kids, I don't see it escalating much from there. Not these days. It's a clear message. No need to go after the old man. Not since his son Bruno was named consiglieri."

Nimitz was biting his lower lip, a habit he had when he was about to think aloud. "We have this tape," he said, "and if they pull it off, it's gold."

"Except for the legal issue of having to inform Rapino his life is in danger," Ozdemir said. "Who knows, we do that, maybe he flips. Knowing they're looking to take him out, why wouldn't he?"

"He have any connection to the old man? I mean direct contact."

"Maybe. Probably not, but he's probably getting all his orders from one of the sons, if not both."

Nimitz played the tape again,

BF: We're going to have to protect ourselves with Rapino.

VF: I was wondering about that. This is not from Dad, though, right? You didn't—

BF: No way. Nothing to do with Dad. This is between us. He takes out that agent, we're both fucked they ever get something on him.

VF: You think he was wired?

BF: You remember what Dad told us? Sometimes you gotta do what you gotta do. (pause) If you gotta wonder about it, you best take care of it. Look at what happened to Richie. He knew, had a hunch, but he didn't act. Twenty-five to life. Besides, with the other guy, Rapino'll make two. That'll get you straightened out. Bottom line is he's gotta go. We can't leave him the option to flip on us.

VF: I'll do whatever I have to.

BF: I'll be there for backup and verification, so don't sweat that.

VF: You mean in case I fuck up?

BF: You can't fuck it up with Rapino. He's too dangerous. I'll be there. Dad'd be pissed at me if I wasn't. Probably kill me if I let you get whacked.

VF: Dad'll be pissed we do this without his permission no matter what happens. He likes Rapino.

BF: Why we never mention it.

VF: He's taking this old rulebook too serious, don't you think? One should be enough. Galante, I mean.

BF: It's his prerogative, Vee. Don't forget how far back he goes with this. Nearly fifty years. Plus you're his son and you don't have a prison record. That's what bumped me up as much as a couple of hits. He can't show favoritism. It's how he was brought up. Old school and old school rules. It could be a help long term. If we can find enough people don't shit their pants over prison time.

VF: Okay, so where do we do it?

BF: Can't be his apartment until we know he's not on camera.

VF: Then where?

BF: We send for him. Tell him he's stepping up.

VF: Won't that tip him off? Especially once he whacks that agent. I mean, I'd be suspicious, I was him. He might think its Dad gave the order.

BF: We'll have to be careful, that's for sure. Rapino is a stone killer. He gets the jump on us, we're fucked.

Nimitz was smiling. "That it'd make me flip," he said.

Ozdemir nodded. "Yep. Me too."

• • • • •

Before Chris brought Katherine to his mother's house for lunch, he explained how his mother was widowed after his father was murdered by mistake by mobsters. He gave her as much warning about his mother as possible, but Katherine was more interested in how he'd dealt with the murder of his father.

"I was eleven at the time," he said. "It hurt. I was pretty fucked up for a while. I didn't understand it. I eventually got over it, but not without a bunch of street fights with kids who couldn't resist poking fun about it. Mom never got over it, and she hates my paternal grandfather because of it."

"Was he involved with the mob, your grandfather?" Katherine said.

"He owned a bar. Word is his wife's brother was a wiseguy, and he helped my grandfather get a loan to buy the place, but Joseph paid off his debt and then his brother-in-law, an uncle I never met, died. My father worked at the bar. Aside from his brother-in-law being a mobster, you don't own a bar in New York back in the day, especially where his was, without knowing somebody connected. My grandfather wasn't involved with anything more than the football tickets with college and pro games and holding envelopes in his register for guys dropping off for their bookies and loan sharks. Their customers loved the football tickets. If they didn't have them, most of their weekend trade would've gone to a bar that did sell them. Used to be a buck a ticket with crazy odds, enticing odds. The guys who distributed the tickets, like my father for extra money, got to keep twenty-five percent of what they brought in each week. My father was dropping off his tickets the day he was killed. It was an accident though. Collateral damage, because the two morons did the shooting hit a few people they didn't mean to shoot. My father was one of them."

"I'm so sorry, Chris," Katherine said.

"Anyway, that's why my mother is so overprotective and can drive me crazy at times. And like I said, she hates my father's father."

"That's quite a bit of drama for one family," Katherine said.

"More than enough, except with my mother it never ends. Just follow my lead with her. She's a little *pazza.*"

Katherine looked confused.

"Crazy," Chris said. "You'll see."

They went to Mary's house carrying gifts. Cake and an expensive serving tray. Chris had also warned Katherine about his mother and how she might freak out over her only child having another woman in his life. Katherine told him to stop making her more nervous than she already was.

She wore black slacks, a white blouse with ruffles and black pumps. Chris wore dungarees, a blue polo shirt and sneakers.

He'd called his mother from Katherine's apartment to let her know he was stopping over with a surprise. He didn't tell her the surprise was Katherine. Mary was taken aback when she saw Katherine. She forced a smile and invited them inside.

Chris did the introductions. Mary and Katherine shook hands.

"I don't know if I made enough," Mary said. "Why didn't you tell me you were bringing someone?"

"I told you it was a surprise," Chris said.

"I'm okay, Mrs. Gallo," Katherine said. "I'm not very hungry."

"Come and sit and let's see if we can stretch it somehow."

Chris said, "She made enough for a small army, trust me."

They sat in the dining room. Katherine offered to help Mary. Mary insisted Katherine was a guest and should relax. Then Mary brought a large pan with a three-pound chicken surrounded by diced potatoes and carrots to the dining room table. There was also bacon draped over the chicken.

"I hope you cooked enough, Ma," Chris said. "Katherine's a lawyer and she's already sued me once."

"Stop that," Katherine said. "I didn't sue him, Mrs. Gallo. He crashed into my car."

Mary returned from the kitchen with a large pitcher of iced tea.

"He did what?"

Chris explained how they met a few years ago and that they'd been going steady until he went undercover.

"I didn't want to worry about him," Katherine said.

"I did that, honey," Mary said. "I did it enough for both of us. I still do it. How'd you catch up again?"

"He used FBI resources to track me down. I moved from Virginia, where I was living when we met, to New York when I took a job here."

"I see. And you two are going steady now?"

"Well, she is pregnant, Ma. Probably pregnant, I should say."

"Really?" Mary said, but it wasn't with any enthusiasm.

Katherine rolled her eyes before she slapped Chris's right arm.

"Ouch," Chris said. "That's the other thing, Ma. She likes to hit me."

"Now stop it," Katherine said.

"Are you joking or what?" Mary said.

"Yes, Ma. I'm breaking your shoes. And hers."

"How did you put up with him?" Katherine asked Mary.

"It wasn't easy," Mary said. "It still isn't."

The three laughed. It was the first time Mary seemed to ease up with her rival.

Katherine explained some of her background, mostly about her family and where she grew up, and how she decided to pursue law school.

"What about after you two broke up?" Mary said. "Chris didn't bother telling me about his new life in the FBI. Did you two stay in touch?"

"Actually, no," Chris cut in. "I was going undercover, Ma. We went over this a dozen times already. I couldn't let anyone know what I was doing, not what I'd become or the investigation I was involved in. Katherine couldn't know either."

"That must've been a lonely time for you," Mary said to Katherine.

Chris broke in again. "Not at all," he said. "She had a dozen or so boyfriends while I remained alone like a priest."

"He really is impossible," Katherine said. "I had two boyfriends, neither of them were serious relationships."

"I see," Mary said, but the unease was back.

They left soon after they finished eating. Mary said she hoped to see Katherine again. Chris gave his mother a hug and kiss, but before they were out the door, Mary said, "Are you going to your grandfather's now?"

"Not today, no."

"Oh, okay."

"Bye Mom."

"Yeah."

Back in Katherine's car, Chris said, "You catch that?"

"She didn't sound pleased. I think she hates me."

"Not yet she don't, but she might. You ever take up that offer and marry me, she'll definitely harbor some angst."

"Thanks for the encouragement."

"I'm joking, kind of, but I meant about visiting my grandfather. She's making it a competition and isn't satisfied you met her first. She's as competitive as she is possessive."

"Sorry," Katherine said.

"Wait until you really are pregnant," Chris said. "Then we'll never get rid of her."

• • • • •

When Special Agent in Charge, Ayes Ozdemir, knocked on Giovanni Rapino's apartment door, there were two other Special Agents behind him. Rapino was wearing gold sweatpants and a white wife beater T-shirt. He looked through the peephole and saw an FBI badge. He opened the door and spoke from there.

"Yes?"

"I'm Agent Ayes Ozdemir with the FBI," Ozdemir said. "Can we talk inside?"

Giovanni went up on his toes to see the two men behind Ozdemir. "What's it about?" he said.

"I'm not here to arrest you. Can we talk?"

Rapino gave it a moment. "Just you," he said. "They can wait there."

Ozdemir nodded and Rapino stepped back inside. When the door was closed, Ozdemir said, "I'm required by law to inform you of a threat against your life."

Rapino nodded and said, "From who?"

"Bruno and Vito Fontana."

"Who these people are?"

"You know who they are."

Rapino shrugged.

"The head of the Cirelli crime family's sons. The family you belong to."

Rapino smirked. "You have proof of this crime family?"

"Do you want to hear them discuss killing you or not."

Rapino shrugged again. "Sure, why not?"

Ozdemir removed a small recording device from his pants pocket. "Ready?"

Rapino smiled.

Ozdemir turned up the volume and replayed the conversation between Bruno and Vito Fontana. When it was finished, Ozdemir asked Rapino if he wanted to hear it again.

"No need," Rapino said. "I don't know these people."

"We're obligated by law to inform you about a threat against your life and now I've done so," Ozdemir said. "But I didn't tell you this so you can strike first."

"Strike first?"

"So you can kill them before they kill you."

"I'm not kill anybody."

"Right. If you do, we'll know you did. Or you can agree to testify against them, and we'll pick them up for conspiracy to commit murder."

Rapino remained silent.

"Why would you protect people looking to kill you?" Ozdemir said.

"Maybe they talk about somebody else," Rapino said. "Another with same name. I don't know these people."

"You do realize we'll be trying to protect you now. I hope you realize that."

"Protect me for what?"

"To make sure you aren't killed by Bruno and Vito Fontana and that you don't kill them."

"I says to you already I'm not kill anybody."

"Jesus Christ—fine. Play it your way. You've been informed about a threat against your life. You're refusing to cooperate and are fully aware you'll be getting protection whether you want it or not. We're obligated by law to do so and we'll do that. Have a nice day."

Ozdemir let himself out. Rapino stared at the door a full 30 seconds before moving to the window to watch them leave the building.

19

Mary Gallo let herself into the kitchen through the back door and stood in silence as Joseph plugged the electric cord from his Farberware coffee pot into the wall outlet above the drain board. Joseph didn't notice her until Artie Adler, reading the *Daily News* at the table, cleared his throat a few times.

"Oh boy," Joseph said as he turned and saw his daughter-in-law. "This is a surprise."

"He didn't tell you I was coming?" Mary said.

"Chris? No."

"Figures."

"Did he tell you?"

The two stared at one another. Adler felt uncomfortable and grabbed the newspaper, stood up and said, "I'm gonna read inside. Give you two a little time alone."

"Well, sit if you're gonna stay," Joseph said to Mary.

Mary took the seat at the head of the table nearest the back door.

"Coffee'll be ready in a few minutes," Joseph said.

"You change the sugar in that bowl yet?"

"Huh? Oh, no. I forgot."

Mary stood back up. "I'll do it," she said. "Where do you keep it, the sugar?"

"One of these cabinets. Let me look."

Joseph opened a few cabinet doors until he found the sugar. He grabbed the bag and handed it to Mary. She looked inside the bag and rolled her eyes.

"When'd you get this, your first communion?"

"I don't use sugar."

"Yeah, no shit?"

"Oy vey."

"You're Yiddish now?"

"He wishes," Adler said from the dining room.

Mary sat at the opposite head of the table from where she had sat earlier and asked for a knife. Joseph opened a cabinet drawer and grabbed a butter knife. He turned it so the handle was facing her.

"Don't tempt me," she said as she took the knife.

Joseph sighed.

Mary went about plunging the knife into the sugar to break it up. "It's all congealed. It's hard as a rock."

"Because I don't use it. Sugar doesn't spoil."

"No, but it's disgusting to have to break it up. You don't want that woman seeing you live like this."

"That woman?"

"Kate."

"Katherine?"

"Whatever."

"Jesus, don't tell me you've got a problem with her too now."

"Oh, shut up, you big horse."

Adler returned from the dining room. "This is too much fun to miss."

"You're the cop, aren't you?" Mary said to him.

"Retired, but yeah," Adler said. "Call him a horse again for me."

"He knows he's a horse."

"I do," Joseph said.

"What are you making for dinner or are you going to order pizzas?"

"Steaks. Steaks and burgers and franks. Didn't you notice the barbecue outside? You had to walk right past it."

"I didn't. I'm not a nosey person."

Joseph's brow went up. "I'll let that one go," he said.

Mary gave him the finger.

"Lovely," Joseph said.

"Should I be impressed you're actually cooking and not ordering pizza?"

"Yes," Adler said. "I was afraid it'd be bagels or pizza."

Joseph pointed at Mary. "You best be nice to Katherine today."

"Don't tell me how to act. Besides, I'm always nice."

"I'm not kidding, Mary. You can chase your son all over again, you give that woman grief."

"That woman?"

Joseph waived her off and said, "Why do I bother?"

Mary emptied the sugar that was in the bowl into the garbage. She replaced it with the sugar she'd broken up inside the bag. Then she said, "Just don't tell me what to do about my son."

"Fine. Ruin it yourself."

"She's a lawyer, for God sake."

"And that's a problem how?"

"Because he's at a disadvantage if it doesn't work out, for one thing. She's smart."

"So is Chris smart, and there are laws for divorce. It's not so easy to screw one another anymore. Not unless you're devious and hide money."

"Chris would never do that."

"And you assume Katherine would?"

"She's the lawyer."

Joseph turned to Adler. "You see what I'm dealing with here? She's worse than you."

"I like her," Adler said.

"I don't need you on my side," Mary said to Adler.

"Okay?" Joseph said to Adler.

"Don't okay me," Mary said, then turned to Adler. "Joseph thinks he knows everything. It wouldn't dawn on him to think a lawyer could screw somebody."

"Always think the worst, Mary," Joseph said. "That should be your nickname."

"And fat slob should be yours."

Adler clapped as he laughed.

● ● ● ● ●

Last night Rapino dreamed about his second cousin, Maria Theresa Costantini. It was the second time he'd dreamed about her since he returned from Italy. She was walking through the halls of a university, then the palazzo at Pizzoferrato, and then into and out of a church. Rapino felt himself following her but couldn't catch up. He watched her get into a small Italian sports car he didn't recognize. He called to her as the sports car headed down a hill and was out of sight.

Rapino took it as another sign that it was too late to change his life. Maria Theresa would serve as a reminder going forward. There was no redemption without a confession of his sins and not to some priest. He remembered what she'd said to him in the town where he was born.

"You can still do what you said you'd do for me," Maria Theresa had said. *"Maybe for the next woman in your life?"*

"What woman?" he'd thought at the time but said something else.

Now he was thinking about it again. What woman? What life? He'd been living a cat and mouse game with law enforcement the same way all *mafioso* lived. It was the same thing here in America or there in Italy, except here the offer to testify against others was more alluring than in Italy. At least it seemed so.

Now that he knew he'd become marked for death by the same people he'd killed for, by his mafia family, there was nothing to stop him from killing the federal agent without their help. In fact, there was nothing to stop him from making it a spectacle and leaving him in the street somewhere rather than in the Atlantic Ocean. He should be found, Rapino was thinking.

Afterward, if he wasn't killed or locked up by law enforcement, he'd go after Bruno and Vito and Aniello Fontana. If he was arrested, he'd give law enforcement everything they wanted, an act more of revenge than redemption. If he managed to escape, he wouldn't hesitate going after the Fontana brothers and their father.

Rapino headed to his gym where he paid for an extra locker for his equipment. He went through his regular circuit routine on the machines twice before showering. When he was dressed again and ready to leave, he waited until the locker room was clear, then removed a couple of handguns from his second locker.

He placed the Ruger EC9s® 9mm into his gym bag and wrapped it with a towel. He also had an older Beretta, the Nano, a pocket size 9mm. He wrapped it in a washcloth and set it alongside the Ruger. He left the gym and dropped his gym bag on the passenger seat before getting behind the wheel of his 2022 Navy blue Cutlass Oldsmobile. He spotted a gray car pulling away from the curb in his rearview mirror and decided to play a game of cat and mouse with the men tailing him. Rapino made two right turns, at 92nd Street and then onto 5th Avenue before turning right again onto 94th Street and finding a parking spot off the corner. He sat there as the gray Honda Accord sped past him, then slowed down. Rapino pulled up behind the Accord and leaned on his horn.

The Accord pulled up, then into a fire hydrant space. Rapino pulled up alongside them and waved at them to follow him.

Then he drove home.

• • • • •

They made love standing up against the island in the kitchen, then again on the couch. Afterward, Katherine said, "You get it out of your system?"

"I'm not sure," Chris said. "I'm not sure the Viagra worked. It's supposed to last four hours, right?"

"You're crazy, you know that?"

"A little. Come, let's get showered and dressed, and then head over to Grampa Gallo's place. I asked him to invite Artie Adler."

"He the ex-cop?"

"Yes, and a very good one at that. He's the one tracked me down."

"And your Mom? Will she be there?"

"I wouldn't bet against it."

"What should I wear?"

"Something makes their tongues hang out."

"Not if your mother will be there."

"Her tongue too."

They showered together, laughing when Chris mocked playing drop the soap. He teased her about the freckles and poked at a few on her upper thighs.

"Little Irish girl legs," he said each time he poked a freckle on her thighs. "Little Irish girl legs."

"Stop that, you nut."

"Turns me on, counselor."

"You're a lunatic," she said.

Chris finished showering first. Katherine turned the hot water up and remained under the spray a few minutes longer.

It was and wasn't a big day for him. Joseph was the last of his family Katherine would meet. If he felt they didn't accept Katherine, he'd disappear on them again. He was pretty sure his grandfather would be okay, but his mother was another story. She hadn't handled their lunch very well. He knew Katherine felt uncomfortable when they left.

He chose his faded dungarees, a clean T-shirt and a blue short-sleeve shirt. He slipped into his sneakers while Katherine dried herself off after her shower.

"You're not going to take an hour to dry your hair, I hope," he said.

"Never mind," she said. "Go pick up a cake or something."

"We'll get one on the way."

"You sure?"

"Positive."

When she was finished drying her hair, Katherine chose a beige shorts suit outfit with brown wedge sandals.

"How much you figure you spend on clothes a month?" he said.

"None of your business."

"Uh-oh, that means a lot."

"It means that it's none of your concern."

"So you are considering my proposal?"

"I'll consider it after we visit my family."

"Will they accept a Yankee in the family?"

"Some of them will, sure."

"And the ones that won't?"

"They're the ones with the most clout."

"Your parents, great."

"Oh, stop it already. You'll do fine. If you don't, I'll still drive you back to New York. I won't leave you stranded."

They left a few minutes later. Katherine drove while Chris changed the radio stations until he heard a saxophone he recognized and turned up the volume to Steely Dan's *Gaucho*.

"Oh, I like this too," Katherine said.

"It's a great album."

"You listen to music when you were undercover?"

"Never. Not until I was home alone. Didn't converse about it either. Those guys, they were either too stupid to engage or too on guard to reveal themselves."

"Are they really falling apart?"

"Can't say."

"Can't can't?"

"Huh? Oh, no. I have no idea. You'd think so with all the flipping they do on one another, but there are still some hard guys willing to do the time. Thing is, once they get out, if they did a long stretch, what are they coming back to? It's a very antiquated worldview. I don't think it can survive today. Not for much longer."

"Antiquated? I'm impressed."

"I can also fart to the national anthem."

Katherine rolled her eyes.

"Anyway, be prepared for some ball breaking," Chris said. "At my expense. My grandfather and his friend are naturals. It's all they do all day, I think, break each other's balls. They'll call it shoe breaking in front of you and my mother. Maybe."

"All men are like that, I think. My brothers certainly are."

"Then we'll get along famously."

"Are you kidding? They'll interrogate you about the mob all day and night. Especially my younger brother. He loves those mob movies."

"Then I'll lie to them. Make myself a hero."

"What do you think is going to happen now with the mob?"

"I don't know. I really don't. Now you have other gangs to worry about. The mob lost a lot of its clout. They don't have the influence they once had. And the other gangs are a lot more violent. Reckless too, I think. Then there're the right wing morons Trump gins up with his bullshit, the ones show up in Army gear with rifles and whatnot. Most of them I think are playacting. Getting their rocks making believe they're at war. They're stupid and not half as violent as they fantasize. Taking selfies while attacking the Capitol? Geniuses. Like he said, he likes 'the not so smart people.' The morons at the Capitol that day, they took pride in being used like that. Mostly, I think they're harmless dopes. Other gangs, some of the Hispanic, the Mexican gangs, they have zero regard for life. Those are the scary ones. Guys undercover in that world, down the border and whatnot, they're risking their lives. Those gangs don't have rules about whacking cops. The cartels may have them, but not the knuckleheads running the streets for them."

"It's still a scary world and I'm glad you'll be done with it."

"I gotta tell you, I'm not exactly thrilled about doing PI work for a law firm."

"It's a lot safer than what you were doing."

"A lot more boring too. I guess the upside is I won't have to make believe I wasn't part of a double murder. That wore on me pretty good until my supervisor in charge explained how easy it was for the bureau to ignore the facts. Jesus, the doublespeak was a turn off."

"I hate to disappoint you, but you're going to find ethical challengers working for a law firm too. Firms are about winning. None of them much care how. One case to the next, it's a vicious cycle. We take on all comers, even when they're horrible people acting purely from greed. Even when their claims are bogus. We take any case with a retainer and even more without one."

"Thanks for that pep talk."

"At least you'll come home nights."

"Yeah, so now that I'm quitting and I'll come home nights and be safe and shit, we can announce, right? Everybody'll be there."

"Georgia first, Special Agent, crazy man. You'll have to meet my people."

"And, like, what? Make Georgia great again?"

"Please. Georgia is getting more blue, but it's still mostly shit-kicking country. I think it was Trump who lost those last few elections there. My father blames Trump. He hates that Skankie Yankie, what he calls him. Not that he'd vote for a Democrat, because he didn't. Lots of Georgians didn't vote for president at all. It was mostly down ballot they voted for."

"Why Trump lost."

"Not according to Trump."

"Yeah, fuck him too. Maybe if we live down there someday, we can make Georgia blue for real. Have a dozen or so kids and raise them as anarchists."

"You're poking fun at my home state."

"While I'm thinking about the wedding night, picturing you in one of those white seductive outfits you see in magazines. I'm big on the garter thing. My favorite movies when I was a kid were the vampire movies where the women vampires all wore garters and the body things."

"Corsets?"

"Yeah. You'll wear that stuff, right?"

"Not until after you pass the family interrogation in Georgia."

Chris spotted a delicatessen on the corner and pointed to it. "Stop there," he said. "They'll have cake."

"That's not a bakery," Katherine said.

"In Brooklyn, any place that carries Entenmann's is a bakery. Park there."

● ● ● ● ●

He'd asked for a black escort because he'd never been with a black woman before. He had specific instruction.

"I want black, eh?" Rapino told the woman handling his call. "Black woman. Dark. Very dark. Tall and thin."

"We can do that for you," the woman said. "Do you prefer an escort with large breasts, normal or small?"

"Tits I don't care. Small, normal. I don't care."

"And how long would you want her for? There's a ninety minute minimum."

"Ninety is good."

"That would be nine hundred dollars."

"Okay."

He gave his credit card information and rolled a joint. Rapino felt the end was near and wanted to enjoy himself before it came. He lit the joint and inhaled deeply. He waited until he felt a buzz, then slowly, with several interruptions in his head he couldn't place, thought about how he would move forward later in the day.

He'd start with the agent, Charlie Mazza. He'd have something to say to Charlie before shooting him. He'd also do his best not to shoot anyone else. He'd need the extra ammunition for the Fontana brothers. He'd go from Mazza to the Fontana brothers and then their father. If he made it through them, he'd let the daughter go. He wouldn't kill a woman unless it was self-defense. The Fontana's had already blown letting him kill Doris Montalvo. Because she had talked to the FBI, it would've been a piece of work he would've handled without regret.

If he walked into Angela Fontana and she wasn't holding a gun on him was different. She'd get a pass.

Before he could continue his thoughts, the escort service called him back with the name of the woman who'd be coming to his apartment. "She's just what you asked for and her name is Tanya."

"Thank you," Rapino said.

"You're welcome. Let us know—"

Rapino ended the call.

He returned to his chair and took another sip of the vodka. He started to think about the people he wanted to kill again but was interrupted with another thought: *How would he get out of his apartment building?*

First, he'd have to avoid the FBI team parked in front of the building. He'd have to do that from the basement door leading to the garages behind the building. Next he'd take his chances and hop a fence and head out at 57th Street. He'd call before leaving and have an Uber waiting for him on 57th Street.

If the FBI was there, he'd have a tail to where he'd kill Charlie Mazza. In that case he'd have to make it quick, assuming the federal agent was in his grandfather's house. If he wasn't there, Rapino could stop at a Carvel someplace and offer to buy the tailing agents a cone or something before he headed home to wait another day.

Then he'd pick up another car somewhere. It's not like he didn't know how.

He poured a vodka on the rocks, sipped some, and then ran his escape in his head a few more times before the combination of the marijuana and booze took control. The buzz he'd attained with the weed and alcohol was putting him to sleep until his door buzzer woke him.

Rapino went to the kitchen area and pressed an intercom button.

"Hello?" he said.

"It's Tanya."

"Come up," he said. "Apartment 4-B."

He pressed the buzzer to unlock the vestibule door and then went to his apartment door to look through the peephole to make sure she was alone. He could see her when she reached the top of the stairs. He opened the door and liked what he saw. Tanya, or whatever her real name was, wore a light green tube dress that clung to her tall and slender body. Her chest was small, but her nipples were perky beneath the material. She had long legs and wore a pair of wedged sandals. A black leather bag was slung over her right shoulder.

"*Bella*," Rapino said.

"Thank you," she said. "Michael is it?"

"No, but is not important. You're FBI?"

Tanya smiled. "Excuse me?"

"You a cop?"

"Seriously?" she said. "Of course not. No."

"Okay, good. Come inside."

She did so. When he closed and locked the door, she said, "Can I have a drink?"

20

Joseph and Adler and Mary were all sitting in the dining room with glasses of lemonade and soda when Chris and Katherine entered through the back door and then the kitchen. They all stood up to say hello. Chris handed Adler two boxes of Entenmann's cakes. Adler turned the boxes to one side and smiled at the sticker.

"Joseph, look, two for six bucks," he said as he held the two boxes of cake up. "He's sharp, your grandson. Last of the big time spenders."

"He's a cheap fuck is what he is," Joseph said. "I'll bet they're both cakes he likes."

Chris turned to Katherine and said, "See what I mean?"

"What's with the back entrance?" Joseph said.

"You never lock it, for one thing," Chris said. "And this way nobody had to get up to answer the door." He turned to Katherine again. "He won't stop now that he started."

"Leave the girl alone," Joseph said as he winked at Katherine. "You are beautiful, Katherine. So, our question is, what the hell do you see in this little shit?"

"Don't you call my son names," Mary said. "Hi, hon," she said to Katherine.

"Come sit here, Katherine," Joseph said. "Next to me."

The table was oblong with space for six chairs, two on each side and the two heads. Mary sat alongside her son on one side. Joseph sat at the head nearest the kitchen. Katherine and Adler sat alongside one another opposite Mary and Chris.

Joseph wanted to hear how they met. Chris told most of the story before Katherine took over. Then Adler said, "You mean to tell me you chose the FBI over this gorgeous woman?"

"He was choosing a career," Mary said.

"What career?" Adler said. "This woman or the farkakte FBI?"

"Watch your language, you," Mary said.

"What does that mean?" Katherine whispered to Chris.

Joseph heard her and said, "Ridiculous. Stupid. Insane."

"What?" Mary said.

Chris waived her off. "Nothing, Ma. I'm moving in with Katherine this weekend."

Mary's eyes opened wide.

"Don't worry, Mary," Katherine said. "If he doesn't do his own laundry, I'll kick him out."

Joseph looked to Adler and said, "Uh-oh."

"Never you mind, Joseph," Mary said. "What do I care where he lives? It's not like he lets me know anything."

"I just told you, Ma. Relax."

"Not to worry," Adler said, "he gets lost again, I'll find him again."

"Yeah, I forgot to thank you for that," Chris said. "Almost getting me killed."

"What?" Mary said.

Adler waived him off. "They don't kill agents anymore."

"What are you two talking about, killed?" Mary said.

Chris said, "They're breaking balls. I mean shoes, Ma. Relax."

"Stop telling me to relax, damn it."

"Oy vey," Joseph said.

"You shut up!" Mary said.

"I didn't say anything."

"Yes, you did."

"It's an expression, Mary," Adler said. "It's Yiddish."

"Yiddish shmiddish," Mary said. "I don't like it when he thinks he's a smartass."

There was a moment of silence before everyone at the table broke out laughing, including Mary.

• • • • •

Rapino took the Uber he'd called to 4th Avenue and 95th Street. He paid the driver and walked along the avenue carrying his bookbag in his right hand until he spotted a white Honda CV idling in a driveway. The trunk was open. A short stack of folding chairs were in the trunk. Rapino looked both ways, then slammed the trunk shut, sat behind the wheel and took off.

He found a spot a few houses from the Gallo address on Seaview Avenue in Canarsie. It was midafternoon, and the park across the street was still crowded around a basketball game going on in the playground area. Dog walkers were also out and strolling along the outer fence of the park.

Rapino had planned on walking up to the front door and ringing the doorbell or knocking. He'd have the Ruger in hand when someone answered the door. If it was Mazza, he might shoot him there and then. If Mazza wasn't there and it was the old man who answered the door, he'd go inside and force the geezer to call his grandson. If it was anyone else that answered the door, Rapino wasn't sure how he'd handle it.

He could also wait a few minutes to see if someone stepped outside. He could force them back inside the house if they did.

He decided his car was too exposed on the avenue and decided to find a better spot to park. He made a U-turn at 89th Street and crossed over to the other side of the avenue, then drove through the first traffic light to 95th Street and turned right. He took 95th Street to St. Jude Place until it became Skidmore Avenue. He went one block alongside the St. Jude Catholic School and turned right onto 93rd Street. Seaview Avenue was one block straight ahead at the traffic light.

The street was a one way and was shaded by several trees on both sides. Rapino parked close to the corner of Seaview Avenue on the left side of the street under the thick branches of a large American elm tree.

He was about to get out of the car when someone knocked on his passenger side window. Rapino turned toward the knock and saw a gun, then a woman he didn't know holding it. She wore black dungarees and a white blouse. He was confused when the door opened and she sat in the passenger seat while holding what looked like a .380 on him. When she reached behind her to shut the passenger door, the handgun turned enough for him to see it was a Smith & Wesson.

He wasn't sure what it was about, but if she was there to kill him, she was clearly close enough to do so.

"Giovanni," she said.

"Who you are?" Rapino said.

"Angela."

"Angela who?"

"Angela Fontana."

Rapino sighed. "I see," he said. "The daughter."

"The daughter."

"The Fontana men are leaving it to their women now?"

"Woman. Singular. I'm the only woman here."

Rapino checked the rearview mirror and saw a group of kids heading their way.

"You're going to shoot me here?"

Angela said, "Why are you here?"

"Me? To kill an agent can testify against me." He motioned toward his left with his head. "He's over there. In a house over there. Other side of the avenue. Why are you here if you don't kill me?"

"I know where he lives. I know where you live too."

"You follows me?"

She nodded.

Rapino suddenly realized who she was. "You're the one takes the pictures of the agent and the old man, the fat guy."

"That's me."

"And your brother, Vito, when he gets his ass kicked by the same agent. You take those pictures too?"

"Me again."

"And now you are killer?"

"You were told not to go after him."

"No, that changed. You don't speak to your brothers?"

"I speak to my father. He's the boss of the family."

"Vito wants this. Bruno agreed, in case you don't know."

Angela paused a moment. "I don't know. It's not what my father wants."

"So, why you have gun?"

"To keep you from killing a federal agent."

"How you know he's here?"

"I don't. I followed you. If you went for coffee, I would've stayed in my car."

"Your father sends you?"

"No."

"Brothers?"

"No."

Rapino shrugged. "I don't understand."

"Sure you do," Angela said. "If you kill a federal agent they will turn the world upside down. If they catch you, you will talk and give everybody up. Or there'd be no avoiding giving you up."

"You mean killing me."

"Definitely."

"So, you do this now, just in case?"

"If I have to, yes."

"Okay, but—"

He grabbed at the gun a moment before she fired. The bullet missed and struck his headrest. He managed to hold onto her right hand and push it up before the second shot went through the roof. She showed teeth as she tried to rake his face with her free hand, but he brought her hand with the gun down forcibly against her right temple. She was stunned enough for him to take the gun from her hand. Then he punched hard at her head again with the heel of the weapon's frame and knocked her unconscious.

Rapino turned to see where the group of kids he'd spotted earlier were. They weren't there. He looked in the driver's side mirror and saw they were using a milk box to climb over the

park fence. He did a quick glance up and down the street using
the mirrors and saw it was safe. Then he tore a sleeve off her
blouse and used it to tie her hands behind her back. He tore the
other sleeve off and tied her ankles together.

He searched the glove compartment for something to gag her
with and found a rag torn from what appeared to be Fruit of the
Loom underwear. He wrapped it around her head and then
covered her mouth. He tied a knot with the rag behind her
head, and then he shoved her down onto the floor of the car. He
removed the magazine without clearing the round in the
chamber and then shoved her gun under the passenger's seat.
He pocketed the magazine, then removed her key fob from her
left pants pocket. Her restraints weren't very secure, but it
would have to make do. He didn't have time to do a better job.

He looked both ways from inside the car before he opened
his door and stepped out. He did another double take on the
street, then headed for the Avenue and got out of there.

• • • • •

His company was eating salad and conversing in the dining
room. Joseph was in his backyard cooking steaks, hamburgers
and franks on the barbecue. Adler stood at the doorway to the
pantry and asked if he needed help.

"My pot," Joseph said.

Adler's brow furrowed. "No way," he said. "Be reasonable."

"I'm out here, nobody can see. Come on, or I have to piss
against a wall. Get my pot."

Adler frowned as he shook his head in disgust. He headed
inside to retrieve the pot, then passed it off to Joseph when he
returned to the doorway.

"Watch the door," Joseph said.

Adler huffed. "Seriously?"

"Just watch the door."

Joseph went to a corner of the yard alongside the house and
did his thing. When he finished, rather than spill the urine in
the yard, he brought the pot to a table and covered it with an
old Frisbee.

"You done?" Adler said.

"Franks and burgers are ready. Come get them and bring
them inside. Buns are on the kitchen table. Steaks'll be done in
another minute."

Adler came down to the grill and used a big fork to move the burgers and franks to the serving plate Joseph had set on the picnic table.

"Your daughter-in-law is drunk," he said as Joseph tended to the steaks.

"Then I'm better off out here."

"I can take over if you want."

"Yeah, right. Bring that shit inside. I'll be another couple of minutes. Maybe hours."

• • • • •

He looked over his shoulder twice before crossing Seaview Avenue and heading to the house where the federal agent's grandfather lived. Rapino could see smoke coming from the backyard.

"*Bene,*" he said. "*Ho fame.* Fuckin' starving."

He'd have to use another car to get out of Brooklyn once the deed was done. If Angela Fontana broke free from her restraints, or if somebody heard her in the car and helped her get out, she'd come looking for him. It was good he kept the magazine from her .380.

Meanwhile, Rapino knew he was going to have to work fast in case she did free herself.

He approached the front door with his hand inside his right pants pocket on the Beretta Nano. He rang the bell and waited. When the front door opened, it was an older guy, but not the grandfather. The older guy opened the screen door and seemed to recognize Rapino. He said, "What do you want?"

It was then Rapino pulled the Nano out of his pocket. "Inside," he said.

"Fuck you," the old man said.

Rapino shot him in the left shoulder, then shoved him, knocking him to the ground. He stepped inside the house and turned to his left where the dining room was crowded with people sitting around a table. The conversations that had been going on in the dining room stopped as everyone turned toward the sound and sight of Artie Adler falling to the floor.

Then they saw the gunman.

"Jesus Christ!" Mary Gallo yelled.

Chris Gallo was up out of his chair. He moved away from those sitting at the table in case Rapino started shooting.

"There you are," Rapino said when he saw Charlie Mazza.

"Leave everyone else alone," Chris said.

"Maybe. What's your real name? I know it's no Charlie Mazza."

Rapino put a foot on Artie Adler's back to keep him in place.

"Can I look at him?" Chris said.

"Your name first," Rapino said.

"Chris."

"*Pezzo di merda.*"

Chris pointed to Adler.

"Not yet," Rapino said. "Later." He motioned at Katherine with his gun. "She your wife, the redhead?"

Chris felt his teeth clenching.

"Don't worry, I don't come here for her."

Chris was calculating the odds of rushing Rapino and still surviving. It was fine if the killer was there for him, but he'd have no guarantees what Rapino might do afterward.

He pointed at Adler again.

"Never mind this old man," Rapino said. "Where's the fat one?"

"Outside cooking," Mary said. "Why don't you leave us alone?"

"Ma, don't," Chris said.

"Your mother?" Rapino said.

Mary turned on her chair. "Yes, I'm his mother. What do you want from us?"

"Ma, please," Chris said, louder this time. "I'll handle this."

"What you're going to handle, mister agent? I have gun. You have hamburgers."

Rapino removed his foot from Adler's back. The old man swung his arm out to try and trip Rapino, but then the killer fired a shot into the back of Adler's right leg and everyone at the table gasped, except for Chris. He hadn't moved.

"Stupid'a fuck," Rapino said to Adler. "Now stay."

"Chris?" Katherine said. Her eyes were wet with tears.

"It's okay," he told her. "He's only here for me." He turned to Rapino and said, "Can we do this outside?"

"No. Too much trouble. We do it here."

"Do what here?" Mary said. "God damn it, you leave my son alone."

"Shut up, old lady," Rapino said. "You give me headache."

Artie Adler managed to get up off the floor and charge Rapino. He made it a few feet before falling to the carpet. Both women screamed as the killer turned toward Adler.

• • • • •

Joseph had started to bring his pot into the kitchen to clean it
when he heard the pistol shot. He moved to the refrigerator and
braced himself against its side. He was out of view from the
dining room when he heard a second shot. Then he heard the
women scream and he stepped into the doorway, his pot half-
filled with urine.

He saw the gunman turning toward the living room and
yelled, "Freeze!"

The gunman turned back toward the command and Joseph
tossed his urine into the gunman's face. Then there was
another shot fired, the bullet missing Joseph. Chris had moved
up close enough to grab the gunman's hand holding the gun.
Chris used his shoulder to drive the gunman into the China
bureau and then tackle him to the floor. Joseph stepped on the
gunman's hand holding the gun. He shifted his weight onto one
leg and the gun dropped from the gunman's hand. Then Joseph
slapped his pot off the gunman's forehead a few times.

"Call an ambulance for Artie," Chris said as he leaned a
knee into the back of Rapino's neck.

Katherine already had her cellphone out and was getting
Joseph's address from Mary. Joseph and Mary went to Adler
and applied pressure to the bullet wound in the back of his
thigh.

The gunman was reaching behind his back for his Ruger, but
Chris had already removed it. He'd pulled his own weapon from
an ankle holster and put it under Rapino's chin. "Keep reaching
for that gun in the back of your pants and I'll blow your head
off," he said.

Then the front door opened and a woman holding a gun was
taking a firing stance at them.

• • • • •

There wasn't time to think about what to do next. Chris was hit
in his left thigh as he drew on the woman. His legs buckled as
he fired his weapon a split second after she tried to fire a second
shot. Her weapon didn't fire. As she turned her eyes toward the
missing magazine in her weapon a bullet entered her throat.
She staggered backward a few steps before falling back onto the
couch. She was gurgling blood and struggling to try and stand
again. Chris's single shot had struck her just below her chin.

Rapino used the opportunity to try to reach for Chris's weapon. He crawled onto Chris's legs and punched at the wound in Chris's thigh. He reached for the Glock in Chris's right hand as Mary grabbed the serving tray with the franks and burgers and slammed it against the back of Rapino's head. She did it again and again and would've hit him a third time had her son not stopped her.

Mary made sure Chris wasn't spouting blood from his thigh, then used his belt to make a tourniquet anyway. Joseph had relieved Katherine and was applying pressure to Adler's thigh wound while Adler held a towel against his shoulder wound. Katherine was standing alongside Mary and Chris. When the tourniquet was secured, Mary gave way for Katherine.

Chris was on his cellphone speaking to his Supervise in Charge, Ayez Ozdemir. "I have Giovanni Rapino here. He just shot up my grandfather's house. Come get him if you want him. Or before I kill him."

Then Chris ended the call and apologized to his fiancé.

The sirens could be heard two minutes later. Police and two EMS wagons arrived within 10 minutes of Katherine's emergency call.

21

Angela Fontana died in an EMS wagon during the ride to Brookdale Hospital. Chris and Adler were treated for gunshot wounds at Brookdale's emergency room. Fortunate their wounds didn't involve their superficial femoral arteries, they would still have to spend at least one night at the hospital. Giovanni Rapino was brought to Brookdale Hospital Medical Center where he was treated for superficial wounds before being taken to the Metropolitan Correctional Center. He spent the next several hours in an observation cell by himself. FBI Special Agent in Charge, Ayez Ozdemir, and the Assistant U.S. Attorney for the Southern District of New York, George Nimitz, arrived later the same night. Two MCC correction officers stood outside the cell as Nimitz and Ozdemir questioned Rapino.

Folding chairs and a small portable table were brought inside the cell. Before questioning began, Nimitz handed Rapino an envelope addressed to his Brooklyn address from Italy.

"You read, eh?" Rapino said.

Nimitz didn't answer. He pointed to a recording device he'd placed on the portable table.

Rapino held the envelope up and said, "I read later. Now, I want deal."

"I'll bet you do," Nimitz said. "Right now you're probably going to jail for a very long time."

Rapino pointed at Ozdemir. "He tells me about Fontana brothers going to kill me. Instead they send sister. Now I want deal."

"Do you want a lawyer present?" Nimitz said.

"Fuck lawyer. I don't need."

"You're sure?"

"Yes, fuck lawyer. What you want to know?"

"You'll have to tell us everything if you really want a deal. You understand that?"

"I understand."

"Everything means everything, Mr. Rapino. Eventually we'll want to know everything you've been involved with from the time you ran with your Uncle and three cousins."

"I say I understand."

"For now we'll want specifics for the last two months, starting who killed Eddie Russo and his mother on Staten Island."

"Me. I did this."

"At the behest of?"

"Behest? Who tells me to do this? Message from the boss, Fontana. He sends his lawyer, Frank Cusmano. He doesn't want to say the words, but I make him. He tells me to kill Eddie Russo. He says we have to honor Carmine Montalvo's demand to kill the man who fucked his wife."

"And you went to Staten Island with our undercover agent, known to you as Charlie Mazza?"

"Charlie fucking Mazza, yes. Not his real name. He doesn't know why we're there. I don't tell him."

"Were you involved with Montalvo's wife?"

"Involved to mean fucking her? Me, Galante, this kid I kill, Eddie Russo. She liked to fuck, eh?"

"Speaking of Galante. Who—"

"Me and the brothers, Vito and Bruno. We go to boat in Jersey, take him to meeting, he thinks, with their father. We drug him and put in bag with weights. We push him off the boat."

"Also on orders from Aniello Fontana?"

"*Si*. He wants to restore old ways. Old rules. Is bullshit, but we do what he says."

"There were murders in the building where you live in Brooklyn. Asian men were killed in another apartment. Do you know anything about that?"

"Nothing."

"You're sure?"

"Nothing. I know nothing about it."

"Angela Fontana. What's the story with her and you? What was she doing in that house?"

"Crazy bitch thinks she's *soldato*. *Soldatessa* for woman. She follows people for her brother and father. Takes pictures. She takes pictures of your boy, Charlie Mazza. How we learn he's agent."

"And how did she wind up in that house?"

"She follows me to near his house, where I park. I don't see her. She has gun, I take it from her. She comes to house later and shoots, but she is shot. I don't know if she is sent by her father or not. She said no."

"Is there anything else we should know? Do you know anything about the murder of Morris Greenblatt?"

"Is me. I go to North Dakota and stab him. This from Vito Fontana, he says from his father. I get credit cards, cash and identification from him."

"You flew to North Dakota for that hit?"

"Yes."

"And you stabbed Greenblatt. The coroner report said his cause of death came from being smothered."

"I smother him after I stab."

"Jesus," Ozdemir said. "And the Internal Affairs cop on the island? Him and Nucci. Was that you too? I fucking hope not."

"This was no me. This was Galante. Had to be boss who gives order. Nucci was underboss."

"You have a wealth of knowledge about this crime family."

"No call it crime family. Call it fuckup operation. Old man lives in ancient times with bullshit rules. Who gets daughter involved in this shit, she's following people with camera? Comes to me with gun. She's dead now, no?"

"She is. Like I said, we'll be having a much deeper discussion about the other people you've killed. You earned your stripes as a hit man and that wasn't yesterday. We'll want to know all of it."

"Or all you have is me on tape? Too bad. I don't testify without deal."

"Like I said, we'll have further discussions about it."

"Fucking Fontana, he deserves what he feels now for his daughter. He goes to claim body?"

"He'll be arrested if he does. Otherwise he'll be arrested in a few hours."

"Stupid fucking people. How you respect stupid fucking people?"

There were a few more questions before Ozdemir ended the session. Rapino waited for the federal agents to leave the cell before he opened the letter from Maria Theresa. He tried to tell if the envelope had been unsealed. He wasn't sure, then ripped the envelop open and whispered as he read it to himself.

Cugino, we all hope this letter finds you healthy and in good spirits, and ready to begin a new life free of the mafia and all crime.

Some bad news. Augusto was killed two weeks ago. Something to do with revenge. Alfredo said Augusto will be

*avenged soon. More killing. I
don't understand this. Why?
His body will be interred where
your parents are entombed, the
same cemetery in Pizzoferrato.
Meanwhile, his mother has lost
her mind over her son's
murder. So much killing. For
what?*

*I don't pray because I'm an
atheist, but I do desire the best
for you and a life away from
cosa nostra crime.*

*Maria Theresa, Alfredo and
Rafael.*

Rapino folded the letter, put it back in the envelope, folded the envelope and slipped it inside his right sock.

• • • • •

Doris Montalvo, was watching CNN from the condo she'd rented in Las Cruces, New Mexico when she saw there was a big mob bust on the east coast. She considered the condo a one-week test drive, but if she liked the development enough and if it was close to the way it was advertised, she'd make the $300,000 purchase and move from Brooklyn immediately.

She'd been in the condo three days and had already dated one of the salespersons, a thirty-four-year old Mexican-American, Rodrigo Sanchez. Last night he'd told his wife he was playing cards and had slept over. Now he was bringing Doris a fresh cup of coffee from the kitchen while she pointed at the television.

"What's that?" Rodrigo said.

"I know some of those people," she said. "I mean I know who they are."

Rodrigo set her coffee cup on a snack tray alongside her recliner and took a seat in the recliner alongside hers. He stared at the television as a parade of men in a looped belly chain were led into the Metropolitan Correctional Center in downtown Manhattan.

He said, "Those are mob guys, right?"

"Every one of them," she said. "I was married to one of them. Not one of them, but another guy. He's dead now."

"Dead how?"

"Killed in prison. What they told me. I really don't know or care. He was an asshole."

"That's crazy."

"It was crazy. Not anymore."

"So, I slept with a notorious mafia woman?"

"You had sex with a former mafia woman. I'm nobody's wife now and don't intend to ever be one again. And next time, don't drink so much so you can go home to your wife. I've grown partial to sleeping alone."

"Okay, but this is really crazy, Doris. I can't believe you were married to a mafia guy."

"Just remember not to tell you friends, Rodrigo. You tell them, I tell your wife."

"Hell no, I wouldn't tell anybody."

"I hope not, because you seem like a nice enough guy, and this can be an ongoing thing if you're smart."

"Damn, woman. You don't trust me?"

"Not as far as I can throw you. And remember what I said about your wife."

Rodrigo crossed his chest. "Swear to God," he said.

"I've seen that routine before. I've also seen men get excited about being with a mob wife. The last one was killed by mobsters who didn't take kindly to it. Guys like on the television."

Rodrigo sat back, his hands held up high. "Okay," he said. "I get it. No problem. I'm cool."

"Good," Doris said.

• • • • •

Mei-Ling and Li-Jie found jobs on the Spanish island of Ibiza as waitresses in a Mediterranean restaurant one block from *Passeig de Ponent*, a walkway along the coast. They'd stayed at a local hostel for two days before finding an affordable apartment not far from their job.

They continued to sleep together on a single mattress and occasionally took care of one another sexually. Neither believed themselves a committed lesbian, although they had shared their bed with another waitress where they worked for their first female threesome.

Thus far they hadn't contacted anyone in their families because they couldn't trust the consequence of making such a connection. Neither knew about Ming Tao and his cohort being killed in their apartment back in Brooklyn. They were both committed to never looking back.

They had the money they'd saved plus the money they'd stolen from Giovanni Rapino, the Italian gangster they had sometimes serviced sexually.

Both women believed that the horrors of their past were over and done with, and that their futures were free and clear of the crimes they'd been subjected to live with. They had committed to never prostituting themselves or stealing again.

They were determined to open their own restaurant someday.

•   •   •   •   •

Officer Sharon Kwan was arrested by undercover Korean officers working a sting operation against police shakedowns in the Astoria section of Queens. Neither spoke as they awaited transportation to their precinct.

The arresting Internal Affairs undercover officer, Min Joon, offered Officer Kwan a bottled water.

"Thanks," she said.

"You should've taken the deal Stone offered," Joon said.

"Fuck Stone. I'm glad he's dead."

"He wouldn't have arrested you. I had no choice."

"You had a choice when you joined the rat squad."

"And you had one when you started taking money from shop owners."

"You'll have to prove that one."

"Your partner already gave you up. It's why he's been out the last two days."

Kwan's face turned red.

"That's right, he flipped soon as we showed him a few videos and he was introduced to the shop owner working undercover. I'm afraid your best chance is to plead guilty, but your lawyer can work that out for you."

"Fuck you, rat."

"Hold onto that attitude," Joon said with a smile. "You're going to need it on Rikers."

• • • • •

Assistant U.S. attorney for the Southern District of New York, George Nimitz, was gloating when Aniello Fontana and his lawyer, Frank Cusmano, were seated at the conference table in the office building at 1 St. Andrews Plaza. A video camera on a tripod faced Fontana and Cusmano.

"Of course, you know this session will be recorded," Nimitz said.

There were three agents in the conference room. Another attorney sat at the head of the table away from the attorney and his client.

A pitcher of water had already been set on a large doily to the left of Cusmano. Individual glasses were spread around the table. Cusmano reached for the pitcher, then poured a glass for himself and his client. Aniello Fontana stared down at his hands resting on his lap.

"So," Nimitz said, "I'm going to assume you don't know about the deal Eugene Carneglia made with our office. We haven't released word about it yet."

Fontana looked up.

"Yes, Aniello," Nimitz said. "Eugene cut a deal to give up his boss, who was the person who put the hit on your two sons."

"What hit?" Fontana said.

"Carneglia was not meeting your sons to discuss anything. He was there to kill them."

Fontana turned to Cusmano.

"We're not really interested in anyone else's situation but Mr. Fontana's," Cusmano said. "This man just lost his daughter."

"Make a proffer, counselor, and make it good. We already have your client on several murders he ordered. Some that didn't pan out but were discussed on tape. The targets of those are all cooperating. He's going to die in a federal prison."

"I'll remind you my client just lost his daughter."

"I'm sorry for his loss. The fact is she had forced her way into a residence in Brooklyn and started shooting. Somebody shot back."

"One of yours."

"One of the FBI's."

"He's a fuckin' dead man," Fontana said.

"He doesn't mean that," Cusmano said. "He's upset."

"Fuck upset. He's toast."

"Aniello, please," Cusmano said, then turned to Nimitz. "You can't hold that against him. He just—"

"Lost his daughter," Nimitz said. "Yeah, you said. Although threatening a federal agent isn't something we take lightly here. It's a big deal."

"Fuck you," Fontana said.

"I'm not sure this is productive," Cusmano said.

"So far it's been a blast," Nimitz said. "Does your client want a deal or does he want to die in jail?"

"Fuck you and your mother," Fontana said. "He started to stand up but was quickly restrained by an agent standing behind him."

"I'll take that as a no, you don't want a deal," Nimitz said.

"My client isn't interested in ratting anyone out," Cusmano said.

"What about his sons? They're both in MCC on a plot to commit murder, among other things. Maybe your client wants to help them out. I mean, they are his sons. Or maybe we should have them brought in to see what they might prefer to twenty-five to life. Before you tell me they just lost a sister, let me be frank and say I don't give a flying fuck. Okay?"

"You motherfucker," Fontana said.

"You talk like you can order another hit, Aniello. You can't. You're fucked. Your entire organization is fucked. Somebody else will grab the reigns, no doubt, but your reign is over. Nobody's gonna kiss your ring anymore, my friend. You're going to jail for life. You're going to die there. All I can do is make your last years a little more comfortable than it will be otherwise. If you don't want to talk, so be it. No skin off my balls. Just nailing you and your punk sons gets my face splashed all over the news. Shame you didn't smile during your perp walk. CNN was there filming it."

"That's enough," Cusmano said.

Nimitz ignored Cusmano. "Your sons can make their own deals," he said. "Or they can choose prison for a long vacation. I could care less. We got you, pal. You and your sons are toast. Burned toast."

Fontana turned to his lawyer. "Come, out of this fucking place."

Cusmano frowned at Nimitz. "Was that really necessary?"

"Please, what this murderous asshole is guilty of? Fuck him."

Aniello glared at Nimitz as he was led to the door. Cusmano frowned at Nimitz.

Nimitz said, "Have a nice day."

22

Joseph was holding his stomach when he walked into Artie Adler's living room. Adler was slumped on his couch, his bandaged leg raised on a thick pillow. It was the day after Adler returned home from the hospital. He wore a sling and a bandage around his thigh where he'd been shot. Joseph was holding a fresh bag of bagels. He'd also brought orange juice and cream cheese.

Joseph sat in an armchair facing Adler's couch and said, "Don't you look pathetic."

Adler flipped him the bird.

"I guess I'll have to set your table now," Joseph said. "You can't get off your *keister* to come to my place, it's on me now."

Adler pointed at Joseph and said, "Yeah? Well don't even think about pissing in my sink, pal. I took a couple bullets for you, it's the least you can do is use the toilet."

"You took two bullets because you're a putz," Joseph said. "Besides, you have a bathroom on this floor, you moron. Why would I need to piss in a pot or your stupid sink?"

Joseph removed the bagels, cream cheese, and orange juice from the bag. He looked at Adler and said, "Now I gotta get the knives and forks too? You're pretty fuckin' useless, you know that?"

Adler used his remote to turn the television on. Joseph was smiling as he made his way to the kitchen and could hear the volume being raised.

"What a putz," he said.

He took two dishes from one cabinet, knives and forks from a drawer, and then grabbed the coffee pot, two doilies and one cup. He walked them back into the living room and cringed at the volume of the television. Adler muted the sound.

"What?" he said.

"I didn't say nothing," Joseph said. "But thank you for lowering that stupid thing."

Adler noticed there was only one cup and frowned at Joseph. He said, "What are you gonna drink from, your hands?"

Joseph removed a new coffee mug from the bag with the bagels. It read: *Get off my lawn!*

"Chris and Katherine got it for me," he said. "Nice, huh?"

"It should'a said moron."

Joseph laughed.

"Can you pour me a cup?" Adler said. "Or I'm supposed to sit here and think about how it tastes?"

Joseph poured Adler a cup of coffee, then poured one for himself.

"Fetch me an onion while your fat ass is up," Adler said. "You bring the scallion cream cheese or the other shit?"

"The scallion," Joseph said. "And the other shit."

Joseph split a bagel and smeared scallion cream cheese on one side. He looked up at Adler and said, "More?"

"Little more."

Joseph added more cream cheese to Adler's bagel. He looked up again and Adler nodded. Joseph put it on a plate and brought it to Adler.

"Here, you can thank me later," he said.

"How're they doing, Chris and Katherine?" Adler said. "Think she'll stick around after what happened?"

Joseph returned to the armchair and sat. "So far so good, far as I can tell," he said. "She must've bought the mug because he couldn't get around."

"Amazon," Adler said.

"What?"

"The website thing. You can buy anything from that place. Putting small timers out of business and monopolizing the shit out of everything."

He stopped to take a bite from the bagel. He chewed, swallowed, and said, "You wouldn't know about these things because you're a moron."

"I know you need to get laid," Joseph said. "Can you get one of those plastic fuck dolls on your Amazon? Get one if you can. Might calm you down some."

"Yeah, sure. You're the one needs to get ..."

Joseph clutched his stomach and then leaned forward to catch the bit of spew in his hands. The spit was spotted with blood.

"You make any plans for that yet?" Adler said, angrily.

Joseph held up a hand. He slowly stood and headed back toward the kitchen. Adler's first floor bathroom was off to the left of the kitchen. Joseph went inside and washed his hands. He wiped his mouth with toilet paper, then washed his face, then hands again. When he returned to the living room, Adler had his cellphone to his right ear and was giving directions.

"The hell are you doing?" Joseph said.

"Calling an ambulance," Adler said. "Enough with this shit. I can't watch it anymore."

"You know what those things cost, you putz?"

"It's on me. You need to get to an emergency room before you drop dead. You do that at home, drop dead, and there's nobody around, you'll stink up the neighborhood, for God sakes."

Joseph was about to curse his friend when Adler spoke into his cellphone. "Yes, that's the address. That's right. Just come up to the front door. We're here now. Thank you."

"I should go home and leave you looking like the putz you are," Joseph said.

"I'll just send them there, you moron."

"I don't like hospitals, Artie. I hate them."

"Nobody likes hospitals, Joe. You need to see someone. At least for the pain relief. You're not gonna treat the cancer, you're gonna die. No reason to do so in constant pain."

Joseph bit his lower lip from pain. "Talk about something else," said. "You're depressing the fuck out of me."

"Fine," Adler said. "How about that Katherine? She is one beautiful woman."

"She is that. Smart too. A friggin' lawyer in the family. Imagine?"

"He better propose, your grandson. I don't know what the hell he's waiting for. After that fiasco at the house, I'm surprised she didn't jump on a flight back home."

"Don't remind me."

"Mary still guarding her son?"

"Mary'll have to get used to Katherine. She can't expect Chris to stay single the rest of his life."

"Was something that day, though, huh? That crazy broad came in with the gun."

"How many times we gonna talk about it?"

"Until the ambulance gets here."

Joseph leaned to his left while holding his stomach. "Fuck me," he said.

"I wish to hell you'd've gotten this taken care of," Adler said. "You're still losing weight but what good is it if you're dying?"

"I'll get back to playing weight the day I croak."

"Don't talk like that."

"What do you want me to say? It's a matter of time. I can deal with it. Now that the kid is okay, I'm fine with it."

"You're a moron."

"Yeah, and you're another Einstein."

Both men laughed.

"I'm gonna miss you, you fat fuck," Adler said.

"If there's any truth to life after death, I'll haunt your ass."

"You would."

"If I could, sure. I'd walk into your bedroom and piss in my pot."

"I hope you know you're not scoring any points with the man upstairs pouring your piss in your sink."

"If it is a man upstairs and he too has a weight issue, he'll understand."

"Moron."

"They're gonna shoot me full of morphine," Joseph said. "I'll be a fuckin' zombie."

"I've seen people die from that shit, Joseph. My wife. She was in a lot of pain and was begging for something before she passed. It was tough to watch."

"Which hospital you call?"

"I called emergency. They'll probably send a wagon from Brookdale. It's close. Maybe they'll transfer you to Sloane or NYU in the city once you're settled."

Joseph looked at Adler a long moment.

"What?" Adler said.

Joseph said, "How do you wipe your ass with that sling? You're left handed, no?"

Adler smiled. "I manage," he said.

"Depends?" Joseph said.

"Touché, fat boy, but you're still going to the hospital now."

They could hear the sirens getting closer.

"Your ride is here," Adler said.

• • • • •

In a conference room at 1 St. Andrews Plaza, a video camera on a tripod faced Bruno Fontana and Frank Cusmano. The Assistant U.S. attorney for the Southern District of New York, George Nimitz, sat across from them mid-table.

"This session will be recorded," he said.

Cusmano nodded. Bruno Fontana stared at Nimitz.

Again there were three agents in the conference room. A second attorney sat at the head of the table. Again, a pitcher of water had already been set on a large doily to the left of Cusmano. Individual glasses were spread around the table.

"I'm not going to waste my time, Mr. Fontana," Nimitz said. "I'm sure you know what we have and how we'll use it. Your attorney has much of our evidence, but not all of it. You're looking at twenty-five to life, same as your father and brother. Your father will die in prison. You're still young enough to want to live some of your life outside. It's up to you."

"I won't testify against my father," Bruno Fontana said.

"You may not have to, but if we needed you too, that would be part of the deal."

Bruno Fontana said, "I won't do it."

"Fine," Nimitz said. He turned to Cusmano. "We're done here. We'll see you with his brother after lunch."

Bruno Fontana and his attorney stood up and left the conference room.

When Nimitz returned two hours later, Cusmano and Vito Fontana were in the same seats the attorney and Bruno Fontana had occupied earlier. Nimitz poured water in all the glasses, then took a sip from his glass.

"Okay," he said. "I'm sure you spoke to your attorney, Vito. Now is your one time only come to Jesus moment. You too are screwed to the wall with the same evidence your father and brother are choosing to fight. They'll lose and probably die in prison. Your father certainly will. Your brother, he lasts the full twenty-five, will get out an old man, about sixty or so? Nobody on the street will give a shit he just did twenty-five. Maybe he lives that long. Maybe. So, what'll it be? Twenty-five to life or a somewhat reduced sentence?"

"How reduced," Vito Fontana said.

"Depends on what you can give us."

"I can give you a drug connection with the Vignieri people."

"With whom from the Vignieri people? I'm sure you already know that the man sent to kill you, Eugene Carneglia, has already made his own deal. He's giving up people too."

"Two captains, a few soldiers."

"Captains agreed to meet with you? You're not even made."

"Because of my father. They met with me because of him."

"Which captains?"

"Rizzoli and Marino."

"How do you have them?"

"On tape."

Cusmano turned to his client. "That's enough."

Nimitz smiled. "I guess your attorney didn't know, huh?"

"Nobody knew," Vito Fontana said. "I'm prepared for this bullshit."

"Who else might you have?"

Vito Fontana counted nine more names off his fingers.

"All on tape?" Nimitz said.

"All on tapes, as in plural. More than one."

"You should let me handle the negotiations, Vito," Cusmano said.

"Fuck you," Vito said. "I know what I have. Either they go for it or not. I'm not gonna play here. It's my fuckin' life, counselor."

"You're facing twenty-five to life," Nimitz said.

"I know what I'm facing. I won't do more than five. You let Gravano walk after killing nineteen people? He got five years for giving up Gotti. You want my testimony, work backwards from that number."

"You're a cocky bastard."

"You want headlines?"

"You don't think that's pushing it?"

"Fuck you. Yes or no?"

"If I say no, you're going away for a long time."

"You won't say no. You need the people I mentioned. You might need a few days to think it over, but you won't say no in the end. Go home and sleep on it. Put me in protective custody and get back to me when you want to put away a dozen made guys instead of just three."

• • • • •

One month to the day of the shooting inside his home, Joseph's ashes were buried atop his wife's ashes and alongside his son's in the Canarsie cemetery. His container was a Rosewood urn, the same as his wife and son. The inscription on the face of the urn provided his name, his dates of birth and death, and the following: "Loving Husband, Father, Grandfather and Friend."

There were ten people attending the burial. Family members and a few friends from back when Joseph owned a bar in Queens. Artie Adler teared up with emotion while giving a short speech about their lifelong friendship and what they meant to one another. He drew laughs when he mentioned Joseph's method of relieving himself.

"Now here's the thing the first time I seen it, it made me nuts, especially when we were in the middle of a meal together. I'd bring him bagels or sandwiches, or we'd barbecue or order a pizza, and always in the middle of the meal, and sometimes afterward, Joseph would have to take a piss. Okay, big deal, right? But Joseph had a special way of handling his business when it came to taking a leak. Joseph wasn't always a big man. That happened gradually from the last few years working at the bar and then after he retired. He was a bigger man the last couple of decades of his life because he'd grown comfortable in retirement. Very sedentary fella, Joseph was. He weighed well over three bills, so heading upstairs to his bathroom, or downstairs to the bathroom in the basement, was more than an annoyance for him. He once told me he thought about adding a bathroom on the first floor of his place, but the cost, he felt, was prohibitive, especially so late in life. He wanted to leave Chris what he had left and didn't think burning thirty grand or so was worth it to take a piss on the same floor. Instead, being the creatively cheap type when it counted, Joseph chose a small pot, the likes of which we'd all boil water for tea or hot chocolate, or maybe boil an egg. He used the pot to take a piss and then poured his discharge into the sink drain."

A few moans erupted from the small crowd.

"I know, I know," Adler said, "but he used steaming hot water to clean it. He would then run the hot water until there was steam coming out the faucet, then he'd clean the pot out and so on. I nicknamed him Joey Piss Pot at some point about ten years ago or so, and the name stuck. Joseph was not amused. The nickname was known to only a very few friends. Come to think of it, as recently as before he went into the hospital, in fact on that crazy day when the shootings took place, while Joseph was in his yard barbecuing, he asked me to fetch his pot. I gave him some shit, but in the end I knew he needed it and retrieved it for him. Then I had to stand guard at the back door while he … you know. As it turned out, that piss pot and the piss inside it was essential in taking down the shooter. Must've tasted like shit too."

The small crowed broke up laughing.

Adler let the laughter fade and said, "Now, I was going to ask Chris if I could have that famous pot, but then I thought about it and felt it should remain in their family. So, on top of everything else he left you, Chris, you also get the pot."

Everyone clapped.

Afterward, Chris, Katherine and Mary set up where the repast was being held at the bar on Cross Bay Boulevard Joseph used to own. Chris and Katherine made the arrangements, having it catered from a nearby Italian restaurant and renting out the bar's basement room for four hours in the afternoon.

Fifteen people, besides family, showed up. The pictures were arranged on two large poster boards Katherine had borrowed from her office. Joseph at 6 months, 1 year, 5 years, 10 years, 14 and 15, and so on up to his wedding and family pictures, including him holding his son Jack, and standing alongside his son the groom and his bride at their wedding. His daughter-in-law Mary, the bride in that picture, stared at it a long time.

Artie Adler was there with a woman he'd recently met. He stood at one of the poster boards and was pointing at pictures of himself and Joseph while explaining their history to the woman he'd brought to the repast.

Chris came up behind Adler and put an arm around his shoulders.

"He was a tough old bird, wasn't he?" he said.

Adler nodded a few times. His eyes were a bit misty. "You have no idea, kid," he said. "When he thought you were with the mob, he was ready to take them all on, and with the cancer I didn't know about yet. And then he wanted to give you money to flee the country."

Chris said, "I still can't believe the two of you tracked me down the way you did."

"His orders. He was scared shit for you. As much as your mother. He broke my shoes until I did what he asked."

"Did you know he was sick?"

Adler nodded. "Eventually," he said. "One of our loudest fights. Said he was stage four, but there was no talking to him about it. Wasn't interested in fighting it. Ignored it like it was a cold. He'd've gone for treatments, he'd be at your wedding. Speaking of which, when do you intend to propose? You have any sense, you'll put a ring on that woman's finger and soon."

"It was up to me, I'd've done that the day I crashed into her car down in Quantico."

"That's one way to meet a girl, I guess."

"I just wish I knew about his cancer. I said some nasty things to him."

"I couldn't say anything once I knew. He was my best pal. I was his. I gave that up, we would've both suffered. As for what you said, believe me, he got over it. He was all about you at the end, kid."

"Would've been nice he made it to the wedding. He'd probably break my shoes about something or other, but I wish he could've made it a few more weeks."

"That where the goalposts are now, few more weeks?"

"I have to propose first, Artie. For real this time, with a ring."

"I wouldn't take my time, I was you."

"Proposal first, then if she agrees, wedding a week or two later. That okay with you?"

"Hey, kid, you're not marrying me."

They both chuckled.

"I know he would've loved to be there," Chris said. "He'd be happy."

Adler gave the woman he was with a kiss on her cheek. "Sarah'll be there for him," he said. "She's gonna fill in as my date."

"I'm sure it'll be a beautiful wedding," Sarah said.

"Thanks," Chris said.

"Speaking of which, you even ready for married life?" Adler said.

"I think so. We've been living together, so I don't expect much to change. I'm not crazy about the new job playing Dick Tracy. This private-eye thing, I don't know. Looks to be pretty boring."

"Yeah, and the upside to that is you're a lot less likely to get yourself killed." Adler turned to Sarah and said, "This guy was FBI. The undercover kid I told you about."

"Oh, this is him?" Sarah said.

"Our own Donnie Brasco."

"Except the real guy was Donnie Brasco cashed in," Chris said.

"You could always write a book," Sarah said. "My son is a writer if you ever need help. He's been published, so he's not some crackpot."

Chris smiled. "Thanks, Sarah. I'll have to think about it. Maybe if I get bored enough chasing down insurance frauds or cheating spouses, I can put something together."

"You let me know if you do," she said. "Your life sounds very exciting."

Chris saw Katherine looking at her phone and went over to her.

"Secret boyfriend?" he said.

"No, he's busy today. It's about that guy, Rapino. He's been put into the witness protection program. A reduced sentence and then witness protection."

Chris said, "Then I'm glad I quit. Ever since Gravano, it's become a joke. The guy kills nineteen people and gets five years. Doesn't make a difference how many people these scumbags kill, there's always a deal at the other end of it. Rapino should spend the rest of his life inside."

"He's only going to be there for five years?" Katherine said. "That worries me, Chris."

"Forget him," Chris said. "A piece of shit like Rapino may get killed in prison. He comes for me I'll take him out next time."

"If you see him coming. I really don't like this. How could they give that animal a deal?"

"I know. Believe me, I know. I was sitting in a car waiting for him while he killed two innocent people. It makes me sick they gave him a deal."

"Will they let you know when he's out?"

"They're supposed to, but that's easy enough to track on our own. Don't worry, I will."

"I thought this was over."

"It is, hon. Time ever comes, I'll make sure of it."

•   •   •   •   •

When word of their cousin's arrest and admission to murders reached Pescara in Italy, Alfredo, Rafael and Maria Theresa decided to take a trip to Pizzoferrato to place flowers in front of the house where Giovanni Rapino was born.

The drive took an hour and 20 minutes. Alfredo drove. Rafael sat shotgun up front. Maria Theresa sat in the back. Their conversations were in Italian and were focused on their cousin in America and the choice to testify he'd finally made.

"I don't care," Rafael said. "It's a shame he turned to the government."

"What you want him to do?" Alfredo said. "He doesn't do that he dies in prison."

"Then he dies in prison," Rafael said. "That's the price one pays."

Alfredo was looking at Maria Theresa in the rearview mirror. He could tell she was upset. He said, "He admitted to seven murders. He had to testify."

"And Augusto is dead from this same shit," Maria Theresa said. "You both make me sick."

"Easy, Maria," Alfredo said. "Giovanni is doing the right thing now. You should be supportive."

"Listening to this conversation? Are you kidding me?"

Alfredo turned to his brother and said, "Maybe we take it easy for now. It upsets her."

"Because she's a communist," Rafael said. "She doesn't show respect."

"Respect?" Maria Theresa said with venom. "You want me to respect a murderer? What the hell is wrong with you? I know you all helped him avenge his mother. I know he killed those two men in Pescara. And you think nothing of it. And now Augusto is dead too. You're all idiots."

"Even me?" Alfredo said.

"Especially you. You're the one they look up to and you think the *Mafioso* is something good. It's crazy. You, all three of you, have nothing in your life. None of you are rich. None of you bothered to educate yourselves. None of you can answer to this God you all claim to worship. How does that work by the way? You kill someone and go to confession?"

"Here she goes," Rafael said. "Thanks, Alfredo. You started her off."

"Don't blame me," Alfredo said. "You're the one who can't shut up about it."

"Why don't you both shut up now," Maria Theresa said. "Let's just go there, lay flowers at the house and the cemetery where his parents are, and then get me back to Pescara so I can forget all of this shit you're talking about."

"Okay, but don't forget, you're the one who wanted to make this trip," Rafael said. "You called me."

"Because I'm stupid to think it would be any different," she said. "Now I know better. Let's just go and get back."

When they arrived at the home where their cousin was born, Maria Theresa placed a bouquet of flowers at the doorstep. Tears flowed from her eyes as she did so. When she saw her cousins making the sign of the cross, Maria Theresa wanted to scream at them again. She didn't, though. She managed to suppress what she felt her anger had turned to, which was rage.

The seven minute drive to the cemetery, *Cimitero di Gamberale*, was peaceful in the car. Once at the mausoleum of Giovanni Rapino's mother and father, Maria Theresa set another bouquet of flowers on the ground beneath their names. She thought about the disappointment the two parents were spared from their premature and horrible deaths and was grateful for at least that. Then she returned to Alfredo's car and begged them to talk about something besides revenge and how they intended to avenge their cousin Augusto next.

• • • • •

Aniello Fontana watched the George Nimitz campaign announcement for the New York 11th Congressional District on the television in a common room at the Manhattan Correctional Center. Fontana was due to transfer to USP Big Sandy in Kentucky. He and several other inmates watching the speech

on the CNN channel laughed when George Nimitz mentioned
he intended to be a law-and-order President.

"The fuck is this guy?" one of the inmates yelled.

"President?" another one yelled. "He's fuckin confused, man."

"Kiss your career goodbye, *pendejo*," another yelled.

Fontana was smiling. He said, "What an asshole. I should've
stabbed this motherfucker when I had the chance. Used a pen
or something. Maybe crack his stupid skull with a water
pitcher. All these guys are no different than us. They cheat and
lie and plant evidence and let people die for the sake of their
cases. Wannabe politicians. Ambitious little pricks. Fucking
jellyfish. No spines. No stones. Tough guys in a crowd of their
own and pussies one on one. Why they need a law degree or a
badge to protect themselves. Probably hide under their beds at
night."

Fontana started to laugh. "He wants to be President and
can't wait to announce."

Later the same night, alone in his cell, Aniello thought about
what would become of his family. Fontana's first born son,
Bruno, had been to prison and knew he could survive it. While
it bothered Aniello that his younger son had broken the code of
silence, *omerta*, Vito had yet to take the blood oath that would
have inducted him into *Cosa Nostra*. Vito's decision to join team
America would save some of his life.

Vito was the mark because he had no prison experience and
was too spoiled. When the feds went after him, they knew he
was the weakest link in their immediate family. Aniello
wondered if he'd always known the same thing.

The crime family he'd ruled for more than a decade was on
its own now. Whether there would be a new power struggle or
not was yet to be seen. Aniello didn't care, except his desire to
change the family name to his own had died with his arrest.

It was the loss of his daughter that upset him the most.
Aniello had been depressed for several days afterward. Her
funeral arrangement had to be made by Fontana's youngest
sister, paid for through the funds his attorney had control over
as executor of Aniello's estate.

All of Cusmano's motions intended to grant Angela's father
and brothers' permission to attend her funeral were rejected by
the same prick who'd announced he was running for President
by mistake.

Angela Fontana was buried alongside her mother's grave in
Brooklyn's Greenwood cemetery.

• • • • •

The day after Aniello Fontana and several other inmates at the Manhattan Correctional Facility watched the United States Attorney for the Southern District of New York, George Nimitz, make a fool of himself on local and national television, including the late night shows and *Saturday Night Live*, a scandal involving an FBI Special Agent in Charge and George Nimitz, in his prior position as an Assistant United States Attorney for the Southern District of New York, came in the form of a lawsuit filed by one Doris Montalvo, the former wife of a captain in the Cirelli crime family.

Allegations of sexual abuse and the lack of protection provided for a woman forced to defend herself against an armed assassin who had broken into her home, a murder plot allegedly caught on federal and local wiretaps by the Organized Crime Task Force, yet never revealed to Mrs. Montalvo, was the breaking news of the day. There was also a recorded conversation wherein Connor Kelly used racist language when referring to Mexicans and implied threats against Mrs. Montalvo.

When asked to comment on the allegations, George Nimitz refused to do so, except to state that he would resign by the end of the week.

• • • • •

Chris's left thigh was still a little sore from where they'd removed the bullet. He was told he was lucky. No damage to his veins or bones, but the bullet had settled in the tensor fasciae latae and had to be removed. Therapy required he walk with a crutch until he no longer needed it.

The trip to Georgia to meet Katherine's family went well. Chris got a kick out of her younger brother. Tim Grady was studying to be a journalist and as Katherine had said, he was enamored with mob movies and culture. He couldn't ask Chris enough questions and was surprised to hear Chris had resigned from the FBI. He suggested they write a book together about his time undercover.

They spent two nights at Katherine's family home, a vintage antebellum, two-story home with a wraparound veranda and a balcony on the second floor. The inside was roomy and filled with antique furniture. When they were alone in her old bedroom, Chris asked Katherine what something like her family's house cost?

Katherine said, "More than a million ten years ago. I have no idea now."

When they returned to New York, Chris moved in with Katherine. She scheduled an interview for him with her firm the following week. He continued recovering while she worked, spending more time on a couch or in bed than he could remember. One day when he was tired of doing nothing, he snuck out of the apartment to meet his mother for help buying an engagement ring. He felt he owed his mother the opportunity to be more involved with his life again. He knew he'd upset her by his periodic and sometimes lengthy disappearing acts.

And his mother had been traumatized to the point of a near heart attack at his grandfather's house. Chris was still fighting the guilt he felt for that day.

They visited two jewelry stores and picked out favorites from each before heading to a diner for lunch. Chris asked her which of the rings she preferred from the two stores. Mary frowned.

"What?" he said.

"They're all so expensive."

"Yeah, but there's no going cheap on a diamond."

Mary extended both her hands. Her engagement ring was on her left hand, her wedding ring on her right hand. "You know what these cost?"

"No clue, Ma, but that was how long ago? Everything is a lot more expensive today."

She lifted her left hand for him to better see. "Unless you use this one."

Chris was surprised. "What?"

Mary removed her engagement ring and placed it on the table.

"Gee, Ma, I don't know."

"You could ask. Maybe she wouldn't mind. You'd be saving a small fortune."

"Forty-five hundred is a lot of money, but it isn't a small fortune."

"You can still ask if you want. I'd feel better knowing it stayed in the family. It's the ring your father gave me."

"Can I borrow it for the night?"

"Of course."

"You're sure about this?"

"I am."

After dropping his mother off at her house, Chris headed back to the apartment to cook dinner for Katherine. He wrapped the ring in blue tissue and scotch tape.

He cooked spaghetti *aglio e olio* for dinner. Katherine didn't notice the strange little package on the dining room table right away and was surprised he'd cooked when she returned home from work.

"Smells so good," she said. "I hope you know what you're doing."

"I grew up in an Italian home," he said. "Don't insult me."

She kissed him hello, then headed to the bedroom to change.

Chris strained the spaghetti in a colander in the sink, then poured the pasta into a large serving bowl. He added the oil and garlic mix on top of the spaghetti, then stirred the combination and set the serving bowl on the dining room table.

When Katherine returned, she saw the spaghetti first, then the taped-up tissue alongside her dish. She purposely ignored it and held her plate up for Chris to fork spaghetti onto it. Chris ignored her ignoring the tissue.

She told him about the interview he'd be having the following week. She knew the woman from Human Resources and thought Chris shouldn't be too flip with her.

"No jokes," Katherine told him.

Chris did his best to make it obvious he was ignoring her. Then she said in an exaggerated southern accent, "So, what's in the tissue, sugar? I hope you didn't blow your nose and think it's a clever joke to play on an unsuspecting Southern girl."

Chris frowned before grabbing her plate and his, and then walking them to the sink. He began to wash them, using dish soap, a sponge and hot water. While he did so, Katherine carefully unwrapped the tissue, slipped the ring on her finger, and then rewrapped the tissue. She set it down and sipped water from her glass, struggling to keep from laughing.

Chris finished the dishes and returned to the dining room. He stopped before sitting and pointed to the tissue. "I can take it back if you want," he said, a touch of anger in his tone.

"Excuse me?"

"Open the damn thing," he said.

Katherine reopened the tissue and looked confused. "Is this a joke?" she said.

"What, not big enough?"

She spread the tissue out on the table and shrugged. He saw it was empty, then looked at her hand. Katherine broke out laughing.

"I should beat you like they used to do in the old days," he said.

"Don't be so sure you can," she said.

"So?"

"Oh, sure," she said. "Of course. What did you think I'd say?"

THE END

Made in the USA
Columbia, SC
30 July 2024

39711541R00143